"I'VE MISSED YOU . . ."

Alexandra lifted her mouth for his fiercely tender kiss. Every nerve ending was afire as he brushed his lips across her cheek, then held her more tightly. She never wanted to stir again, never wanted him to let go.

It was then that she noticed the strip of faded blue satin tied to a button of his uniform coat. She lifted the ribbon and let its frayed ends trail through her fingers.

"It's been everywhere with me," he whispered. "Through every battle . . ."

"You need a new one." Alexandra fingered the gold fringe at his shoulder, her eyes drinking in every detail of him. "You make a handsome captain," she said. Then she heard the beat of distant drums; time was slipping away. The British were coming . . . and they wanted Philadelphia.

Dalton felt the faint tremor that shuddered through her. He drew back and saw that her eyes were wet, her face pale. "Alex," he soothed, laying the back of his hand gently to her cheek.

"Please come back to me," she whispered.

He drew her close again, pressing her head to his chest. "I will, love." His voice was thick, revealing his torment. "I promise."

They held each other and seized what they could from their stolen time together, and the silence between them was bittersweet, yet filled with love.

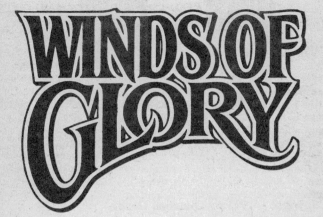

WINDS OF GLORY

GRETCHEN GENET

PINNACLE BOOKS
WINDSOR PUBLISHING CORP.

For Jim

PINNACLE BOOKS

are published by

Windsor Publishing Corp.
475 Park Avenue South
New York, NY 10016

Copyright © 1993 by Gretchen Genet

Pinnacle and the P logo are trademarks of Windsor Publishing Corp.

First Printing: January 1993

Printed in the United States of America

"Know, my good friend, that no distance can keep anxious lovers long asunder, and that the wonders of former ages may be revived in this."

George Washington

MORRISTOWN

NEW JERSEY

DELAWARE RIVER

BATTLE OF
LONG ISLAND
AUGUST 27, 1776

LONG ISLAND

STATEN
ISLAND

PENNSYLVANIA

BATTLE OF
PRINCETON
JANUARY 3, 1777

BATTLE OF
MONMOUTH
JUNE 28, 1778

BATTLE OF
TRENTON
DECEMBER 26, 1776

BATTLE OF
GERMANTOWN
OCTOBER 4, 1777

SCHUYLKILL RIVER

VALLEY
FORGE

PHILADELPHIA

BATTLE OF
BRANDYWINE
SEPTEMBER 11, 1777

DELAWARE RIVER

ATLANTIC OCEAN

SEAT OF WAR
IN THE NORTHERN COLONIES
1776 TO 1778

PENNSYLVANIA

NEW
JERSEY

WISSAHICKON CREEK

GERMANTOWN

DOWNSTREAM
FARM

GERMANTOWN ROAD

WILLOWBROOK

SCHUYLKILL RIVER

RIDGE ROAD

PHILADELPHIA

THE NECK

SWEET BRIAR

FORT MIFFLIN

DELAWARE   RIVER

FORT MERCER

PHILADELPHIA
AND ITS ENVIRONS
1776

I.

JACK FLASH

Chapter One

The thief stole through moon-dappled darkness to the wood's edge. Kneeling on damp grass, he removed a brass-bound spyglass from his vest pocket, telescoped the barrel, and played the glass over the hollow below, where a house of baronial aspect blazed with light. Sweet Briar, nestled among tall poplars, was the country manor of Charles Villard—merchant, aristocrat, third generation of inherited wealth.

As a breeze drifted up from the vale, the thief inclined his head and imagined he could actually smell the riches displayed so lavishly before him. The fragrances of petunias and chrysanthemums, blossoming in manicured gardens, sweetened the late September night. Smoke from cookfires flowed from a great quadruple chimney in the mansion's east wing, bringing tantalizing smells from a busy kitchen—roasting meats, fresh-baked pies, steaming vegetables picked today from the kitchen gardens.

Sweet Briar, with its white servants, Scottish head gardeners, parks, stables, and well-kept groves, rivaled the most impressive and elegant English ménage. The house itself was an architectural masterpiece. Broad flights of stone steps with iron balustrades led to doorways of generous proportions. Above each doorway, Palladian windows of clear, rose-colored glass glowed like fine wine in candlelight. To the west of the great house, the land sloped gently away to the Schuylkill River, a silvered expanse edged with feathery black forests.

Money. It was thick here, lying in wait within those ivy-draped walls. And a good thief, a clever thief, could have a

11

piece of it if he kept his wits about him.

He panned the spyglass over the long, circular drive and saw two pinpoints of golden light bobbing in the distance. Before long, he heard the sound of metal-rimmed wheels crunching gravel, the lively clip-clop of ironshod hooves. A large black coach, drawn by four matched grays, materialized from the gloom. From its scarlet and blue trim, the thief knew the coach belonged to Evelyn Wright, aging paragon of Philadelphia society. Charles Villard's aunt.

As the coach halted before the mansion's columned front entrance, two liveried footmen jumped down from their perches, opened the doors, and let down the steps. With the aid of their blue-clad arms, three passengers alighted—an elderly gentleman and two primped ladies. The thief paid particular attention to the ladies. Lantern light glittered on jewels adorning their fashionably curled hair. Around Evelyn Wright's creased throat lay a sapphire, opal, and diamond treasure that made him sigh in nervous anticipation. A wonder her skinny neck didn't snap under the weight of all those stones. The necklace must be worth a fortune. The thief meant to have it.

The coach doors closed, the guests entered the house. The liveried footmen carried three portmanteaus inside, then reappeared and climbed back onto their perches behind the coach. With the sharp crack of a whip, the coach started away. Charles Villard's guests, along with their valuables, would be staying the night.

Compacting his spyglass, the thief backtracked through the woods to a clearing where he had tethered his horse, a dark bay mare with one white stocking and a wide bright blaze. Though unremarkable to look at, the horse was sturdy, swift, and obedient—essential qualities for a robber's mount. As her master approached, the mare's head rose, ears pricked forward. She whickered a soft greeting.

"Ssh," he said, bringing her head against his chest and rubbing her ears. "You want the dogs to hear us?" He fed her a piece of carrot from his pocket and spoke softly to her while she crunched. "Secret, you should see what's down there. A fucking fortune in stones, just waiting for me to take it." As he talked, her gentle, curious eyes watched

12

him in the moonlight. They seemed to be asking a question.

"I ain't scared," he said staunchly. "Bloody stupid maybe, but not scared. What about you? You won't be lonely out here, will you?" Smiling, he patted her neck. "I didn't think so. You're a tough girl."

Freeing her reins, he looped them about her neck, loosely knotted the ends, then turned and started along a deer path leading deeper into the trees. Like a well-trained dog, Secret followed behind him, nudging his back from time to time with her muzzle. When they reached a swift-running brook, the thief secured her to a sapling, tying her reins low to the ground so that she could drink if she wanted. Then he stood by her flank and opened his saddlebag. Inside was a black cloth hood, which he fitted over his head, and a black sack, which he tied to his belt. From leather saddle holsters, he removed a brace of pistols, primed and loaded, with right and left hand locks so both guns could be fired at once. They were handsome, graceful weapons of exceptional quality, with brass barrels and ornate sterling silver mountings highlighted with gold wash. They were stolen weapons. He thrust them into his belt.

The thief was ready to assault Sweet Briar. He only hoped Sweet Briar was unprepared for a visit from him.

Leaving the woods, he crossed the lawn in a crouch, using shrubs and trees for cover, his footfalls deadened by heavy dew on the grass. He was concerned about the kennel hounds, whose sharp ears and baying throats could bring the watchmen down on him. There were four guards, and the thief knew from watching Sweet Briar all week that they were lackadaisical men with a fondness for card playing. Right now they were probably doing just that in one of the porters' lodges. Still, an alarm would bring them running with their pistols drawn.

The thief reached the house without incident and sank down among the trailing branches of a yew bush. There he waited, breathing shallowly and listening to the sweet sounds of a violin accompanying a pianoforte. Inside the house, he imagined, Charles Villard was leading his guests to the candlelit dining room, where gleaming silver and china adorned a long, linen-covered table. Where stewards cooled wine in silver vessels and served course after course from a food-laden sideboard.

Keeping low, his black clothes blending with the shrubbery, the thief rounded the house in search of the dining room, which was easy to find. Its windows glowed with the golden light of two multitiered chandeliers hung with crystal drops.

The thief crept beneath the windows. Raising his hooded head cautiously above the level of the sills, he peered inside and almost laughed. Two couples were seated at the enormous table. Not clustered at one end so they could easily converse, but spread to the farthest reaches of the room so they had to speak loudly in order to be heard. Which pleased the thief because the night was warm, windows were cracked, and he could overhear every word said in the dining room.

He recognized all four people at the table, though he had met only one—Charles Villard, master of Sweet Briar and looking every bit the part. Villard was resplendent in a formal suit of black silk velvet over an ivory satin waistcoat, all copiously embroidered with a floral border pattern in pastel silks. His handsome, slender face was framed by his own blond hair, meticulously puffed, rolled, and powdered.

Standing, Villard raised his wineglass in a toast. "How fortunate I am," he said, "to have the fairest of Philadelphia grace this table." He bowed to his aunt, who was seated on his right, then fixed his gaze on the young woman at the far end of the table. His look intensified. "To you, Alexandra, on your twenty-first birthday."

Alexandra Pennington returned his smile. A blush warmed her face, but her eyes did not leave his.

"To your health, your wisdom, and your exceptional beauty," said Villard, "which grows more astonishing with each day."

The thief rolled his eyes. As usual, Villard was oozing charm, but he had a point. Alexandra Pennington was lovely, and the thief found his attention speared by Jonathan Pennington's young widow. He had glimpsed her from a distance many times. Now, watching her sip wine, he wondered why he had never felt inclined to take a closer look. In the blazing candlelight, her skin had a

14

golden hue suggestive of honey. He liked the color of her hair, dark brown shot with amber, full of shine. Her spirited blue eyes and delicate features formed an appealing face that made him want to know more about her, intimate things. But he knew this was as close as he would ever come to that fantasy.

"You honor me, Charles," she said in a clear, steady voice. "But I'm afraid your compliments are overstated."

"Overstated? I was thinking just the opposite."

"Another beautifully told lie," she said, "which I accept."

There was laughter all around.

The thief drew his gaze from Alexandra's face to her pearl and diamond pendant necklace, which was not as flashy as Aunt Evelyn's, but was still a choice piece. Something to bear in mind later on when he went to work.

For now, he sat with his back against the house wall, directly beneath an open window, and listened to the conversation in the dining room. The discussion, not surprisingly, centered on the rising political storm that was electrifying the Colonies and promised fury when it broke. These days, such talk was on everyone's tongue, and the collective viewpoint in the dining room was predictable. They were Loyalists in there, dining beneath a hundred expensive spermaceti candles, sampling fine brandy and rare roast beef, and appreciating none of it beyond its momentary value.

"Thank God the King has finally decided to deal with the traitors," said a tart female voice. Evelyn Wright, a sparrowlike woman who shared her nephew's thin, pale good looks, seethed with indignation. "The city's become a cesspit of rebels. Honest people are terrified to speak their minds. One wrong word could get them tarred and feathered and tied to a tree on some dark road. It's outrageous."

"Damn if I'll hold my tongue," said George Pennington. He meant it, and because he did Alexandra glanced worriedly at her brother-in-law. A stately old gentleman, George Pennington was an outspoken Loyalist who had publicly condemned the Congress, then refused to retract his statements. His bravery was commendable, if fool-hardy, for such behavior had landed many people in

15

prison or seen them banished from the province. Pennington's friendship with Chief Justice Benjamin Chew was perhaps the only reason he had not been dragged before the Committee of Safety to face charges.

"George, you really should be careful of what you say," Alexandra advised him.

But Pennington shook his head. "I won't keep quiet while smugglers and pompous lawyers stir up poor folk with nonsense. Fair trade and moderate taxes," he scoffed, disgusted. "They're afraid of losing their profits, that's the real motive for their insidious propaganda. Impudent rascals. They should all be hanged."

"Indeed," said Villard. "And so they shall be if they continue to push."

"Push?" There was acid in Evelyn Wright's tone. "Nephew, they put Mr. Washington in command of an army. If that isn't pushing, what is?"

"An army?" Villard smiled. "Be serious, Aunt Evie. It's a mob of yokels and shopkeepers, all come together like a flock of migrating birds. There's no organization or discipline among them. Their leaders are insanely jealous of one another." He paused, chuckled, sipped wine. "I understand the world has never seen so many captains in one place as at Cambridge. Everyone wants to be an officer, and no one wants to take orders. They have to steal ammunition and guns because they have none, and the fools are begging a fight with the Royal Army."

"Let's pray it doesn't come to that," Alexandra said quietly.

"They need to be taught a lesson," Evelyn insisted. "If bloodshed is the answer, so be it. Law and order must be restored in the Colonies, or we'll end up at the mercy of men like Jack Flash."

Outside the window, Jack Flash sat up straighter, his whole being suddenly intent.

"I heard he robbed Tom Warren the other night," said George Pennington in a somber voice.

Villard nodded. "On the Frankfort Road."

"What happened?"

"There was a body lying in the road. Naturally the coachman stopped to inspect it, but it turned out to be a ruse—old clothing stuffed with straw. The villain

16

dropped from a tree and robbed poor Tom and his wife."

"Bastard!" Pennington said.

Jack Flash smiled a little.

"A lot of poor people think he's a hero," Alexandra said.

"Ignorant people, you mean," Villard shot back. "Rebels. He's targeting Loyalists, and they love him for it. Their approval is making him bolder. Who knows where he'll strike next?"

Jack Flash, felon of the broadsheets, tipped his head back with a grin.

"Enough disturbing talk," Villard said and motioned a steward to pour more wine all around. "Ladies, George, this is supposed to be a birthday celebration. Let's not have it fall short of a splendid time."

Oh, sound the trumpets, Jack Flash thought.

He continued to wait. And wait some more. His neck grew stiff, his backside numb from sitting too long in one position. Much later, he took out his watch, opened the cover, and checked the time. Half-past ten. How long did it take to eat a goddamned dinner?

Three hours, give or take several minutes. At long last he heard chairs scrape on the dining room floor as Villard and his guests left the table.

Jack Flash left the bushes on his hands and knees, then slipped along the back of the great house until he came to a broad, raised terrace. Standing in its shadow, he surveyed the three stories above him to determine where the guest bedrooms were located. He knew the servants' quarters were above the kitchen, which ruled out the east wing. The third floor was also out—too far to expect guests to climb. Jack Flash turned his attention to the west wing and looked for lights, for the maids would have been instructed to leave a candle burning in each guest room.

On the second floor of the west wing, three windows glowed softly. An easy climb up an ivy-covered trellis. As Jack Flash thought this, the terrace doors above him suddenly opened and footsteps sounded on brick. Jack Flash flattened himself to the wall as voices penetrated the night. Very slowly, he tilted his head back to look up.

Alexandra Pennington and Charles Villard stood a few feet over his head, so close he could have reached out and touched the toe of Villard's red-heeled shoe. Had the couple looked down, they might have noticed him. But they were too intent on each other to pay much attention to their shadowed surroundings.

Charles Villard took her hand, lifted it to his lips, and pressed a lingering kiss to her fingers. "I've been waiting all night for this moment," he said. "Dear Alexandra, I enjoy your company immensely."

"And I yours."

Stifling a sigh, Jack Flash wondered how long they would gush nonsense and keep him trapped there.

"You must know why I brought you out here," Villard said.

Alexandra hesitated, looking up at him. "I'm afraid I don't."

To her astonishment, after kissing her hand again, Villard sank to one knee and said with naked yearning, "Marry me, Alexandra. Say yes, and I'll be the happiest man alive."

There was a shocked pause that Jack Flash felt to his boots.

Still holding her hand, Villard slowly rose. "I've startled you," he said. "Forgive me, but I thought surely you understood my feelings."

"Charles, we hardly know each other."

"On the contrary, I know all I need to know about you. I adore you."

Silence above. Jack Flash waited, intrigued, as Alexandra considered her response. "You're a persistent man," she said at last, and he knew from her voice that she was smiling.

"My feelings make me persistent." Moving closer to her, Villard cupped her chin. "I'm afraid I have little control over them, and the fault is entirely yours." He bent his head and kissed her.

Moments later she whispered, "Charles, it's too soon. I need time."

"I understand," he said. "I'll wait, because to me you are everything a man could ever want. For now I ask only the privilege of courting you, so that I may prove my devotion."

Below in the shadows Jack Flash was all ears, and when Alexandra gave her consent to be courted, he grimaced at the thought of her ending up with Charles Villard. Then the terrace doors closed and the night again belonged to him.

Moving to the vine-draped trellis, he tested its strength. The trellis seemed sturdy enough to support his weight, but he hesitated, gripped by sudden apprehension. He had never done anything this brazen in his career as a thief. He thought of Evelyn Wright's necklace, calculated the price it would fetch, and decided the reward was worth the risk. Gathering himself, he climbed swiftly to a second-floor window, jacked it open, and pulled himself inside an elegantly furnished bedroom. The light from a single candle gleamed on dark mahogany, tooled leather wall coverings, and a tall, gilt-edged looking glass. The twelve-foot-high ceiling dwarfed even the massive four-posted bed, which was larger than any he had ever seen. On the bed, a pink sleeping shift and a robe were laid out. He lifted the nightgown and fingered its soft material. Evelyn Wright's?

With a sigh he returned the shift to the bed. Why make this easy for him? Moving to the door, he pressed his ear against it and heard music. Somewhere in the house, the violin and pianoforte duet had resumed. Villard and his guests were dancing downstairs, swirling like brightly colored peacocks across a polished floor. Soon they would retire, and when Evelyn Wright came upstairs, Jack Flash must be ready to seize his prize.

He cracked the door, stuck his head into a deserted hallway, then moved on silent feet to the next bedroom, which was as breathtaking as the first.

And just as frustrating. Another sleeping shift had been laid out, lavender with tiny blue roses embroidered around the neckline. He opened the portmanteau at the foot of the bed and rifled the clothing inside, searching for a monogram or some other clue to denote ownership. He found nothing.

Then he spied an ivory-handled hairbrush on the vanity and quickly inspected it. Strands of long, dark hair, caught in stiff bristles, told him what he needed to know. As he put the brush down and turned toward the door, footsteps echoed in the hallway, accompanied by a high-pitched giggle. Hissing a curse, he dove to the floor and rolled under the bed just as the door opened.

"Ain't he something?" said a girl's voice. "Fawning like a lovesick pup. Bobby says he's a changed man, actually civil these past two weeks."

"It won't last, not with him."

"You think he'll marry her?"

"That depends on her, don't it?"

"Are you bloody daft? With his looks and money? If he asks her, she'll accept on the spot. Wait and see."

Jack Flash inched toward the foot of the bed, peered through a slit in the dust ruffle, and saw two uniformed maids lounging in armchairs near the fireplace, looking for all the world like they owned the place. With a soundless sigh, he lowered his forehead onto folded arms.

Over the next hour, he learned their names were Hallie and Susan, and they talked endlessly about someone named Bobby, who was hung like an ox and apparently just as brainless. It was well after midnight when Susan finally roused herself, declaring that she should go next door to wait on Mrs. Wright, the nasty bitch. Susan left, Hallie dozed off in a chair, and Jack Flash remained trapped under the bed.

Alexandra Pennington arrived at one o'clock in the morning and woke Hallie with a gentle shake. Springing up, the girl rubbed sleep from her eyes and apologized for napping.

"Nonsense," Alexandra said with a laugh. "Waiting is the most exhausting job in the world."

Amen, thought Jack Flash.

"Would you please help me with my gown?" Alexandra asked, unhooking the bodice front.

"Yes, ma'am." Moving behind her, Hallie drew the white satin gown off Alexandra's shoulders, taking care not to damage the silk fringe trim. "I'm to ask if you'd like a bath, ma'am. There's heated water downstairs, and I could have the tub brought up. Won't take a minute."

"Is there water in the pitcher?" Alexandra asked, nodding toward the washstand.

"Yes, ma'am."

"That will be fine. I'm really too tired to bathe."

"Yes, ma'am."

Hallie carefully hung the white gown in the armoire.

Matching embroidered slippers with gold diamond roses followed, then a pale blue petticoat of quilted satin.

Jack Flash's mouth had gone dry. She wore stays. God only knew why. Her waist was wonderfully slender, her breasts high and proudly jutting. He thought they would settle when the stays came off. He was wrong.

"I can manage now, Hallie."

"Yes, ma'am," she said and dipped a curtsy. "Will there be anything else, ma'am?"

"No, thank you."

"Very good, ma'am. Good night."

"Good night, Hallie."

The door closed. Wearing only a fine linen shift, Alexandra Pennington opened her portmanteau and brought out a stiff leather jewelry case. Moving to the vanity, she removed her pendant necklace and earrings and, under Jack Flash's watchful gaze, put them carefully into the case. The jeweled enameled bows from her hair went in next. Then she unpinned her hair and brushed it with long, smooth strokes until it shone. As she worked, candlelight defined her suppleness through gauzy linen, and his eyes drank in long legs that rose into gently flared hips. She was exquisite.

She was taking off her shift. After a moment, without realizing it, he stopped breathing and simply stared as the world stood still and his imagination soared to a dizzy, impossible height. A voice in his head said he ought to look away. Instead, riveted, he watched her bathe at the washstand, memorizing details that until now only her dead husband had been privy to.

Finally she drew the lavender sleeping shift over her head, blew out the candle, and climbed into bed. Lying motionless on his stomach, chin resting on folded hands, he listened to her movements above him as she fussed with the covers and got comfortable. Her sleek image was burned into his mind.

It was still branded there when he heard her soft, even breathing and knew she was asleep. Easing from under the bed, he came to his knees and let his eyes adjust to the dim light. Then, like a cat prowling the darkness, he padded to the vanity, slipped her jewel case into the sack at his belt, and thrust Alexandra Pennington from his thoughts.

21

Jack Flash let himself into the hallway, where a single candle burned in a sconce. Now for Evelyn Wright, who was snoring like a drunken sailor. For a moment, as he cautiously opened her door, he thought he had made a mistake. This must be George Pennington's bedroom. But no, it was Evelyn Wright wheezing, snorting, and muttering to herself on the bed.

The drapes were drawn over the window, allowing only thin shafts of moonlight to penetrate the gloom. Fortunately, he had visited this room earlier and remembered its layout. In near blackness, he negotiated an obstacle course of furniture to reach the vanity, where he discovered a delicate scent bottle and a set of hair bows, but no jewelry case or necklace.

Goddamnit. Where had she hidden it?

As he turned, his hand brushed a tall candlestick. He heard it wobble, lunged blindly for it, and missed. The heavy pewter piece struck the floor with an ungodly clatter. Frozen, the hair on his arms prickling, Jack Flash listened to Evelyn stir, mumble, smack her lips, and begin snoring again. Incredible. The sleep of the dead.

His pulse was beating too quickly. As he stood there, an urgent desire to flee came over him, but he refused to leave without Evelyn's necklace. Perhaps he should wake her, shove a pistol under her nose, and demand it from her.

Then something glimmered at him from the vanity—a wink of sapphire blue near where the candlestick had been. Smiling, he scooped up the heavy necklace. It joined Alexandra Pennington's jewelry case as Jack Flash left the room.

A candle still burned in the hallway. Glancing both ways, alert to the slightest sound, he went left toward the stairwell, conscious of the weighted sack bumping his thigh with each step. He had gone several paces when a door behind him suddenly opened and fear hammered his heart. As he spun around, a pistol materialized in his hand, then wavered.

Alexandra Pennington stood in her bedroom doorway, staring with wide, frightened eyes at the black-clad apparition before her. The hood added to his considerable height. Slits cut for his eyes made him look sinister and threatening, and though he quickly retreated from her,

22

intent on running, she cringed in terror and her scream split the stillness.

By the time the servants and Charles Villard responded to her alarm, Jack Flash had left the house by a downstairs window. He hit the ground running. Light-footed as a deer, he sprinted across the lawn, melted into the treeline, and became just another shadow among shadows.

Chapter Two

"I can't believe his nerve," Alexandra fumed, pacing the sunlit parlor of her country house. "Despicable bastard. It was bad enough that we couldn't feel safe on the roads, now he's invading our homes." Going to a window, she stared outside at the broad maples lining Willowbrook's drive, but her mind's eye beheld a different vision—a tall man wearing a black hood. The thought of Jack Flash skulking around her in darkness was unnerving. She shivered, feeling violated.

"The fault is mine," Villard said.

Turning from the window, Alexandra saw his guilt-ridden look and tried to put him at ease. "Don't be silly, Charles. You're no more responsible for what happened than I am."

"My watchmen were lax," he said. "I should have made sure they were doing their jobs." His father would have seen to it, he imagined. Right now, Richard Villard would be saying his son deserved all manner of embarrassment for being careless with the help. But Richard Villard was not around anymore to find fault. He was planted in Christ's Church yard where he belonged. Still, on occasion, he managed to taunt his son from the grave. Now was one of those times.

"Thank God you weren't harmed," Villard said.

"Don't laugh, but I think I frightened him as much as he did me."

"You said he aimed a pistol at you."

Alexandra turned back to the window. "Only for an instant."

Appalled that he could have lost her in that instant, Villard urged, "I think you should move back to your city house. It isn't safe for you to stay here."

Alexandra disagreed. Just being at Willowbrook was a comfort to her. She loved the tree-shaded stone house with its sloping, wooded grounds overlooking the Schuylkill River. Built as a summer retreat, the house was private and rural, yet convenient to Philadelphia, which lay a few miles to the south. Compared with Sweet Briar's lavish elegance, Willowbrook was a modest reflection of her late husband's simple tastes. Frugal John Pennington had never felt the need to display his wealth, only to accumulate it. He had made certain his young wife would want for nothing in the event of his death.

Lost in remembrance, Alexandra summoned an image of John, smiling as she envisioned his long, stringy frame, his wavy brown hair streaked with gray, the powerful chin, and the large brown eyes that had withheld nothing from her. That his visage was so sharp and true in her mind was hardly surprising. John Pennington had been in her memory since she was old enough to know anyone.

A longstanding friend and business associate of her father, John had been a frequent guest at her family's home in Boston. Whenever he had visited, Alexandra was always first down the walkway to greet him, her skirts flying, her smile overjoyed. A child verging on womanhood, she had been fascinated by John's worldliness and flattered by his regard of her as an equal. He never talked down to her and heard every word she said. During his visits, she monopolized his time with youthful possessiveness, never dreaming where it would all lead.

When her father died of throat distemper and creditors flocked like vultures to their door, John had been there to stave them off. Alexandra thought him a shining hero for coming to her mother's aid. Then one night, after he had spoken privately with her mother, she learned there was a price for his generosity. In return for settling her mother's debts, a marriage had been arranged.

Suddenly, alarmingly, Alexandra's life was no longer her own. John Pennington, her trusted friend, the person in whom she confided everything, was to become her *husband*. And she was barely fifteen! Certainly she was more grown-up than other girls her age, but still unseasoned. And John was so very *old*. He had lived three times her years. Worse, with no regard for her preference, he had schemed behind her back to buy her, for that was what it amounted to in Alexandra's mind.

The wedding ceremony was simple and private, the transition from child to wife immediate and frightening. From a world of schoolmasters, dancing lessons, and studies of social graces, she was thrust into John Pennington's daunting life in faraway Philadelphia. She felt betrayed by him. She imagined herself of no more significance to him than a business contract.

How wrong she had been. From the moment they were wed, John had enriched her life with the kind of devotion for which all women yearn. Her greatest terror had come that first night in his bedchamber, but there, with patience, gentleness, and respect, he had made the unimaginable bearable, and eventually quite enjoyable. In time her fears and resentment were laid to rest, and the difference in their ages came to seem unimportant. John encouraged her individuality, taught her responsibility, and entrusted her with the care of his household and his heart.

Alexandra had been content with him. But she had often wondered, lying in his bed late at night, what had passed her by in life because of him. Children might have filled the void, but as years elapsed and none came, she despaired of ever having a family. John, anxious to reassure her, blamed their lack of success on his years and his flagging health. He told her not to fret on his account. She had always been enough for him, and always would be. To the end, he never left her in doubt of the happiness she brought him.

As Alexandra drifted back to her parlor at Willowbrook, a familiar, vulnerable feeling rushed over her. Just when she had begun to feel whole again, Jack Flash had come to remind her of how easily life's balance could be disturbed or shattered. She had lost a cherished friend in John, and for months that loss had filled her with empty turmoil. Gradually she had found new footing, her sorrow had eased into acceptance, and with it came the realization that, for the first time in her life, she could make her own choices.

She made one now. "I refuse to let a thief change my plans," she told Villard. "I'm staying here until November."

"Then you'll need more men to guard the place."

"Edward Brock is handy with a musket. I believe he would lay down his life defending Willowbrook. He and Mary served John faithfully for twenty-five years, you know."

"Edward is only one man, Alexandra."

"There's Christopher Clue." As she said his name, she looked out the window toward the carriage house, where, framed in its open double doors, Clue was repainting the bright yellow trim on the Pennington coach. His tuneless whistling, drifting across the yard, made her smile.

"He's only a boy," Villard said.

"Hardly. He'll be nineteen next month," she pointed out. "And he's very mature for his age."

"When he's sober."

She had no answer for that. Her young coachman often drank too much and spent sotted nights with a milkmaid in Derby, a situation Alexandra pretended to be unaware of. Watching Clue now, she wondered if servants experienced true, deep-felt passion or if they simply squandered flesh when the urge struck. The latter, she imagined, or else Clue would marry the girl instead of merely plumbing her. But that was neither here nor there. Whatever Clue's romantic notions were, she knew his sense of loyalty was deep-rooted and would not be ruffled by the threat of a visit from Jack Flash.

"I shall be fine here," she insisted. "Would you care for some tea, Charles?"

"Please."

She crossed to the bellpull, conscious of his gray eyes following her. He made no effort to conceal his appraisal, which was both flattering and disconcerting. After spending years with a quiet, unobtrusive man, Charles Villard's aggression took some getting used to.

She faced him and asked, "I wonder what's keeping Sheriff Dewees?"

"A pint of ale, no doubt," Villard said drily.

"With the demands of his job, I wouldn't be surprised."

"Ordering deputies about, you mean? The man rarely leaves his office. They should turn it into an ale house for him and be done with it."

"Promise me you won't flay him alive when he gets here."

Appearing to give it some thought, Villard said, "I promise to flay him in a civilized manner."

Alexandra smiled at him across the room. Charles Villard was an easy man to look at, tall and straight-backed, impeccably tasteful in soft doeskin breeches and vest and a white linen shirt. His golden hair, lightly powdered, was drawn back with a black bow. As he returned her look and she saw his expression grow intimate, her face warmed with the memory of his ardent proposal on Sweet Briar's terrace. Glancing away, she was aware of a pleasant sensation, knew it to be enticement, and wondered if she could be happy with him. She decided the answer was worth pursuing.

The tea came. With it came William Dewees, Sheriff of Philadelphia County. A burly man with broad, dark features, Dewees walked heavy in his boots, and Alexandra heard him long before Mrs. Brock showed him into the parlor. One glance at his reddened face and she knew Villard was right—Dewees had dallied with a pint of ale. Perhaps several, from the look of him.

Dewees bowed expansively to Alexandra, ingratiated himself a moment on Villard, then took an armchair near the hearth and wiped his perspiring brow with a kerchief.

"Devilishly warm today," he said to no one in particular.

"Would you like some tea, Sheriff?" Alexandra asked.

"Yes, thank you."

She poured for him, and as he took the teacup in his meaty hands, he said, "Sorry to hear about last night, Mrs. Pennington."

"Billy," Villard said in a flat voice, "we are all sorry. Just tell us what you intend to do about it."

"I'm doing all I can, Charlie."

"Educate me."

For a moment Dewees looked affronted, then quickly sought to mollify his influential acquaintance. "I assure you every clue is being investigated, but there are pitiful few of them. He's like a phantom, comes and goes without leaving a trace."

"He's a flesh-and-blood criminal who has committed eight robberies in the past six months." Villard cocked his head. "How much do you figure he's stolen so far, Billy?"

"Quite a lot."

"Last night alone he took a necklace worth several thousand pounds."

"Plus a less costly one," Alexandra put in, "but it had great sentimental value. It belonged to my mother."

"I'm terribly sorry," Dewees said again. "I'll do everything in my power to get it back for you."

Villard's eyebrows rose. As he stared at Dewees, his silence was somehow more scathing than words.

Uncomfortable, Dewees took out a pencil and notebook and began questioning Alexandra about her encounter with Jack Flash. "Can you describe him for me, Mrs. Pennington?"

She would never forget him. "He was tall," she said. At the time, he had seemed a towering figure.

"Did you notice anything distinctive he was wearing? A ring, clothing, his boots?"

"His clothes were plain, all black." She was silent a moment, lost in those panic-stricken moments when she was face-to-face with the robber. "His cuffs were frayed, and his breeches were almost worn through at the knees. Not a gentleman's clothes, certainly. But his pistols were fine quality. Silver mountings with gold decorations."

"He probably stole them," Villard said.

"Did he speak?" Dewees asked.

Alexandra shook her head. "Not a word. He just looked at me, then ran like the devil was chasing him. I hate to say this, Sheriff, but he could have been anyone."

Having heard those exact words before, Dewees gave her a rueful smile. "Perhaps we'll get lucky," he said. "He may have dropped something outside the house."

Villard took a small silver box from his vest pocket and offered it to Dewees, who declined the snuff. "I had my servants comb the grounds and the near woods," Villard said, pinching some dark grains onto his hand. "They found some tracks, nothing distinguishing. But I suppose you'll want to check for yourself." He inhaled the snuff, stroked his nostrils. "You should also inquire into the whereabouts of certain individuals last night."

"Certain individuals?"

Villard snapped the snuffbox closed. "Oh, for God's sake, Billy," he said irritably. "His victims are all Loyalists! It's obvious he's one of those damned Independents. You know they're behind the violence in Philadelphia."

"Thirty thousand people live in the city," Dewees reminded him. "God alone knows how many of them are Independents. They don't all wear their colors on their sleeves so I can sort them out. I only see what's on the surface."

Eyes narrowed, Villard watched him a moment. "Then you had best start digging."

There was a sudden chill in the warm room. "Of course, Charlie," said Dewees, who had just discovered how icy pale Villard's eyes could be. Those eyes were telling him that his job was in jeopardy, and he had no choice but to believe it. Villard had powerful allies in the Assembly, men who could buy and sell the sheriff's office on a whim. "I'll put every available man on the case," Dewees promised and saw Villard relax a little.

"Indeed you should. And keep me informed."

Dewees said he would and, forsaking his now-cold cup of tea, stood up and excused himself. When he had gone, Villard went to a window and watched him ride away on a lanky mare, a poor horse with a dull coat. A fitting horse for Dewees, Villard thought. The oaf was as clumsy in the saddle as he was on his feet.

Silence had invaded the parlor. Retrieving the sheriff's teacup and saucer, Alexandra put them with the teapot on a small footed tray. "That was a civilized flaying?" she asked.

"I'm sick of his excuses." Villard's voice was sharp. He seemed to quiver with anger. "When I think that you could have been shot last night, it makes me want to thrash him. I can't bear the thought of you being hurt."

His concern softened Alexandra's annoyance. Crossing the room to him, she touched his arm and felt tensed muscles beneath the soft material of his sleeve. "I think

30

you should have a glass of wine, Charles."

"I think I should have several." He sat in a chair, and Alexandra brought him the wine along with a sheet of paper. "What's this?" he asked.

"A notice I wrote. I'm going to have it printed on handbills and distributed at the market next Saturday."

As she stood behind his chair and looked over his shoulder, Villard scanned the paper and saw:

REWARD

For the return of a pearl and diamond pendant necklace, set in silver and valued at five hundred pounds, which was feloniously taken from Mrs. Jonathan Pennington. Whoever returns said property or offers information leading to its recovery shall receive FIFTY POUNDS reward.

Inquiries to Mrs. Pennington at Willowbrook will be accorded discretion.

Villard finished reading and looked up.

"What do you think?" she asked.

"It worries me," he said, taking her hand. His thumb rubbed the backs of her fingers as his solemn eyes held hers. "I think you're asking for more trouble."

Chapter Three

Clouds raced on a crisp blue sky. The morning frost had burned off beneath the sun, but a stiff breeze from the Delaware River chilled the air and brought the salty tang of the ocean to Philadelphia's waterfront. Along its southern quays, where the wharves were large enough to accommodate the most lofty, deep-keeled merchantmen, the clamor from busy warehouses and ship holds drowned the cries of seagulls wheeling overhead.

As Alexandra stepped from Villard's coach onto King Street, the sights, sounds, and smells of America's busiest seaport assaulted her. It was Saturday, market day, and quaysides teemed with tradesmen arriving from the Jersey shore with wares to be sold. The smell of boiled caulking pitch was rank in the air. Hogsheads of grain and flour, rolled from warehouses by burly men, rumbled over cobbles to the docksides, where they were lowered into dank, dark holds for a voyage to a sister colony. Sailors on shipboard and workers on the docks shouted to each other in voices strong enough to carry to mid-river.

Far out on the water, canvas top sails unfurled and grew hard-bellied as sleek vessels glided downriver. Others waited at anchor for a turn at the wharves. The ships carried cargoes from all over the world—linens from Ireland, wines from Portugal and Madeira, expensive woolens and cutlery from England, rum and molasses from the West Indies, and even Rhode Island oysters that were believed to be superior to any others.

Uncertain where to look first, Alexandra asked Villard, "Which one is the *Golden Fleece?*"

"That one," he said, nodding at one of many great ships towering above the wharves. The *Golden Fleece* was for sale, and Villard had come to make an offer to her owner, the ship's captain. He had brought Alexandra and Evelyn Wright along, and afterward planned to escort them to Centre Square, where a hanging was scheduled for three o'clock.

Evelyn surveyed the ship critically. "Her sails need repairs," she told her nephew.

"Sharp-eyed Aunt Evie. I'll make note of that to her captain." Villard offered Alexandra one arm, Evelyn the other. "Shall we go aboard?"

They climbed a steep, ridged gangplank with a rope barrier. As Alexandra lifted the hem of her skirt to step onto the deck, a lewd voice floated down from the rigging, where sailors scrambled like squirrels along the yards. "Higher, girlie!"

Glancing up, she saw grinning faces high above her.

Villard was also looking overhead. "Pay no attention," he said.

"They don't bother me."

"I suppose I can't blame them." Villard regarded her warmly. "You do catch the eye."

Alexandra smiled her thanks at him. She was wearing a periwinkle blue gown trimmed with Flanders lace and accented with violet bows that matched the ones on her hat. The gown's slashed skirt revealed a quilted lavender petticoat, exactly the shade of her velvet cloak. The colors were the latest fashion, and the look on Villard's face said they suited her.

A bearded, heavyset man approached them, introduced himself as the ship's cargo master, and asked their business. Hearing the name Villard, he pointed with a tally stick toward the poop deck. "Sir, the captain's in his cabin. He's expecting you."

"Will the ladies be safe on deck?" Villard asked.

To which the cargo master looked offended. "Of course, sir."

After Villard left to see the captain, Alexandra stood with Evelyn at the starboard rail and watched lashed bundles of timber being lowered into the ship's hold with a block-and-rope whip. As each bundle was stowed, the cargo master notched his tally stick with a knife.

"When Charles leaves that cabin," Evelyn said, "he'll be master of this ship, mark my words."

"No doubt," Alexandra said, polite but preoccupied. She was absorbed in watching a ship at the next wharf, from which sailors were unloading livestock from Europe. Part of the ship's deck was partitioned into stalls and pens that were crowded with horses and cattle, all anxious to leave their floating prison.

"Charles has three other ships, did he tell you?" Evelyn wanted to know.

"No, he didn't."

"He's very well off," Evelyn said. "And so clever and handsome, isn't he? Of course, being his aunt, I suppose I have a jaded eye. But the fact is, there are many hopeful hearts in this city who would gladly tie a knot with him."

Oh, no, Alexandra thought, wondering how much Evelyn knew about her nephew's marriage proposal. "Is that so?" she asked, her smile forced.

"Oh, yes, dear! At the last Assembly Ball, all the mothers were plotting and arranging for their daughters to dance with him. This past winter, Mrs. Cranston threw a sleighing party just so she could maneuver her little Jane alone with him." Eyes wistful, Evelyn placed a hand over her breast and sighed. "The poor girl's heart was broken when he came down with a touch of quinsy and couldn't attend. But her mother is a determined woman. She'll try again, as will every other mother until he's taken."

Alexandra kept quiet.

"Only a fool would hesitate to marry him," Evelyn said.

Now Alexandra was sure Charles had told his aunt. The realization dismayed her, for Evelyn was a notorious gossip, incapable of keeping a secret, and her loose tongue had been known to cause people grief. Alexandra was always mindful of what she said to her, but apparently Charles was not.

Evelyn seemed to be waiting for a response. Before Alexandra could think of one, a horse's enraged scream punctured her thoughts and drew her attention to the livestock ship she had noticed earlier. The distance to the ship was not great, and she had an unhindered view of five brawny sailors trying to manhandle a handsome chestnut

34

stallion onto the aft gangplank. The horse was putting up a terrific fight, thrashing and kicking at his tormentors. Desperate to get loose, the stallion rose up in mane-swirling elegance and danced backward across the deck, front hooves pawing air, rear hooves skidding on wood as he strained against the lead rope.

The lead rope suddenly snapped. Sailors scattered and dove for cover. In hot pursuit of one of them, the stallion lunged across the deck, lost his footing, and crashed into one of the stock pens. Recovering, the horse again reared up and struck out with sharp, deadly hooves, his murderous screams making Alexandra cringe.

Every sailor on deck had taken refuge inside the pens and on gangplanks. Except for one young man. Alexandra did not notice where he came from, but suddenly he was standing alone on the deck, facing the hot-mouthed stallion, who was savaging a door to one of the stalls.

The man was no sailor, she realized, not in those homespun clothes and ancient riding boots. He had a country-bred look about him, tall and well-built with hair as black as a raven's wing. He was either utterly fearless or daft as he waited for the stallion's challenge.

When the maddened beast focused on him, ears pinned back, eyes rolling whitely, the young man slowly extended his hand and began to talk. Although Alexandra could not hear a word he said, she saw the remarkable effect his voice had on the horse.

The stallion stilled, quivering. After a moment, his ears pricked forward, flicked back, came forward again. Muscles twitched beneath the glossy chestnut coat. Tossing his proud head, the stallion stamped a great front hoof on the deck, not with rage, but with indignation, as though stating his case. Then, still wary, the animal stretched out his muzzle and tested the stranger's scent.

As Alexandra watched, riveted, the black-haired man started forward.

"He must be mad," Evelyn breathed.

"He seems to know what he's doing."

Indeed he did. He stopped a few feet from the stallion and let the stallion come to him, let the beast smell him and nip his sleeve and become used to his touch and voice. Only then did the young man take hold of the halter. He

35

led the stallion around the deck several times, talking to him all the while, stroking his thick, arched neck and soothing the nervousness out of him.

When at last he led the horse toward the gangplank, Alexandra drew a tense breath. At the companionway, the stallion balked and planted himself, refusing to go forward.

A curious thing happened then. The young man leaned his forehead against the stallion's cheek, and they stayed that way a few moments, neither moving. Then, gently, the young man blew air into the stallion's flared nostril. When he did it a second time, the horse shivered a little and thrust his muzzle against the young man's chest, the gesture almost playful. Finally, responding to the steadying voice of his handler, the stallion placed one hesitant hoof on the plank. Then another.

Alexandra smiled.

Still nervous but willing, the stallion headed down the gangplank to the wharf, coaxed along by skilled, patient hands. Horse and man reached the dock without further incident, and the sailors on the ship cheered roundly. With a wave, the young man acknowledged their shouts and started along the quay with his charge in tow.

As they neared the wharf where *Golden Fleece* was docked, Alexandra's regard of the high-strung, well-bred stallion increased. Someone had paid a small fortune for the beast. She hoped his owner would appreciate the risk and effort expended to deliver him safely.

When the young man was within earshot, she began to clap for him, much to Evelyn's embarrassment. "Alexandra!" she said sternly. "He'll think you're a hoyden."

Ignoring the caution, Alexandra continued her ovation, and the sound of applause made the young man pause and look up. He met her eyes and seemed to freeze.

"Bravo!" she called down to him.

His startled face broke into a smile. He bowed to her, low and exaggerated, then straightened and started off again with a light, jaunty step. Watching him cross King Street, Alexandra was aware of a warm feeling and knew it to be part admiration. She was still watching when he disappeared into a shadowed alley leading to Front Street.

Chapter Four

Alexandra saw him again that same day. He was at the Centre Square, where the spectacle of the scaffold had drawn a large crowd from the High Street Market.

The chestnut stallion caught her attention first. Standing restively at the fringe of the crowd, the stallion tossed his head and nipped at a dark bay mare alongside him. Astride the mare, relaxed in the saddle as he eyed the tall gibbet, was the young man from the wharf. Curiosity gripped Alexandra as she studied him. He was hatless. His luxurious shock of coal black hair was unpowdered and tied back with a leather thong. As he glanced over the gathering, his gaze came upon hers and held, and Alexandra found herself staring into his good-looking, amiable face. Again, as at the wharf, she had the sensation of recognition on his part, but she had no idea who he was.

For modesty's sake, she looked away and felt Villard draw her protectively to his side. "Stay close," he cautioned her. "Watch out for thieves."

There was no better prey for pickpockets than a curious throng around a scaffold. Alexandra pulled her cloak more tightly about her.

"A good attendance today," Villard noted. "The justices will be pleased."

Hangings and whippings were always held on market days to ensure an adequate number of spectators. Philadelphians complained about having to walk a few blocks beyond the city proper to reach the State House, yet they went much farther without protest to attend executions and, until recently, horse races. Centre Square,

37

with its half-mile course, had been the scene of horse racing in Philadelphia until the First Continental Congress banned the sport along with other frivolous gaming and extravagances. Now the common was used to drill militia companies and for public executions.

"I see the Whartons are here," Villard said. "Aunt Evie will be sorry she missed them."

Alexandra did not miss Aunt Evelyn, who had declined to attend the hanging because, in her words, "I can't bear watching them twitch."

Villard took out his watch and checked the time. "It won't be long now."

No sooner did he speak than they heard the distant rattle of drumsticks on tightened skins. The sound rolled across the common, silencing the crowd, and all heads turned toward the market road. A cart came into view, drawn by a plodding horse and flanked by armed militia. With sunlight glinting on their sharpened bayonets, the guards slow-marched the prisoner to the scaffold.

Barefoot, wearing a soiled shirt and tattered breeches, the convict stepped from the cart and glared with hate-maddened eyes at the crowd.

"He certainly doesn't seem repentant," Alexandra whispered to Villard.

A scuffle broke out near the foot of the scaffolding, but the disturbance was quickly ended by militiamen wielding blade-tipped muskets. The crowd again quieted. The executioner moved to the foot of the scaffold stairs and unrolled a parchment. In a bellowing voice, he read an account of the prisoner's abominable crimes and the sentence that had been passed on him.

Asked if he had any last words, Thomas Coggin, condemned horse thief and rapist, spat on the ground and said nothing. But there were partisan mutters from the crowd, for Coggin had stood against the law, against the rich, and the published reports of his infamous deeds had transformed him into a dark hero to some of his peers.

Alexandra's palms felt slick as she watched Coggin ascend the scaffold with a purposeful air. After his hands were bound behind his back, a leather jerkin was pulled over his head, concealing his spiteful expression. With a shake of his head, Coggin refused the protection of a minister's prayer. Guided by firm hands, he mounted the executioner's ladder and stood ramrod stiff as the noose came around his neck.

The air grew hushed. As the ladder was knocked away, Alexandra found somewhere else to look, her fingers clutching Villard's arm. Above the hiss of the crowd, she heard a throttled grunting that went on and on as Coggin's resisting body clung to life. Moisture stung her eyes. Coggin was a low-bred thief and a rapist, but his prolonged agony pierced her, making her close her eyes and whisper a prayer for his unfortunate soul.

Blinking back tears, she focused on a now-familiar sight—the handsome chestnut stallion. Beside the horse, his face grave, the black-haired man was watching the condemned thief swing from the gibbet.

"Are you all right?" Villard asked, leaning his head close to hers.

"I'm fine." She shot a glance at the scaffold, where Coggin was twitching a death dance. His spasms gradually lessened until, with a last terrible jerk, his corpse hung still and silent, turning in a slow circle. In two hours, the body would be taken down and removed for burial. Until then, it would serve as proof of the Court's ultimate power.

The macabre scene over, murmuring voices arose as the crowd began to recover from its grimness. Within minutes, laughter and lively conversations defied the stark reality, dangling crooked-necked from the noose.

Alexandra found her gaze drawn back to the chestnut stallion. Several people had gathered to admire the horse, and as she watched, the black-haired man dismounted to speak with them. "Do you know that man?" she asked Villard.

Following her look, he frowned slightly and said in a toneless voice, "Dalton Philips."

Alexandra was familiar with the name. "The horse breeder?"

"Amongst other things," Villard replied. "He also raises cattle and sheep. He owns a farm on Wissahickon Creek."

"I've seen his advertisements in the *Gazette*," she said. But always, when reading them, she had envisioned a

39

plain, soiled bumpkin with farm animals for sale. Now she amended her assumption, for Dalton Philips seemed far from ordinary, and his clothes, while not good quality, were clean and neat.

She told Villard about the incident at the wharf that morning. "It was quite amazing the way he handled that horse."

"He's a fair horseman," Villard allowed, looking anywhere but at Dalton Philips.

Detecting an underlying chagrin in his tone, Alexandra guessed its source and nudged his arm. "He's raced against your horses, hasn't he?"

"And won every time," Villard admitted with a sigh. "Just once, I would like the satisfaction of beating him. He rides his own mounts, can you believe it?"

"He can't afford a jockey, I suppose."

"No. His farm is struggling."

"Is he a Loyalist?"

"A fence rider," Villard said. "He refuses to be drawn into political quarrels."

"You seem to know him well."

"Not by choice." Villard looked to his right where, surrounded by interested listeners, Dalton Philips was explaining something about the stallion. "He likes rubbing elbows with the gentry so he can find buyers for his horses, but all the better gentlemen ignore him."

"Are his horses of good quality?"

"Better than the man."

Her narrowed eyes admonished him. "That's unfair, Charles."

"It's true," he insisted. "You would understand if you had ever spoken with him."

"Then I will speak with him, because I would like a closer look at that stallion. You must admit he's impressive." She took Villard's arm. "Shall we?"

"Whatever you like," he said, but without much enthusiasm.

Dalton Philips was ready to mount up when he saw them coming his way. He paused, one foot in the mare's stirrup, and watched them with a puzzled look, as if unsure it was actually him they wanted to see. When he realized it was, he lowered his foot and faced them.

40

To Alexandra's discomfort, Villard did not remove his hat when he said, "Good afternoon, Mr. Philips."

"Mr. Villard," he replied in the same lukewarm manner.

Now the hat came off. "May I introduce Mrs. Alexandra Pennington?"

Fixing his gaze on her, Dalton Philips nodded courteously. "A pleasure, ma'am," he said.

He might be a farmer, but close up he was remarkably handsome. His eyes were deep green with thick lashes. Cat's eyes, quick, bold, and thoughtful, seeming to probe inside her. The sensation was not unpleasant.

"I saw you at the wharf this morning," she said.

He smiled, vaguely embarrassed. "I remember."

"You were thrilling to watch."

"Thank you."

Alexandra guessed him to be a few years older than herself, unless she counted his eyes. In them were depths she could not begin to fathom. Reaching out, she stroked the stallion's glossy neck. "His disposition has certainly improved. He seems like a different horse."

"He wanted off that ship awfully bad," Dalton said. "Can't say I blame him a bit."

"Is he yours?" she asked.

Dalton nodded. "His name's Mercury. He just arrived from Ireland."

"Irish bred?" Villard asked, suddenly interested.

"In Dublin," Dalton replied.

At that, Villard sighed and looked sympathetic. "Then you've wasted your money."

"What makes you think so?"

"Everyone knows the best horses are bred in England."

After considering the stallion a moment, Dalton said, "He looks right grand to me."

"Forgive me for saying so, but I've seen better quality."

"Not in the Colonies."

Listening to their exchange, Alexandra sensed a deep-rooted antagonism between the two men, simmering beneath a veneer of manners, and she wondered if gaming was their only area of conflict. There would be no attempt at civility, she imagined, were she not present.

41

"You're looking at the finest racehorse in America," Dalton said.

Smiling, Villard pursued him. "Would you care to back that claim with a friendly wager?"

"Against what horse?"

"My three-year-old gelding, North Wind. I'm sure you've heard of him?"

"Many times," Dalton said. "He's a fast ride, but they don't come no faster than Mercury. Quick as a bolt, he is."

"How would you know when you haven't even tried him?"

"Don't have to," Dalton shrugged. "I can tell just by looking, you see."

"Five hundred pounds says North Wind will beat him."

Alexandra saw astonishment flicker in Dalton's eyes, then swift calculation. "You're forgetting the ban on racing," he said.

"I'll do as I please on my own property." Villard spread his hands and coaxed, "Come now, Mr. Philips. You've beaten me to a fare-thee-well in the past. It's only fair that you give me a chance to recoup some of my losses. Unless, of course, you're afraid to race?"

Dalton watched him a moment. "I can't match your bet, Mr. Villard." It was said with a touch of defiance, and it made Alexandra take a closer look at plain, worn clothing and scuffed boots.

"Then I'll take your stallion as payment if you lose," Villard said.

Dalton hesitated, and Alexandra sensed his struggle with temptation. Five hundred pounds must be a fantastic sum of money to a farmer. But the stallion was young, probably untrained for racing, and had spent the past six weeks on board a ship. Only a fool would accept the challenge.

"I accept," Dalton said, "if you'll give me two weeks to prepare my horse."

"One week."

In the pause, Alexandra watched Dalton's face and knew what was coming. "One week," he agreed.

Villard beamed in satisfaction. "Saturday next at Sweet Briar? Three o'clock?"

"I'll be there," Dalton said, then nodded farewell to Alexandra. "Good day, ma'am."

"Good day, Mr. Philips."

Gathering his mare's reins, Dalton swung himself into her saddle, touched his heels to her flanks, and was off at a lively canter. At his urging, the mare stretched into a fluid gallop, trailed closely by the chestnut stallion.

That Dalton Philips rode beautifully came as no surprise to Alexandra. Watching him cross the square, she asked Villard, "Why did you challenge him?"

"Why not?"

"Because you know he can't afford to lose that horse. It would be a terrible blow to him."

"It will teach him not to be boastful."

Alexandra weighed his remark a moment. "He was boastful, wasn't he?" she conceded.

"Obscenely."

"I still intend to bet against you, Charles."

His mouth sagged. "You wouldn't!"

"I certainly would. That horse is magnificent. Besides," she said, linking arms with him, "I have a soft spot for second-raters."

"I shall feel terrible when I win," Villard said.

Meeting his pained look, Alexandra laughed at his concern. "Now who's boasting?"

Chapter Five

Alexandra had always prided herself on being a good horsewoman. She exhibited natural grace in the saddle and could keep up with a hunt through the most rugged terrain. Once, on a dare, she had raced her dappled gray mare against Timothy Matlack on his prize filly, and had beaten him soundly, much to his embarrassment.

Today her mare was as frisky as the October wind that gusted through Sweet Briar's hollows and rustled the leaves that were turning the vivid colors of autumn. Dressed in a woolen riding habit, Alexandra rode beside Villard along the race course where, later that afternoon, Dalton Philips would compete against Villard's jockey, an employee at Sweet Briar's stable.

Reining his horse closer to hers, Villard clasped the gloved hand she held out to him. "How much did you bet on Philips?" he wanted to know.

Alexandra smiled. All day he had been burning to ask the question, and had finally done so. "One hundred pounds," she said lightly.

"Good God." His fingers squeezed hers as if in consolation. "What scheming opportunist took advantage of your urge to gamble?"

"George." Her brother-in-law, although unable to attend the race, had been delighted to accept her wager.

Villard said, "I thought you were joking about betting against me."

"No, I was quite serious."

"So I see."

As they topped a grassy knoll, the brick mansion came

into view. Scattered across its south lawn in colorful array were a dozen dancing couples, friends of Villard who had come to Sweet Briar to watch the contest. At the moment, his guests were being pampered with wine, music, and an abundance of food laid out on linen-covered tables.

A shrill laugh, carried by the wind, made Alexandra grip her reins tighter. Frowning, she watched a short, plump man in a gaudy yellow suit toss his wineglass high in the air. He pirouetted, teetering on red-heeled pumps, then caught the glass behind his back. Applause followed his performance.

"Why on earth did you invite that silly man?" she asked.

Villard studied his friend Stephen Lindsay, owner of a glassworks in the city. "He does look atrocious in that suit, doesn't he?"

"Like a chubby canary."

Villard laughed. "Other than that, what's wrong with him?"

"He's loud-mouthed," she said, "and always drunk."

"He means no harm. Besides, everyone here is drunk. He fits in nicely."

But Alexandra could not dismiss her dislike of Lindsay. "He's a do-nothing. His only concern is where and when the next party will be held."

"And what do you think he should be concerned about?" Villard asked.

She turned troubled eyes on him. "The rebel army at Cambridge, perhaps?"

"Sweetheart, believe me," he soothed, "their audacity will amount to nothing."

"How can you say that when people all over the Colonies are drilling for battle?"

They were also making firelocks, casting mortars, shells, and shot, and making saltpeter. To Alexandra's unease, Philadelphia was decorated with flags inscribed "Liberty or Death." The impetus of rebellion was greater in other parts of the Colonies, but everywhere Americans were itching to strike a blow, even those who continued to speak in terms of reconciling colonial interests with British sovereignty. The radicals in Congress claimed their military preparations were not meant to destroy British rule, but to protect American rights. Meanwhile,

45

through the urgings of those same extremists, the cries for independence grew louder, stronger, and more dangerous with each day.

"Perhaps Mr. Washington doesn't frighten you," Alexandra said, "but he does me. He might deliberately do something to ruin the Crown's chances for a peaceful solution."

"I say England should get busy with her muskets rather than her pens," Villard said. "There's only one way to deal with treason against the King. Crush it."

She flinched from the truth in his words. But while the idea of using force appalled her, she was even more alarmed to contemplate rule by the demagogues and firebrands who were preaching principles of equality and democracy. It was madness to want to change a tried and true system that had sustained the Colonies for one hundred and fifty years. Thoughtful men, reasoning men, could scarcely deny that America's natural alliance and loyalty was to England.

However, the rebels were doing just that. They were rushing headlong toward an armed conflict with the mother country. What had once struck Alexandra as impossible now seemed increasingly likely—civil war. American challenging American. Tories and Whigs held in hatred and fear of each other.

"Suppose the rebels win a battle?" she asked.

"Absurd."

"Just suppose they do," she insisted, for she did not share Villard's conviction that the rebel army was harmless.

"Then I'll fight," he said with dignity, "to defend my home and my King against rabble. If the trouble escalates, Loyalists will have to fight. It's as simple as that."

It was brutally simple, and it frightened her to think of him facing loaded muskets. Never mind that those muskets were in the hands of misguided farmers and tradesmen. Bullets were bullets. Dead was dead.

"Don't look so forlorn," he said gently.

"I can't help it."

"Dare I hope your concern is for me?"

In that moment, meeting his earnest eyes, Alexandra felt closer to him than ever before. Her fingers tightened

46

around his. "You know it is."

When they reached the gathering on the lawn, a groom was waiting to take their horses, and a steward stood ready with two glasses of wine.

"Heigh-ho!" a voice hailed them.

Her face carefully blank, Alexandra watched Stephen Lindsay approach, his yellow satin suit shimmering in the afternoon sunlight.

"The lovebirds returneth," he cooed and sketched a feathery greeting in the air. "Sweet Alexandra, I do hope that blush on your cheeks is from stolen moments of lust, and not this raw wind."

Alexandra bristled. It seemed Lindsay could not speak without leering or attempting to cause someone, anyone, embarrassment. "Hello, Stephen," was all she said.

He seemed oblivious to her cool tone. He was quite lathered. "Delicious party, Charlie," he said. "But then, you always excel at entertainment."

"I do try."

"And a glorious result you achieve. The entire world should be told of your consummate generosity."

Alexandra's gaze flicked from one man to the other. For the life of her, she could not comprehend why Villard tolerated this empty-headed fool. More than that, he went out of his way to include Lindsay in his circle of friends, most of whom were a decent, intelligent sort. Perhaps he felt sorry for Lindsay, whose best attribute, as far as she could tell, was his skill at fawning.

As the musicians struck up a quick, joyful tune, Lindsay folded his hands over his heart and looked wistful. "Ah, 'The World Turned Upside Down,'" he sighed. "Just hearken to that sweet flute. How refreshing! Those churlish fifes and drums are the only music one hears anymore." Signaling a steward to refill his wineglass, he asked Villard, "Is North Wind ready for the race?"

"Indeed," said Villard, confident. "Sammy's been working him on the course all week."

"If Philips had any backers, I would bet a frightful sum on North Wind. He's a sure winner."

"Have you seen Mr. Philips's stallion?" Alexandra asked Lindsay.

"No, I haven't," he admitted.

"Then your optimism may be premature." She was not sure what inspired her to do it, but her next words were, "It so happens I'm backing Mr. Philips's horse, and I'll be happy to accept any wager you care to make against him."

Lindsay sputtered in surprise.

"One hundred pounds?" she asked. "Does that strike your fancy?"

Lindsay glanced open-mouthed at Villard, who seemed irritated, but said nothing. Shrugging, Lindsay looked back at Alexandra. "I must say I admire your pluck, Alexandra. Very well, one hundred pounds it is." He suddenly paused, distracted. "Charlie," he said, nudging Villard's arm. "The bumpkin hath arrived."

"Where?"

"Over there." With his chin, Lindsay indicated the line of carriages in the drive. "Alexandra, isn't that your coachman he's speaking with?"

Alexandra looked and saw Dalton Philips deep in conversation with Christopher Clue. From their expressions and easy gestures, she realized this was not the first time the two men had met.

"It is," she said.

"Perhaps we should leave him there," Lindsay suggested with an air of distaste. "He appears more at home with the help."

At that, Villard flashed Lindsay an annoyed look. "Stephen, show some manners. Mr. Philips is here at my invitation, and I expect you to be courteous to him."

"I'll go and get him," Alexandra said.

"But—"

"I want to give him some advice about the course." Smiling, she handed Villard her wineglass. "You don't mind, do you? After all, I have a substantial sum riding on him."

She left without waiting for his reply. Let him suffer Lindsay if he liked; she had better things to do. As she scanned the prettily polished crowd, her smile became full-fledged and mischievous. Wouldn't they just die to see her fraternizing with a livestock farmer? Especially Charles, and it would serve him right for subjecting her to that loud-mouthed canary.

The first thing she noticed about Dalton Philips was

that he was wearing the same clothes as when she first saw him. And they were not as clean as before. When he turned and saw her, she smiled a warm welcome. "Hello, Mr. Philips."

"Hello, ma'am."

Now she was close enough to detect something else about him. He smelled strongly of cheap lye soap, but it did not mask the odor that came from working with livestock. Ignoring the musky scent, she took his arm and asked her coachman, "Christopher, would you look after Mr. Philips's horse? He and I need to discuss the fine points of the race course."

Clue's quick, cheerful face lit up. "Mrs. Pennington," he said in a sly voice. "You didn't bet on this scoundrel, did you?"

"Indeed I did. Because he's going to win. Aren't you, Mr. Philips?" she asked, looking at him.

He seemed momentarily tongue-tied. Beneath her fingers, his arm felt tense. "I'll do my best," he said.

"I have no doubt that you will." With that, Alexandra drew him away with her. In no hurry to return to the party, she guided him in the opposite direction, and they followed a well-kept pathway that meandered through a series of terraced gardens. Along the way, she described the race course in as much detail as she could remember from her ride.

"You should take a turn around it before the race," she advised.

"I intend to," he said, then shot her a sidelong glance. "Did you really bet on me, ma'am?"

His wondering look made her want to laugh. "Yes."

"And what did Mr. Villard think of that?"

"What could he think?" she said, amused. "It's my money."

Villard, torn between amazement and outrage, was watching them stroll arm in arm through the topiary garden. Alexandra Pennington on a farmer's arm. To Villard's mind, her elegance made Dalton Philips seem all the more crude and awkward. Observing his furtive glances at her, Villard's lips twitched. Who could blame the clod for gawking? She must seem a goddess to him.

Excusing himself from the gathering, Villard walked to

49

Sweet Briar's stable, where his jockey was saddling North Wind in the paddock. At the paddock gate, Villard paused a moment to savor the black gelding's splendid conformation. North Wind was an enormous creature, a full sixteen hands and every inch of it champion. Crossing to the horse, Villard patted his sleek, muscular shoulder.

"How is he today, Sammy?"

"Tip-top, Mr. Villard."

"Did you get a look Philips's stallion?"

"Yes, sir."

"And?"

Sammy hesitated. "A good-looking horse, sir," he conceded. "But North Wind is about to flatten him."

That was exactly what Villard wanted to hear. Smiling, he patted Sammy's shoulder much as he had North Wind's. Then his amusement faded and something sinister came into his eyes. "Beat him," he said. "I don't care how you manage it, just beat him."

"We'll win, sir," Sammy said and knew he better had.

Chapter Six

Dalton Philips had come to Sweet Briar for money. A staggering amount of money. To get it, he was willing to endure a pompous crowd, leering glances, and the discomforting sensation of being out of his element. All week he had prepared himself for these obstacles.

But he had not, in his wildest thoughts, expected to stroll through gardens with Alexandra Pennington on his arm. For once he was glad he had bathed, frigid as the creek had been that morning. Still, having a clean body did not inspire his wits or make his heart calm. His mind seemed paralyzed as he groped for replies to her questions. But what bothered him most, and what he tried hard to overcome, was the sense of subservience she triggered in him. His instinct was to humble himself. Old habits died hard.

"Would you like some wine?" she asked. They had reached the lawn where the party was in progress, and Dalton saw a number of heads turn to stare his way. His chin rose a notch as he smiled at her.

"Maybe after the race," he said.

"Will you stay afterward?"

Was she hopeful or just being polite? "If you like," he ventured to see what she would say. Before she could reply, a voice behind him said, "Mr. Philips, how good of you to show."

Turning, Dalton came face-to-face with Charles Villard and struggled to keep his smile in place. "I said I'd be here."

"So you did. Frankly, I thought you might change your

mind about risking your horse."

"No, sir." Goddamnit, don't grovel for him.

"You're a brave fellow," Villard said, then took out his watch and checked the time. "It's nearly three o'clock. Are you ready?"

"Soon as I take Mercury around the course."

The next thing Dalton knew, Villard had extricated Alexandra Pennington from him with a slick maneuver. "On to the fray, man," Villard urged. He was smiling, but his humor died in his eyes. "My guests are growing restless."

Thus Dalton was dismissed. As he started away, Alexandra called after him, "I'll be cheering for you, Mr. Philips."

She would be the only one, he imagined.

The race course began on the south lawn, went past the stable complex, rounded a hay barn, and followed a mown path across a broad, sloping meadow. Beyond the meadow, the path plunged through a long, wooded defile where its width narrowed to less than ten yards. Then leaving the woods and veering up a grassy hillock, the race course came full circle back to the south lawn. A half-mile of uneven terrain, twice around.

When Dalton finished his trial lap, Villard's jockey was waiting at the starting marker, sitting coolly astride a prancing North Wind. Dalton knew Sammy Finn from race days at the Centre Square track.

"Hello, Sammy," he greeted him.

"Dalton." No warmth here either. Wearing Sweet Briar livery, Sammy looked briskly businesslike, as did his horse.

Mercury snorted and flared his nostrils at the gelding's scent, but Dalton quieted him. The stallion's ears were pricked, his eyes were liquid clear as he fought the bit, eager to be off. The warm-up lap had merely whetted his appetite.

Villard and his guests, drinks in hand, stood off to one side. As Dalton glanced their way, he met Alexandra's waiting eyes, saw her encouraging smile, and smiled back at her, rejuvenated. This was his day, Mercury was prepared to beat the devil, and five hundred pounds waited at the rainbow's end.

Reining the stallion to the marker, he was conscious of the nervous, quivering energy set to explode beneath him. He looked over at his opponent. "Clean ride, Sammy?"

Eyes looking straight ahead, Sammy didn't answer.

Villard raised a red scarf in the air. "Are the riders ready?"

They were.

The scarf fluttered to the ground. Dalton touched his heels to Mercury's flanks. Massive muscles bunched and flexed as Mercury shot forward into a smooth, effortless gallop, Dalton lying low along his withers as the stallion's long strides ate up the lawn. Just behind them, North Wind's thudding hooves were leaving impressions in the soft turf.

They swept past the stable, then the hay barn loomed ahead. As Dalton guided Mercury around the barn, North Wind swung alongside them, then spurted forward and took the lead. Crossing the meadow, the stallion strained to overtake the gelding, but Dalton held him on a tight rein, letting North Wind set the pace.

Mercury settled down. The meadow slipped by beneath them in a golden blur, then trees whipped past on either side as the horses entered the wooded leg of the course. Up ahead, Sammy was using his crop with a vengeance, flailing on a glossy black rump, but North Wind could not shake the chestnut demon galloping in his wake.

"Attaboy," Dalton coaxed his horse. "Make him work, tire him out."

The course fled uphill. The horses burst from shadows into sunlight, thundered over a rise, and bore down on the starting marker. As they raced past the spectators, Dalton was vaguely aware of shouts and shrill whistles urging the riders on. He still held the stallion in check, but moments later, when the hay barn again came into view, he let Mercury go.

After spending a rigorous week with the man on his back, Mercury understood the urgent signals that now came from knees, heels, and hands, pressing and squeezing, and Dalton, his spirit soaring with his horse, felt a change beneath him as raw power was unleashed. In that moment, he knew the race belonged to Mercury. Mercury was running because he loved to, not because he must, and the stallion made his move with an aggressive, unswerving will to win.

He floated up on North Wind's flank. Glancing back, Sammy saw then coming on like a bad dream, threatening his slim lead, and he laid leather to his sweating black horse. But Mercury was flying, his mane whipping past Dalton's shoulder as they pulled abreast of the leader.

The horses plunged neck and neck into the narrow, wooded passage. Dalton could hear North Wind grunting with effort. As he glanced over at him, a sudden, stinging pain lashed his neck. Jolted, Dalton saw Sammy's arm coil again, saw the riding crop in his fist and cold purpose in his eyes. Before he could react, Sammy delivered a savage strike to Mercury's muzzle, and the stallion swerved wide. Branches clipped Dalton's face and clawed his arm as he ducked low, sawing on the reins, and brought the stallion back on course.

North Wind had retaken the lead. Until that instant, Dalton had refused to think about losing the glorious animal under him. Now he could think of nothing else. Crouched over Mercury's withers, he pressed his face to the stallion's hot, damp neck and urged, "Go, boy. Goddamn you, move. *Move!*"

Muscles surged beneath the chestnut pelt. With an incredible increase of speed, Mercury again drew even with North Wind, matched him stride for stride, then inched ahead. Going flat-out, the horses broke from the woods and lunged up the grassy hillock toward the homestretch, with Mercury in front by a nose. From the corner of his eye, Dalton saw Sammy cock his arm for another strike and fury welled in him.

His hand shot out, snagging the crop. As he flung it away, Mercury collided with North Wind and both horses stumbled. Recovering, they plunged on toward the finish line, their hooves pounding the ground and flinging up clods of earth as they went. When they swept over the marker, the stallion was ahead by a full length.

As the horses galloped past her, Alexandra's heart was racing with them. Elated, she watched Dalton and Sammy rein in and circle back toward the finish line, but when they dismounted and faced each other, her exhilaration ebbed as she realized something was terribly wrong between them. They seemed ready to attack each other.

She followed Villard toward them and heard Dalton say, "You bloody bastard!" to Sammy's defiant face. Hands balled into fists, a furious Sammy squared off with him.

"Stop!" Villard commanded, seizing Sammy's arm and flinging him backward. "What's the meaning of this?"

"Ask him, sir." Sammy stabbed an accusing finger at Dalton. "He's the cheater."

Villard looked at Dalton for a response.

"He struck my horse and me with his crop."

"That's not true, Mr. Villard," Sammy said hotly. "I did nothing of the sort."

Dalton lifted a hand to his neck. "Then what's this?" he demanded, fingering a two-inch red welt.

"I only did that after you deliberately jostled me. You were trying to knock me off my horse!"

"That ain't what happened," Dalton said in a low voice, and Alexandra saw him trembling a little. She also noted Sammy's furtive eyes and shifting stance and read these as signs of guilt. Even so, the grumbling from Sweet Briar's guests favored Villard's jockey.

Encouraged, Sammy told his boss, "He's lying, sir."

"And he smells like a pigsty," Stephen Lindsay sneered.

As Dalton's head whipped toward the loud, derisive voice, Alexandra saw that his eyes were on fire. She wanted to box Lindsay's ears. For a tense moment, she thought Dalton would advance and take his revenge on the imbecile. Instead he looked back at Villard and said with strained calm, "I won the race. Now let's you and me settle up so I can leave."

At that, Lindsay strode forward and plucked at Villard's sleeve. "You're not going to pay him?" he whined, incredulous.

"Of course I am. He did win, Stephen."

"Rubbish! He jostled your horse, I saw it clearly. He's nothing but a cheat." Murmured agreement followed Lindsay's assertion.

Eyeing the fiery red mark on Dalton's neck, Alexandra started to come to his defense, but her words were cut off by Villard, who, to her relief, seemed as angry at Lindsay as she was.

"Stephen," he said in a warning tone, "if you cannot be

55

civil, then be quiet. Mr. Philips is my guest. I will cover your loss if I must, but I won't tolerate your rudeness to him. The fact is, no rules were laid down beforehand. If jostling occurred during the race, then it must be allowed."

"It wasn't on purpose," Dalton protested. "He was striking my bloody horse."

Villard nodded, his face grim. "If you say so, then I apologize for Sammy's behavior."

Startled, Sammy drew himself up. "But, sir—"

"I've heard enough!" Villard snapped and silence fell. After a moment, he beckoned Dalton with his fingers. "Come along and I'll pay you."

"No."

With failing patience, Villard stared at him. "My good man, I said I'd honor the bet."

"Keep your money," Dalton said, taking stock of the hostile faces around him. "It ain't worth having lies spread. Good day, Mr. Villard."

When he tugged Mercury's reins and started forward, people moved out of his way. Once clear of the crowd, he slipped his foot into the stirrup and swung himself onto the stallion's back. Head high, as fiercely proud as the horse beneath him, he left Sweet Briar without looking back.

Watching him go, Alexandra felt a nagging shame for the treatment he had received, but that was nothing compared with the guilt she felt for keeping silent.

Chapter Seven

"I'm so glad you moved back to the city," George Pennington told Alexandra with a happy smile. "I've been so bored these past few weeks. Now I have someone to visit on cold afternoons."

It had been an unusually frigid November, and Alexandra was bundled against the frosted morning. Her scarlet cloak, made of a heavy wool weave, was lined with fur, as was her red satin hat. The hat was pulled down low to cover her ears, and its scarlet ribbons were tied beneath her chin. Although the temperature inside her coach was comfortable enough, ice-glazed windows made it difficult to view the scenery. When they entered the city proper, the coach lurched as its wheels left a hard-rutted roadway and rolled onto smooth cobblestones.

"You could have visited me at Willowbrook," she told her brother-in-law.

"I meant to. But for some reason or another, I never got around to it."

Alexandra knew what the reason was. Concerned, she reached over and squeezed his arm. "Haven't you been feeling well?"

"I feel fine," he said, but she had known him too long to be fooled by his nonchalance. The flesh of his face was as wan and transparent as the thin November sky. His bones were so pronounced he seemed skeletal.

To her doubting look, he said, "I could have walked to the market, you know. You didn't have to come round for me."

"Troublemakers should not be permitted to walk the streets."

"Oh my," Pennington said. "I sense a rebuke coming."

"A well-deserved one," she said.

His brown eyes crinkling, Pennington straightened his wig with his fingertips, loosened his shoulders with a shrug, and faced her with fragile dignity. "Fire away."

"Will you be serious?"

"I assure you, dear girl, I'm quite serious."

"I heard you started a quarrel at the City Tavern the other night."

"I did no such thing," he said. "I was provoked into defending my honor."

"By slandering Mr. Washington before a Whig crowd?"

"I did not slander him. I spoke the truth about him."

"You called him an ass," she said.

Pennington smiled. "And so he is."

Sighing, Alexandra moved her feet to the warmer and wondered why George Pennington could not be more like his brother John. Her late husband had always been reluctant to express his views in public, whereas George could not seem to call enough attention to himself. And his opinions had earned him dangerous enemies—radicals who favored violence over words. Furtive, dirty little men who met in dirty little alleys to hatch their vicious schemes.

"George, I'm afraid for you," she told him.

"I know you are," he said, taking her hand between his thin, knobby ones. "And I do appreciate it. But if I keep silent about something I know is wrong, something that damages everything I believe in, then what is the point of my being in the world?"

Alexandra was quiet, mulling over his words. Finally she said, "I understand your feelings. I'm a Tory, and I despise the rebels as much as you do. But I also care about your silly bones, so I want you to promise me that you'll stop being an instigator." When Pennington merely frowned, she said, "Please, George. So I can quit worrying about you."

"Oh, dear," he said in a pitying voice. "Poor Charles hasn't a prayer against you."

"What do you mean?"

"He's already smitten. Show him those glistening blue eyes and that tremulous look, and he'll melt," said George, wavering his fingers to imitate what he envisioned, "into a warm puddle at your feet."

Into the silence came the clip-clop of horses' hooves and the rumble of coach wheels on cobbles. A dog barked somewhere nearby.

"How neatly you changed the subject," Alexandra said with a grudging smile.

"Oh, look!" he said, glancing outside. "We're at the market."

Normally Alexandra came to the market with her maidservant, Mary Brock. Today she had left Mary at home in order to speak privately with George Pennington about his reckless behavior. But her stubborn brother-in-law was through listening, and Christopher Clue was opening the coach doors for them, leaving her with no choice but to pick up her shopping basket and step outside.

The market building, considered by many as the most important building in the city, was one story high, supported by enormous brick pillars, and extended five hundred feet along the center of High Street. Some sections sold fish, some freshly butchered meats, and others sold butter, and vegetables and fruits in season, all brought to town in the covered wagons lining the broad avenue outside. Everything under the great, arched roof was as neat and clean as a dining hall. Crowds of people of every rank thronged into the market from cross streets, and the noise that saluted the ears was a great, buzzing murmur that resounded through the cavernous building.

"Where shall we go first?" Pennington asked as Alexandra took his arm.

"I need butter and cheese."

"This way, then."

"And also some mutton from Mr. Thompson."

"This way, then," said Pennington, changing direction.

"And don't let me forget bread."

"I have already forgotten the first item."

"How convenient it must be," she said, "to have such a short memory."

"It does come in handy. No one ever asks important favors of me for fear I'll forget to do them." Steering her

59

past a man in a tall beaver hat, Pennington went on, "But it isn't that my memory is short, mind. Merely selective. I should think by now you would know that."

Alexandra realized he was still talking to her, and some part of her was listening. But the rest of her did not hear a word he said because a familiar face had snared her attention. Across the crowded aisleway, Dalton Philips was standing before a dairy stall where small pyramids of cheese, eggs, and butter were on display. Encouraged by the seller, he took a coin from his coat pocket, scooped out an edge full of butter, and sampled it.

"Alexandra!"

"Yes, George?"

"Good heavens, have you lost your ears?"

"I'm sorry," she said, then rushed on, "George, there's someone over there I must speak with. Would you mind waiting for me at Mr. Thompson's stall? I promise not to be long."

Pennington rolled his eyes. "That wistful look again. Oh, very well."

"You're a dear," she said, kissing his cheek. As Pennington went on his way, Alexandra turned and looked for Dalton Philips. He was no longer at the dairy farmer's stall. In fact, he was nowhere in sight.

Dodging bodies, she crossed the aisle and caught a glimpse of him moving toward the fish market. She went after him. He disappeared in the milling throng, reappeared for a moment, then disappeared again as she dogged him. When next she saw him, he was reading a broadsheet tacked to a wall in the fish market. At least, he was attempting to decipher it, but the task seemed a laborious one for him. As Alexandra watched, he grimaced, chewing his bottom lip, and then his mouth worked as he sounded out a difficult word. For some reason his struggle touched her to the quick.

Since the race at Sweet Briar, she had conjured his image many times, usually with guilt, but sometimes with an unexpectedly warm sentiment. Studying him now, with him unaware of her and at his ease, she realized her memory had fallen short. He was dressed no better than before, and his boots were mud splattered, as was the hem of his greatcoat. But there was nothing commonplace about the handsome face that suddenly grew wary, as though sensing her stare, then looked straight at her.

Caught out, she moved to join him. "Hello, Mr. Philips." Her fear of meeting resentment was swept aside by his smile.

"Mrs. Pennington!" he said with undisguised pleasure. "It's good to see you. How have you been?"

"Very well, thank you. And you?"

"Never better."

Her image of him had been so wrong. She had forgotten the vitality in his face, how richly black his hair was, the boldness and defiance and humor of those green eyes and strong jaw. Glancing away, she studied the broadsheets tacked to the wall beside them. "Spending time with the felons?"

He laughed. "Just having a curious look."

"At this one?" she asked, indicating a Proclamation which read:

ONE THOUSAND POUNDS REWARD
For the apprehension of a Villian known as Jack Flash, who has been concerned in many daring Burglaries and Robberies in and near the City of Philadelphia, so that he should be convicted thereof in due Course of Law.

"It caught my eye," Dalton said. "So did this one." He tapped a handbill that someone had posted beside the Proclamation.

Recognizing her notice offering a reward for her necklace, Alexandra said drily, "It might as well be taken down, for all the good it's done."

"No results?"

"None."

"I'd count myself lucky," Dalton said, suddenly serious.

"You think the notice is dangerous?"

He nodded. "It's the wording, you see. Like asking Jack Flash to visit you and do more mischief."

"A chance I'm willing to take. Anyway," she shrugged, "he's never hurt anyone."

"Yet," Dalton said and searched her face. "The necklace must be important to you."

"It was a gift from my mother."

"I'm sorry you lost it."

A moment went by. Then Alexandra, because she felt compelled and because she liked this unpretentious man, told him, "I'm sorry for what happened at Sweet Briar."

She was afraid the reminder would put ice between them. Instead he smiled again. "That was some day," he said.

"It was disgraceful how you were treated."

"I survived."

"That's beside the point," she said, wanting him to understand how badly she felt about the incident.

He must have realized it, for he said, "It wasn't your doing. I'm just glad you didn't lose any money on me."

"I should have made money, and so should you. You won the race."

"I did win," he agreed. "And I ran a clean race. That's worth something." With that, he went on to another subject. "I was riding by Willowbrook the other day and saw your caretaker. He said you moved back to the city."

"Yes," she said, "to my house on Fourth Street. It's just above Spruce."

"I know the place. Christopher Clue pointed it out to me once." To her questioning look, he explained, "I sold Clue a mare a while back, that's how I know him."

"You sold him Sunshine?"

Dalton nodded.

"I've ridden her," Alexandra said. "She's a sweet horse."

"Gentle as a lamb. Just what Clue needs to get home at night without—" Dalton caught himself, aware he had said too much.

"Yes, I know," she said, amused by his dismay. "He's been known to get drunk and fall out of the saddle."

"I never said that."

"You didn't have to," she said. "Though Christopher may not remember, I helped him stumble into the house on several of those occasions."

Dalton's eyes widened a little. "Did you now?"

"But don't tell him I said so," she added quickly. "I wouldn't want him embarrassed. He's the best coachman in the city, even if he can't stay on a horse."

"I won't breathe a word," Dalton promised, smiling.

"Good," she said and felt awkward in the pause that followed. There didn't seem to be anything left to talk about. She had made her apology to him, George Pennington was waiting, and so, not knowing what else to say, she said, "It was good seeing you again, Mr. Philips."

"And you, ma'am."

"Perhaps you'll stop and visit us sometime. I'm sure Christopher would like that."

"Thank you, ma'am. I will."

Alexandra said goodbye and turned away. Threading her way through the market crowd, she felt him watching her, and her awareness of his attention made everything else lose significance. Suddenly she could think of a hundred questions to ask him. She wanted to know where he was from, what his life had been like, how he had acquired his great skill with horses. More and more, he aroused her curiosity. And, to be honest with herself, he attracted her.

But nothing could come of her interest, now or ever, because of a glaring drawback that she could not ignore anymore than he could help. Dalton Philips was a farmer.

Chapter Eight

That evening Alexandra dined alone on boiled mutton, carrots, beef tongue laid in mashed potatoes, and a fine Madeira that Mary Brock brought up from the cellar.

"The beef tongue is excellent," Alexandra told her and received a gratified smile. Mary, a nervous woman with a simple, hearthside soul, looked ever on the verge of panic, but also as though a word of kindness or praise would fill her with happiness.

"I marinated it overnight," she explained. "It's Edward's favorite dish. A shame he has to be away tonight." Her husband Edward was visiting an ailing friend in Chester, and was not expected back until tomorrow.

"Is there enough beef tongue for you and Christopher?" Alexandra wanted to know.

"Oh, yes. And pudding for dessert."

"Please remind Christopher to leave the Madeira alone."

"I already warned him, ma'am."

From that, Alexandra knew the rascal had helped himself to the bottle. "Warn him again, please," she said, wondering if it would do any good. With Clue, an open bottle of wine was as good as empty.

Mary left for the kitchen, and Alexandra made a mental note to speak with her coachman about his abuse of her liquor supply. She was framing the exact words to use when someone rapped on the front door. The knocking came again and again, so insistent that Alexandra went to see for herself who was calling.

Opening the door, she found a hatless George Pennington sagging against the jamb, his wig askew, his clothing torn and disheveled. Blood trickled from a cut on his forehead.

Alarmed, Alexandra steadied him. "George, what happened?"

His breath was a harsh rasping in his throat. Frantic to tell her something, he raised a feeble hand, but was too winded to speak.

She heard the mob before she saw them. The droning of coarse voices made her step outside and look up the street where, in blazing torchlight, a group of jeering, hard-eyed men with soiled coats and wicked cudgels was coming steadily toward her house. Alexandra did not waste a moment.

"Come inside, George," she said, ushered him ahead of her, then slammed and bolted the door behind them. Guiding Pennington to a chair, she called urgently for Clue.

Moments later Clue appeared from the kitchen, trailed by Mary Brock. "What is it, ma'am?"

"A mob."

"Christ Almighty."

"Fetch the City Troop and Mr. Villard," Alexandra said. "Go out the back way. Hurry, Christopher!"

By then the mob's angry shouting was louder, penetrating the anxious stillness in the room. Mary Brock stood wringing her hands as Clue hesitated to leave.

"Send Mary, ma'am," he said. "I should stay here."

"Are you mad?" Alexandra demanded. "Suppose those animals get hold of her?"

Clue winced at the thought.

"Go!" she ordered.

Spurred into action, he went out through the kitchen, and Alexandra turned her attention to George Pennington, who was clutching his chest, his face deathly white.

"Bastards stole my horse!" he gasped.

Taking his hand, Alexandra rubbed it briskly between her own. "Mary, bring Mr. Pennington some brandy. And make sure the kitchen door is locked."

When Mary returned with the brandy, Alexandra took

the glass from her shaking hands and fed George several sips. "Better?" she asked, striving to keep her voice steady.

He nodded.

A sudden, piercing shout made her glance at the front windows, where torchlight flickered beyond the closed draperies. The mob was in her front yard, and from the sounds they were making, they smelled blood.

"Pennington, you bastard scum!" yelled a brutal voice. "Show your yellow hide!"

"They'll destroy your house," Pennington said weakly. As he started to rise, Alexandra pressed him back into the chair.

"I'll stall them," she said, "until Christopher brings the City Troop."

"You can't!"

Alexandra knew she had to try. She recalled what had happened to the last victim of a Philadelphia mob. His house had been broken into. His library was torched and his servants pricked with stolen bayonets. The women, including his wife, were molested. Everything in his house that would break had been smashed; dirt and dung was smeared on his walls and rubbed into his rugs. Then the mob had shaved the poor man's protesting head bald. From the house, the mob had moved in a stampede to the stable, where they wrecked wagons and carriages and painted the master's favorite riding horse bright red, with touches of yellow on its tail and blue on its muzzle.

Frightened, but determined to protect George Pennington and her property, Alexandra went to the door, took a moment to brace herself, then opened the door and stepped outside. She found herself facing a wall of crude-looking men who went suddenly silent. In the blazing torchlight, their glaring faces radiated such awful fierceness that she was hard-pressed not to retreat at once. As she squared her shoulders and measured them, they came back to life and jeered her.

"Where's Georgie?" someone growled.

"I've sent for the City Troop," was her answer. "I advise you to leave before they come."

Contemptuous of her warning, the mob howled with laughter, and Alexandra felt their amusement like a physical blow. A gray-haired man stepped toward her and spat green phlegm onto her brick walk. Squat, muscular, and shabbily dressed, his bright eyes leered at her from a face like old, dried leather.

"Where's Georgie?"

"He's gone."

"Girlie," the man smirked, "send him out, or some of these boys might throw you down and take turns fucking you."

The door was only a few feet behind her, but she knew there was no safety in fleeing. They would follow her inside, grab poor George, and maybe kill him. Hurry, Christopher, she thought frantically.

"Who are you?" she asked the vulgar man. "And what do you want with George?"

"Sam Peters. We come to shut his fat mouth."

"He hasn't hurt anyone," she said. "Go away and leave us alone."

"Loyalist pig!"

"Grab that fucking whore!"

"Move out of the way," Peters warned her, "or you'll get it."

Alexandra's back stiffened. Her eyes glittered with magnificent scorn. "How dare you threaten me?" she demanded.

"You bloody loyalist bitch—"

"Get off my property, or I'll have you in jail."

Peters was unbelievably quick. His hands shot out, seized her bodice, and jerked her to him. When she kicked his shin, he slapped her twice. Hard. Reeling from the blows, Alexandra felt a second pair of arms come around her from behind, and the stench of unwashed bodies assaulted her senses, reviving her. Terrified, she screamed and thrashed as fumbling hands squeezed her breasts and lifted her skirts to the freezing night. Despite her efforts she could not get loose, and her tormentors did as they pleased while the rest of the mob cheered them on.

Her heart was wild with panic when suddenly, from the corner of her vision, she saw something large explode from the shadows and bear down on her attackers. Sam Peters sensed danger, looked over his shoulder, and was hammered by a vicious blow that snapped his head around and made him release Alexandra. For an instant, she saw her rescuer's face beneath a three-cornered hat, saw a murderous light in his eyes as his fist shot past her head and bashed the man behind her.

Catlike, Dalton Philips spun to face the next challenger, and when a sinewy, bearded man lunged for him, he struck with a boot to the groin, then whipped his elbow into a groaning face. A bone crunched, blood spurted from a battered nose. Grabbing Alexandra, Dalton thrust her toward the house. In the same motion his hand moved under his greatcoat and came out with a pistol, which he leveled at the nearest threat.

"Get back, all of you!"

The command, fired in a lacerating voice, brought instant obedience. The front ranks shrank back like a receding wave.

"I'll kill the next man who touches her," Dalton vowed. As his eyes raked the now-silent mob, no one doubted him. His withering stare lingered on faces he knew. "Whose bloody idea was it to come here?" he demanded. "Yours, Sam Peters? And you, Nate, where's your goddamn sense? You ought to be ashamed, you load of drunks."

"Fuck off, Dalton," Peters spat. "We come here for Pennington. Send him out."

Dalton didn't move.

"Send the fucker out," someone snarled, "or we'll come in and get him!"

Menacing approval rippled through the crowd.

"That would be bloody stupid," Dalton said, "because the first man through that door gets a bullet." Turning his head fractionally, he spoke over his shoulder to Alexandra. "Get inside. Now."

She went, and he backed into the house after her, his pistol covering their retreat. As he closed and bolted the door, a stone thudded against it. Another one smashed through an upstairs window with a shattering of glass.

"Did they hurt you, ma'am?"

Alexandra shook her head and located her voice. "Thank you, Mr. Philips."

"Don't thank me yet. Those bastards ain't done with us."

Numb, Alexandra stared at him. She had not imagined him cowardly, but neither had she dreamed him capable of the swift, skillful savagery he had displayed outside. She saw him survey the faces in the room—a frightened maidservant, a shaken old man, and herself, trembling uncontrollably.

"Well," he said, with what seemed to her an amazing calm, "I think we'd better go upstairs and find a room with a nice, sturdy door."

George Pennington, leaning on Mary Brock, went ahead. Following behind them, Alexandra felt Dalton's hand press the small of her back.

"Do you have any guns, ma'am?" From his tone, he might have been requesting a cup of tea.

"A musket," she said, "but my caretaker has it at Willowbrook. I sent Christopher after the City Troop. They should be here any minute."

"Good enough," Dalton said.

They went into the guest bedroom, which overlooked the front yard. Alexandra convinced George Pennington to lie down on the bed and instructed Mary to look after him, but the poor woman, quaking visibly and gripping a bedpost, appeared not to hear her.

Dalton had moved to one of the windows. Parting the drapes, he frowned at what he saw, then went to a heavy cherrywood dresser and began to shove it toward the bedroom door. When Alexandra tried to help him, he waved her off.

"I can manage it. Watch outside and tell me what they're up to."

Quickly doing his bidding, she peered down at flaming torches held by men with hatless heads, their wild hair blowing in the night. "They're looking inside," she told him.

"They don't know we only got one pistol, or they'd have busted in by now."

"They're probably afraid you'll shoot one of them."

"I will," Dalton said, "if I have to."

Alexandra believed him. Glancing around, she saw that

69

he had wrestled the dresser in front of the door and was now eyeing a three-legged occasional table in a corner of the room. Crossing to the table, he asked her, "Are you fond of this piece?"

"Do what you like with it."

He turned the table on its side, gripped a thick, carved oak leg with both hands, braced his boot against another leg, and heaved. Wood splintered as the leg ripped away. Hefting the club, Dalton smacked it against his palm with a satisfied nod.

"Young man?" said George Pennington, sitting up on the bed.

"Yes, sir?"

"Break off another one of those."

Grinning, Dalton complied. "Here you go, sir," he said, handing him the makeshift club. "Aim for their shins. They won't feel it on their thick heads."

"What's your name, son?"

"Dalton Philips."

"Mr. Philips," said George, "if you should ever find yourself in need, allow me the honor of repaying your courageous assistance."

"Don't mention it, sir."

Just then the shouting outside rose to a coarse, ugly crescendo that pierced Alexandra to the bone. Looking down at the yard, she saw her red-painted fence, with ball-and-chain weighted gates, lying in pieces on the ground. Boxwood shrubs lining the front walk were being deliberately trampled and mangled. Trancelike, she watched strong hands uproot her lanternpost and fling it into the street like so much rubbish. As the destruction continued, she had the sensation of floating in someone else's nightmare, her realities misshapen and shifting like some trick of reflecting mirrors. This could not be happening. Dear God, listen to their hate-filled voices.

All at once she became aware of Dalton standing beside her, near enough for her to feel a faint heat from his body. He smelled like a stable. Right now, she wouldn't have cared if he smelled like a chamber pot, she was so glad of his presence.

70

"Thank God you're here," she said, still watching the mob.

"You did invite me."

His matter-of-factness made her smile. "I had a different sort of visit in mind."

"So did I."

Something in his voice made her forget about the mob for a moment. Then, as a loud crash came from downstairs, she grabbed his arm. "They're inside," she whispered, staring at him.

"They might not come up here," he said just as softly. "But they'll wreck the downstairs, so prepare yourself." He squeezed her shoulder, then moved to the door.

Moments later, there came from below such a hellish racket, Alexandra thought it could not be real, it must be her imagination. Glass shattered, wooden paneling splintered and cracked as walls deflected flying debris. The house rumbled to furniture upending and tumbling across polished hardwood floors. But what shocked and galled Alexandra most was the depraved laughter she heard amidst yells and curses. Her beautiful things were being demolished for the enjoyment of barbarians!

Movement outside caught her attention. Her face stricken, she watched as several looters, their arms loaded with booty, darted across her yard and disappeared into the darkness beyond the street lamps. One of the thieves was carrying her grandmother clock, which had been made by Rittenhouse and was very valuable. She would never be able to replace it.

Sudden footsteps on the stairs stilled her breathing. Glancing at Dalton, she saw him braced against the dresser, his pistol and club held ready, no expression on his face as he waited to see what came next.

Horsemen came. More than a dozen of them, brandishing pistols and shouting like demons as they galloped swiftly along Fourth Street from the north. Watching them approach, Alexandra recognized several members of the City Troop, and her knees went weak with relief.

Sheriff Dewees was also among the riders, and behind him on the same horse rode Christopher Clue. Red-faced from the cold, his thick coppery hair streaming wildly,

Clue held on for his life as Dewees galloped madly with the pack.

With guns leveled, the horsemen bore down on the vandals in the yard. Inside the house, stampeding feet trembled floorboards as the mob fled through doorways and clambered out windows. Driven before the furious, mounted charge, small groups of men scattered like windblown leaves into the night. As the sheriff's horse went by, Alexandra saw Christopher Clue leap to the ground, yelling at the top of his lungs, and chase a fleeing villain on foot.

A pistol cracked down the street. Someone screamed in pain, then more shots rang out as tongues of fire flared in darkness. Hoofbeats faded as riders pursued remnants of the mob into alleyways and across frozen fields. And then, miraculously, it was quiet in the house.

As the lull continued, Dalton said, "I think we're rescued." He shoved the dresser aside, cracked the door, and peered out into the hallway. Everything was still, but he said, "Stay put, everyone. I'll go have a look." He slipped from the room and quiet descended again.

Minutes later, Alexandra was examining the gash on Pennington's forehead when murmuring voices rose from below. Footsteps came running up the stairs. "Mrs. Pennington?"

"In here, Christopher."

When Clue came in, his face anxious and flushed with excitement, Alexandra was so happy to see him that she hugged him. Embarrassed, he stepped back and glanced around. "Is everyone all right?"

"We seem to be," she said. "Where's Mr. Philips?"

"Gone."

"What?"

"I saw him downstairs for a minute, then he left when the sheriff came in." To her distraught look, Clue shrugged helplessly. "He said things seemed under control, and he had to be going."

"He can't have left," Alexandra said and went downstairs to check for herself. She was unprepared for what awaited her. A human hurricane had ripped through her elegant rooms, dismembering furniture, gouging walls and floors, smashing fine china, crystal lamps, and her beautiful gilt-edged mirror above the drawing-room mantel. The marble mantelpiece itself was cracked and chipped. Shards of silvered glass crunched underfoot as she waded slowly through the destruction, awed and infuriated to tears.

Every window on the first floor had been broken, and cold air poured inside, making her shiver. Numb with despair, she watched Clue bank a fresh fire on the drawing-room hearth.

Sheriff Dewees appeared from the kitchen and offered his condolences. "We came as quickly as we could, Mrs. Pennington."

"I know. Thank you, Sheriff."

"We caught some of the devils," he told her. "When we learn the names of the ringleaders, they'll be severely punished."

Alexandra nodded, not really caring. When Clue pressed a small glass of brandy into her hand, she drank it straight down. As she stood there, several deputies entered the room and shook their heads in disbelief when they beheld the enormous damage. Nearby residents, emboldened by the presence of lawmen, filed inside for a curious look at the aftermath of a mob's fury. Before long, the house thronged with people.

At the height of the confusion, Charles Villard arrived and searched the crowded rooms for Alexandra. When he located her, relief swept him, intense and complete. He threaded his way to her side.

"Dear God," he said, seeing how pale she was. Taking her hand, he drew her into a small breakfast room off the parlor, closed the door behind them, and held her against him. "Sweetheart, are you all right?"

Alexandra, grateful to have his arms around her and feel his warmth seeping into her, said she felt better now that he was there.

"Thank God you weren't harmed," he whispered, pressing his lips to her hair.

"You can thank Dalton Philips."

She might as well have rammed a hot poker into his eye. Villard drew his head back and stared at her. "Dalton

73

Philips was here?"

"He stood off the whole mob in front of the house," she said and described how Dalton had bravely snatched her from danger. "I don't know what would have happened if he hadn't come when he did. He left before I could thank him." Then her face contorted with another worry. "Charles, they wrecked my house. Goddamn them!"

Embracing her again, Villard stroked her hair and back. "There," he said. "It's all right, I have you. You're safe, sweetheart, that's what matters." As she clung to him, he continued to hold her and murmur soothing words, but while his voice was tender, his face was a bitter mask.

Chapter Nine

To Villard's disgust, word of Dalton Philips's heroism made the rounds of Philadelphia drawing rooms. Instead of dying out, as Villard hoped it would, the excitement was kept alive by George Pennington, who simply would not tire of embellishing the story. Each time Villard heard Alexandra's name in connection with Philips, his resentment increased. He had been upstaged by a lowbred farmer. Worse, as Alexandra's suitor, he must acknowledge Philips's defense of her in a gentlemanly manner.

And so, a few days after the incident, Villard found himself at a small tavern tucked away in Strawberry Alley. The inn, known as the Sign of the Death of the Fox, was a rough-cast, two-storied building that bore the date mark of 1703. Out front, the little space to the lane was filled with bleached oyster shells to resemble a seaside tavern. Inside, the crowded taproom was dim, vibrant, and cozy warm from a roaring fire. Steam rose from mugs of hot buttered rum, tobacco pipes flared red in shadowed recesses. But hottest of all was the ongoing debate among the tavern's patrons, who came from all ranks.

"It's a rotten island," said a man whose gruff voice was at odds with his spruce, tailored appearance. "Why should America be tied to that mass of vice and corruption?"

"Because the Congress says so," came a surly reply. "And because British troops are here to make sure of it."

"And I say we should quit this goddamn caution and face the inevitable!"

The answering volley was a mixture of support and

75

disagreement. Drunkenness seemed to be the only common denominator of the group.

Ignoring their heated discussion, Villard scanned the smoky taproom and spotted his quarry at a corner table. Dalton Philips, quiet and attentive, was sitting alone. Excellent.

Villard approached him. A tallow candle stub, guttering in a sconce near the table, threw shadows over Philips's face and played havoc with Villard's imagination. One moment the farmer seemed to be smiling, the next he looked grim.

"Good evening, Mr. Philips."

"Mr. Villard."

"May I join you?"

In answer, Dalton removed his booted foot from a second chair at the table, and Villard sat down and braced himself. The words were more difficult to say than he had imagined. "It seems I owe you a debt of gratitude."

"What for?"

Impudent bastard. Look at his smug face. "For rescuing Alexandra, of course."

"Oh, that," Dalton said. A shrug, nothing more.

Villard seethed. The dirty son of a whore was going to make him work at this. He wished the tavern were not so crowded. He loathed being seen with Philips.

"I appreciate your coming to her aid," he said. "From what I hear, she's very fortunate that you happened to be in the area."

"Actually, I was there on purpose."

Villard blinked. "Educate me?"

"I was on my way to her place when I saw the mob," Dalton explained. "I ran into her at the market, you see, and she told me to stop by if I wanted. Lucky thing I did."

Something cold and nauseating suddenly coiled in Villard's stomach, threatening his composure, but he managed to retain his courteous bearing. For appearances' sake he would buy Philips a drink, and then leave before too many people saw them together.

Just then a tavern maid appeared from the kitchen, and Villard signaled her. When she arrived at the table, he said in a wooden voice, "Get Mr. Philips whatever he wants to drink."

"Another pint, Jenny," Dalton said, surrendering his tankard with a smile and a wink. After she left, he looked back at Villard and waited for him to speak.

"Alexandra and I will soon be announcing our engagement."

"Well, congratulations," Dalton said, "for being almost engaged."

"We plan to marry next year."

"Do you now?" Dalton smiled. "She must be beside herself with joy." His tankard of foaming ale arrived. He took a long pull, wiped a thumb across his mouth. "You're not drinking, Mr. Villard. What's the matter? Don't like the company?"

Villard measured him. "You're still in a tiff about the race, aren't you?"

"That was no race," Dalton said. "That was a sham."

"I offered to pay you."

"And your friends offered to smear my name."

Burning to rub salt into the wound, Villard gave a careless shrug. "To be honest, I didn't see what occurred between you and Sammy during the race. Perhaps his anger was justified."

Dalton watched him a moment, sipped ale. "Or perhaps the little shit was following your orders."

Silence hummed.

"It seems we are not to remain amiable," Villard said.

"It seems we never were," Dalton said and raised his tankard. "But thanks for the drink. I know how much it hurt to buy it."

Pushing slowly to his feet, Villard stared down at him with frosty eyes. "You'll never know," he said and walked away.

Chapter Ten

After spending just one week in Philadelphia, Alexandra closed up her city house and returned to Willowbrook for the winter. She had never been more grateful for having the means to make such a move. The countryside, dreary and boring as it was in wintertime, seemed a haven compared to Philadelphia, where mob violence and murders were no longer shocking events. A quick glance through a newspaper told the grim story of the city's decline from cultural jewel of the Colonies to a seething political cauldron. These days, it was as dangerous to be a Whig in Philadelphia as it was to be a Tory, for vengeful fanatics infested both parties.

Before leaving the city, Alexandra visited a gunsmith's shop and purchased a pistol—a small, beautifully crafted weapon with inlays of ivory and silver wire.

"That's not a proper pistol," Christopher Clue said when he saw it. "That's for plucking squirrels off the lawn."

Alexandra laughed.

"Can you handle a pistol, Mrs. Pennington?" he asked, skeptical.

"John taught me," she said and, gripping the weapon with both hands, demonstrated her shooter's stance for him.

"Very good, ma'am."

"Trust me, Christopher. I can load and fire a gun as well as I need to. I just pray I never have to."

"We won't be bothered here," he assured her.

Alexandra did feel safe inside Willowbrook's thick stone

walls. After just a few days there, her traumatic confrontation with the mob began to fade from her thoughts. Images that had burned so vividly in her mind, robbing her of sleep, gradually became washed-out vagaries.

Except for one image. And so, when she was settled in for the winter, Alexandra sat at her writing desk in her bedroom and penned a letter of gratitude to Dalton Philips. She rewrote the letter three times before the wording satisfied her. Finished, she sealed the letter with wax and took it to Clue.

"I want you to deliver this to Dalton Philips at his farm."

Clue, who was oiling a harness in the carriage house, perked up at the prospect of an afternoon jaunt. "Right away, ma'am."

He left on his mare and returned four hours later to say that Dalton Philips was not at Downstream Farm. "But I found him at the Flying Goose," Clue said, smiling and bright-eyed.

Alexandra took a closer look at him. He was saturated as a mop. "So I see."

"He bought me a pint."

"Just one?" she inquired sweetly.

"Two, actually. Then it seemed only fair to buy him one."

"Naturally." One thing about Clue, drinking never made him unpleasant, just more cheerful and generous.

"I hope you're not upset with me," he said, scratching his head. "It's just that Dalton tells such funny stories. He's a funny fellow. Quick."

"Did you give him the letter?"

Clue looked momentarily blank, then came back to his senses. "Yes, I remember now. I handed it to him as I was leaving."

"Are you sure?"

"Sure as I'm standing here, ma'am."

Tottering would have been a better description, but it turned out he was right. Three days later, a letter from Dalton Philips arrived by post, and Alexandra took it into the parlor to read it.

To Mrs. Pennington, Willowbrook

    This is wensday, december 6. On monday I reséved your letter and was pleased and also releav'd to learn you are safely at Willowbrook. I am sory you had to remove from town as I am sure you have done nothing to hurt anybody nor have given any offence to any Person at all. If word shold reach me that anyone comes to disterb you or molest you in any way I will show them a proper resentment.

I also ask you to remember thair are some sinsere and lawfull people among the mobs who are sadly caut up in the madness of others. But they shold not feel at Liberty to disterb and terrify a person to death. If you shold ever need my assistence I will be thair in a minit.

Remember I am

Humbly yours,
Dalton Philips

Alexandra didn't know whether to laugh or feel flattered. As she read his letter through again, she imagined him choosing his words with care, trying hard to sound formal as he scratched away with an unpracticed hand. His handwriting was wavering, his spelling atrocious, yet it was all somehow endearing. Dalton Philips's education had obviously been sparse, but he did not lack sincerity. Or gallantry.

Chapter Eleven

Just before midnight, New Year's Eve, Peter Buckley gave a mighty stretch and told his younger brother Henry, "I think I'll go see Lizzie for a bit."

"You can't leave," Henry protested, dismayed. "Mr. Villard is paying us to watch this place." They were in Charles Villard's countinghouse, which stood next door to his city mansion on Chestnut Street.

"What he doesn't know won't bother him, will it?"

"Peter—"

Ignoring his brother, Peter got up from the table where they had been dicing, went to a window, and looked next door. Golden candlelight spilled from the great house onto snow-coated Chestnut Street, which was lined with conveyances. Peter could hear music tinkling faintly. As he watched colorfully gowned women and foppish, well-groomed men glide past windows to a dance, the urge to celebrate the new year grew stronger in him.

"They're having a high time over there," he said. "He'll never miss me."

"Mr. Villard doesn't miss a trick."

"I won't be gone long."

Henry fell silent, brooding. A small fire snapped on the hearth to keep the brothers warm, but even so their breaths misted in the chill room.

"He's probably drunk," Peter said with a shrug.

"He'll throttle us both."

"He'll never know! I said I won't be long. Lizzie doesn't mind if I'm quick."

"All that doxie wants is something shoved between her legs."

81

Eager to oblige her, Peter grinned wolfishly. "I'll pay you to watch for me," he said.

His interest pricked, Henry waited.

"Two shillings."

"Three."

"Done," Peter agreed and picked up his hat.

"You'd better be quick."

"Like a flash." Shrugging into his greatcoat, Peter let himself out a side door into a small, fenced yard, and Henry, unhappy but resigned to his brother's impulsiveness, followed him outside. The night was cloudless with a brilliant full moon. The silvery orb shone so brightly on the snow-encrusted city that the night watchmen had extinguished street lamps to conserve oil.

Henry watched his brother's dark shape cross the yard and slip through the gate. "Hurry!" he hissed, wondering if Peter heard him or even cared. Alone, shivering in his shirtsleeves and waistcoat, Henry had an unnerving vision of Mr. Villard making a surprise inspection of his countinghouse.

In the next instant, something slammed into Henry's back and bore him face-first to the frozen ground. When he tried to rise, a hard knee bashed his spine, a powerful hand thrust his face into the snow and held it there. Ice crystals crammed up his nose and packed his mouth. For a terrifying moment, he thought his attacker meant to suffocate him. Then strong fingers clenched in his hair, jerking his head back, and the sting Henry felt at his throat was a knife point. A low voice, close to his ear, made his insides shrivel.

"Don't make a sound."

Henry lay still, snow dribbling down his chin as his heart thudded in his chest.

"Get up slowly," said the voice. "And if you like your throat the way it is, don't try anything."

Henry stood up obediently and felt his assailant pat him down for weapons. But his pistol was inside the countinghouse, hanging in a shoulder holster that was slung on a peg.

"We're going inside," the voice said, and Henry felt the knife prick the small of his back, prodding him forward. As they entered the countinghouse, he flicked a glance at his holstered gun, hanging just a few feet away. It was on his mind to lunge for the weapon when strong hands suddenly spun him around and slammed him back against a wall. Glancing down, Henry saw a long, thin blade aimed at his chest. One quick thrust, and it would pierce his heart.

"You're Henry Buckley, is that right?"

It was right, but Henry was too jolted to speak to the hooded man facing him. *Jack Flash*.

"Show me where the money is, Henry."

"There's no money," Henry blurted, then flinched as the robber let him have a quarter inch of razor-sharp steel. A red stain appeared on Henry's white shirt, radiating from the knife point.

"Henry," Jack Flash scoffed. "Why would Mr. Villard hire two men to guard an empty house?"

"Because he's rich?"

"Exactly."

"But there's nothing here, I swear it!"

Henry's mouth went dry as dust as the black-hooded outlaw moved forward a few inches and towered above him. For an insane instant, he considered grabbing for the knife, but Jack Flash looked strong and capable, and his eyes, glittering behind the hood, were utterly merciless. His voice had a deathlike quality that held Henry immobile.

"Are you going to make me hurt you?"

"It's upstairs."

"Good boy, Henry. Show me."

Henry showed him.

The silver he and Peter had been hired to guard was inside a heavy strongbox with iron fittings. The strongbox was padlocked and, as Henry explained in an unsteady voice, the key was elsewhere.

Jack Flash surveyed the locked chest a moment. "Carry it downstairs," he ordered. When Henry had done so, Jack Flash handed him an iron poker from the fireplace.

"Break it open."

Gripping the poker with sweat-slick palms, Henry darted a look at the villain.

"Don't be daft, Henry." Jack Flash sounded amused. His knife had disappeared. In his hand now was a beautifully ornamented pistol with its hammer drawn back to full-cock. "I can pull the trigger a bit quicker than you can swing, don't you think?" It was his pleasant manner, more than anything else, that frightened Henry, who knelt with the poker and attacked the padlock.

It took him a few minutes to complete the job. Conscious of the gun at his back, Henry gave a hard twist, his face reddening with strain, then tumbled forward as the lock staple snapped. When he lifted the strongbox lid, revealing six fat leather purses, Jack Flash tossed him a heavy cloth sack.

"Fill it."

Coins clinked as Henry did as he was told. Finished, he stared up at the tall, black-clad man who seemed to hesitate. To Henry's mind, his life hinged on the outcome of that hesitation.

"Face down on the floor," Jack Flash ordered, "hands behind your back." Moments later, Henry's wrists had been bound with a leather thong and his mouth was gagged. Taking Henry's greatcoat from a peg, Jack Flash knelt and covered him with it. "Do you have a family?" he asked.

Henry swallowed, nodded.

"If you want to see them again, stay put."

Chapter Twelve

It was a new year, 1776. The old one had ended with a prosperous romp for Dalton Philips. As he rode north on Wissahickon Road, the sack inside his saddlebag clinked against Secret's flank, sweet music that made him smile. Mr. Villard, he thought, the Sons of Liberty thank you.

Five miles north of the city, the mare took herself off the main road onto a rutted dirt lane that wound through acres of gloomy pines. When the evergreens thinned, a fieldstone farmhouse came into view, standing solid and compact on the east bank of nearby Wissahickon Creek. Like its outbuildings, the house was dark and silent.

Dalton rounded a small forage barn, passed a large pig pen and shed-row stalls for cattle and sheep, and arrived at a weatherbeaten stable. Dismounting, he looked toward the farmhouse and saw a lantern appear in a downstairs window.

A door opened. The flickering light came outside and bobbed toward him. Not that the spry little man carrying the lantern had need of it. The light was for Dalton. Timothy Leeds, whose toothless grin Dalton could now see, was nearly blind from cataracts and did almost everything by touch, smell, and very sharp hearing.

"Hello, Twigs," Dalton greeted him. "You're up late."

"Took you long enough, boy."

"Don't tell me you was worried."

Milky eyes shone with affection. "Not a bit," Twigs said and shuffled into the stable, lighting the aisleway for Dalton and Secret.

When they reached Secret's stall, Dalton tossed the

heavy money sack near Twigs's feet, and the old man caught his breath at the sound of coins striking the earthen floor. Setting the lantern down, he knelt on the floor and his hand went unerringly to the sack. "Oh, yes," he breathed, feeling inside. "This will buy a few muskets."

While Dalton removed Secret's bridle and saddle, Twiggs fetched him a full water pail and a soft-bristled brush. Dipping the brush in water, Dalton gently scrubbed off Secret's white blaze, which, like her front stocking, was actually a thick coating of pipeclay. As he worked, a barn cat slunk from the shadows and rubbed against his legs.

Twigs had gone back to inspecting the stolen silver with jittery fingers. Hearing coins clink, Dalton glanced down at the wispy white head and smiled to himself. The old man was like this every time, frazzled but jubilant.

Squeezing fistfuls of coins, Twigs's grooved face and burnt-out eyes bloomed with delight. "It's a bloody fortune," he said in awe.

"It'll raise the price on Jack Flash's head, I imagine."

"Mr. Villard must be shitting marble."

"I feel bad for the Buckley brothers," Dalton said quietly.

"Were they careless?" Twigs demanded.

"Very."

"Then they deserve whatever happens to them."

Twigs, a fiery little failure in his own right, had a flair for igniting flames under others. Year by year he became shabbier and whiter, more stooped and sad eyed. But while age ravaged his body, his mind grew increasingly hot-tempered and zealous, a bright spark shining in gray dimness. A spark that constantly sought tinder to bring his schemes to life. His appetite for rebellion was a keen blade sharpened by persistent misfortune and wielded by limitless energy. Men of his kind fostered greatness or tragedy. There was no middle ground.

"You must be hungry," he said, getting up.

"Starved."

"I roasted a chicken. Come in when you're ready." Twigs left the lantern behind, but took the money sack with him. A little later, in the farmhouse kitchen, he set a heaping plate in front of Dalton. "Happy new year, boy."

"It's off to a fucking cold start," Dalton said. "My ass nearly froze to the saddle."

The kitchen was snug, though. A fire hissed and popped on the hearth, throwing wavering, orange-red light into shadowy corners. One wall of the room displayed a musket with a seventeen-inch bayonet fixed to its muzzle. Hanging below the musket was a French officer's saber, thirty inches long with an ivory grip, its black scabbard ornamented with silver on the tip, middle, and throat. Save for the two weapons, the room was bare of decoration.

"Did I mention that Captain Thorne is in New York?" Twigs asked.

"A hundred times, I think."

"We need to exchange jewelry for coin. He's offering English money."

"I'll leave Friday," Dalton said and took a bite of cold chicken leg. He chewed, swallowed, fingered a knothole in the planking table. "But I'm not selling the pearl and diamond necklace."

"The one you took from Mrs. Pennington?"

"That's right."

"Why not?"

"I'm giving it back," Dalton said. "Anonymally."

"Anonymously."

"However you fucking say it."

There was a long pause before Twigs asked, "Do you have a special interest in the Tory lady?" He took the ensuing silence as a yes. "Ah," he said. "The fly has met the spider."

"What's that supposed to mean?"

"Do I need to spell it out?"

"She's not like the rest of them."

At that, Twigs threw his head back and laughed. "Oh, God, this is ripe!"

"Come on, Twigs. Don't go on like that."

"Is it her crack you're after, boy?"

Dalton's stare sharpened. "Watch your mouth," he warned. "She's a nice lady, and I happen to like her. What's wrong with that?"

"Nothing," Twigs shrugged, "if that's all there is to it. But that's not what I'm hearing, is it?"

Dalton's mouth compressed. Twigs had the damndest way of reading a person's thoughts with those sharp little ears, always tilting his head at odd angles to home in on a person's voice. Once he was on your tail, he was like a baying hound, refusing to break off pursuit.

"Quit dreaming," Twigs said. "If she's leaving her scent for you, it's only to amuse herself. Deep down she's the same as all those rich bastards who think the rest of us were put here to serve them."

"She don't treat me like that."

"And how does she treat you?" Twigs fired back. "The same as she treats Mr. Villard? Do you measure up to him in her eyes, boy?"

Stung, Dalton stared unseeing at the table top. After a moment, Twigs reached over and squeezed his arm. "You're the best man I know, Dalton," he said in a gentler tone. "But Alexandra Pennington looks at you and sees a nobody. And that's all she'll ever see, because she's blind in a worse way than me."

It was quiet in the room except for the crackling fire. Sighing, Dalton pushed his unfinished plate away. There was no point in arguing, especially when Twigs could be right, so he said, "Anthony Wayne's drilling a battalion in Chester County."

"So I heard."

"Is there anything you don't hear?"

Twigs just smiled.

"I want to join him."

Now it was Twigs's turn to sigh. "You're doing more good as Jack Flash," he said.

"You keep saying that, and maybe it's true, but it don't feel right anymore." Receiving no answer, Dalton got up and began to pace. "I'm tired of planning jobs, and I'm sick to death of holding my tongue. I want everyone to know I'm for independence."

"Is it recognition you want or independence?" Twigs asked brutally. "Because now's the time to make that selfish choice."

Dalton pretended to ignore him. Crossing the kitchen, he took the saber down from the wall, slid the blade from its scabbard, and tested the razor edge on an imaginary opponent. The heavy sword felt good in his grip, like an extension of his arm.

"What is it you think you're missing?" Twigs persisted as steel hissed through air. "A bloody row? Washington hasn't done a damn thing but sit on his ass at Cambridge. Meanwhile, Jack Flash has outfitted three companies of soldiers." The sword continued to slash at nothing, but Twigs knew Dalton was listening. "When we have ourselves a real battle—and by God, we will—three companies could mean the difference between winning and losing."

Dalton slotted the saber into the scabbard and rammed it home. "It ain't right what I'm doing."

"God, you can be thick!" Twigs said, banging the table for emphasis. "Do you think this war will be won by honest men? It'll be decided by nasty, dirty, bloody, stinking scum."

"Speak for yourself."

Twigs couldn't stop a smile.

And Dalton, filled with determination and the daring hope of youth, said, "I want to fight as a soldier."

"And you will," Twigs said, "when the time is right."

"Ain't that for me to decide?"

"One more job."

Dalton knew that tone. He was silent a moment, interested against his will. "Who?"

"A lawyer by the name of Robert McPherson. A filthy rich Tory." Then Twigs, with sly intent, barbed his hook. "He's married to Evelyn Wright's daughter."

Evelyn Wright's daughter. Charles Villard's cousin. Bending his head, Dalton rubbed the back of his neck with his fingertips. "All right," he said at last. "Once more. Then Jack Flash is a piece of history."

Chapter Thirteen

The first heavy snow came. It began one nightfall and continued until the next morning, thick, soft flakes that swirled around rooftops and drifted across roads and fields. When the sun finally emerged from plumy gray clouds, the whitened landscape glinted with a brilliance that hurt the eyes.

The snowfall brought Charles Villard to Willowbrook in a high-prowed red sleigh drawn by a spirited white filly. Hearing the jingle of its belled harness, Alexandra looked out her bedroom window and saw the sleigh in her yard. Eyes shining with anticipation, she quickly changed into heavy clothing.

When she arrived downstairs, Villard was having tea in the parlor. He greeted her with a warm kiss on the cheek, then said, "I thought you might need a change of scenery, so I came to take you for a ride."

His instincts, as ever, were infallible. Isolated from Philadelphia society, Alexandra had begun to yearn for activity, and a sleigh ride seemed exactly the right prescription for her boredom.

As they left the parlor, she took his arm and said, "You're the most considerate man I know."

"No, just selfish," he confessed. "The truth is, I was lonely for your company. I wish you hadn't left the city."

"I had to leave, Charles. I didn't feel safe there."

He nodded, resigned, then said in a lighter voice, "The repairs on your house are going well. You'll be amazed when you see the place."

A few weeks earlier, when he had offered to oversee the

repair work, Alexandra had hesitated to let him handle her affairs. It was a form of commitment, and although she was growing increasingly fond of him, she was not yet ready for wedlock. Unseemly though it was for a woman of her age and social standing to remain widowed, she was determined to enjoy her freedom awhile longer. More than a husband, she craved what she had been denied in her youth—romance—and Charles Villard was filling that greater need with flair.

Each moment she spent with him was a lesson in intensity. He could be witty and fun. He could be charming and tender and make her feel every inch a woman. From the start, he had demonstrated a resolve to win her, and Alexandra's affection was warming to his persistence, so that she found herself being drawn inexorably toward a permanent bond with him. But for now, to her contentment, he seemed satisfied to progress their courtship at her pace.

He ushered her outside the house, and they found Clue admiring the white filly harnessed to the sleigh. "What do you think of her?" Villard asked him.

"She's a beauty, sir." As Clue stroked the filly's neck, the horse snorted vaporous clouds and stamped a dainty hoof in the snow. "Lots of fire in her."

"She's a bit headstrong," Villard admitted, "but she settles down nicely once she's moving. I call her Solitaire."

"A perfect name for her. She certainly does stand out." Clue surveyed the sleigh, noting its leather-cushioned seat and padded prow, the solid brass handrails gleaming like new. "We should get one of these, Mrs. Pennington," he said. "I could hitch Sunshine to it. She was a carriage horse before I bought her, you know."

"I think that's a wonderful idea," Alexandra said as Villard handed her into the seat.

Villard got in beside her, settled a thick woolen blanket over their laps for warmth, and took up the reins. When he slapped them hard against Solitaire's rump, the filly gave a shrill whinny and rose on her hind legs for an instant. Coming back to the ground, she broke into a canter, jarring the sleigh's occupants, then settled down to a swift, nervous trot.

Clue watched with concern as the sleigh moved down

the drive. From his brief observation, he knew the filly was skittish and needed a gentle, but firm, touch on the reins, not Villard's domineering hand.

"Bloody idiot," Clue muttered, shaking his head. "He's going to get someone hurt."

In the sleigh, Villard was of a similar mind. "Do you trust Christopher Clue?" he asked Alexandra.

Startled, she replied, "Implicitly."

"And the Brocks?"

"With my life. Charles, what on earth are you getting at?"

"I just want to be sure you're in good hands."

"Of course I am. Why would you think otherwise?"

"Haven't you heard about Tom Bartholomew?"

Alexandra shook her head, then listened as he explained, "Two of his servants attacked him the other night. They tied him hand and foot, took all his valuables, and set fire to his house. He was burned alive."

"Oh, my God," she whispered, horrified.

Villard guided the filly between two stone pillars marking the end of Willowbrook's drive. When the sleigh was gliding north along the Ridge Road, he looked over at her with serious eyes and said, "That's what this rebellion has inspired. Commoners have gotten the idea that there should be no class structure and that the wealthy should be punished for living well. Which is ludicrous, not to mention dangerous."

"I have no problems with my servants."

"No?" Villard smiled a little. "Is your coachman still helping himself to your liquor?"

Alexandra looked away in chagrin. "That," she said, "is between Christopher and me. And it isn't an indication that I'm about to be set upon by hostile servants."

"I'm sure that's what the King thought when those Yankees burned the *Gaspee*."

"A poor analogy."

"Perhaps," he conceded. "But all the same, common folk are getting out of hand. Just look what they did to your house."

When Alexandra fell silent, beseiged by memories of that night, Villard said gently, "I'm sorry. I shouldn't have reminded you."

"It's all right."

"Anyway," he pointed out, "things are looking up. Montgomery's defeat should take the sting out of the rebels."

On New Year's Eve, during a raging blizzard, rebel forces under Richard Montgomery and Benedict Arnold had stormed the British fortress at Quebec. The hard-fought battle had seen the rebels come within an ace of taking the town. Had their numbers not been depleted by a torturous wilderness march to reach the Canadian stronghold, they might have succeeded. As it was, Montgomery was killed early in the fighting, Arnold was badly wounded, and the Americans had withdrawn into the frozen Plains of Abraham to lick their wounds.

News of the rebel disaster had heartened Villard, who was still smarting over the robbery at his countinghouse that same night. "It should all be over soon," he said. "Especially with England sending more troops to crush the rebellion."

"Foreign troops," she said uneasily, watching the snow-laden scenery drift by. "I read in the *Gazette* that the ministry has hired mercenaries from Hesse-Cassel."

Villard shrugged. "The Royal Army is already spread too thin. The King must do whatever is necessary to control the Colonies."

Alexandra, who had a deep love for her birthplace, was disturbed by the idea of Hessian soldiers coming to America to spill blood. "I think it's absurd," she said. "It's like a father summoning the police to spank his disobedient child. No, it's worse than that. Those soldiers were bought like slaves or horseflesh. They're fighting for money and plunder. They care nothing about England, and probably a good deal less about us."

"They're professional soldiers," Villard said in a soothing voice. "And they'll be taking orders from General Howe."

"They're foreign butchers, and I can't believe the King would send them to slay his subjects."

"Alexandra—"

"The moment German troops set foot on American soil, thousands of lukewarms will swing to the rebel cause. Doesn't he realize that?"

Now Villard was amused. "Perhaps you should write and tell him so."

"Perhaps I will," she shot back.

A moment passed, then he quietly reminded her, "You're supposed to be enjoying yourself."

Alexandra took a deep, calming breath and studied the way ahead. After cresting a hillock, the winding road plunged toward a copse of evergreens, where heavy-laden boughs formed a long, whitened tunnel and slanting shafts of sunlight dappled the ground. The only sounds to be heard were jingling harness bells and the rhythmic beat of snow-muffled hooves. As the sleigh glided among the pines, Alexandra was captivated by the pristine stillness of her surroundings.

She was quiet for so long, Villard took her hand and said, "I didn't mean to upset you."

"It wasn't you, Charles."

"If ever something is troubling you, please don't hesitate to confide in me."

"You see how considerate you are?"

He tightened his grip on her hand. "It comes naturally when I'm with you."

"And I appreciate it," she said. "But you were right. We should be enjoying this day."

"I want us to have many more together."

Awaiting her reaction, Villard was relieved to see her smile and feel the answering pressure of her fingers against his own. God, she was lovely. In daylight, by candlelight, by any light she was breathtaking, and he longed for the day when she would become his wife.

Many of his friends were also anticipating the result of his suit, and a few tasteless ones, including Stephen Lindsay, had even wagered money on the outcome. Which made Alexandra's procrastination all the more frustrating, but Villard knew better than to browbeat her. She was headstrong and required careful handling. Patience was the key to possessing her. But just now, looking at reflected sunlight on her hair and the deep blue of her eyes, his restraint was being severely tested. The desire he felt was overwhelming.

As the sleigh rounded a sharp bend, Villard saw a large pine branch lying across the road just ahead. Mounded in drifted snow, the bushy limb resembled a carcass at first glance, and Villard pulled back reflexively on Solitaire's reins. The filly stopped short, muscles twitching as she nervously eyed the branch. There was room enough to go around it, so Villard slapped the reins against a white rump. Startled, Solitaire sprang forward several strides, then shied from the strange-looking object in the road. When she tried to turn back the way they had come, Villard fought to control her.

"Oh, no you don't," he said sharply.

Alexandra's fingers tightened on the handrail. "She's frightened."

"She has to learn obedience," Villard insisted. Taking up the whip, he lashed Solitaire's backside. The horse went rigid, snorting in pain, and stubbornly held her ground. Determined to be obeyed, Villard got to his feet and whipped her again, putting more power behind the blow. Still Solitaire refused to budge.

When the whip fell a third time, the filly screamed in protest and tried to kick her tormentor. Failing that, she bolted to the right to escape the stinging lash, and her headlong flight took them straight at a brush-tangled bank.

Alexandra felt the sleigh lurch as its runners leaped a ditch and skidded sideways. Thrown back against the seat, she gripped the handrail as Solitaire surged uphill, plowing through underbrush as she went. A wall of trees loomed ahead. As the filly plunged toward a narrow gap between two stout elms, Alexandra saw the collision coming and could only brace herself. The tree trunks stopped the sleigh with sledgehammer impact, hurling her forward into the prow.

Sometime later, opening her eyes, Alexandra found herself lying on the floor of the sleigh, looking up through snow-covered branches at patches of blue sky overhead. A dull pain throbbed in her temple. Lifting a hand to her forehead, she encountered sticky wetness. Her fingers came back coated with blood.

"Charles?" she asked and received no answer. Dismayed, she pushed to a sitting position and saw him lying beside her, his face ashen.

"Oh, God." Leaning over him, Alexandra touched his

95

face, felt his warm breath against her hand, and fought down her panic. He was alive, but his deathlike pallor was alarming. Fingers searching, she discovered a hard swelling above his left ear.

"Charles," she said, stroking his face, but he was unresponsive. Fear for him made her eyes fill. She shook him gently as blood dripped from her forehead onto his coat. "Charles, can you hear me?"

When her efforts failed to rouse him, Alexandra got to her feet and tested her shaky limbs. Her bones seemed intact. In fact, other than a slight ringing in her ears and the warm wetness on her face, nothing seemed amiss.

Looking around, she saw that Solitaire was still attached to the sleigh, but the horse was quivering badly and seemed in no mood to be handled. Worse, the sleigh was firmly wedged between two trees and the harness was fouled in the underbrush. There was only one thing to do—walk to the nearest house and bring back help.

After covering Villard with the woolen blanket, Alexandra stepped from the sleigh into calf-deep snow, made her way down the bank, and crossed the ditch to the road. Shaking snow from her skirt, she suddenly paused, listening to the muffled sound of hoofbeats. Hope buoyed her as a rider came into view, and when she realized who it was, her relief was complete.

Dalton Philips could hardly believe what he was seeing. Reining to the side of the road, he dismounted and left his mare untethered. His focus was Alexandra. "Jesus God," he said, surveying her bloodied face with concern. "Are you all right, ma'am?"

"Yes. Just shaken up."

"You're bleeding badly."

He was right. There was an annoying amount of blood dripping down the side of her face, but that was the least of her worries. "Charles is hurt," she said, taking Dalton's arm and urging him toward the snow-drifted bank.

"Bad?"

"I don't know. He's unconscious."

When they reached the sleigh, Dalton leaned over Villard and peered into each of his eyes a moment. He checked the pulse in his throat, felt the lump above his ear, and turned his head carefully from side to side. Straightening, he looked at Alexandra, who was sitting on the seat, her face anxious.

"He should be fine when he wakes up."

"Thank God," she breathed.

"You must have a nasty headache."

"It's only a cut."

"Looks like a good one," Dalton said, sitting beside her. "Here, let me see."

Alexandra felt his fingers take her chin and tilt her head back. As he examined the gash at her hairline, she found herself studying him in return, and when his eyes met hers, she was suddenly conscious of her disheveled appearance. She realized she could not have looked worse—her face bloodied, her hat missing, her unbound hair falling in ringlets to her shoulders—but he didn't seem to mind.

He untied the scarf from around her neck and folded it lengthwise several times. Then, smoothing her hair from her brow, he wound the scarf around her head and reached behind her to knot it. Finished, he drew back and surveyed her face.

As the silence expanded, all she could think to say was, "That's much better."

Dalton smiled, then glanced at Villard. "We'd better get him home. I'll see if I can get the horse untangled."

He left the sleigh and circled around in front of the nervous, white-eyed filly, talking soothing nonsense as he went. "Easy, girl. I know you're scared, but it's just me coming." When he was close enough, he held out a hand and let the horse nuzzle his palm. "You see? Nothing to be afraid of."

With a ragged sigh, Solitaire lowered her head to be petted, and Dalton obligingly rubbed her ears. "You've got yourself in a mess," he said. "Just stand still and I'll get you loose." Stroking her neck, gentling her with his voice and touch, he moved slowly toward her flank, unsnarling harness from underbrush along the way. As he laid his hand on her back, the filly's hind leg suddenly lashed at him in a powerful, vicious blur. Caught off guard, Dalton dove out of harm's reach and landed facedown in the snow.

Alexandra was on her feet. "Mr. Philips!"

"Stay there," he said, getting up. "I'm not hurt."

97

Again he approached the filly's left side. As he ran his hand lightly over her pelt, Solitaire flinched and pulled away, rolling her eyes at him. "Calm down, you little fireball," he said. "What happened to make you mad?"

Just then Dalton noticed the welts left on her rump by the whip, and although his tone remained gentle, his disgust was apparent as he moved to examine the marks. "Attagirl," he soothed. "I ain't gonna hurt you, I'm just having a look. I know the whip smarts, I know it does. Makes you bloody crazy, don't it?"

To Alexandra's relief, Solitaire stood docilely as Dalton unbuckled the leather keeper securing the sleigh's wooden shaft to the harness saddle. Circling to the filly's right side, he unfastened the keeper from the right shaft, unhooked the tracers from the sleigh, and crossed them over Solitaire's back to keep the ends from dragging. Solitaire moved willingly as he walked her slowly away from the sleigh until the shafts dropped free of the keepers. Talking in a low voice, Dalton led her off the bank, tethered her to a tree beside the road, then returned to the sleigh for Alexandra.

"I'll take you back down," he said.

The next thing Alexandra knew, he had swung her into his arms as though she weighed no more than a pillow. Startled, she stared into his face, inches from her own. "I can walk, Mr. Philips."

"Your dress is soaked," he said. "Your feet must be freezing."

"But—"

"Mrs. Pennington, you're shivering. I'll carry you."

She almost refused, except he was right—her toes were numb with cold. But by the time they reached the road and he set her down, her quickened pulse had pumped new warmth into her extremities. She thought he might use his mare to pull the sleigh free, but he went back up the bank alone, planted himself behind the splintered prow, and leaned his shoulder against it. After some vigorous shoving, the sleigh came unstuck, and Dalton pushed it downhill to the road.

Villard was still unconscious, but Alexandra was encouraged to see some color returning to his face. As she watched, Dalton picked him up as easily as he had her, propped him in a corner of the seat, and tucked the blanket around him.

After hitching Solitaire to the sleigh, Dalton retrieved his mare and led her over to Alexandra. "This is Secret," he said. "She ain't saddled proper for a lady, but if you wouldn't mind riding her ahead of the sleigh, I think the filly would do better following another horse."

"I've ridden astride," Alexandra said. So saying, she took hold of the saddle, pulled herself onto the mare's back, and settled her bulky skirts around her. She was thankful that Dalton pretended not to notice her exposed calf. His eyes were on her face as he gave Secret a pat.

"You shouldn't have any trouble with her," he said. "Just remember, she's trained for racing. It don't take much to make her move."

"I'll remember."

Alexandra waited for Dalton to get into the sleigh and take up the reins, then she nudged Secret's flanks. Within moments she realized the graceful little mare had deceptive power and speed. Even at a trot, Secret's stride was smooth and effortless. She was a joy to ride, responding to the slightest pressure from heels or knees, moving with a willingness that stemmed, Alexandra imagined, from trust and affection.

Glancing behind her, she saw the white filly trailing at a matched pace, with little guidance from Dalton. His presence was a balm to Alexandra's nerves. With a grateful sigh, she looked back at the road.

The white horse was moving along so well, in fact, that Dalton turned his attention to Villard, who suddenly moaned and raised a hand to his throbbing head.

"Mr. Villard?"

Villard's eyelids fluttered. With some effort, he focused on the man beside him, and when he realized who it was, his eyes closed as though to blot out the sight. "What in the hell are you doing here?" he mumbled.

"Saving your ass."

Hearing this, Villard tried to piece together what had happened to him, but his memory was in fragments. He only knew that somehow he was once again indebted to Dalton Philips. The thought made him nauseous. Then, in a rush, he remembered something that made him sit up straighter. "Where's Alexandra?"

"Straight ahead."

Villard looked, saw her riding the mare, and relaxed against the seat with a sigh. As the details of the accident filtered back to him, his menacing stare settled on Solitaire, the cause of his humiliation.

Noting his look, Dalton said, "She's a bit high-strung to be used as a sleigh horse."

"The stupid animal tried to kill us, all because of a branch in the road. She absolutely refused to go around it."

"So you whipped her."

Villard glared at him. "What of it?" he demanded.

"Why didn't you just get out and move the branch?"

"Because there was room to go around it."

A moment went by. "Horses are funny critters," Dalton said. "It usually don't take much to set them off. You lay a whip to some, they're liable to tell you to get fucked."

"Don't lecture me."

"I'm just stating a fact."

"The devil take you and your facts," Villard snapped, his temper erupting. "I happen to know a little something about horses."

Eyeing his bruised face, Dalton couldn't stop a smile. "A little something is right," he said.

Gray eyes hardened with rage.

The sleigh runners hissed in the silence as the two men considered each other. Up ahead, unaware of their conflict, Alexandra rode Dalton's mare as though the horse were her own. And Villard, his restraint crumbling as hatred welled uncontrolled, saw only Dalton's amused face and wanted to kill him.

"Listen carefully, you gutter bastard," he said. "I don't like you. I don't like the way you act or the way you smell, and I especially don't like having you near things that belong to me."

"Are you always this much fun when you wake up?"

Villard had to pause and get himself under control. "Take my advice," he said, low and threatening. "Stick to cleaning stalls and leave what's mine alone. This is your only warning."

Dalton was thoughtful a moment, then said, "Let me

see if I understand you. You're telling me to stay away from Alexandra Pennington?"

"How perceptive."

"And if I don't, something bad will happen to me?"

Villard's face was murderous. "What do you think?"

"I think your parents were too closely related."

A tremor shook Villard. Dalton made a tempting target, his hands occupied by the reins, but Villard's balled fists remained at his sides and his composure held. There would be a better time and place.

"The fact is," he said, "Alexandra pities you. 'That poor, dull farmer,' she calls you. Allow me to translate. You're nothing, worthy only of her sympathy."

That struck a nerve. Dalton's jaw clenched. "You almost got her killed today," he said with quiet fury.

Alexandra chose that moment to glance over her shoulder at them, and when she saw Villard sitting up, wide awake, she smiled with relief. For a horrified instant, Villard could only stare at her bloodstained face and clothing, then he summoned an answering smile and waved reassuringly to her. His enthusiasm dissolved the moment she looked back at the road.

"Remember my warning," he told Dalton in an ominous voice.

Dalton would never forget it.

When they arrived at Willowbrook a few minutes later, Alexandra tied Secret to the hitching post and went straight to Villard, her face anxious. "Are you all right?"

"Yes, I'm fine," he said, caressing her cheek. "Let's get you inside, sweetheart. You must be freezing." Then turning to Dalton, he forced a smile that seemed filled with gratitude. "How fortunate we are that you came along. If there is any way we can repay you—"

"Don't mention it," Dalton cut him off.

"Mr. Philips," Alexandra said, "at least come inside and get warm."

"Soon as I unhitch the horse, ma'am."

Though Dalton avoided her eyes, Alexandra did not miss the disturbance in his voice. Puzzled by his withdrawal, she said, "I'll send Christopher out to help you, then come into the parlor for some tea."

"Yes, ma'am."

Alexandra went inside with Villard, and Dalton went through the motions of unhitching the filly, who showed no signs of her former wildness. Just the opposite, Solitaire seemed drained by her ordeal, even dispirited, so Dalton put aside his own chagrin and took a moment to fondle her ears.

"Pretty girl," he said softly. "You'll feel better after you get some grain in you."

The front door opened. Expecting Christopher Clue, Dalton looked, then stood still as a deer as Alexandra came down the front walk to him. She was wearing the same wet clothing and her face was still bloodstained. Her eyes, as they gauged him, were concerned.

Worry had drawn Alexandra outside. She was afraid Dalton would leave again without giving her a chance to thank him. She also wanted to know what was troubling him, but his solemn expression gave away nothing. For no reason that she could understand, guilt stabbed her. "Have I offended you somehow?"

He looked as though she had struck him. "Never, ma'am. Don't even think it."

"Then what on earth is wrong?"

"Ain't nothing wrong."

He spoke with such conviction, she almost believed him. After a moment, Dalton shifted uncomfortably under her stare and his attention returned to the filly. Even before Alexandra asked the question, she knew he was going to disappoint her. "Will you stay for awhile?"

"I'd like to," he replied, "but I'm supposed to meet someone in town. Fact is, I'm late."

Her disappointment was keener than she had anticipated. Before she could say another word, he led Solitaire to the hitching post, tethered her there, then swung onto Secret's back and reined over to where Alexandra stood.

"I'm extremely grateful to you, Mr. Philips."

He shrugged the thanks away. "I was glad to help out."

"You're a generous man, but I don't like the way you keep disappearing."

That earned a smile. "You'd better get back inside," he said. "You'll catch cold."

After he left, Alexandra could not stop thinking about him. She wondered what had driven him off.

Other than some bruises and a splitting headache, there didn't appear to be anything wrong with Villard. Except, perhaps, that he was too quiet and his eyes were unnaturally bright.

Despite Alexandra's protests, he insisted on driving the sleigh home. "When you fall off a horse," he said, "you should immediately get back on."

"This isn't the same."

Her concern pleased him so much that he embraced her and kissed her cheek. "Forgive me," he whispered against her hair.

"Charles, it was an accident."

"No," he said with regret. "I am to blame. I lost my temper with the horse, not thinking what could happen. Had you been badly hurt, I couldn't have lived with myself."

As her arms tightened around him, Villard felt a surge of affection that was so strong it astonished him. He bent his head and kissed her again, this time on the lips, his mouth telling her, without words, how much she meant to him.

It was late afternoon when he climbed into the sleigh and left Willowbrook. He did not go his city house. Instead he headed for Sweet Briar at a brisk pace, driving south along the Ridge Road, across the center common, and down toward the Neck, as the tongue of land between the converging rivers was known. The Neck was a lovely, wooded place where lavish mansions, built as summer retreats by wealthy Philadelphians, adorned the river-banks. Today, in the dead of winter, it was a quiet, lonely place that suited Villard's deteriorating mood.

At Sweet Briar's stable, Sammy Finn saw the bright red sleigh gliding up the drive and sighed in frustration. Sammy spent his winters at Sweet Briar, tending the horses, and he knew the master's habits. With Mr. Villard, surprise inspections of his country estate were a form of recreation.

Sammy waited for him in the paddock. Right away, he noticed Villard's bandaged head and bloodied clothing. Next his gaze was drawn to the sleigh's cracked prow and slightly bent left runner. Lastly, with a sick feeling, he stared at Solitaire. Having hand-picked the flashy white horse for his employer, Sammy knew he would be held accountable for her performance today.

Anxiety made his mouth dry. "Did she give you trouble, sir?" he asked. When his question was ignored, Sammy's concern intensified.

Climbing from the sleigh, Villard said, "Unhitch her, but leave her in the paddock."

"Yes, sir."

Villard left, and Sammy removed the filly's harness, then brought her a bucket of water, which she drank straight down. Hearing footsteps behind him, Sammy turned and saw his employer returning to the paddock.

Charles Villard was carrying a musket. He opened the paddock gate and approached the filly with a purposeful air. "Stand back," he told Sammy, whose mouth sagged in shock.

"But Mr. Villard—"

"Shut your goddamned face and get out of the way!"

Sammy moved back, suddenly afraid for his life. He watched Sweet Briar's master check the charge in the pan, heard the click of the musket's lock, saw Villard fit the brass butt plate to his shoulder and sight along the barrel. The flint fell, the musket spat flame and smoke, and the filly's front legs buckled. As Sammy stared in horror, the beautiful white horse went down with a belly-deep groan, a round red hole neatly centered in her forehead.

Villard had stepped clear of billowing smoke to see the result of his shot. What he saw apparently pleased him, for his mouth thinned in a smile.

Chapter Fourteen

The sun was setting when Dalton burst into the kitchen at Downstream Farm. "You'll never believe what I've got," he said, waving a pamphlet.

Twigs, busy at the bread oven built into the side of the chimney, cocked his head and waited.

"It's this little book called *Common Sense*," Dalton said. "Everyone's reading it!"

Twigs grunted, then poked a long-handled shovel into the oven and withdrew the first of four steaming loaves, which he carried one by one to the table.

"It's about our independence," Dalton said and received another grunt. "Ain't you curious about it?"

"In a minute."

Dalton lit a candle and sat at the table. His impatient fingers drummed wood as Twigs shuffled unhurriedly to a cluttered sideboard, inventoried a row of bottles with his fingertips, and selected one. After pouring two tankards of rum, he brought them to the table and sat down.

"Now then," he said, holding out his hand, beckoning with his fingers. Dalton gave him the booklet. "Jesus God, boy!" Twigs said when he felt its thickness. "You'll be a year reading this."

Anxious to get started, Dalton snatched the book back from him and fanned its pages. "It's written anonymally."

"Anonymously."

"Right," Dalton agreed. "Who do you suppose wrote it? Franklin?"

"Wrong."

"Must have been Adams, then."

"Wrong again."

Dalton stared at him. "Who then?" he demanded.

"Paine. Who else?"

"How do you know?"

A gleam appeared in milky eyes. "Because a little bird told me he was writing something important."

"A bird named Dr. Rush?"

Twigs guzzled rum, then belched. "Read it to me, boy."

Dalton needed help with three words in the first paragraph alone. He spelled the words out, Twigs pronounced them for him and explained their meanings, and Dalton labored onward. It got easier. His thirst for knowledge and the author's simple eloquence went hand in hand.

To Dalton's delight, Paine was unafraid to use the words "separation" and "independence" as he blasted the royal brute in England and laid bare the very foundation of the British Constitution. The Constitution, said Paine, allowed some people to wallow in luxury while forcing the greater part to live in poverty. It was nothing more than an instrument that made legislators of wealthy men who, raised in comfort, ambition, and pride, knew nothing of law and right but were experts at tyrannizing over their fellow men.

"Listen to this," Dalton said and read: "'Male and female are the distinctions of nature, good and bad the distinctions of heaven; but how a race of men came into the world so exalted above the rest, and distinguished like some new species, is worth inquiring into, and whether they are the means of happiness or of misery to mankind."

Twigs nodded, wholly absorbed. "Go on," he said softly.

The hours passed unnoticed. With each page Dalton turned, his blood was stirred anew with ideas that echoed his deepest convictions, but which he could never have expressed with such clarity. The final passage of *Common Sense* burned him like a brand:

These proceedings may at first seem strange and difficult, but like all other steps which we have already passed over, will in a little time become familiar and agreeable: and until an independence is declared, the continent will feel itself like a man who continues putting off some unpleasant business from day to day, yet knows it must be done, hates to set about it, wishes it over, and is continually haunted with the thoughts of its necessity.

Closing the book, Dalton stared hypnotically at the flickering candle flame, his thoughts moving like a stream of pure fire in the wake of Paine's words.

"That," said Twigs, "is a bloody masterpiece."

Dalton just nodded, forgetful of Twigs's blindness.

"The world is about to change, boy. The rich have been exploiting the poor long enough."

Dalton knew all about poverty and exploitation by the rich. Eyes glittering, he raised his mug in a toast. "God damn the King."

Chapter Fifteen

Daylight was failing. Dense, swirling snow fell thick and fast on the pine-shrouded hollow where Jack Flash was at work.

Earlier that afternoon, as Dalton Philips, he had shadowed a Tory named Robert McPherson to a counting-house on Water Street. From the shadows of a cooperage, Dalton had watched and waited until McPherson left the countinghouse accompanied by his burly coachman, a fidgety-eyed man whose cloak concealed a pistol. Rightly so, because the bulge beneath McPherson's well-fitted topcoat was undoubtedly a sack of coins. A rich lawyer, McPherson was a partner in a large Philadelphia mercantile house. More importantly, in Dalton's estimation, he was related to Charles Villard.

Money. It seemed to go round in select circles.

The wind was picking up, driving swarms of white flakes into the gray evening. Donning his black hood, Jack Flash settled his three-cornered hat over his head and pulled the brim down low to shield his eyes from stinging snow. No one would be expecting him in this freak March blizzard. Soon McPherson's coach would pass this way en route to the Neck, where the lawyer's grand house stood at the fork of Shakhanfin Creek. If all went as planned, the coach would make an unscheduled stop, and Jack Flash would end his career on a high note.

Wrapped in his cloak, he crouched in a thicket beside the road. It was cold as the devil. He blew on his hands to warm them, then stiffened as hoofbeats reached his ears. Moments later a horseman rode by, head bent, shoulders shivering inside his greatcoat as the wind whipped his back. The rider faded into the dusk, the soft silence of the storm returned, and Jack Flash shifted anxiously. If his quarry didn't hurry, the road would become impassable.

As the minutes crawled by, the cold seeped into his bones, sheeting snow whitened his still form. He was almost ready to give up when he heard the rattle of coach wheels and a whipcrack of leather laid to a sluggish horse.

Jack Flash rose on the balls of his feet, his blood humming as a large black coach appeared from ghostly gloom. McPherson's. The driver and footman, hunched over against the whirling storm, failed to see the shadow that bounded from a thicket and sprang lightly onto the footman's perch, startling him speechless. Before the footman could react, powerful fists snagged his cloak and heaved, and he was suddenly airborne, clawing at nothing. He thudded to the snowy road with a grunt. The coach sped on.

Drawing his pistol, Jack Flash climbed on top of the coach, inched his way forward, and pressed the cold muzzle behind the coachman's ear. "Move and you're dead."

The coachman went rigid.

Jack Flash relieved him of his gun, then locked an arm around his throat and squeezed hard. The coachman began to thrash, but he was no match for the strength that held him. Fifteen seconds passed. Twenty. The coachman began to weaken. At thirty seconds he passed out, and Jack Flash quickly released him and climbed forward onto the driver's bench. Grabbing the loose reins, he steered with one hand and checked the unconscious man with the other. Feeling a strong, steady pulse and regular breathing, he sighed with relief and gave his attention to the road ahead.

A hundred yards farther on, at a safe distance from where he had dumped the footman, he stopped the coach beneath the gnarled branches of an ancient oak. The monstrous tree stood atop a steep bank that hid Secret from view of the road. By now, he imagined, the little mare was coated with snow and anxious for the warmth of her stall. Jack Flash didn't intend to keep her waiting much longer.

Leaping down from the bench, he threw open the coach

door and found not only Robert McPherson inside, but also Evelyn Wright. Her withered face paled as she beheld the hooded figure in the doorway.

Jack Flash motioned with his pistol. "Get out," he commanded.

Frozen in disbelief, neither moved.

"Get out, goddamnit!"

McPherson flinched and got to his feet. A polished, well-fed man with three chins and protruding black eyes, his cloaked bulk momentarily filled the doorway, blotting out Jack Flash's view of Evelyn Wright.

When he saw her again, she was aiming a pistol at him. He leveled his own gun instinctively. For a fractured instant he considered pulling the trigger, but something stayed his finger as Charles Villard's aunt shut her eyes and the pistol's weight dragged her trembling hand downward.

She fired.

Jack Flash saw flame and smoke gush, heard a sharp crack as lead left the barrel, and felt something stab deep into his thigh. Hot pain spread under the bone, lancing upward through his groin like a blade of fire. As he staggered back, McPherson lunged at him and grabbed for his gun. They struggled briefly. Then Jack Flash, in pain and rage, flung him away like a rag doll.

Turning, he launched himself at the steep bank below the oak, scrabbled for purchase, and started up with only one purpose in mind. Escape. No time to worry about the wound. From the warmth on his skin, he knew there was a fair amount of blood, and the throbbing from knee to groin made him gasp as he clawed his way upward. Reaching the top, he lurched through undergrowth and brambles that snagged his clothing and pulled him off balance so that he fell headlong into raking thorns.

He stumbled up, clutching his leg in agony, and spotted Secret, a dark shape against swirling whiteness. She whickered softly as he approached her, then flared her nostrils at the odor of his blood. Leaning against her, his arms going around her neck, he buried his face in her damp, warm coat as the world spun out of control.

Slowly his wits returned, his head came up. How long before McPherson set the sheriff after him? The thought made him shiver. Jack Flash, the fearless robber, was suddenly a fugitive, panting and frozen wet and filled with terror. He had to mount Secret from the wrong side, but she barely moved a muscle as he swung himself up, dragged his throbbing leg over her rump, and collapsed with a sharp cry into the saddle.

Dalton headed north toward home. He followed a riding path that crossed drifted fields, skirted icy marshes, and plunged through wooded defiles on the fringes of farms. At last he emerged from a grove of hemlocks onto a field in the Northern Liberties. He had tied a tourniquet around his thigh, but even so had a bootful of blood. Shuddering in the raw wind, his world swimming and tilting, he leaned forward and hugged Secret's neck as though drawing on her strength. A spasm racked him. God, he felt cold.

"It hurts, Secret," he moaned. "It fucking hurts."

He knew he was leaving a bloody trail, but there was no help for it, and he was beginning not to care. All he could think of was reaching Twigs, a warm fire, and a pint of rum. His body felt remarkably light. His thoughts began to stray.

There was a time when he knew nothing, then suddenly awoke to find himself clinging to the mare's neck. It took him a moment to realize they were on the Wissahickon Road. Secret, left to her own devices, was following the familiar track home. But home was still miles away, and the open road meant capture and death to Jack Flash.

As he thought this, the thud of approaching hoofbeats penetrated his stupor and shot new life into his leaden limbs. His cold-stiffened fingers yanked the reins, wheeling Secret toward a copse of trees. As they left the road the mare stumbled on uneven ground, and for the first time in years, Dalton lost his seat on a horse.

He saw the tree trunk coming but could not avoid slamming into it. White light exploded around him. For a moment his body seemed to float, tumbling in slow motion, then the cold ground rushed up to meet him. As he lay unmoving, a warm rivulet flowed across his cheek to the corner of his mouth. He tasted blood. Some part of him knew he was lucky to be breathing, and that was the last thing he knew for awhile.

Chapter Sixteen

Alexandra opened her front door to Sheriff Dewees.

"Good evening, Mrs. Pennington," he said. "I'm sorry to disturb you at this hour."

She held the door wider. "Please come in, Sheriff."

A blast of frigid air followed him inside and threatened to extinguish the branch of candles in Alexandra's hand. Shivering, she closed the door and drew her night robe more closely about her. A lace-edged mobcap covered her dark hair. "Has something happened?" she asked.

"I'm afraid so," Dewees said and removed his cocked hat, dumping a brimful of snow to the hallway floor. In the wavering light, his face was grim. "Jack Flash stopped a coach on the Neck and tried to rob it."

Alexandra winced in dismay. "Not again."

"This time was different," Dewees said. "He was wounded. Pretty badly, we think. We lost his tracks not far from here."

"Good Lord," she breathed.

"I stopped to warn you to be on the lookout and to have your men keep their guns handy. He's liable to be desperate."

"We'll be careful," she said. "I hope to God you find him."

"We'll get the scoundrel," he vowed, jamming his hat over his head. "Good night, ma'am."

"Good night, Sheriff. And thank you."

When Dewees was gone, Mary Brock edged from the shadows of the hallway into the candlelight. Her eyes were huge as she stared at Alexandra, who was leaning against

112

the door in a kind of trance. "He's Jack Flash," Mary whispered, anxiously wringing her hands.

Alexandra located her voice. "So it seems," she said. "Where the devil is Christopher?"

"He's coming, ma'am."

"Tell him to hurry."

Alexandra went upstairs to her guest room, where a fire was blazing on the hearth and Dalton Philips was lying on the bed. His eyes were closed, his breathing was shallow and uneven. Closing the door, Alexandra stood very still and watched him, unable to comprehend the truth about him. This selfless man, who had saved her from a mob and come to her aid on a lonely, frozen road, was a notorious thief. He had robbed her at Sweet Briar. He had aimed a pistol at her heart and frightened her half to death.

He moaned and stirred.

Moving to the bed, Alexandra placed the candle branch on the nightstand and sat beside him. Glazed green eyes looked into hers. His voice was a whisper. "Where's my horse?"

"In my barn." Alexandra touched his shoulder in reassurance. "Edward Brock is bedding her down. Don't worry, she's fine." Her gaze moved to the mess of blood that was his left thigh. "But you certainly are not."

Just then the door opened, and Christopher Clue came in carrying a large serving tray. On the tray were lint and bandages, a bottle of brandy, and a washbasin filled with water. "Hello, Dalton," he said in a tone that put Dalton at ease.

"How are you, Chris?"

Clue put down the tray and appraised him. "Better than you," he concluded.

Dalton managed a smile. "It's just a scratch."

Sitting on the bed, Clue inspected the wound. "It's a bit more than a scratch, you numbskull," he said. "The ball went clear through. Must hurt like bloody hellfire."

"That about says it."

"Hold still now."

Dalton hissed as the tourniquet was loosened and pain stabbed torn flesh. "The bullet missed the bone," he croaked.

"Well, split me. You're a genius."

113

"It'll heal itself. It just needs cleaning."

"It needs a doctor."

"No!" Dalton's eyes were bright with alarm as he gripped Clue's wrist. "A doctor means a dance on the gallows, Clue. You've tended wounds before. Just pretend I'm one of your horses."

"You're about as daft as one."

Dalton stared at him, waiting, dreading a refusal.

At last Clue gave a deep sigh and nodded. "I'll fix you up as best I can," he said, "but you might be better off hanged."

Dalton sank back on the pillows. "Was that you that picked me out of the snow?" he asked.

"You weigh a ton."

"A grateful ton."

"I couldn't leave you there to freeze, could I?"

"You could have whistled for the sheriff."

At that, Clue glanced at Alexandra. "I reckon no one in this house wants that, Dalton."

Alexandra had been silent, but now, finding Dalton's eyes on her, she said firmly, "That does not mean anyone here approves of your thievery."

"I never dreamed such a thing, ma'am."

"Christopher, did you bring scissors?" she asked.

Clue held up a pair of long shears.

"Cut off his clothes," she said.

"All of them?"

"All of them."

Jolted, Dalton held up defensive hands. "Just the leg, ma'am."

"All of his clothes, Christopher."

"Now please, ma'am!" Dalton said, close to panic. "It ain't necessary."

She ignored him. "Christopher?"

Clue set to work.

And Alexandra told Dalton, "Stop fussing and lie still. Your clothes are filthy and they're coming off."

He opened his mouth to reply, then flinched in agony as the shears slid along his injured thigh, parting blood-soaked wool as they went. A sheen of perspiration formed on his face. Silent and miserable, he stared at the ceiling and drew ragged breaths.

114

Moved by his distress, Alexandra poured brandy into a glass and held it to his lips. "Drink some of this," she urged.

He drank obediently as the scissors snip-snipped. His embarrassed, fevered eyes would not meet hers.

"I was married for almost six years," she told him, low and conspiritorial. "You haven't got anything that would surprise me, so just relax." But as his severed breeches came away, revealing a lean, hard-muscled body, Alexandra knew she was wrong. John Pennington had never looked like this.

"Christopher, help me sit him up," she said.

Together they pulled Dalton to a sitting position, raised his arms over his head, and removed his damp gray shirt. Casting the shirt aside, Alexandra stilled, staring at rows of ridged scars covering Dalton's back, their crisscrossed pattern suggesting a brutal, methodical whipping. Clue also saw the marks and met her shocked look. Neither said a word.

When Dalton was lying flat again, Clue began cleaning the swollen, puckered wound to determine the full extent of the damage. As he worked, tossing aside bloodied wads of lint, his expression grew tense. Finally he wiped a hand over his mouth. "Shit, Dalton," he said, then shot Alexandra a sheepish look. "Pardon me, ma'am. It's just that I've never dealt with anything like this before. It needs to be sewed."

"Then sew it," Dalton said in a faint voice.

Clue muttered, "Oh, Christ," and turned beseeching eyes on Alexandra. "Mrs. Pennington, if I'm going to stitch this bloody mess, first I need a drink."

She studied him a moment. He did indeed look unsettled. "Just one, Christopher."

"Just one, ma'am," he agreed. "To steady my hands."

After Clue went downstairs, Alexandra dipped a clean cloth in the water basin and wrung it out. Leaning over Dalton, she wiped perspiration from his face and neck, wanting to bring relief to his heated skin. He smelled of sweat, brandy, and blood. His hand shook slightly as he reached for hers and gripped it hard.

"I'm sorry for all this trouble."

"It's all right," she comforted him. "Just lie still and try

115

not to hurt."

His smile was more a grimace. "I wish I could order that happy event."

Hours later, Alexandra slipped into her guest room and found Dalton asleep, one arm outflung, his body drained to exhaustion. Lifting the bedcovers, she checked his bandage and was relieved to see that his bleeding had stopped. As she covered him again, he stirred, murmured something unintelligible, then drifted back to sleep. His breathing seemed normal, his skin felt cool beneath her fingertips. Encouraged by his improvement, her fear for him abated. Apparently he was as tough as he was bold.

His endurance tonight had evoked her admiration. She remembered how, when Clue had stitched the wound, blood had dripped to the mattress and Dalton had shivered like a leaf in a storm as his white-knuckled fists clenched the bedcovers. But no sound had passed his lips. She also recalled the terrible scars on his back and knew he was no stranger to pain.

Studying his tranquil face, captivated by the sight, Alexandra had the extraordinary sensation that she had always known him. It seemed so natural to lean over him and smooth damp hair from his forehead. As she did this, his eyes opened and looked at her, and for an instant she was lost in their pull.

"How are you feeling?"

"Bloody stupid," he said in a thick voice.

Alexandra smiled. "I'm not sure we can cure that," she told him, "but we'll do what we can about your leg." His answering smile suffused her with warmth. "Are you hungry or thirsty?"

Dalton shook his head.

"Then rest. I'll look in on you later," she said and went to the door.

"Mrs. Pennington?"

Alexandra paused and looked back at him.

"I won't forget your kindness."

This time her smile was forced, because neither could she forget that he was Jack Flash.

Chapter Seventeen

"I never met such a curmudgeon," Clue complained. "What hole did he crawl out of?"

Propped up in bed on pillows, Dalton said, "You don't want to know, Chris."

Clue suspected he was right. Wielding sharp shears, he bent over Dalton's bandaged leg and clipped through stiff layers of lint and cloth. "You'd have thought I shot you myself," he said. "The old gaffer was downright abusive to me."

Because he was scared, Dalton thought, then wondered what would have become of Twigs had Jack Flash been killed the other night. The image of his best friend wasting away in an almshouse, left to rot among sick, helpless, and unwanted souls, was repulsive to him.

"Twigs ain't so bad," he said, "once you get to know him."

"Perish the thought."

Dalton smiled. "At least now he knows I'm all right. Thanks for making the trip."

"Buy me a pint sometime, we'll call it even."

A pint. Small reward for all Clue had done. Dalton watched him peel the bandage away from the wound, which suppurated clear fluid from entrance and exit holes. The ball had punched through muscle, miraculously missing the bone and leaving the artery intact. His thigh was discolored from knee to hip and still throbbed like hell, but there was no leakage of blood or pus and the swelling had noticeably decreased.

"It don't look too bad," he said.

117

Clue's narrowed eyes and quick fingers made a thorough inspection of the injury. "It's better," he agreed, "but you're going to be laid up for a while."

"Not here."

Detecting unease in Dalton's voice, Clue said, "Mrs. Pennington doesn't want you to leave until you're able."

"I'm able."

"Don't be pigheaded. You start this leg bleeding again, you could end up losing it."

Dalton fell silent.

So Clue, humming an off-key tune, began applying a fresh bandage to the wound. As he worked, he felt his patient flinch every so often. Stealing a glance at him, Clue saw lines of pain etched on Dalton's face and knew he was feeling worse than he let on. Though Dalton tried to disguise it, bloodloss had made him weak as a newborn. He was a far cry from the robust man Clue was used to. He was Jack Flash, and that knowledge was electrifying.

After tying off the bandage, Clue looked up into green eyes that were filled with remorse.

"I ain't proud of what I done, Chris."

"Now, Dalton—"

"I don't blame you for thinking the worst of me."

Clue sighed and rubbed his jaw. "You want to know the truth?" he asked. "I was tickled when you robbed Mr. Villard. That pompous bastard needed to be brought down a peg. But I didn't appreciate you robbing Mrs. Pennington. She's a good woman. She didn't deserve it."

The room was suddenly quiet. Immersed in guilt, Dalton stared past Clue with a faraway look. "I'll make it up to her," he said, and with all his heart he meant it.

That evening, when Alexandra entered Dalton's bed-chamber, he was sleeping soundly. The fire had died to embers on the grate, and the air in the room felt chill. Moving quietly on slippered feet, she knelt before the hearth, stacked wood on glowing coals, then sat back and watched flames lick and curl around dry logs. After a time, she glanced toward the bed.

Dalton looked back at her. "Hello, ma'am."

"I didn't mean to wake you."

He shrugged as if it didn't matter.

As Alexandra approached the bed, her shadow fell across him, making it difficult to see his eyes and know what he was thinking. "Christopher tells me your leg is mending."

"It feels much better."

There was a pause. Alexandra looked down at her hands. "Dalton, we need to talk."

"Yes, ma'am," he said, so soft she barely heard him.

Moving an armchair close to the bed, she sat down and watched his grim face in the flickering light. Perhaps she was mad for doing this, but her mind was made up.

"First I want to put your mind at ease," she began. "This morning I spoke with Christopher and the Brocks about your situation. We all remember what you did for us the night the mob came to my house, and we want to repay you. So rest assured your secret will be safe with us." Pausing, she let the silence expand as resolve hardened her look. "But now I want your promise that Jack Flash will never again show his face in Philadelphia."

"He's dead, ma'am."

Although Alexandra didn't care for his choice of words, the intent behind them felt genuine. She nodded, satisfied, then his low, dismal voice pierced her.

"I'm sorry for stealing from you."

He seemed so ashamed that her impulse was to reassure him, but she caught herself in time. Repaying her debt to him was one thing; forgiving his crimes was quite another.

She was about to tell him so when he said, "For what it's worth, Dalton Philips never benefited from Jack Flash."

It was such a ridiculous statement, she could not help mocking him. "Really."

"It's true."

"Then who is his beneficiary?"

His chin rose a notch. "The American Army."

Shock whiplashed her. For a moment, she could only stare at him. "You're a rebel?"

Dalton nodded, no longer ashamed but defiant. "And proud of it," he said, looking dauntless with the firelight bisecting his face.

"Oh, this is gorgeous," she said. "Frankly, I would

119

rather you were a common thief."

"I didn't ask your approval, did I?"

"Don't you dare."

Silence crackled. Then Alexandra shook her head and even laughed. "A rebel," she said, as though she still could not believe it. Her glittering eyes bored into him. "Your kind is more dangerous than the worst criminals."

"Because we want liberty?"

"Liberty," she said with contempt, "is just a word. We can rule ourselves here, but we still need the King."

"What for? So we have someone to bow to? And who will rule us, ma'am?"

"People of wisdom and intelligence."

He smirked at that. "Rich, flaming aristocrats, you mean. Like those frolicking bastards in England who want to drain us dry."

"Since when are you an expert on England?"

"I was born and raised there," he shot back. "I've seen how the horsey rich live, and it ain't no different here. Poor people have no say."

"Of course you have say," she said with an angry, dismissive gesture. "You rebels spout about freedom, yet common people enjoy more advantages here than anywhere in the world. There are opportunities for everyone, and you still have the protection and bounties of the Empire. What more could you want?"

"The right to be heard," he said.

"I'm listening," she challenged.

"It don't make sense for us to be chained to some fat old man sitting on a tiny little island half a world away. He runs his bloody Empire like pieces on a checkerboard. Why should his British merchants be rewarded from our hard work? Answer me that."

"There's plenty of reward spread here."

"True," Dalton agreed. "Mostly to privileged folk who wouldn't know an honest day's work if it bit them on the behind."

Her mouth compressed. "So you think everyone should be treated as equals."

"I do."

"And yet you don't mind being a puppet for a handful of pompous men."

"What pompous men?" he demanded.

"Hancock, Adams, Jefferson, Morris." She cocked her head. "Shall I go on?"

"Don't let me stop you."

"Not one of them will ever lift a musket and fight honorably. No, they'll spin fancy words and plot and debate in drawing rooms while rabble does their dirty work."

"I ain't rabble," he said belligerently. "I'm a Patriot, and so's the rest of us who want independence. We want our God-given rights, and we're willing to die for them."

Alexandra rolled her eyes and sighed. "God-given rights," she said sweetly. "To do what, pray tell? To throw stones through my windows? Destroy my property? Terrify me half out of my wits?"

Dalton hesitated.

"It's disgraceful conduct," she said. "It has nothing to do with rights."

As he watched her, firelight etched dark hollows beneath his mouth and cheekbones. Finally he said, "I don't approve of the mobs."

"No, you would rather rob people on dark roads or go onto a battlefield and shoot lead into good English boys."

"Ma'am—"

"It's a revolt without dignity, with total disregard for British interests."

His voice had lost its force. "I don't feel much like arguing with you."

"Of course not! You're wrong and you know it."

"It ain't that," he said weakly, wiping a hand over his brow. He shivered a little. His stare grew unfocused, but Alexandra, in her anger, failed to notice.

"You rebels want everything handed to you on a platter. Life isn't meant to be—"

A moan escaped him. Startled, Alexandra saw his eyes roll back in his head as the blood seemed to drain from his face. To her alarm, he clutched his chest and began to shudder.

"Dalton?"

He seemed not to hear her. His body had gone rigid, his face was contorted and reddened, just as John Pennington's had been on the night he died. Horrified, she sat on

121

the bed and gripped his shoulders. "Dalton?" she asked.

A spasm racked him. His trembling body arched up, then went suddenly limp as, with the tiniest whimper, he stopped breathing.

"Dalton!" Fear scalded her. As she started up to get help, strong fingers seized her arm, pulling her back, and Dalton's laughing eyes opened.

"Look at you," he scoffed. "Carrying on over a rebel."

For a moment she was speechless.

"Don't it seem odd?" he asked. "Us being enemies?"

"Damn you!"

"Oh, I see," he said. "A minute ago you didn't care if I was General Washington himself. But now that I'm not dying, it's safe to hate me again."

Alexandra jerked from his grip and glared at his amused face. "I don't hate you," she said. "I feel sorry for you."

His smile wavered.

"Because I see no happy end to your idiotic convictions. God help me, you might be a rebel, but there is something quite likeable about you, and I don't want to see you punished for treason." She paused, drew a deep breath, then gave him a grudging smile. "You bastard."

Dalton laughed.

"You should be on the stage."

"All prinked up?"

"Like a Yankee-Doodle dandy."

"That's the spirit, ma'am."

"Stop calling me that," she said. "It makes me feel old. I have a name, you know."

"Alexandra," he said softly, searching her face. "Pretty name, that. Does anyone ever call you Alex?"

"My husband did."

"You were married six years?"

She nodded. "Almost."

"You married young," he said.

"I had just turned fifteen."

"How old was John Pennington?"

"Forty-five."

His mouth opened in shock. "Jesus God."

"Don't look at me that way. We were a good match."

"If a bit lopsided."

Her back stiffened. "I resent that."

"That was rude, wasn't it?" His eyes grew apologetic. "I'm sorry."

"I was very fond of John."

"I believe you," he said, raising warding hands.

Realizing how defensive she sounded, Alexandra swallowed and looked away.

"Did you know him long before you married him?" Dalton wanted to know.

"All my life. He was a close friend of my father. My family all called him uncle, but he and I were especially close. When my father died, John was there to soften the blow. I don't know how we would have managed without him." She was silent a moment, staring at her hands in her lap. "Then one day my mother said that John had asked for my hand and that I was to marry him. It was a shock," she admitted.

"I guess so, having to marry your uncle."

"Not a real uncle."

"Did you love him?"

The question stopped her cold. She could not say why, exactly, unless it was the gentle curiosity in Dalton's voice or his intent eyes, which held her whole. After a time, very softly, she said, "Yes. He was a dear man. But I've often wondered if there should have been a different kind of love between us."

As soon as the words were out, Alexandra wanted them back. With a glance at Dalton, she asked herself why on earth she had confided so much to him. "We should talk about something else," she said.

Dalton put his hands behind his head and got comfortable. "What would you like to talk about?"

"You."

"A dull subject."

"Where is your family?"

"I wouldn't know."

She frowned at him. "Your mother and father?"

"Never knew them," he said with a shrug, then smiled. "I warned you I was dull."

He had no memory of his parents? "Then who raised you?" she asked.

"A man named Ben Philips. He was a farrier, looked

after me till I was ten."

"What happened then?"

"He croaked," Dalton said. "Fell face down in a dung pile," his hand demonstrated the event, "right in the middle of shoeing a horse. Talk about being planted in dirt. It was awful."

Though she tried, Alexandra could not keep from smiling. "How did you manage after that?"

"I got by," he said, "cleaning stalls and whatnot. Then a friend of Ben's found me work at Foxborough Manor in Yorkshire, a real grand place with a big stable. I was a mucker first, then a groom. Sometimes I even got to be a jockey."

"Did you like it there?"

Dalton considered his answer. "It was all right," he said, but without much enthusiasm. "I mean I didn't starve, and plenty of people do."

"Why were you whipped?"

Caught off guard, Dalton averted his eyes. A long silence followed before he said in a subdued voice, "I took something that didn't belong to me."

Alexandra waited for him to look at her.

"The master's daughter."

Her eyebrows rose.

"We didn't do anything wrong," he insisted. "We was just good friends." After a moment he sighed and his eyes warmed with some long-ago memory. "We grew up together, you see. She taught me my letters and such."

Alexandra said, "Oh," wondering what *and such* meant.

"She was always at the stable for one reason or another. We flirted sometimes. You know, harmless stuff. Anyway, one day her father saw me kiss her."

"And he whipped you for that?"

"Oh, no," Dalton said, and the scorn in his eyes was absolute. "He did it nice and lawful. First he planted some coins under my bed, then he accused me of stealing a horse from his barn and selling it. He even bought himself a witness."

"That's despicable!"

"He wanted rid of me," Dalton said. "He told the Court I was a notorious liar."

"And the magistrates believed him?"

"One of them was his brother."

Appalled, she asked, "Didn't you have a lawyer?" The moment she said it, Alexandra realized how foolish the question was.

"Lawyers want money."

"Of course." Her face felt warm. "Go on."

Dalton shrugged. "There wasn't much I could say except I didn't steal his bleeding horse. I never took anything from him in my life."

"So you were whipped?"

He nodded. "Plus I can never set foot in England again." He gave her a rueful smile. "All for a kiss."

Alexandra's heart went out to him. "I'm sorry," was all she could think to say.

"Don't be," he replied. "It turned out for the best, didn't it? I ended up in America."

But Alexandra shuddered to think of the undeserved agony he had suffered. She had seen men flogged, seen their flesh ribboned by metal-tipped thongs until blood streamed down their backs and overflowed their boot tops. In her mind, she saw him bound to a stained post, his teeth clenching a leather wedge while the cat clawed him.

All for a kiss.

Dalton was quiet, his expression neutral. From his appearance, Alexandra could almost believe he had come to terms with his past. But she took a closer look at shuttered green eyes. A wounded man prowled in them, the victim of cruel and unjust power. She imagined the scars on his back were nothing compared with the ones on his soul.

Chapter Eighteen

Winter gradually lost its bite. The nights were still cold and snow clung in tenacious patches in the deep woods, but there was warmth at last in the sunlight as the green season arrived and overspread the thawing land.

Dalton left Willowbrook early in April. When Alexandra said goodbye to him, they were alone in the kitchen, where morning sunlight slanted through windows and a cookfire crackled on the hearth. He was leaning on a wooden crutch fashioned from an oak branch. Wearing a shirt, breeches, and stockings that had once belonged to John Pennington, his shining black hair tied with a black bow, he could have been a gentleman standing before her. Instead he was a thief who gloried in being a rebel.

Alexandra said, "Promise me you'll look after that leg."

"I promise," he said. In his eyes was a look she could not define. Nor could she name the feeling that welled in her as he laid the back of his hand gently to her cheek. "Thank you, Alexandra."

Those three words, softly spoken, encompassed much more than gratitude and caused an immediate quickening of her pulse. She gave a casual response, hiding her excitement, and afterward could not remember exactly what she had said in farewell.

When he was gone, she went into the guest room before Mrs. Brock had a chance to disturb things, and found the bed made in a fashion only Dalton could have accomplished. Sitting on the mattress, Alexandra closed her eyes and absorbed the ghost of his presence. Her head filled with the memory of his warm, strong touch, and the quickness of his smile, and of friendship so easily shared. After a time, she lay back on the pillow and, whether she wished it or not, Dalton Philips followed her deep within the privacy of herself.

A door slammed downstairs.

Alexandra sat up abruptly, as though startled, and moved off the bed. She stood for a moment, then began stripping the covers off the mattress, her movements brisk and purposeful.

What in God's name was wrong with her? She had harbored a felon. He had taken her beautiful necklace, stolen money from Charles, and robbed others at gunpoint. Worst of all, he was a traitor who wanted to destroy her way of life. She should be glad to be rid of him. But even as the thought formed Alexandra knew it was empty.

Gathering up the sheets, she went to the door, then leaned against it and waited for the turmoil inside to abate. The bundle in her arms gave off a familiar, musky scent that invaded her senses and threatened her determination. Straightening, she exhaled a long breath. There was only one sane thing to do.

She went out and closed the door on Dalton Philips.

"How are you, Twigs?"

"Me?" Bony hands clutched Dalton's shoulders. "Jesus, boy, you scared me half to death!" Twigs seemed to want to embrace him but held back.

Dalton had no shyness. He crushed the gray stick of a man to him and heard Twigs say, "It's my fault. I should have listened to you. You wanted to quit and I pushed you—"

"Twigs," Dalton said, holding him at arm's length. "The choice was mine. Anyway I'm back, all in one piece, so let's forget about what's done."

But Twigs would not be consoled. "It isn't safe for you to stay here."

"I ain't leaving."

"But that woman knows about you!" Roving, sightless eyes were alive with fear. "Suppose she talks?"

"If it wasn't for her," Dalton said, "I'd be dead or sitting in jail. I trust her, Twigs."

"What about her servants?" he demanded.

"Them too."

Twigs was scornful. "You're a fool."

Dalton made no reply, secure in his belief that no one at Willowbrook would betray him.

Realizing the argument was lost, Twigs sighed and said, "Let's go inside," then went ahead as Dalton hobbled into the kitchen and sank down on a bench at the table. The ride from Willowbrook, slow as Clue had driven the wagon, had jarred his leg unmercifully. He flexed it with care, grimacing at deep, gnawing pain.

Across the table, Twigs was fidgeting with the pewter buttons of his shabby brown waistcoat. "Both mares foaled last week," he said. "We have another bay colt and a chestnut filly."

The news pleased Dalton, for the foals would bring much-needed money to Downstream Farm. "Seems like you managed all right without me," he said.

"I paid the Mueller boy to clean stalls and feed up for me. I told him you were in Baltimore, looking at horses. Between the two of us, we got things done."

Dalton smiled to himself. Knowing Twigs, the old man had done the lion's share of the work. His competence always amazed Dalton, but Twigs would need permanent help running the farm in the months ahead, because Dalton planned to be gone. "Soon as my leg heals," he said, "I'm joining Colonel Wayne's battalion."

But Twigs shook his head. "You'll never be ready in time. Wayne has orders to march to New York within a week."

Disappointment stung Dalton. "New York?"

"Haven't you heard?" Twigs asked. "Howe loaded his whole damn army onto ships and left Boston Harbor. Washington thinks he's going to make a pass at New York."

Dalton's fist banged the table. "Goddamnit!" he exploded. "Fighting time's come and here I sit, useful as a drop of dog spit."

"Calm down, boy," Twigs laughed. Getting up from the table, he went to a cupboard and brought back a jug of hard cider, which he plunked down in front of Dalton. "Drink up," he said. "Things aren't as bad as they seem."

"Easy for you to say." Scowling, Dalton uncorked the jug with his teeth and drank deeply.

"You remember Tom Mifflin?" Twigs asked.

"I remember you had dealings with him."

Thomas Mifflin, a Philadelphian, was a brigadier general in the Continental army. "When you reach the army," Twigs said, "look him up. He'll know what to do with you."

"He will?" Dalton asked.

"There's a lieutenant's rank waiting for you." The shocked hush made Twigs grin. "You didn't think I'd send you up there to be a bloody private, did you?" he demanded. "You've got a grand horse and a wicked sword, and you're the devil with both. Be a damn shame to waste you in the ranks, especially after all you've done."

"A lieutenant?" Spoken softly, as though afraid of shattering the miracle.

"You can thank Jack Flash."

As the reality seeped in, Dalton felt a sensation that was indescribable. A lieutenant. An American officer leading Patriots against the stinking proud Bloodybacks. He had risked everything for a dream, and that dream was about to be unleashed. When the mighty British lion hurled its challenge, America would answer with fire and steel, and the world, for better or worse, would be changed.

Chapter Nineteen

The Delaware River was open again to the great ships. The thick ice that had clung all winter to its banks had melted away, thawed by a warming current. Gulls wheeled on a mild breeze. Bright sunshine sparkled the waters and drenched Philadelphia's bustling quays and shipyards. But while spring flourished, bringing new life to the greening land, Charles Villard prepared to flirt with death.

In his comfortable quarters on board the *Golden Fleece*, Alexandra waited for him to join her. Her canvas chair faced galleried windows that spread from quarter to quarter and looked astern, offering a view of the broad Delaware. Across the shimmering river, crisp blue sky defined the Jersey shoreline, a verdant strip of land adorned with farmhouses, windmills, and miniature wharves. Alexandra absorbed the view without really seeing it, for her mind was on a stubborn, golden-haired man who was about to court disaster for the sake of a business venture.

Golden Fleece had been cleared to sail on the afternoon tide, and when the ship's anchor was hoisted, Villard would begin a dangerous voyage south to the Carolinas. Dangerous because American privateers were roaming the coastal waters like hungry sharks, scouting for potential prey, and although their targets were chiefly British naval vessels, Tory-owned merchantmen were also frequent victims of attacks.

The sea raiders sailed under letters of the marque from the Continental Congress, whose authorization allowed rogue captains and their crews to escape the designation of pirates. Over a thousand ships had been commissioned throughout the Colonies as privateers. They ranged in size from one hundred to five hundred tons, carried as many as twenty guns, and were manned by rebels eager to bag prizes.

Golden Fleece had been outfitted with a dozen ten-pounders and boasted an experienced crew. But she was designed to carry cargo, not to outrun other ships, and her bright new sails would be highly visible to scavengers lying in wait on the horizon.

Consumed with apprehension, Alexandra listened absently to watery thumpings from below, the leathery flap of feet on the quarterdeck overhead, gulls shrieking their annoyance at one another. Finally footsteps echoed in the corridor outside the cabin. Recognizing the tempo of his stride, Alexandra came to her feet as the door opened and Villard entered the room.

He smiled at her. "That didn't take long, did it?"

Alexandra said no and returned his smile, but her eyes gave away worry.

"Sweetheart, what's wrong?" he asked.

"I don't understand why you can't send a representative."

Crossing the cabin to her, he ran his hands down her arms and surveyed her anxious face. "Because the contract is too important to be entrusted to someone else."

"Important enough to risk your life for?"

His fingers laced with hers. "That depends," he said and looked thoughtful. "Am I worth two sloops?"

"Charles!"

His laughter rang in the room. "Don't worry, I'll be fine."

"How long will you be gone?"

"Three weeks, perhaps four. It's difficult to say."

Sighing, Alexandra studied their entwined hands. "I shall be a wreck the entire time."

"Do you mean that?"

"Of course I do."

A moment passed, then his hand rose to cup her chin, tilting her face up to him. In a quiet voice he asked, "Do you realize it has been seven months since I proposed to you?"

Surprise rippled through her. Staring at him, her thoughts moving fast, she read his tender look and knew what was coming.

"In September," he said, "on your birthday, it will be one year. A year's courtship is all a woman can expect from a man, especially when he would give anything to marry her this minute."

The appeal in his eyes held Alexandra motionless.

And Villard, sensing her mood was right and finding himself unable to contain the desire in his heart, seized the moment and spoke with a great yearning. "Alexandra, you're the most precious thing in the world to me. In all my life, I have never cared about anyone the way I care about you. I would be so good to you."

She stared at him intently, seeing him in her future, a man she could confide in and laugh with, and they would communicate with gentle touches and knowing looks. As the silence lengthened and he waited for her response, Alexandra imagined she could be happy as Charles Villard's wife. The words came of their own accord. "September is a beautiful month for a wedding."

At first he just stood there. Then he drew her to him and hugged her close. "I'll always love you," he whispered.

Hearing this, feeling his arms securely around her, Alexandra believed she was following the right path with a man suited to her in ways that mattered. She was grateful to him for not rushing her.

September seemed a long way off.

Chapter Twenty

A thunderstorm swept down on Willowbrook with unexpected fury. From her bedroom window, Alexandra watched the landscape darken as black clouds rolled overhead to a steady, powerful rumbling, a warning of what nature had in store. It seemed that night was falling until lightning glared and the world was revealed in stark brilliance.

The rain came with a low hiss on the trees. Within moments the far woods were a dark blur. Suddenly Alexandra leaned closer to the window, peering hard at movement not caused by the storm. A horseman appeared from the slanting gray torrent and cantered along the drive toward the house. The rider's head was bowed to shield his face, but she would know him anywhere. She recoiled slightly. Then her fingertips went to the windowpanes, her eyes tracking his progress as sensations twisted inside her—elation, surprise, guilt.

His chestnut stallion, frightened by the storm, fought the bit and suddenly reared up as thunder cracked like a cannonshot and forked lightning slammed to the ground. Alarmed, Alexandra watched him bring the horse under control. As he rode on toward the house, a sigh of relief escaped her.

She left her bedroom, hurried down the back stairs to the kitchen, and found Mary Brock nervously kneading a mound of dough and flinching with each thunderclap. At the kitchen table, unperturbed by the storm, Edward Brock and Christopher Clue were eating dinner.

"Mr. Philips is here," Alexandra said and was pinned by

133

three pairs of eyes.

Clue smiled and shook his head. "Only Dalton would be out in this weather."

"Please help him get his horse into the barn."

Donning his hat and coat, Clue went out into the storm, and Alexandra waited in the kitchen. She told herself there was no reason to feel anxious. When Dalton walked through that door, nothing special would happen and her heart would calm because all she would see was a common farmer.

The door opened, and he came inside with Clue, and the air in the room suddenly changed. He seemed taller than she remembered and walked with a slight limp. Rivulets of water poured from his hat and oiled cloak as he glanced around the kitchen. Seeing her, he smiled and took off his hat, and Alexandra realized he would never seem ordinary.

"Hello, ma'am."

"Hello, Mr. Philips."

After nodding a greeting to the Brocks, Dalton removed a soggy bundle from beneath his cloak and held it out to her. "The clothes I borrowed," he said. "I appreciate you loaning them to me."

Alexandra had meant for him to keep them. But as she took the bundle from him, her every nerve conscious of his nearness, she was glad he had decided otherwise. "It's good to see you again," she said.

"And you, ma'am."

In the ensuing pause, rain drummed like a fury on the roof. Dalton stood uncertainly, his smile wavering as his fingers fiddled with his hat. He looked so nervous that Alexandra took the hat from him and hung it on a peg. "I was about to have dinner," she said. "Would you care to join me?"

He relaxed visibly. "Yes, very much."

A little later, Edward Brock showed them into the dining room, where the long, oval table had been set for two. Edward, a slight, balding man with a bland manner, settled Alexandra at one end while Dalton sat gingerly on a velvet-covered chair at the other. With expert efficiency and a minimum of words, Edward poured wine, served soup, then left them alone.

Lifting her soup spoon, Alexandra noticed Dalton

134

watching her across an expanse of heavy white damask. His expression was puzzled. "Is something wrong?" she asked.

"Do I have to sit all the way down here?"

She smiled in surprise. "Not if you don't want to."

At that, he gathered up his plate, silverware, and wineglass, and moved to a chair adjacent to hers. "That's better," he said, sitting down. She watched him arrange his silverware, then rearrange it. Finally he sighed. "Can I ask you something?"

Alexandra waited.

"What's the purpose of two spoons and two forks?"

Her impulse was to laugh at his ignorance, but instead she explained that the large spoon was a soup spoon, the smaller one was for the main course, the fork nearest the plate was the dinner fork, and the other one would be used for dessert.

After which Dalton scratched his head and said, "Can't you just use the same fork for dinner and dessert? I mean, the fork don't know the difference."

"People do," she said. "It's the proper way to set a table."

"Seems like a lot of extra work."

A smile played on her lips as she met his serious look. "Are you hungry?"

"Starved."

"Then quit complaining and eat."

By the time the main course arrived, the rain had slackened off, Dalton had quit trying to figure out which fork was which, and Alexandra realized just how much she had missed his buoyant company. Watching him spear a chunk of chicken with his knife, she said, "Your leg seems much better."

"It's almost as good as new." The chicken, still on his knife, went into his mouth.

She waited until he had swallowed, then asked, "Does it bother you at all?"

"Off and on," he said with a shrug. "Mostly when I ride."

"You chose a terrible day to go riding."

"Actually," Dalton said, "I was out in the storm on purpose. I'm getting Mercury used to loud noises, you see.

135

We're leaving for the army at week's end."

It was a blow Alexandra didn't see coming. "Oh," she said, then sipped wine to mask her dismay. Say something else, she thought, but no brilliant words came to mind and the moments dragged by as Dalton watched her.

Finally he said, "I'm going to be a lieutenant."

"How nice."

He sounded so proud to be made an officer, but surely he knew that in battle, officers were the first targets to be picked off. British marksmen would shoot lead at him, redcoated infantrymen would try to skewer him with their bayonets, and mounted dragoons would swing sabers with razored edges in the hopes of severing his life. She felt suddenly ill.

"Alexandra?"

He was staring at her, his face concerned, and it broke her heart to think of him silenced and cold and turning to dust beneath the earth.

"You look like you've seen a ghost," he said.

"It must be the wine."

After that, she had no appetite and her concentration suffered. When the meal was over, Dalton pulled out her chair for her, as any gentleman would, but when she stood up, he blocked her path.

"I didn't mean to upset you," he said. "I just wanted you to know I was leaving."

Alexandra was afraid of tears as she searched his face. "Please look after yourself."

He was quiet a moment, his regard of her intense. Then breaking off his scrutiny, he snapped his fingers and said, "Hey, I almost forgot. I brought you something." He reached in his waistcoat pocket, and when his hand came out again, something sparkled in it. Smiling, he held up her pearl and diamond necklace.

"Dalton," she said softly, delighted and astonished. "You still have it."

"And these," he said, reaching into his pocket again. Out came her earrings and enameled hair bows, which he laid on the dining room table. "Turn around, Alexandra."

She did as he said and felt his fingers brush her skin as he fastened the necklace around her throat. Then taking her shoulders, he turned her to face him. His hands remained

136

on her shoulders, and Alexandra knew from his eyes that he was going to kiss her, and she told herself it would be a harmless kiss, as between friends. He had only to lean down a few inches. He did it slowly, allowing her the opportunity to pull away.

She waited for him.

She was expecting it, she wanted it, but even so the kiss surprised her, the intimate warmth of his mouth and his tongue touching hers as his hands moved over her back, bringing her closer. The kiss between friends became a deep, glorious exploration that made her tremble. After an eternity, which was only a matter of moments, she recalled who it was that held her, and the shock of her desire for him, the overwhelming intensity of it, made her pull away in sudden panic, forcing him to let go.

She hugged her arms and stared at the floor, too unnerved to meet his eyes. Her thoughts were frozen, but her body startled to sensations—the lingering heat of him, the remembrance of his mouth tasting hers, first gently, then with hunger. It took a moment to bring herself under control. With a shaky sigh, she looked up and saw hurt on his face.

"That shouldn't have happened," she said and wished her voice sounded firmer.

"Why not?"

There was no kind way to tell him, so she didn't soften the blow. "Because we're unsuitable for each other." Seeing his stung look, she was immediately sorry for saying it.

"Unsuitable how?" he demanded, and her face felt unbearably warm. He was going to make her spell it out, but as she cast about for the right words, he cut her off. "Because my pockets don't clink when I walk?" he asked. "Is that what it takes to impress you?"

"Dalton, you don't understand—"

"Oh, I do," he said in a low, angry voice. "You're ashamed for having thoughts about me."

"It would never work out, don't you see?"

"Then why did you kiss me just now?"

Alexandra faltered.

"To flatter yourself that you could make me want you?" His eyes raked her. "Well, you have."

She heard his bitterness and felt inexplicably at fault. "I'm sorry," she said, "but I cannot return your feelings. There are too many differences between us."

A muscle jumped in his cheek. "You're right," he said. "I ain't rich, and I never learned any manners. And I hope to God I never learn to tell a dessert fork from a dinner fork."

"It's more than that."

"Yes, it is," he agreed. "It's being afraid to do what you want because of what other people think. You're so bloody worried about appearances, you don't have time for feelings. But I don't have that problem, you see, because I haven't gone through life wearing blinders."

Pierced by his contempt, Alexandra drew herself up. "You're very quick to judge me," she said. "You. A thief who also happens to be a traitor. But your shortcomings aside, there could still be nothing between us because I'm betrothed to Charles Villard."

Silence throbbed. Dalton stared at her as though seeing her for the first time, then slowly his anger ebbed into keen disappointment. "Goodbye, Alexandra," he said and turned away.

She almost called him back. The words were on her tongue, begging to be spoken, but she said nothing. Hearing the back door close, she went upstairs to her bedroom and watched from a window as he left. Her heart was beating too quickly, her eyes were hot and moist as indignation and regret collided inside her. Leaning her forehead against the glass, she tried to swallow the ache in her throat, but the discomfort persisted.

"Bloody stupid farmer!" she whispered. "Who the hell do you think you are?" Even as she cursed him, Alexandra knew her anger was selfish. Because the truth was he had taken only what she had granted him, with a passion she was scarcely prepared for, and in return she had crushed him. She flinched from the memory of his scorn, appalled to realize she deserved it not only from him, but from Charles, whose trust she had cheaply abused.

A sound penetrated her misery—iron-rimmed wheels crunching gravel. She looked up and saw Evelyn Wright's carriage approaching the house.

"Oh, gorgeous," she groaned as the carriage and Dalton

Philips passed each other on the driveway. Infuriated, she moved away from the window. Of all the times for Evelyn to visit. Now the prying, irritating woman would pester her with questions about why Dalton was here. Composing herself, Alexandra unfastened her necklace and laid it on the dressing table, then went downstairs to greet the chatterbox.

True to form, Evelyn's mouth began running the moment she came through the door. "Was that Dalton Philips I just saw leaving?"

"Yes, it was," Alexandra said in a toneless voice, ushering her toward the parlor.

"Was he here for any special reason?"

"He was caught in the storm and stopped here to escape it."

They entered the parlor, where Evelyn draped herself in an armchair. "The storm ended ages ago, dear. Did he stay and visit?"

"As a matter of fact, Mr. Philips and I were talking business. I'm thinking of buying a riding horse, and I wanted his advice."

"One of his horses?"

"No. Would you like tea?"

"Thank you, dear. I would love some." Evelyn, her eyes speculative, watched Alexandra tug the bellpull. "I was under the impression that you already had a riding horse."

"Is there a rule against having two?" Alexandra asked, more sharply than she had intended.

Evelyn's eyebrows rose. "Of course not," she said. "But I'm sure Charles could find one exactly suited to you. By the bye," she smiled as though the world had suddenly brightened, "that's what I've come to tell you. His ship was sighted on the Delaware. He should reach Philadelphia by nightfall."

Relief for his safe return swept Alexandra, then panic stabbed the hollow hurt inside her. Dalton's angry departure had left her shaken and guilt-ridden, and she hoped Charles would not come to Willowbrook before she had a chance to collect herself. Tomorrow she could face him, but not tonight.

Chapter Twenty-One

Carrying a branch of candles, Edward Brock opened Willowbrook's front door and saw Charles Villard standing outside. "Good evening, sir," he said, his voice and expression impassive. "I trust your voyage was—"

Villard shouldered past him and entered the house uninvited. Removing his cloak, he flung it at Brock as his glittering eyes swept the hallway. "Where's Alexandra?" he demanded.

Brock, despite his slight size, was not easily intimidated. Together with Mary, he had been a Pennington fixture for nearly three decades, and Villard's hostile demeanor was not enough to shunt him from his duty, which was to protect Alexandra and which sometimes required him to stretch the truth.

"Madam has taken ill," he said. "She has retired for the evening. Perhaps I could give her a message for you, or you might call on her tomorrow."

Villard said, "I'll see her right now," and headed for the staircase. Ignoring Brock's protest, he took the stairs three at a time and walked straight to her bedroom door. A telltale crack of light showed along the floor. He pounded on the door, then flung it open without waiting for a response.

Alexandra was seated at her writing desk, holding a quill pen poised over a sheet of stationery. As Villard approached the desk, she returned the pen to the inkstand and started to put the letter away. Villard snatched it from her.

"Charles!" she cried, dismayed. When she tried to

140

recover the letter, he caught her wrist in an iron grip.

Just then Edward Brock appeared in the doorway and quickly assessed the scene. "Release her, Mr. Villard," he ordered, moving into the room.

Villard's eyes blazed at him. Before he could speak, Alexandra said, "It's all right, Edward."

"Mrs. Pennington, I told him that you were indisposed."

"Edward, please. Let me handle this."

Brock's stony silence conveyed his disapproval of the situation. Finally he said, "I'll be just outside if you should need me."

His statement was a warning for Villard, who ignored him. After Brock withdrew, Villard stared hard at Alexandra.

"Charles, you're hurting me."

He let go of her wrist, then looked at the letter and saw:

Willowbrook, 15th May, 1776

Dear Mr. Philips:

My conscience will not permit me to let my unkind remarks stand as they were left. I had no desire to injure you, and you should know I find your company enjoyable

With a sharply drawn breath, Villard looked at her. His voice, like his eyes, was bleak. "Explain this."

"It's exactly what it looks like," she said. "A letter of apology."

"Educate me, sweetheart. Why in God's name do you need to apologize to that bastard?"

She winced at his venomous tone. "Because I offended him this afternoon, and I—"

"What the hell was he doing here?"

Whatever guilt Alexandra might have been feeling was swept aside by his rudeness. She eyed him defiantly. "Don't tell me your dear aunt neglected to give you all the details."

"She only mentioned that he was here."

"How considerate of her to leave the rest to your imagination. The fact is," Alexandra explained, "Mr.

141

Philips was caught in a terrible storm, and Willowbrook was the nearest refuge."

Villard waited.

"I invited him to have dinner with me."

"You did what?"

"I invited him to dinner," she said, enunciating each word as though speaking to a slow-witted person. "For God's sake, Charles! Perhaps you've forgotten, but we both owe him a debt of gratitude. I was merely trying to repay him in some small measure. Is that so terrible?"

He glanced at the letter, then shook it at her. "You still haven't explained this."

Annoyed as she was, Alexandra detested having to lie to him, but admitting the truth was unimaginable. "It's nothing, really," she said, looking anywhere but at him. "Mr. Philips's table manners are atrocious. I made a thoughtless remark to that effect and wanted to apologize for it." The story was partially true, which helped her to tell it, but afterward guilt needled her and she had trouble meeting Villard's stare.

"Is there anything else between you and Philips?" he asked, as though afraid of what her answer would be.

Alexandra shook her head and said, "No," meaning it.

"Why did you tell Edward Brock to send me away?"

"Because I've had a horrible headache all day, and I asked him not to admit any visitors. I didn't mean you, of course, but he takes everything I say quite literally." It was another deception, and she felt like a coward for hiding behind Edward's loyalty. Her instructions to him had been specific—make excuses for her if Charles Villard came calling. Now Charles was here, and she told him, "I wasn't expecting you tonight."

"I had to come."

She relaxed a little. "I should have known you would."

After a moment, Villard sighed and dragged his fingers through his hair. "I'm sorry for bursting in here," he said, his voice low with regret. "I've behaved like a jealous fool."

A smile touched her lips. "Yes, you have," she agreed, "but I'm still glad you're back."

With sudden longing, Villard drew her into his arms and let his misgivings slip away as he held her. "I've been thinking about this moment for days," he whispered. "Four weeks felt like forever."

"It did seem like a long time."

"Too long. I'll never leave you again." As he spoke, his gaze traveled her cozy bedroom, absorbing its feminine appointments: the lace-edged pillows and coverlet on the four-posted bed; the canopy hangings of frilly white dimity; a pair of satin slippers on the floor by her writing desk; ivory combs, hair brushes, and colored perfume bottles arrayed on the dressing table.

A sparkle caught his eye. Villard blinked in surprise. Releasing Alexandra, he went to the vanity and stared down at her necklace. The same necklace Jack Flash had stolen, he was certain of it. Astonished, he picked it up and faced her. "How on earth did you recover this?"

Alexandra was hard-pressed to meet his penetrating look. For an instant, she considered telling him the truth about Dalton and clearing her conscience, then thrust the urge away. She had given Dalton her word and was honor bound to keep it, but her complicity with him made her feel treacherous.

"My reward notice finally paid off," she lied.

"You're joking!"

"There's the proof," she said, nodding at the necklace. "It was returned a few nights ago."

"By whom?" Villard wanted to know.

Bracing herself, Alexandra told him the story she had concocted to explain the reappearance of her necklace, a story her servants would corroborate if questioned. "Thursday night," she said, "a man showed up and said he had come to claim the reward money. As I promised in my notice, I didn't ask any questions." She shrugged. "The exchange was made, then he left."

Incredulous, Villard bombarded her with questions. "Did you recognize him?"

No.

"What did he look like?"

Scrawny, unkempt, his clothing shabby.

"Was he armed?"

Yes.

"Good God!" Villard was alarmed. "Could he have been Jack Flash?"

143

Alexandra shook her head. "He wasn't tall enough."

"You're positive it wasn't he?"

Her face was burning. "Charles," she said, "I'm not sure of anything, except that he had my necklace and I was relieved when he left."

Villard did not seem at all convinced by her tale. As he measured her, a flash of insight suddenly leaped in his eyes. His expression grew calculating.

He knows I'm lying, Alexandra thought, wondering how long she could maintain the pretense of calm with her heart racing the way it was. She feared more questions were coming, harder ones that would undermine her promise to protect a criminal. She wished she had never laid eyes on Dalton Philips.

At last Villard looked away. He stood very still, staring at nothing, then rubbed his jaw and sighed. "I'm glad you got it back," he said. "I know how much it means to you."

It was all Alexandra could do to mask her relief. When his arms opened, she moved into his embrace and pressed her face to his shoulder, hiding her shame.

Chapter Twenty-Two

It was quiet enough in the barn to hear moths fluttering around lanterns. In the center aisleway, secured to cross-ties, Mercury stood quietly as Dalton brushed his coppery pelt until it gleamed in the soft light.

To Twigs, sitting on a nearby hay bale, the vigorous brush strokes were like an echo of his anxious heart. "You'll rub the hide off him, Dalton."

"It might be the last good grooming he gets for awhile."

"You just want him looking grand when you trot into camp."

Dalton smiled. "He don't need brushing for that, do you boy?" He patted the stallion's satiny flank, then resumed his work. "He's footing proper since I put the new shoes on him. Not clipping himself anymore."

Twigs just nodded.

As the silence lengthened, Dalton was aware of a growing heaviness inside him, an ache like a dull blade in his gut. Glancing along the hard-packed aisle, he saw dark heads with shining, curious eyes peering at him from several stalls. Down the row, a brood mare whickered gently as her foal awoke. Straw rustled as the foal lurched onto spindly legs and began to suckle. A female barn cat, with golden eyes aglow, glided from shadows and threaded boldly among the stallion's legs, then rubbed her slender body against Dalton's shin.

The brush stilled in his hand. He drew lungfuls of warm, musty air permeated with the odors of sweetened grain, manure, and tangy lime. His roots went deep into this place. Every inch of soil, fence, and timber bore his touch, his mark. Most of the animals he had raised from newborns after helping them enter the world.

He glanced at Twigs, at his bent white head and gnarled fingers, which toyed aimlessly with a lead shank. As though sensing his stare, Twigs's head rose, bright eyes fixed on nothing, and Dalton felt an uncomfortable thickness in his throat. Most of all he would miss the old man.

He put the brush aside and said briskly, "Reckon it's time to saddle up."

Mercury grew restless the moment the saddle blanket hit his back. He snorted, pawing the ground, then startled the silent barn with his throaty command. The strident sound aroused age-old instincts in the brood mares, and their answering whinnies made Dalton smile as he settled the saddle over the pad and reached under Mercury's belly for the girth.

"Forget it," he told the stallion. "You already had your fun."

A few weeks earlier, when both brood mares were in foal heat, Dalton had bred the stallion to them, with the mares hobbled and twitched to protect Mercury from a maiming kick. The act of breeding had intensified the stallion's orneriness, but Dalton preferred that to the prospect of having Mercury's line end with a bullet. With any luck the mares had caught, and by this time next year the stallion's progeny would be romping in the pasture.

As Dalton buckled the girth, Twigs warned him, "Stay away from those camp whores. The pox will kill you as sure as steel, just slower."

Dalton retrieved Mercury's bridle from its peg. "I ain't joining the army for girls."

"Don't fool yourself, boy. You'll get lonely."

Metal clinked as Dalton unfastened Mercury's halter, slipped the bit into his mouth in the same motion, and worked the headstall over his ears. "Never that lonely."

"No?" Twigs asked. "My guess is, you'll be trying hard to forget how Mrs. Pennington flattened you."

Dalton's hands stilled. Eyes narrowed, he studied Twigs's canny face. "What the devil are you talking about?"

"You went to see her the other day."

"To return the clothes I borrowed. So?"

"So," Twigs said slowly, "ever since then you've been walking around here like someone cut out your heart."

Dalton concentrated on adjusting the bridle.

"I hear she got herself engaged to Mr. Villard."

His face grim, Dalton double-checked the girth's tightness. Unbuckling a strap, he gave a savage yank to reach the next notch, then changed his mind and returned the buckle to its original position.

"Were you surprised when you found out?" Twigs ventured.

Dalton sighed. "Is there a point to all this?"

"Yes. Don't hurt yourself because of her."

"Twigs, I wasn't born yesterday."

"Just remember those army doxies will spread their legs for anyone, and you can't always tell by looking if their crack's rotten."

Dalton planned to put Alexandra Pennington from his mind, but not by sleeping with whores and risking the pox. He touched the grip of a pistol hanging in a leather saddle holster. Gunfire, battlesmoke, a redcoated enemy; all would come to him and help him forget.

"In case you're wondering," he said flatly, "you were right. Apparently I ain't good enough for her. So fuck her and King George. What matters is winning our independence, and by God it's going to happen if I have anything to say about it. I'm going to be the worst damn nightmare those Bloodybacks ever met."

He backed up a pace and looked Mercury over. The stallion's coat shone with fiery color, his neck arched as he wrestled with the bit. Dalton had seen horses aplenty during his lifetime, but right at this moment he knew Mercury was above all the others, graceful and noble, a full-blooded champion who made a man feel privileged just to sit astride him.

His heart beating strongly, Dalton took a last look around. The air in the barn was cool, yet he could feel a warm dampness between his shoulder blades. For days he had been preparing for this moment. His saddlebags were full, his musket and pistols were meticulously clean, the firelocks oiled. Edged weapons had been honed to razor

147

sharpness, their bright blades now sheathed in scabbards. Waiting.

He was ready.

As he led Mercury from the barn, Twigs followed close behind them. The horizon was smeared by long tongues of cloud, molten gold feathering into pink and violet. Dalton studied the farmhouse as the first shafts of sunlight glinted on its windows, and he saw the steep roof and chimneys of his home silhouetted against a pale blue sky.

He faced Twigs and held him in one long glance to fix his image in his mind. The wrinkled face was intent. Jubilation, sorrow, fear, all were there.

"Don't worry about the farm," Twigs told him. "I'll have help starting Monday, and we'll look after the place for you. You just look after yourself."

Dalton stepped forward and embraced him, shocked to feel how frail he was, all skin and bones in baggy, threadbare clothes. "I'll miss you, Twigs."

"The same here." After a moment Twigs urged him away. "Go on, boy, get moving. We said all that needs saying."

Dalton turned away, grabbed Mercury's saddle to mount up, then paused as drumming hooves pulled his attention to the lane. A group of horsemen thundered from the blackness of evergreens and bore down on the paddock, and when Dalton saw Sheriff Dewees in the lead, he knew his luck had run out.

Twigs, also sensing doom, clutched Dalton's arm and tried to shove him bodily onto the stallion's back. "Go!" he cried. "You can outrun them!"

But Dalton stood motionless because the riders had reached the paddock and a dozen pistols had been drawn, trained not just on him, but on Twigs. Surrounded by horsemen, Dalton stared into the hard eyes of Sheriff Dewees.

"Good morning, Mr. Philips."

"Mornin', Sheriff," he said and was surprised to find himself so calm. His eyes flicked to the bore of Dewees's gun, then returned to his face. "What can I do for you?"

"You can stand still and keep your hands away from those pistols." Dewees assessed the stallion's gear. "Going somewhere?"

"Matter of fact, I am. General Washington's having a party in New York, and I'm invited."

Shaggy eyebrows lifted in surprise. "Well now," said Dewees. "I never realized you were so inclined. I suppose that makes you a Loyalist hater."

"It makes me a Patriot."

"Where were you last night?"

"He was right here with me," Twigs said hotly.

"Shut up, you old fool," Dewees snapped. "You'd gut your own mother to protect him." His gaze swung back to Dalton. "Where were you?" he repeated.

"Sheriff, what's this about?"

"There was a robbery last night at Matt Whittaker's place on Eighth Street. Matt and his wife were savagely beaten."

Dalton's palms were suddenly damp. "I'm sorry to hear that," he said, fighting down panic. "But what has it got to do with me?"

"Precisely what I'm wondering."

Dalton watched him a moment. "Like Twigs said, I was here all night."

"That's odd," said Dewees with seeming perplexity. "An hour ago I spoke with a man who saw you near the Dog Marsh around midnight."

"He's mistaken."

"Then you won't mind if we have a look around."

"Suit yourselves," Dalton shrugged, relieved that all traces of Jack Flash had been removed from Downstream Farm.

At a nod from Dewees, the deputies scattered to search the farm buildings, and Dalton, a bitter taste in his mouth, wondered who had committed last night's robbery and, more importantly, who had pointed the sheriff in his direction.

He stared at the ground with a sinking feeling. Not her, he thought, heartsick at the idea. Images flashed through his mind like pieces of a dream, moments he would never forget. He could still feel her mouth against his own and smell the perfume from her hair. Alexandra, trembling and confused as she broke from his embrace, had reduced him to helpless anger with her rejection. He had been wrong about the depth of her feelings for him. Had he also

149

misjudged her sense of honor?

Something shattered inside the house, jerking him back to the present. In their search for evidence, the deputies were showing little regard for his property. Tools clattered from shelves and pegs in the storehouse; planking rumbled in the hayloft as neatly stacked bales were overturned; another crash of pottery came from the farmhouse kitchen. One man was even nosing around in the springhouse. Dalton watched and waited, no expression on his face as he listened to the careless destruction.

After what seemed like an hour, several disappointed-looking deputies emerged from the farmhouse and reported their lack of success to Sheriff Dewees. Moments later the sheriff was informed that nothing incriminating had been found in the barn or the storehouse. Heartened by Dewees's thwarted look, Dalton began to relax. Then the deputy in the springhouse gave a shrill whistle and motioned for the sheriff to join him.

Dewees was gone several minutes. When he returned, a mud-caked gunnysack swung from his hand. Metal clanged as he dropped the sack on the ground at Dalton's feet and fixed him with baleful eyes. "We found this buried in your springhouse."

Dalton's stomach was like a clenched fist inside him. Not trusting himself to speak, he stared at the coarse, bulging gunny with a feeling of dread.

The sheriff knelt, worked open the drawstring, and withdrew a gleaming silver teapot with beaded moldings and the initial *W* engraved on its belly. Again his hand dipped into the sack, this time removing a fistful of heavy tableware. Decorative silver handles bore the same bold engraving as the teapot.

Grimly satisfied, Dewees looked up at Dalton. "The Whittakers had all their silver monogrammed."

His words startled Dalton into denial. "I've never seen that silver before," he said. "Someone planted it here."

"You're under arrest." Dewees stood up and motioned to his men. "Tie him up. If he resists, shoot him."

As Dalton's wrists were lashed behind his back, Dewees stood eye to eye with him. "I forgot to mention," he said in a voice to match his menacing look. "The man who saw

150

you last night also identified you as Jack Flash."

Twigs surged forward. "It's a fucking lie!" he yelled hoarsely. "He was here all night, I tell you!"

Ignoring him, Dewees started to turn away, but bony fingers snagged his waistcoat like talons and yanked him around with surprising strength.

"Listen, you bloody bastard," Twigs growled. "I'll have you split like a—"

"Twigs!" Dalton shouted. He was angry now. Blazing. His voice cracked like a whip. "You ain't helping nothing, so back off!"

A reluctant Twigs obeyed.

Straightening his waistcoat, Dewees leveled a finger at Dalton. "One more thing," he said. "Mrs. Whittaker is in a very poor way from the beating she suffered. She may not live. So don't try anything on the road or one of these boys will blow your head off."

Dalton was taken to the new jail on Walnut Street. Though completed in 1773, the building had yet to be used for county purposes. The bulk of the city's prisoners still resided in the Stone Prison and the Workhouse at Third and Market Streets.

The Walnut Street jail, also built from stone, was two stories high, with a gloomy basement, and was surmounted by a bell tower. A high flight of stone steps led to the main doorway. Inside the jail, Dalton was greeted by cool, shadowy silence. After the dazzle of morning sunlight, the entrance hall seemed like a dungeon.

Keys jingled. An iron grate swung quietly on oiled hinges to reveal a dim passageway. Footsteps echoed as Dalton was marched between rows of unoccupied cells and then down a circular flight of stone steps to where it was darker and cooler still, and where the solitary confinement cells stood empty and waiting.

Lanterns were lit. Dalton, his hands still bound behind his back, was prodded into a narrow, stone-walled room that was furnished with a table and two chairs. His gaze swept the chamber. Not a cell, he decided, but an interrogation room. He watched Sheriff Dewees position a chair in the middle of the floor and point wordlessly to it.

With a sigh, Dalton sat down.

Somewhere between the front entrance and the basement, Dewees had managed to lay his hands on a bottle. Now he removed the cork, tipped the bottle to his mouth, and swilled rum like water. One of his men, a thick blond giant with massive shoulders, lounged in a corner of the room and studied Dalton with dull eyes.

"Now then," said Dewees, leaning back against the table, the bottle resting on his thigh. "I want some answers. How I get them is entirely up to you."

Dalton waited.

"After you robbed the Whittakers—"

"I didn't rob them. I was home all last night."

"You were seen near the Dog Marsh less than an hour after the robbery occurred."

"Whoever said so is daft as a pecker."

Dewees's fingers drummed the table. His eyes conveyed a silent message to the hulking blond giant, who levered away from the wall and disappeared from Dalton's field of view. Moments later, Dalton felt a disturbance of air on the back of his neck.

Dewees cocked his head, massaged his jaw. "How tall are you, Dalton?" he asked and received a steady stare. "Matt Whittaker described his assailant as a tall man, lean and very strong."

"Like some of your deputies?"

"He also wore a black hood."

"So should some of your men," Dalton said, "ugly as they are." A powerful hand seized his shoulder. Tilting his head back, he saw the blond hulk towering above him, eyes aflame, and shrugged. "Just making a point."

A balled fist hammered his cheek and almost knocked him off the chair. As he straightened, the side of his face stung hotly, but the pain was lost in a surge of fury. It took every ounce of willpower to restrain himself, but he stayed in the chair, his body quivering with suppressed anger.

"Once more," said Dewees, quiet and tense. "Where were you last night?"

"Fucking your wife."

This time Dewees did the honors himself, crossing to Dalton in one long stride. No puny man, the sheriff wielded his fists like mallets, and thudding blows snapped

152

Dalton's head to and fro. When the beating stopped and the room righted itself, Dalton spat a bloody mouthful at his attacker.

Sheriff Dewees returned to the table. Again the bottle rose to his lips and rum sluiced down his throat. He wiped a sleeve across his mouth, his glittering stare never leaving his prisoner.

"You've been a thorn in my side for months," he said. "But no more, damn you. Your neck's going to stretch, and I'm going to celebrate while you dance."

There was a knock at the door.

"Come!" Dewees growled.

Two men entered the room. Dalton recognized one of them as the deputy who had discovered the sack of silver in his springhouse. The second man was a stranger. Of medium height and build, with lank, greasy hair, his stooped posture made him appear smaller and older than he was. Dalton placed his lined face at around thirty wasted years. In his flinty eyes, which were never still, a hard glimmer revealed a grasping soul.

Sheriff Dewees welcomed him with enthusiasm. "Ah, Mr. Dobbs," he said, dropping a friendly hand on his shoulder. "Thank you for coming so promptly." Fingers tightening, Dewees turned him to face Dalton. "Do you recognize this man?"

Dobbs squinted his soulless eyes, then nodded. "Indeed I do. That's Dalton Philips."

"Tell me when and where you first saw him."

"About two years ago, at a horse race at Centre Square track. He won that day." Dobbs grinned, exposing jagged gray teeth. "Rode like the devil, he did. After that, I bet on him every time he raced."

"Now then," said Dewees, in no hurry, "where else have you seen him?"

"At the Dog Marsh last night," said Dobbs and his eyes grew large. "God, it was frightful. I was going home my usual way, down the path from the common, and I heard a horse coming behind me. Being alone and unarmed, I thought it best to hide myself in the bushes."

Dobbs's voice lowered, his stoop grew more pronounced as he glanced up, sketching the air with his hand. "There was a moon last night, so I could see things clearly. When

153

the rider came along, he was dressed all in black and wore a black hood. Well, sir, I knew right away he was Jack Flash, and my heart started going like a kettledrum. He stopped his horse right in front of me and took off his hood." Darting eyes assessed Dalton, then Dobbs aimed a stubby finger at him. "It was him."

Anger burned like acid in Dalton's throat. He came to his feet, only to be slammed back into the chair by the blond giant. "You're a liar," he said, glaring at Dobbs.

Unperturbed, Dobbs shook his head and faced Dewees. "I'm certain it was him, Sheriff."

"You'll swear to it?"

"In any court."

"Thank you, Mr. Dobbs. You've been most helpful."

As Dobbs left the room, Dalton's glittering eyes followed him. "Bastard," he said through his teeth, but Dobbs never looked back.

After the door closed behind the shifty man, Dewees rubbed his hands together and looked pleased. "Well, Dalton," he said, "you've passed each test with flying colors. The evidence was found on your property, a witness has identified you. Now for the final proof." Dewees glanced at his deputy. "Remove his breeches."

Dalton thought he had heard wrong until the blond man came at him. With a curse, he sprang catlike from the chair and put it between them. "Get back," he snarled, and the look in his eyes made the deputy hesitate.

Sheriff Dewees laughed at the scene. His amusement quickly ebbed, however, when Dalton lunged and slammed his forehead into the deputy's chin, stunning him. Dalton then leveled him with swift, well-placed kicks. In the end Dewees was forced to lend a hand and received a bloodied nose and a throbbing crotch for his efforts. But the sheriff found what he was looking for— fresh scars on Dalton's thigh, the result of Evelyn Wright's poor aim.

Dewees rose panting to his feet, wiped blood from his face, and told the deputy, "Put braces on him. He's too dangerous to leave loose."

And so, wearing manacles on his ankles and wrists, Dalton was dragged into a gloomy cell and chained to a thick iron staple embedded in stone. Below the staple, a hard, narrow bunk was bolted to the wall. The heavy door banged shut, a key turned in the lock, and he stood alone in pitch blackness, numb through and through. After a time he experimented with the chains to establish his boundaries. There was just enough allowance for him to lie down on the bunk, get up and stretch, or arch a stream of urine into a corner, as he did now. Metal clanked with each of his movements. Already his skin was chafed raw by the iron shackles.

He sank down on the bunk and searched his mind for an anchor, something to keep his rising fear at bay. At least the jail was new and as yet uninfested with crawling vermin that could make a man itch himself mad. Or with fevers that spread from victim to victim like the kiss of death. But it was utterly silent and still in his tomb, and there was nothing to divert the black despair that welled up and slowly consumed him.

He was a bloody fool for trusting Alexandra Pennington.

Chapter Twenty-Three

Wielding an ivory comb, her lips clamping a dozen hair pins, Mary Brock piled Alexandra's hair into a simple fashion, wound a gold ribbon through dark ringlets, and arranged the shiny frill in a bow at the back.

"There you are," Mary said, admiring her handiwork.

Alexandra studied her reflection in the dressing-table mirror. "Do you like it as well as the other style?"

"Oh, much more! It's very becoming. He'll think you spent hours on it."

Alexandra smiled. In fact, she had already spent half the day preparing for tonight's party at Sweet Briar. The gown she had chosen to wear was beige silk, woven with pale yellow stripes and small brocaded flowers in pink, blue, and green. The pleated silk trimmings on the robe, stomacher, and petticoat were edged with matching braid.

"Which gloves will you wear?" Mary asked.

"The yellow ones."

Mary beamed. "They'll be perfect with your dress."

Just then a sharp rap came at the door, and Clue's voice called, "Mrs. Pennington?"

"Come in, Christopher."

The moment she saw his anxious face, Alexandra knew something was wrong.

"I'm sorry for barging in," he said, crossing the room to her. "But I just heard some news from the postman, and I knew you'd want to be told right away."

Apprehensive, Alexandra waited.

"Dalton was arrested this morning."

The words came like a shot through the heart. It was a

moment before she could speak, and even then all she could think to say was, *"Why?"*

Clue shrugged helplessly. "There was a robbery in town last night. I don't know the details, but the sheriff arrested Dalton and accused him of being Jack Flash."

Alexandra stared in open-mouthed shock, her fingers twisting the folds of her dressing gown into two tight balls. Robbery was punishable by death, especially if it could be proved that the robber was Jack Flash. If convicted, Dalton would swing into eternal infamy from a gibbet. She had a vision of him twitching at the end of a rope, the life choking out of him, and her eyes closed as the walls seemed to sway at her.

"Mrs. Pennington?" Clue asked, touching her shoulder.

Her glittering eyes opened again. "It makes no sense," she said with despair. "Why would he do such a thing when he knew we could condemn him with a word?"

"Somebody did it," Clue pointed out, "and Dalton's the one being blamed. He's in the Walnut Street jail."

Alexandra cringed to imagine him locked in a bleak cell. Her mind felt battered, her thoughts reeling with unfocused urgency and a startling, stronger sense of dread at losing something vital to her. She could not sit there and do nothing. "Christopher, hitch up the coach," she said. "Hurry."

"Where are we going?"

"To see George." If anyone could get answers for her, George Pennington could.

At Alexandra's urging, Clue made the trip from Willowbrook to Philadelphia in remarkable time, the coach veering and lurching over the rutted Ridge Road as he drove the team at a reckless pace.

George Pennington's residence, called Oakwood after the mature, stately trees that graced the property, fronted Cedar Street between Seventh and Eighth. A spacious house of elegant construction, its extensive grounds and garden were beautifully laid out, the brick walks complemented with costly statuary. Like many fine city houses, Oakwood had no front nor back, but more accurately had two fronts and no back, for the rear entrance rivaled the front in ornamentation.

When the coach stopped behind the house, Alexandra

157

got out without waiting for Clue's assistance. Gathering her skirts, she hurried up a flight of broad stone stairs to Oakwood's door and rapped the brass knocker.

A negro manservant answered her summons. Seeing her, his teeth gleamed in a white crescent. "Good aft'noon, Mrs. Pennington! A pleasure to see you, ma'am."

"And you, William. Is George at home?"

"Yessum." William stood aside and bowed her into the hall. "'Bout ready to have his tea in the front parlor."

George Pennington was delighted to see her. Rising stiffly from an armchair, he took her hands and pressed a fond kiss to her cheek. "'Pon my soul, it's good to see you! I was beginning to think you'd forsaken the city altogether." Then noting her anxiety, his grip on her hands tightened. "What is it, my dear?"

The words tumbled from her. "Mr. Philips was arrested for robbery. They threw him in *jail*, George."

Pennington, his compassion aroused by her great distress, said gently, "Yes, I know." He glanced at William, who was pouring tea at a small, slipper-footed table. "William, leave the tea," he directed. "I believe a spot of brandy is in order."

Taking Alexandra's arm, he steered her to a sofa and sat down with her, and after the brandy arrived and William had poured for them, Pennington dismissed his servant. Alone with Alexandra, he drank liberally from his glass. "Ah, much better," he sighed. "My mouth was dry as a beggar's loaf."

Alexandra barely tasted the brandy. "What have you heard?" she asked.

"Quite a lot." And so, urgently pressed, Pennington told of the foul deed that had stunned the entire city. "Jack Flash robbed the Whittaker place last night," he began. "By all accounts, his conduct was brutal. The poor souls were viciously beaten. Mr. Whittaker was pistol-whipped and his arm broken like a matchstick. And Mrs. Whittaker," Pennington shook his head uncomfortably. "Nasty, nasty business."

He paused to sip brandy, then continued. "When I heard Mr. Philips had been charged with the crime, I was flabbergasted. I immediately called on Benjamin to learn

158

the facts of the matter." Chief Justice Benjamin Chew was Pennington's good friend and fount of information. "I'm afraid his news was disturbing. Evidently, there was substantial grounds for Mr. Philips's arrest."

"What grounds?"

"For one thing, Sheriff Dewees found the Whittakers' silver buried at his farm."

Alexandra felt a sudden coldness around her heart.

"For another, a witness has identified him."

"What witness?"

"A man named Dobbs. He claims to have seen Mr. Philips just after the robbery occurred." Pennington told her of Dobbs's alleged encounter with a black-garbed, hooded horseman, whose identity was unveiled beneath a bright moon. "According to Mr. Dobbs, the man was Dalton Philips."

Alexandra emptied her glass.

And Pennington, studying her closely, said, "A grand jury will hear his case next Friday. Sheriff Dewees feels confident of indictments for felony and robbery, and assault and battery." Pennington's expression became grave. "And for murder, should Mrs. Whittaker die in the meantime. They say she was so badly beaten that even her own husband cannot recognize her."

Alexandra kept silent, her eyes dark with misery.

So Pennington pushed to his feet, took her empty glass, and refilled it from a decanter. "Damn sad, if you ask me," he said, pressing the freshened glass into her hand. "Mr. Philips seemed like such a fine fellow. It's hard to imagine him as that villain."

"Dalton isn't a villain," she blurted.

Pennington, easing back onto the sofa, darted a curious look at her. "Alexandra," he said carefully, "the evidence against him is overwhelming."

"I don't believe a word of it."

"But Sheriff Dewees—"

"Damn his eyes!" she exploded. "He's a lazy, incompetent ass! Until Jack Flash appeared, he couldn't see fit to bestir himself from his desk or his bottle. Now his comfortable job is in jeopardy, and I daresay he would sacrifice anyone to redeem himself!"

Pennington drew his head back in surprise. "The fact

159

remains, he found the Whittaker silver at Downstream Farm."

"Doesn't that strike you as convenient?" she challenged.

"In God's name, I have little tolerance for the man, but I sincerely doubt that he *arranged* for Mr. Philips to be arrested."

"Perhaps not, but someone else could have. Someone greedy for the reward money on Jack Flash." Alexandra got up and began to pace. "Just who is this Dobbs character?" she asked. "Do you know anything about him?"

"Only what Benjamin told me," Pennington said with a shrug. "He lives in a bungalow near the Dog Marsh, but spends most of his time leaning on his elbows at the Bunch of Grapes."

"Oh, that's bloody damn gorgeous," she said, then grimaced at his wondering look. "Forgive me, George. I'm not myself today."

"I expect my brother taught you that phrase."

"And several others," she said, angrily brushing her hair from her forehead. "So this Dobbs is a drunkard who lives in the marshes?"

"That's a rather oversimple description. To be fair, he does hold a job at a printing shop."

"Where he makes a fortune in wages, I suppose."

Pennington smiled wryly. "I expect not."

They watched each other a moment, then Alexandra went to the fireplace and leaned a hand against the mantelpiece, her back to him.

"A thousand pounds reward must be a great temptation to some people," she said. "Enough that they would knowingly condemn an innocent man." Even as she said this, Alexandra reminded herself that Dalton was far from innocent. But she could not, in her wildest thoughts, imagine him pistol-whipping a defenseless man or beating a woman to within an inch of her life.

Dobbs was lying.

She needed to know more about him, and she needed the information quickly. She faced Pennington. "George," she began, unable to keep the urgency from her voice, "I know Dalton Philips, and I would stake my life that he did not rob the Whittakers." Her next words came out a touch

160

defiantly. "You see, our acquaintance is more than just casual."

To her relief, Pennington's reaction was mild—a raised eyebrow, a gleam in his eyes that was part concern, part intrigue.

"Therefore," she said, "I must ask a great favor of you."

"Name it, my dear."

"I want you to use your influence to learn everything you can about Mr. Dobbs, because I don't believe he's telling the truth."

Pennington regarded her a long moment, and her face warmed under his shrewd scrutiny. Finally he sighed and patted his heart. "Oh, to see a woman in distress," he said wistfully. "Very well. I'll see what I can find out."

Alexandra walked over and hugged him.

Chapter Twenty-Four

After a week in solitary confinement, cut off from people and daylight, Dalton's internal clock lost all sense of accuracy. He marked time by the delivery of his meals, when a lantern-bearing deputy would enter his cell and, using a long wooden handle, would slide a food tray and a water jug within his reach. Dalton's inquiries about events in the outside world invariably went unanswered, and by the time his eyes could bear to focus on the lantern's brightness, the deputy and the light would be gone.

He slept as much as possible. When sleep eluded him, he did everything he could to keep from dwelling on the future. He exercised to the extent his shackles would allow. Sometimes he composed rhymes with a patriotic flavor and even sang to himself, inventing new lyrics to popular ditties.

> "Yankee Doodle went to war
>   to thump the bloody British.
> Come to find, at fighting time,
>   their lot was mighty skittish.
> Yankee Doodle, fuck 'em good,
>   Yankee Doodle, fix 'em.
> Mind their muskets and their swords
>   and with your saber stick 'em."

One day, as he lay with his hands behind his head, footsteps echoed outside his cell door and made him sit up abruptly. Feeding time already?

Keys jingled, the lock gave a sharp, metallic click, then

the heavy, iron-bound door swung open. A lantern was thrust into the cell, and Dalton, now on his feet, shielded his eyes against the painful glare.

"You 'ave company, pigshit," said a gruff voice. "Five minutes, that's all you git."

Dalton's eyes stung from the light. Though blinded by tears, he knew his visitor at once, for there was no mistaking that shuffling, hesitant gait.

"Twigs?"

Dalton could see him now, a blurred outline groping toward the bunk, and chains clanked as he stretched out his arms to guide him, and then embrace him.

"Good God, boy!" Twigs's voice was hoarse with emotion. "I thought they'd never let me in to see you!"

Dalton wanted to reply, but he was not sure what sort of sound he might make if he tried, so he kept silent. After a moment Twigs drew back, his hands trailing down Dalton's arms to the iron cuffs restraining him, and as his fingertips discovered the raw abrasions caused by the manacles, his breath hissed and his frail body went rigid. "Those bastards!"

"I'm all right, Twigs,'" Dalton assured him. "Here, sit down. Tell me what's happening out there."

They sat on the bunk, their heads almost touching, and spoke in whispers so that the guard outside the door could not eavesdrop on their conversation.

"I hired a lawyer for your trial," Twigs said.

"Using what for money?"

"He doesn't want money."

Dalton was suspicious. "Why not?"

"Because you're famous," Twigs grinned. "They're singing songs about you in the taverns."

"They are?"

"Every night! Jack Flash is a hero, a Patriot. He made the Tories quake in their boots."

Dalton snorted a laugh. "I'll bet the Tories are singing a different tune."

"But not quite as loud," Twigs said with a sly look. "They're afraid of stirring things up. The fact is, you're more dangerous to them in here than you ever were out there."

"You could have fooled me."

"It's true," Twigs insisted. "Two nights ago, a mob surrounded the courthouse and threatened to burn it down if you were sentenced to hang."

Dalton smiled, his eyes narrowing. "Did they now?" He punched Twigs lightly on the arm. "Sounds like you've been busy."

"Oh, I'm just getting started," Twigs said and there was menace in his voice. "That bitch is going to pay for putting you here."

The words lashed Dalton with sudden and overwhelming force. Without thinking, he locked his fingers into Twigs's shirt and shook him. "You leave her alone," he snarled, his voice unrecognizable and all the more deadly for its softness. "I mean it, Twigs, don't you touch her!"

Startled, Twigs gripped the hands that held him fast. "Easy, boy," he soothed. "I was only going to scare her."

"If you so much as look at her wrong—" Dalton broke off and bit his lip, staring at Twigs's amazed face. "Jesus!" he whispered fiercely, his grip slackening, his fury dying like a snuffed candle. He sagged against the wall and pulled a hand through his hair. "Goddamn you," he muttered. "Always meddling where you shouldn't."

Twigs, still shocked at being threatened by the man he looked upon as a son, rubbed his chest where Dalton had seized him. "She's the cause of all this," he said, defensive. "She betrayed you!"

Dalton said nothing and felt everything.

"Maybe she didn't go to the sheriff," Twigs conceded, "but she told Mr. Villard about you, and that bastard fixed you but good."

Dalton burned at the thought, sensing it was true, the awareness cutting him as deep as any knife. If he closed his eyes and concentrated on Villard, he recalled an ominous voice in a frozen landscape, warning him to withdraw or face the consequences. He could easily imagine the cold-hearted dog plotting his downfall.

He rubbed his forehead with his fingertips. "What about Dobbs?" he asked in a flat voice. "Can you connect him with Villard?"

"Not yet." Twigs was grim. "He's a crafty little rat, slippery as a newt. Twice I had him followed, but each time he disappeared like smoke." Bony fingers gripped

Dalton's arm. "But don't worry, there's still time. Your trial isn't until the middle of June."

Though Dalton didn't say so, he feared that Twigs, with all his resources, was still no match for the elusive Mr. Dobbs. Dalton had seen Dobbs's eyes close up, had heard him speak lies as though imparting gospel, and he knew it would take a miracle to pin him down.

As always, Twigs seemed to latch onto Dalton's thoughts, for he said, "I won't let you down," and squeezed his shoulder. "Before I'm through I'll know everything there is to know about that lying sack of shit, and then some."

As it turned out, George Pennington had better luck investigating Dobbs. When he had gathered a significant amount of information on him, he sent Alexandra a note asking her to come to Oakwood. She arrived that afternoon looking much the same as when he had last seen her—anxious and full of fight.

Rain clouds were scudding over the city, and the air was unseasonably cool. In Oakwood's front parlor, where a small fire had been lit to dispel the chill, windows shivered in their frames as freak gusts sprayed droplets against the panes, turning the scenery to a wavering gray blur.

Although Pennington was dressed to withstand an October gale, his hands felt cold when Alexandra took them, so her first concern became his health. "Aren't you feeling well?" she wanted to know.

"I feel splendid." He moved to a side table and poured two glasses of his favorite peach brandy. "In fact, I have tremendous energy these days."

Alexandra was skeptical, for his eyes, while as lively as ever, were underscored with dark circles and watched her from a wan face. She noted the way his hand kept pressing the small of his back, as if to stifle an ache there.

"Shall we sit near the fire?" she asked, accepting a glass from him.

"If you like."

But Alexandra did not take a seat on the sofa with him. Instead she stoked the blaze and, in a whispering of silk, began to pace before the hearth. "Have you some news?" she asked.

Pennington nodded. "Please bear in mind that the

165

information comes secondhand from an acquaintance of mine, Harry Mullen. Once a week he rides messages to Maryland, so I asked him to make some inquiries for me while he was in Baltimore." To her questioning look, Pennington explained, "Mr. Dobbs resided in Baltimore before coming to Philadelphia."

"What did he do there?"

"Much the same as what he does here. Drank a lot, lived in a squalid waterfront building, held a meager job. He was also a heavy gambler—horses, cards, dice."

"Why did he leave Baltimore?"

Pennington held up a hand. "I'm getting to that," he said, then nursed his brandy a moment before continuing. "Do you know what an affidavit man is?"

Alexandra stopped pacing, her pulse quickening. "Someone who will swear to anything, given the right incentive."

"Usually money," Pennington said in a dry voice. "Which brings me to the most interesting part of the story. Two years ago, Mr. Dobbs testified at the trial of a man accused of raping and murdering a pregnant woman. His testimony was so persuasive, the defendant was acquitted."

"Good God," she breathed.

"There's more," he said. "After the trial, the dead woman's husband threatened to kill Mr. Dobbs."

"So he left town."

"With a full purse," Pennington pointed out. "From all indications, he arrived here with a considerable amount of coin, which he has long since gambled away."

Alexandra's eyes glittered. "And now he's after more blood money," she said. "Well, he isn't going to get away with it."

Pennington was quick to caution her. "The records in Baltimore show only that he testified at a murder trial. The rest amounts to hearsay."

"Notable hearsay."

Pennington sighed. "Alexandra," he said, "Dobbs has already persuaded a grand jury to indict Mr. Philips. If he takes the stand at his trial and proves convincing . . ." Pennington's voice trailed off as he shrugged. "I'm afraid the evidence is against Mr. Philips."

166

"The evidence," she said flatly, "is fraudulent. Dalton did not rob the Whittakers."

"I agree the matter is not cut and dried."

"Nor will it end that way if I can help it."

"What are you planning to do?" he asked.

"At the very least, I shall make certain the facts about Dobbs reach the right ears, beginning with Mr. Philips's lawyer." She chewed a thumbnail, thinking hard. "There's still time to expose this farce. Dalton's trial isn't for several weeks."

At that, Pennington frowned and concentrated on his glass.

His unease was not lost on Alexandra. "What's wrong?" she asked.

Pennington hesitated, avoiding her eyes, then gave a careless shrug. "Nothing of any consequence."

"Then why won't you look at me?"

"Oh, dear," he murmured.

"Out with it, George."

He surrendered with a sigh. "It seems that Charles has also taken an extraordinary interest in Mr. Philips's case."

Alexandra went still. "How so?"

"By trying to hurry it along. Indeed," Pennington eyed her regretfully, "he has done everything except stand on his head to expedite matters."

Alexandra moved to the sofa and sat down.

"I'm afraid he succeeded," Pennington said. "The trial date has been moved up to next week."

Her eyes were as bleak as the rain-soaked afternoon. "Are you sure Charles was responsible?"

"Absolutely. He has many powerful friends in the city. I wouldn't have thought he would use them to this end, but I suppose his enthusiasm is understandable. He lost a good deal of money to Jack Flash."

Numbed by the news, Alexandra wondered if Villard's motivation went beyond money. Her mind recoiled from the suspicion that he was acting, at least in part, out of jealousy.

"Is there any way to postpone the trial?" she asked and heard the desperate plea in her voice. Pennington gave her such a penetrating stare that she faltered and looked down at her hands clenched in her lap. Slowly her gaze returned to his. "You must be wondering about my conduct."

"I confess, my curiosity is monstrous. But I'll not pry, Alexandra."

"You deserve an explanation."

"By all your actions there can be only one," Pennington said quietly. "You care a great deal for Mr. Philips."

Her eyes closed. "Yes," she whispered.

"I assume he feels the same toward you?"

She nodded, then pressed her fists to her temples as if suppressing unwanted thoughts. "It was ridiculous even to imagine," she said. "A farmer courting me."

"You told him as much?"

"I said he was unsuitable for me." Without warning tears stung her eyes. "I hurt him, George."

"I expect so," he said. "No man wants to be told he's unworthy of the woman he admires."

"But why would he even hope for my favor?" she cried angrily. "He has no education, no prospects, little means. His status speaks it all!"

"Does it?" Pennington shot back. After a moment, he sighed and his face was grim. "I wonder if money or title have ever brought any man a moment of true happiness." He gestured around at the luxurious room. "You see how I live, in comfort, every stick of it inherited because my father could not take it with him. All my life I have never wanted for any material thing, but God knows I have regrets that no amount of wealth will mend."

His eyes clouded with such sudden pain that Alexandra laid a consoling hand on his arm. Pennington, made uncomfortable by her sympathy, hurried on. "We shall all someday reach a grave," he said. "The best we can hope for is to enter it fulfilled." His hand covered hers, his fingers cool despite the fire's warmth. "A word to the wise, my dear. Don't squander your life on what is accepted rather than what is desired. You will never feel complete if you allow your heart to become a place of compromise."

As she weighed his advice, Alexandra felt more confused and miserable than ever.

"Forgive me," he said, reading her turmoil. "That was presumptuous. I didn't mean to imply that you won't be happy with Charles. I know you care deeply for him, and I'm sure he's very devoted to you."

168

She forced a smile. "No offense taken."

"But keep my opinions to myself, hmm?"

"Don't you dare."

He patted her hand. "Well then," he said, "getting back to Mr. Philips's situation. I suppose you're aware that he's a rebel?"

Her breath drew in sharply. "Yes," she admitted. "But he's also a very brave man who quite probably saved both our lives. He would never ask anything of you in return, so I'm asking for him. Can you get his trial delayed?"

Captive to her imploring eyes, Pennington shook his head and even chuckled. "By God, you're irresistible."

"Can you?" she insisted.

"I imagine his lawyer is already seeking a postponement."

"And as you well know, he will run into a brick wall."

Pennington nodded. "No doubt." After that he was silent, staring with seemingly empty eyes at the fire.

"George?" she prompted.

"I was just thinking," he said, still watching the leaping flames. "You would be amazed at the state of our judicial system. It's a shambles, really, and getting worse by the day. The backlog of cases to be tried is horrendous, all because of those damned radicals in Congress. They've instituted more disruptive measures than a porcupine has quills. No one seems to know who's in control anymore, the Assembly or that wretched Committee of Safety." Pennington looked at her then, a slow smile curving his mouth, wispy gray eyebrows dancing. "Who can say what will happen by the time Mr. Philips's trial rolls around?"

Alexandra felt restored. "Thank you, George," she said with relief.

He raised a cautioning finger. "I promise only to speak with Benjamin," he said. "And I must warn you, whatever he accomplishes may only delay the inevitable."

Chapter Twenty-Five

Alexandra handed her damp cloak and hat to Sweet Briar's liveried butler. "Please tell Mr. Villard that I must speak with him."

"Yes, madam," he intoned. "This way, please." And he led her to the west parlor to wait.

Hands clasping and unclasping nervously, Alexandra wandered the spacious room, her shoes cushioned by a thick, floral-patterned carpet. The decorated ceiling of Adamesque design, the paneled walls, and the splendidly carved mantel combined to give the room an aura of stateliness that was far removed from Willowbrook's cozy parlor.

Her gaze was drawn to the pediment above the fireplace mantel, where the impaneled portrait of a stern-looking gentleman glared down at her. Richard Villard. With his chin elevated, his gray eyes pompous and scornful, he seemed to be sitting in judgment on his lofty perch. Several feet above his bewigged head, a carved and painted reproduction of the Villard family coat of arms embraced the portrait like a grandiose crown.

"He was a champion bastard," said a voice behind her. Turning, Alexandra saw Villard standing in the doorway. He sauntered into the room and surveyed the painting with distaste. "Notice the way his mouth pulls down at the corners," he said, "like a hooked eel. I must say, the artist captured the very essence of the man. My father always looked as though he had swallowed something rancid."

Alexandra was stuck for a reply, but Villard seemed oblivious to her discomfort. Like night into day, a change

170

came over him. His frown evaporated. His eyes shone with affection as he lifted her hand and kissed it. "This is a pleasant surprise," he said. "I was just working on my ledgers. What drudgery!"

"I'm sorry for the interruption, but I had to see you."

"And I'm delighted!" he said, taking her elbow and guiding her to a satin-damask sofa. As they sat down, she smelled whiskey strongly on him. His voice and manner were exuberant. "You picked a miserable evening to travel," he said. "It's raining like a curse out there."

Alexandra started to explain the reason for her visit, then abruptly stopped when the butler appeared with a refreshment tray, which he placed on the sofa table. She waited until he was gone, then began again. "Charles—"

"Would you like something to drink?"

"No, thank you."

"Some cheese, then?" He smiled at her, glassy-eyed. "This is marvelous cheddar. It's from New York."

"Charles, I came here to ask you something important."

At last he grasped her seriousness. Blond eyebrows rose. "By all means," he said, searching her face. "Would you mind if I have a whiskey while we talk?"

"Of course not."

Unstopping a crystal decanter, Villard filled a small glass, downed half of it, then leaned back and got comfortable. "Now then," his attention centered on her, "what is that lovely frown all about?"

"Why are you using your influence against Mr. Philips?"

Villard could not hide his astonishment. Sitting up straighter, he took a long pull from his glass while his thoughts raced. "I suppose George told you?" he asked, sarcastic.

"What difference does it make how I found out? The point is—"

"The *point* is," he interrupted loudly, "Mr. Philips dug his own grave."

"Perhaps," she said. "But you needn't be so anxious to fill it in."

Villard stared at her. "Have you forgotten that Jack Flash robbed me twice? I simply want to see justice served. Is that so hard to understand?"

"It seems to me that you're trying to *deprive* Mr. Philips of justice."

"Good God!" Villard shot to his feet, whiskey spilling from his glass to the carpet. "Just whose side are you on?" he demanded.

His arrogant tone stung Alexandra into an equivalent anger. "It isn't a question of taking sides. It's a question of right and wrong, and I happen to think it is wrong to use one's connections to condemn a man."

"Tell that to the Whittakers."

"I don't believe he robbed them."

Villard grew still. "Enlighten me?"

"The circumstances of his arrest are suspicious."

"Sheriff Dewees doesn't think so."

"Wasn't it you who called the sheriff a bungling fool?"

Villard made no reply. Glass in hand, he moved away from her, his fingers trailing over the polished surface of a cherrywood tea table.

"Sweetheart," he said with his back to her, "I can understand your sympathizing with Mr. Philips. After all, he did rescue you from that mob. But don't you think this is carrying it a bit too far?"

Ignoring his question, Alexandra asked one of her own. "Are you acquainted with the so-called witness, Mr. Dobbs?"

Villard faced her. "Only by name."

"His credentials," she emphasized the word scornfully, "are questionable. In Baltimore he acquired a reputation as an affidavit man." As she spoke, Alexandra watched Villard's eyes and thought she saw panic flicker in them. She hesitated, then heard herself ask, "Did you have a hand in Mr. Philips's arrest?"

Villard's glass banged down, denting the tea table and making her flinch. "Goddamnit, I resent your question! How dare you suggest such a thing?" He seemed to quiver with anger as his hard, unblinking stare bored into her. "Mr. Philips is a criminal! He was caught with the evidence and deserves to be brought to trial, so let the goddamned Court decide whether he's guilty or innocent!"

Jolted by his outburst, Alexandra kept silent as shock moved sudden and cold over her flesh. This was a Villard

172

she had never met. She watched him wipe a hand over his face, then saw the fury leave his eyes as his shoulders sagged.

"Alexandra, I'm sorry." Now his voice was soft, hardly more than a whisper, and her thoughts spun as he came to the sofa and knelt before her. "I didn't mean to shout at you, but I cannot believe you would accuse me of doing something so dishonorable."

Taken aback by his transformation, Alexandra could think of nothing to say in return. Her gaze went unbidden to the portrait above the mantel, and she imagined that Richard Villard was somehow listening and damning her for the attack on his son, who leaned forward and gripped her shoulders. "Sweetheart, listen to me," he said earnestly. "Perhaps I shouldn't have interfered with Mr. Philips's case, and henceforth I will let the matter resolve itself. But I swear to you, before God, that I played no part in his arrest."

He seemed so sincere, so injured by her suspicion, that Alexandra grappled with confusion. When her silence continued, his fingers tightened on her shoulders, his face grew incredulous. "Dear God, what do you take me for?"

"You had no right to meddle."

"All I did was get his trial moved ahead by two weeks."

"All you did?" she repeated, aghast. "We're talking about a man's life, not a social event."

Villard's gaze slid from hers. He was quiet a moment, weighing her remark, then hung his head. "You're right," he said dismally, staring at the floor. "But I couldn't help myself. When I heard he had been arrested, I thought it served him right for trying to seduce the woman I love."

Warmth rushed to her face. "Charles, nothing like that happened."

His head rose. His eyes were filled with anxiety. "Philips has more than a passing interest in you. He once made a point of telling me so."

That was news to Alexandra. Astonishing news.

"It drove me crazy with jealousy," Villard said. "That's why I meddled, not because he might be Jack Flash, but because I feared his attraction to you." He paused, swallowing. "Sweetheart, I throw myself on your mercy.

173

What I did was wrong, and I'm sorry."

The mantel clock ticked in the stillness. Villard caught her hand and brought it to his cheek, imploring her, "Please try to forgive me."

Struck by his urgency, Alexandra searched his face and saw deep remorse. Hesitation tore at her. At last she said, "Promise me that nothing like this will ever happen again."

"On my love for you, I swear it."

He had spoken the words with feeling, but her uncertainty lingered. Again she felt the portrait's malevolent stare, the soulless gray eyes probing like daggers, and sensed that Richard Villard was scorning her doubt.

Charles Villard, on the other hand, seemed anxious to put the matter to rest. "It's for the best you found out. I don't want any secrets between us. Now suppose we forget this ugly conversation," he urged.

But Alexandra could not forget what he had done. At his insistence, she drank a glass of wine to calm her nerves, but was feeling no better by the time she started for home. In the solitude of her coach, oblivious to the jostling ride as wheels plowed through muddy ruts, she agonized about the scruples of her future husband.

Who, meanwhile, was feeling not an ounce of guilt. Shortly after Alexandra left, he set out on horseback for the marshes at the western edge of the city. Though the night was damp and chill, he perspired beneath his riding habit and double-caped cloak.

Mr. Dobbs was waiting for him at a prearranged place— a wooded glen on a dry finger of ground jutting into swampy lowlands. Villard approached the meeting site with care, for the surrounding territory was treacherous, littered with pockets of slimy water deep enough to swallow a man and his horse.

The rain had tapered to a fine drizzle. High overhead a dim glow suggested that the moon rode behind thinning clouds, but there was little light to speak of beneath the canopy of leafy branches. Even so, Villard quickly spotted Dobbs—a dark, bent figure leaning against a tree—and from the dull gleam of rotting teeth he knew the shifty beggar was smiling.

"Evening, Mr. Villard."

The low, nasal voice almost made him shudder. Dobbs offended his sensibilities in every imaginable way, but because Dobbs was essential to his plan, Villard swallowed his revulsion and ordered, "Come here."

Dobbs's shadow separated from the tree, then lunged to catch the small leather purse Villard tossed at him. "Your downpayment, as we discussed."

Another flash of decayed teeth. "You won't be disappointed."

"Let's hope not."

"Mr. Philips is as good as hanged." Coins jingled as Dobbs hefted the purse. "Just don't forget the price we agreed on."

"If your testimony leads to a conviction, I'll double the amount."

A hush fell. Somewhere nearby a bullfrog boomed, causing Villard's mount to prance uneasily beneath him. Dobbs recovered his voice. "That's mighty generous of you."

"I expect you to earn it."

With that, Villard reined his horse in a tight circle and headed back the way he had come. Watching him vanish into the dripping forest, Dobbs wondered who the snotty bastard had hired to impersonate Jack Flash. Judging from the condition of the Whittakers after the robbery, it was someone who enjoyed inflicting pain.

Then Dobbs shivered with the memory of a cold, softspoken voice and bottomless gray eyes. It wouldn't surprise him if Villard had done the job himself.

Chapter Twenty-Six

Dalton's trial was postponed at the last minute, much to the delight of his supporters. Although his lawyer claimed credit for the timely delay, Dalton believed the praise belonged to an old man whose skillful propaganda had inflamed the common men's sentiments in Jack Flash's favor.

Twigs, always quick to exploit opportunity, was using the ongoing power struggle in Congress to full advantage. As the radicals slowly and steadily took political control of the capital, their need for support from every quarter grew proportionately. They were not about to cross swords with the rebel faction over a mere outlaw's fate. Hence Twigs, through his various mouthpieces and underlings, could say and do pretty much what he liked to help Dalton's cause.

He fanned embers into infernos. At the markets and in tavern taprooms, hotheaded Independents threatened justices and talked openly of freeing Jack Flash. Rumors circulated that reprisals would follow if the Court sentenced him to hang.

Toward the middle of June, a change occurred at the Walnut Street jail. Dalton was released from solitary confinement and moved to a cell overlooking the weed-choked prison yard. Although his wrists remained shackled, he was allowed the freedom of his new cage. He spent hours at the window, enjoying blessed daylight on his face while absorbing the familiar sounds and smells of the city.

As the hot days of June bore down on July, and the rebel

grip on Philadelphia tightened, the courts were thrown into utter chaos. Late in the month the Pennsylvania judicial system broke down entirely. The old government virtually ground to a halt, Governor John Penn had no credentials, and the rebels ruled the colonial capital.

Dalton, fearing a long delay as much as the final result, saw weeks blur into months as he awaited his fate. His lawyer kept him informed of legal developments, while news of the war was brought by Twigs, who was allowed to see him once a week. The lawyer's visits grew sporadic, but Twigs arrived every seventh day like clockwork. Hungry for information, Dalton always asked first about the enemy's movements, and what he heard was alarming.

A large concentration of British forces was converging on New York—Sir William Howe's troops from Halifax, thousands of redcoats and Hessians from Europe, and Clinton's regiments from Charleston. Combined, they would comprise the most formidable assemblage of British military power in history. General Howe had his eye on New York City with its splendid harbor, a strategic base from which he could advance up the Hudson. A strategic base that General Washington, with his untried, untrained Patriot army, was determined to defend.

Dalton was afraid the city would prove untenable under fire and that the surrounding rivers, islands, bays, and inlets would spread American forces too thin. "It ain't worth keeping," he told Twigs. "We should burn the place to the ground and leave the Lobsters with nothing."

Twigs pursed his lips in thought. "We should," he agreed, "except we can't afford to alienate New Yorkers by burning their cities. Anyway, there's still a chance the war will die before it's even born."

"Says who?"

"The Howe brothers. They've been appointed peace commissioners by the ministry. Sir William still thinks he can bring the Colonies to a compromise."

"Sure," Dalton smirked, "and I can fly to the fucking moon."

Twigs laughed. "I wish the fighting would start here, but I suppose New York's as good a place as any to prove ourselves."

At that, Dalton closed his eyes and wrestled with

177

frustration, for he could only wait and wonder while others did the proving. He was rotting in jail while soldiers in the north were preparing for battle.

In July, the smell of blood went to men's heads like wine. Fanned by clever propagandists, the flames of impatience and discontent consumed all that remained of America's flimsy respect for the mother country. Anyone still foolish enough to preach reconciliation and reunion was pelted with stones by children or publicly whipped. The whippings took place at the cart's tail while the offender was paraded through the streets, preceded by a fife and drums playing the "Rogue's March."

Down with the Loyalists! It was no longer a muttering, but a battle cry. Among the Philadelphia upper class, where Toryism had come dangerously close to being fashionable, a new breed of hot-and-cold Loyalist was emerging. Fearful of taking sides and jeopardizing their property, they kept quiet and let others bear the brunt of criticism and violence. Only the bravest of the Loyalists were open Tories, but even they suffered from an inability to unite behind their ideals. Most were content to wait and see which way the political tide turned.

Alexandra was stunned when, on July second, the Congress passed a resolution of independence. The old guard of Pennsylvania moderates, Robert Morris and John Dickinson, absented themselves from the proceedings that day, thereby allowing an almost unanimous colonial vote in favor of independence. It amounted to an open declaration of war.

Alexandra was torn between damning the Congress and blaming the King's ministers, whose hardened attitudes had paved the way for such a resolution. Two days after the resolution was passed, Congress adopted Jefferson's revised Declaration of Independence, and on July eighth it was read aloud for the first time to a crowd of boisterous Philadelphians. Alexandra, escorted by Christopher Clue, was among the listeners.

"We shouldn't be here," Clue said, nervous beside her.

"I want to hear this travesty."

Clue darted a glance around. "Please keep your voice down," he urged. Then he forgot his apprehension as the speaker, standing on a balcony overlooking the State

House yard, unrolled a document and hushed the crowd with his resonant voice. The words he spoke held Clue captive. Liberty for the individual. The creation of a society of free and equal men. Government by the consent of the governed.

Clue, having observed the fires of rebellion with a passive eye, and having felt certain the movement was doomed to eventual failure, was astonished to realize that a full-scale struggle for independence would indeed be waged against Great Britain. The Congress of the thirteen United States of America had declared the Colonies:

> **Free and Independent States;** that they are absolved from all Allegiance to the British Crown, and that all political Connection between them and the State of Great Britain, is and ought to be totally dissolved; and that as Free and Independent States, they have full Power to levy War, conclude Peace, contract Alliances, establish Commerce, and to do all other Acts and Things which Independent States may of right do.

"Dear God," Alexandra whispered. "Those *fools.*"

Around her the crowd began cheering and waving hats, and some militiamen who were present fired their muskets into the ground. Even Clue wore a dazzled grin. But his humor fled as the crowd surged toward the State House and Alexandra, propelled by the rush, was separated from him. Clue dove after her, caught her arm, and elbowed his way clear of the throng, pulling her along behind him.

"We'd better leave," he insisted, watching the frenzied activity around the State House entrance. Someone had fetched a ladder and propped it against the ornate doorway. Encouraged by the crowd, a young man climbed up the rungs and, wielding a chisel and hammer, began prying the Royal Arms off the State House wall. As wood splintered and sections of the British lion and the royal crown tumbled down, the mob began chanting, "BURN IT! BURN IT!"

Clue tugged Alexandra's arm. "Please, Mrs. Pennington."

Numb with disbelief, she went with him.

179

For the next few days, as news of the Declaration was spread by couriers on fast horses, reports reached Philadelphia of similar incidents taking place throughout the Colonies. In New York, after Washington's announcement of independence to his army, rebel troops pulled down a statue of King George on the Bowling Green. The gilded lead statue, which showed His Majesty crowned and mounted on horseback, was broken apart by an enthusiastic mob, and the pieces were being shipped to Connecticut, where munitions makers would turn them into thousands of bullets.

At Willowbrook, Alexandra kept track of unfolding events from a safe distance. The pages of the *Gazette* were a primary source of information as well as outrage. Before her eyes, the center of gravity was shifting from the genteel and polite of Philadelphia to the plebeians of the city and the rough country peasants. In mid-July, by order of the Congress, a Convention was formed to draft a new state constitution—the product of the victory of farmers and artisans over the ruling class.

Before long, the Convention was engaged in a heated debate over what to do with the criminals stagnating in Philadelphia's jails. When Alexandra learned that many of the members were in favor of swift prosecutions in order to clear the books and start afresh, her indignation changed to anguish.

The news so distressed her that she sent Clue to the State House each morning to await the Convention's decision. As the proceedings dragged on, and the pressure to reach a solution mounted, Alexandra alternately prayed for Dalton Philips and cursed him for making her a wreck. At night, waiting to fall asleep, she was plagued by a recurrent vision of him mounting a scaffold while she watched from the crowd, powerless to stop his execution.

Chapter Twenty-Seven

"Lace," insisted Evelyn Wright, dabbing a napkin to the corners of her mouth.

Alexandra regarded her with annoyance. "I've already decided on satin."

"Goodness no, dear." A flick of Evelyn's wrist dismissed the notion as absurd. "It simply must be lace."

"Must it?" Alexandra wished she had declined the invitation to lunch at Sweet Briar. The droning was giving her a headache.

"Yards and yards of lace," Evelyn said. "It's the very thing this year, don't you know?"

"Perhaps you didn't hear me." Alexandra spoke quietly, but firmly. "I've decided to wear satin."

Realizing she was getting nowhere, Evelyn looked across the dining room table at her nephew. "Charles, do you have a preference?"

Villard started and looked blank. "Excuse me?"

"Alexandra's wedding dress. Would you prefer that it be satin or lace?"

Alexandra bristled. Her wrath nearly exploded when Villard said vaguely, "Lace, I suppose," then went back to eating his lunch without even a glance at her.

Evelyn smiled in triumph. "You see?"

Alexandra saw that Villard was too preoccupied to care whether his bride arrived at the altar wearing satin or lace or filthy rags. Lately he had been like a stranger to her, distant and morose, untouched by her attempts to reach him and restore their relationship to its former easy intimacy.

Part of the trouble, she knew, was financial. Since April, when the Congress had closed American ports to British shipping, trade in the Colonies had suffered. Cut off from his London suppliers, Villard's revenue had declined while profiteering among Whig merchants grew rife. Then, early in July, one of his ships bound from the West Indies disappeared at sea, whether the victim of a storm or a marauding privateer, no one knew for certain.

Alexandra only knew she could not bear much more of his moodiness. Whenever they were together, he seemed to want her sympathy more than anything else. Instead of affection, he gave her gifts. His conversation often consisted of one-word replies to her questions, which, later on, he would not remember her asking.

She longed to tell him that his apathy hurt her, that she would not tolerate being taken for granted, but for now she held back because his aunt was present. Painfully so.

"It will be the most fabulous event in years," Evelyn sighed. "By the bye, dear." She patted the table as if to emphasize the importance of what she was about to say. "I've thought of someone else who must attend."

Alexandra's voice was challenging. "You have already invited half of Philadelphia."

"Oh, but we simply must invite the Cranstons."

"But we simply will not."

Disconcerted, Evelyn threw her nephew an injured look. "Charles?" she demanded, dragging him from his reverie.

A moment passed as he gauged the tension in the room. Noting the high color on Alexandra's face, the indignation in his aunt's stare, he swallowed a sigh. Apparently some part of him had heard their exchange, for he said, "I'm afraid Alexandra is right. This is a wedding, not a pageant. Besides, I hardly know the Cranstons."

Evelyn dropped her gaze, sniffed, poked at her asparagus with a fork. "I fail to see why some of my friends should be excluded," she pouted. "After all, Charles, I've been like a mother to you since my dear brother passed away, God rest him."

To Alexandra's vexation, Villard yielded without further discussion. "All right, Aunt Evie," he soothed her.

"We'll invite whomever you wish."

Hands clenched beneath the table, Alexandra stared at her plate and kept silent, afraid of what she might say if she opened her mouth. This was not the time to voice her disgust, but she fully intended to do so, for if Charles showed so little regard for her feelings now, what was in store for her in the months and years ahead?

September, once so far away, was rushing at her.

Footsteps disrupted her angry thoughts. Looking up, she saw Sweet Briar's butler enter the dining room, walk straight to Villard, and proffer a silver card tray bearing a wax-sealed letter. Taking the letter, Villard waved him away with an impatient gesture, then broke the seal. Paper rustled as he unfolded the note and scanned it.

In the stillness, Alexandra watched his face and saw astonishment freeze his features. As his shock gave way to fury, his fingers curled into a fist, crushing the note. Trancelike, he rose and said with strained composure, "Ladies, will you excuse me?"

"Charles?" Alexandra asked in concern.

He left the room without replying. Her own annoyance forgotten, Alexandra glanced at Evelyn, who looked back at her with eyebrows raised and said, "I wonder what that was all about?"

The answer lay on the table where he had left it. Fearing he had lost another ship, Alexandra got up and went to his chair to retrieve the note. From there, she could see Villard in the small parlor across the passageway. His back was to her. He was pouring whiskey into a glass.

She picked up the crumpled paper and heard Evelyn hiss, "Do you think that's wise?" Ignoring her, Alexandra smoothed the paper out on the table and read the brief message.

The Convention has declared amnesty for all prisoners.

She leaned a hand on the table, riveted by the miraculous words that did not seem real, even as she read them over again, her pulse soaring. *Amnesty!*

Her gaze returned to the man across the hall, and a chill brushed her spine because now she understood the reason

183

for his wrath. He had wanted Dalton Philips to be executed. He had pushed for it, hoped for it, and now he was furious that his wish had been denied.

To Villard, his condition felt much more acute than mere anger and disappointment. After coming so close to his goal, failure was unbearable to him.

Later that day, he learned the motive behind the Convention's decision. The expansive move was aimed at winning widespread public support for the rebel government by offering "amnesty for debtors, or for any criminal offense or offenses, or practices against the present virtuous measures of the American States, or prisoners of war." In short, all felons, regardless of their crimes, would soon be released from prison. Which posed a problem for Villard beyond his immediate discontent.

And so, early the next evening, he headed into the marshes for another clandestine meeting. It was a beautiful dusk, cool and still with a lingering mist from the river. There had been little rain of late, and the bogs had receded to form slimy green pools where frogs and snakes and furtive things slithered, including Mr. Dobbs.

He appeared like a wraith from behind a tree. From his appearance, he might well have slept in the low-lying mire beside the Schuylkill. His suit was rumpled and soiled, his oily face unwashed. For several reasons, including distrust, Villard did not feel inclined to dismount while they talked. He was there for only one purpose—to send Mr. Dobbs beyond the reach of Dalton Philips. He was worried about being charged with a crime, but more than that he loathed to have the world know he had stooped to hire the likes of Mr. Dobbs.

"You have something for me?" Dobbs wanted to know.

The purse Villard removed from his saddlebag was heavy with gold. He made as if to hand it over, then snatched it back as Dobbs's greedy hands shot out and closed on air.

"Hey!"

"My dear Mr. Dobbs." Villard's voice was sharp, cutting. "What a vermin you are."

The shabby man drew back and looked wary. "We had a bargain."

"On the contrary, *you* are getting a bargain, whereas I

am paying for services not rendered." Villard smiled his contempt. "Therefore, indulge me a moment while I summarize what this money is now purchasing."

Dobbs waited.

"You will disappear," Villard said, "forever. Change your name and forget you ever heard mine."

"I understand all that—"

"Shut your goddamned face while I'm speaking!"

Dobbs shut up.

And Villard struggled to compose himself. "You insolent bastard!" He hurled the purse at him, then watched him open the drawstring and finger the shiny coins inside. "Is it enough?" he demanded.

It was more money than Dobbs had ever seen in his life. "Oh, yes," he breathed. "Just the right amount. It will take me very far away indeed." Hearing a firelock click, Dobbs looked up into the dark bore of a pistol, the merciless eyes behind it.

"Farther than you can imagine," Villard said and blew a hole through his shiny forehead. The impact pitched Dobbs backward onto the spongy ground. Dismounting, Villard knelt by his splayed body and noted with satisfaction that the ball had lifted the top of his skull away. There was some evidence of the kill, bright red splatters on green moss, but by morning the insects and night creatures would have removed these signs.

Sitting cross-legged on the ground, Villard waited for the blood to cease flowing. Around him the marsh pressed in like a wall, crickets droned their shrill chorus, vegetation rustled as animals scurried past in their hunt for food. Another man might have feared nightfall in those fetid woods, but Villard was comfortable in darkness.

When the time came, he had no qualms about handling the corpse. Indeed, he rather enjoyed the idea that he had rid the world of a blight. Grabbing Dobbs beneath the armpits, he dragged him backward through swamp grass and across rotting logs toward a glimmer of silver river beyond the woods.

Villard was panting when the trees finally thinned and he hauled his burden to the lip of the embankment. For a moment he considered the view, alert for any observer, but he was quite alone.

In the deepening twilight, he staggered down to the river's edge, entered the shallows, and waded out past the reeds with Dobbs in tow. Standing chest deep in chilly water, he thrust the body from him and felt exhilarated as the current swept it away.

Chapter Twenty-Eight

Jack Flash was a free man, and Alexandra was miserable because he had gone to join the rebel army. That was what her heart told her as she scanned a broadside tacked to a wall in the High Street Market. The notice was addressed: TO ALL BRAVE, HEALTHY, ABLE-BODIED, AND WELL-DISPOSED YOUNG MEN. It was a call to arms for the defense of the Liberties and Independence of the United States against the hostile designs of foreign enemies. The recruiting poster proclaimed, among other things, that a soldier who joined the army would receive a supply of good and handsome clothing, ample daily rations, and sixty dollars a year in gold and silver money.

A pack of lies, she thought scornfully. False promises to tempt the poor man who believed he had nothing to lose. How elegantly the deception was worded, as though participating in a war meant ". . . spending a few happy years in viewing the different parts of this beautiful continent, in the honourable and truly respectable character of soldier, after which, he may, if he pleases, return home to his friends, with his pockets FULL of money and his head covered with laurels."

If he survives, Alexandra thought with despair. She turned away from the poster and nearly collided with Clue, who had been reading over her shoulder. His intrigued look incensed her.

"I'm ready to leave," she said.

"But you haven't done any shopping."

"I'll come back on Saturday."

187

Frowning, he followed her from the busy market building to the hot, dusty street, where they had left the coach in the care of a shopkeeper's son. Clue flipped him a shilling for his trouble, then opened the coach door for Alexandra and handed her inside. As she pulled off her hat and flung it to the seat, he lingered in the doorway.

"As long as we're in town," he suggested, "why don't you call on Mr. Pennington?"

"So you can swill free rum in his kitchen?" Alexandra heard the venom in her voice and paused, shocked at herself.

"No, ma'am," said Clue, hiding his hurt. "I just thought a visit might cheer you up."

"I'm sorry, Christopher. That was dreadful of me."

He shrugged away her concern. "No harm done," he said, but his averted eyes implied otherwise. As he started for the driver's bench, she called him back.

"Drive to Mr. Featherman's shop," she said. "You need a new suit of clothes."

"Me?" Clue hooked a thumb at his chest, his face incredulous. Mr. Featherman, an English tailor, operated an exclusive establishment.

"Yes, you," she said, pleased by his reaction. "Mary tells me that everything you own is patched."

"But the cost—"

"Is irrelevant." Alexandra silenced his protest with a wave. "I can't have my coachman running around looking like a pauper. Consider the clothes a well-deserved bonus."

Clue just watched her.

"Well?"

"If you insist, ma'am."

She did insist. So Clue drove up Market Street and turned north onto Third, intending to circle the block to Second Street, where Mr. Featherman had his shop. But along the way he suddenly hauled back on the reins as a horseman rode directly in front of the team.

Alexandra threw out a hand to brace herself as the coach lurched to a halt. "Good Lord," she said under her breath, alarmed. Had they struck someone down?

Looking out her window, she froze in astonishment to see Mercury blocking their path, with Dalton Philips astride him. Dressed in traveling clothes, Dalton carried a musket across his thighs and a brace of pistols in leather saddle holsters. A silver-ornamented saber hung from his shoulder belt. Behind him, the tip of a bayonet scabbard protruded from the makeshift pack lashed to his saddle. He was armed to fight a war all by himself. Indeed, with his shoulders squared and his eyes glittering, he exuded the awful aggression of someone about to launch an attack.

As he reined his stallion alongside the coach and stared down at her, Alexandra realized his hostility was meant for her alone. She opened her mouth to say something, but his cold voice stopped her from speaking. "I want to talk to you."

Without waiting for her permission, Dalton dismounted and tied Mercury to the back of the coach. "Drive slow, Chris," he said.

"Where to?"

"Don't matter. Anywhere."

Alexandra flinched as the far door was flung open. Framed in the opening, Dalton watched her a moment before grabbing the door jamb and pulling himself into the coach. Clue slapped the reins and the vehicle began to move, but Alexandra hardly noticed because Dalton, with the entire facing seat at his disposal, had chosen to sit next to her.

They regarded each other in silence, and in those strained moments Alexandra took in a barrage of sensuous details—the familiar odors of horses and strong lye soap, the red marks on his wrists from being shackled, his thinner face, and his accusing green eyes with smudges like faint bruises beneath them.

His flat voice shattered the spell. "Did you tell anyone about Jack Flash?"

Dismay welled up in her. He believed she had thrown him to the wolves. "I gave you my word," she said. "I told no one."

Dalton was quiet, watchful. He seemed to want more from her, and Alexandra, troubled beside him, offered it. "I would never betray you. When I heard you were arrested, I was terrified for you."

"I didn't rob the Whittakers," he said.

189

"I never thought you did. Dobbs was lying."

His eyes narrowed, but he was otherwise still. "How do you know?"

"I had him investigated."

"You did?" There was wonder in his voice.

She nodded. "I thought he was after the reward money."

The clip-clop of hooves and the creak of carriage wheels filled the pause. Dalton glanced out his window and seemed absorbed in the view up Third Street toward Callowhill. After a time he said, "Someone sent my lawyer a letter about Dobbs. It was written anonymally." His penetrating gaze came back to her. "Was it from you?"

She gave a small shrug. "I thought the information might be useful to him."

"Did you now?" Dalton studied her a long moment. Then, although his eyes were still remote, his body relaxed against the seat. "The thing is," he said, "there was someone else involved, because Dobbs didn't rob the Whittakers and he didn't bury the silver at my farm. He was just supposed to lie and collect money from someone that don't like me a whole lot."

Disconcerted, Alexandra kept silent, not because she doubted what he said, but because she knew who it was he suspected, and she feared he was right.

"But I'll never be able to prove anything," Dalton said, disgusted. "Dobbs is gone, the little maggot. I can't waste time looking for him. There's going to be a battle in New York, and I intend to be there for it."

Alexandra swallowed the dryness in her throat. She could argue with him that his cause was hopeless, that American farmers and tradesmen were no match for British soldiers. But she knew he would not be swayed, and she did not want to waste these moments because she knew she might never see him again.

Her pulse was quickening. Irresistibly drawn, she touched the angry red mark on his wrist, surprised at her own boldness as her fingertips traced his scar and her eyes rose to meet his guarded look.

"I was wrong," she said softly.

"About what?"

"When I said I could not return your feelings."

Dalton hesitated for a second. "What makes you think I

have any feelings left?"

In answer, she placed her hand against the side of his face and saw his eyes change, saw restraint wiped away by longing. Something deep within her stirred. The air around them seemed suddenly charged with energy. She whispered his name, and Dalton, because he could not help it and because he wanted her closeness, responded by gathering her into his arms as though to keep her there forever.

Alexandra shivered to powerful sensations. Everything she felt in his embrace was new, galvanizing. She lifted her face to him and felt him gently kiss her cheek, then her lips with rising need, his mouth tasting hers and his tongue delving intimately until nothing outside the coach mattered, only here and now in this private world where every shade of feeling was explored and prolonged. Their mouths came apart only to start over, find a better angle, join a little deeper.

At length he took his lips from hers and drew her closer into his warmth, and for awhile they just held each other as their heartbeats slowed and the world intruded.

"I was afraid you were gone," she murmured against his throat.

"I couldn't leave without seeing you again." He rubbed his cheek in her hair, luxuriating in her nearness. "I couldn't stop thinking about you."

Alexandra could feel him trembling slightly and tightened her arms around him. "Dalton, I don't want you to go."

"It won't be forever." His hand rose to cradle the back of her head as his wondering eyes looked down at her. "Will you wait for me?" he asked with as much hope as he dared.

A well of tenderness surged in her. She nodded, her heart full to aching. "I love you."

For the space of a breath he simply watched her. Then he took her face between his hands, and the kiss he gave her was filled with the hunger of days and nights spent in a lonely cell, yearning for the gift that had just been given him. The gift was devotedly returned, and as the coach gently rocked and swayed on its way, and the city around them seethed with thoughts of bloody retribution, they clung to each other and stole precious moments from what should have been, but which might never be again.

Sometime later, Clue stopped the coach and looked back from the driver's bench as Dalton got out. They were on Third Street at the entrance to Elbow Lane, and across the street was the Workhouse and the Stone Prison, both now empty of debtors and criminals.

Dalton took notice of the prison buildings. He swung himself onto the stallion's back and reined to the coach window, where Alexandra was waiting for him. Leaning sideways off his prancing horse, he kissed her full on the lips.

By then Clue was grinning, pleased and surprised. He turned and looked straight ahead, but before long he glanced over his shoulder again, just in time to see Alexandra hand Dalton a blue satin ribbon from her hat. Dalton got a look on his face then that Clue would never forget. He watched him thread the ribbon through a buttonhole of his sleeveless waistcoat. Then Dalton reached for her hand, gently kissed her palm, and closed her fingers into a small fist to retain the kiss.

Alexandra withdrew into the coach, and Dalton nudged Mercury forward to speak with Clue. "Look after her, Chris. And yourself."

"Don't worry about us," Clue assured him, then lowered his voice so Alexandra would not hear him say, "Just thump the buggers."

Dalton's face was solemn as he put on his three-cornered hat. "That'll take some doing," he said. "The British have been winning wars for ages." Then he slowly smiled and a fierce glimmer came into his eyes. "But they never had to fight Americans."

As Dalton rode off on his handsome horse, with his shiny blue ribbon fluttering on his chest, Clue felt a strange mixture of envy and relief at being left behind. Embracing a cause seemed a noble undertaking, but in war it meant braving bullets and destroying other lives, both frightening prospects to Clue. Some men were born warriors. He had no delusions about being one of them.

After Dalton disappeared from view, Clue gathered up the reins, then suddenly froze, staring at a passing coach trimmed in scarlet and blue. Evelyn Wright's outraged face peered from a window. Frowning back at the meddlesome woman, Clue wondered how much she had seen. Plenty, judging from her expression. In seconds she was gone, a pall of dust rising in her wake, and Clue was seized by a terrible sense of foreboding.

Chapter Twenty-Nine

It happened sooner than Clue expected.

He was the only man at Willowbrook when the trouble arrived. Edward and Mary Brock had gone into town to visit a friend. Clue, in shirt-sleeves and brown breeches, his face smudged with axle grease, was working in the carriage house when Charles Villard galloped up the driveway on a sweat-stained roan.

"Oh, shit," Clue groaned and left the carriage house to intercept him. By the time Villard had tethered his lathered horse to the hitching post, Clue had planted himself before the fan steps leading up to Willowbrook's front door.

Villard strode up the walkway, a riding crop clenched in his fist, and stood face-to-face with Clue. "Get out of my way."

"No, sir," Clue said firmly. "You can see her another time."

Villard cocked his head. "Is that so?"

Without warning the crop flashed out and stinging leather caught Clue full across the face. He staggered back in surprise, a hand raised to his burning cheek. He was shorter and more slender than Villard, and in that moment was frightened of him, but he held his ground.

"Mr. Villard," he said with as much calm as he could manage, "I asked you to leave."

"You filthy dog!" Villard crowded Clue backward. "Who the hell do you think you're talking to?"

A madman, Clue thought, looking into icy gray eyes. "Mrs. Pennington is—"

The front door opened and there stood Alexandra. Afraid of what Villard would do next, Clue backed up the stairs to protect her.

Pantherlike, Villard followed him. He paused on the stoop and stared past Clue at Alexandra. "You were with him again."

There was no need to ask who he was talking about. "Yes," she said simply.

"I think you had better talk to me."

She touched Clue's arm. "It's all right, Christopher."

"No, ma'am." His wary eyes were fixed on Villard. "It isn't."

"Christopher, please move aside."

Clue turned his head slightly, and when Alexandra saw the red line on his cheek where blood had drawn to the surface, shock flooded her. Noting the riding crop in Villard's gloved hand, her eyes blazed at him. "Did you strike him?" she asked in astonishment.

"He raised his fist at me."

"That's a lie!" Clue protested.

"Will you hide behind him, Alexandra?" Villard demanded. "Or will you have the decency to explain yourself to me?"

Alexandra's voice was scornful. "I'll say what needs to be said." With that, she took Clue's arm to draw him inside. "Christopher, let me handle this."

For a second, her firm tone persuaded him that she could. Then he remembered the evil he had felt a few minutes earlier, emanating from wintry eyes, and balked in the doorway. "Please, ma'am," he said, "send him away."

Instead she tugged his arm and insisted, "Stand aside."

Clue obeyed, and Villard swept past them into the hallway, his long, angry strides taking him into the parlor. When he disappeared from view, Alexandra turned to Clue and asked in a low voice, "Why did he strike you?"

"Because he's raving mad!" Clue whispered. "Can't you see that?"

"You did nothing to provoke him?"

"I told him he couldn't see you, not in the mood he's in." As she turned toward the parlor, Clue gripped her arm, desperate to make her understand. "You shouldn't be alone with him, Mrs. Pennington."

She placed a reassuring hand over his. "Wait here." Then she left, silk skirts whispering in the silent hall, and Clue stared after her despairingly.

In the parlor, Villard had poured himself a brandy and was looking out a window at the hazy, sunlit grounds. Closing the door behind her, Alexandra leaned against it and watched his rigid back, noting how the glass shook in his hand. Her own body, like her voice, trembled with outrage. "How dare you hit Christopher?"

"He's an insolent puppy," Villard said without turning around. "He needed a lesson in humility."

Alexandra's breath drew in sharply at his brutal tone. "He's my friend," she shot back, "and you had best keep your hands off him. Damn you, Charles, look at me!" When he faced her, she searched his face for some sign of repentence and saw none. Fury surged in her. To Villard, putting a welt on Clue's face amounted to nothing worse than disciplining an animal. "My God, what is wrong with you?" she demanded. "Have you no more conscience than a beast in the field?"

"You have the gall to lecture me about conscience?" he cried, suddenly fierce. "You have humiliated me. You kissed that bastard in the middle of Third Street, in broad daylight, for everyone to see."

"I was saying goodbye to him."

"Not good riddance?"

"No," she said firmly. "Nothing like that."

His nostrils flared. "Educate me?"

Alexandra studied the man she had promised to wed, a man whose resentful soul was consumed with a jealousy that at last was justified. His eyes were fixed and so horribly bleak, it was hard for her to imagine that they had ever held warmth. "I cannot marry you, Charles."

For a moment he seemed incapable of speech. *"What?"* It was a snarl, a threat.

"It's finished between us." As she spoke the words, a great sense of relief swept her.

Villard's face reddened, a muscle twitched in his cheek. "You don't know what you're saying."

"I know exactly what I'm saying," she retorted. "You're the most cold-hearted, selfish man I've ever known. You only care when it suits your purpose. God help me, I once thought I loved you, but no more," she said flatly. "Our betrothal is ended."

His intense stare had not wavered from her face. "I can't believe this," he said in a thick, incredulous voice. "That stinking, vulgar farmer has poisoned you against me."

"Dalton did nothing of the sort. The credit belongs entirely to you."

"Dalton," he sneered the name. "How low you have sunk, Alexandra."

"No, Charles. I have never felt more enlightened."

At last Villard grasped her resolve and rage knifed him. He fixed on her lovely face while his mind wrestled with an overload of emotions, unwilling to accept that she had thrown him over for a bumpkin. It was incomprehensible. Once word got out, his friends would ridicule him. He would be the laughingstock of the entire city, and Dalton Philips would be crowing loudest of all.

His smoldering eyes raked her. "You used me," he said. "While you were playing parlor games with me, you were spreading your legs for that stable cleaner."

Alexandra recoiled as though slapped. Then her chin rose, her shoulders drew back, and contempt seemed to flare in her dark blue gaze. "If I have sinned, it was in taking so long to realize what a pathetic, hollow man you are."

"How long did you know he was Jack Flash?"

The question caught her off guard. She hesitated, and Villard pounced on her instant of confusion.

"I thought so," he said. "You protected that whoreson from the law."

"I would do it again," she said in defiance. "And you may as well know I did everything I could to get him out of jail, just as you tried to bury him." She measured him a moment, then challenged, "Where did you send Mr. Dobbs?"

His face changed then, and the look that came over him made her insides shrink as if a demon had passed over her grave. "Would you like to see?" he asked, his voice soft and amused.

Alexandra faltered under his brittle stare. "I want you to leave, Charles."

197

Instead he advanced on her. Retreating from the malice in his eyes, she tried to put a chair between them, but he moved with incredible quickness. His hand shot out, seizing her hair, and yanked her forward until their faces were inches apart.

"You bitch!"

Alexandra was suddenly afraid to move or speak because his hate-maddened eyes were promising punishment if she did. Jeweled hair ribbons flew as he shook her.

"Did he fuck you like one of his horses? Use a crop on you? Spurs?" Villard twisted her head back until she whimpered in pain. "Or do you prefer hobbles, sweetheart?"

"Charles, let go!" was all she could manage. Through a blur of tears she saw his balled fist rise and poise above her face like a mallet. His breath quivered, his face contorted as he fought to control himself, and Alexandra stared in horrified amazement at the cruel creature lurking beneath his careful polish.

Just then the parlor door crashed inward. Villard shoved her away and spun to face Clue, who took in the scene with a strangled cry and hurled himself across the room to Alexandra's defense.

As she tumbled over a chair to the floor, there was a crash of glass and splintering wood. Sprawled facedown among the remains of an antique vase, Alexandra heard the meaty thump of a fist striking flesh. The sound came again and again, accompanied by grunts of pain that she realized were coming from Clue. Heart hammering, she pulled herself up, looked over the toppled chair toward the fireplace, and saw him lying flat on his back with Villard astride him.

Clue's lower lip was split. Blood streamed from his nose as vicious blows broke through his guard, bruising his face and making a mockery of his defenses. Through a haze of pain, he saw the livid face above him, the eyes wild with intent, and he knew Villard meant to kill him. With that thought in his brain, he heaved against the weight pinning him down. His fingers seized a ruffled shirt to throw the madman aside, but the ruffles tore away in his hand. In the next instant, a fist hammered his cheekbone, cracking his head against the brick hearth, and the room exploded crimson and white and whirled around him.

When Clue stopped struggling, Villard's hand darted out and seized an iron poker from the hearth.

"No!" Alexandra sprang up. "Charles, for God's sake!" She flung herself at him, grabbed his raised arm and held on with a strength born of terror.

Clue forgotten, Villard came to his feet, bringing Alexandra along by the hair, and with his eyes boring into hers, he closed his fingers around her throat and squeezed hard. Alexandra pried at his hand, but his grip was like iron. As she clawed for his eyes, he jerked his head back and watched her thrash, his teeth bared in a grin. After a time her chest began to burn, her knees grew weak, and she heard a churning sound like being underwater.

All at once he released her. As she swayed on her feet, gasping for air, Villard placed a palm against her chest and shoved her backward at Clue, who had made it to his knees. He caught her around the waist and cushioned her fall. When Villard moved to stand over them, Clue sheltered her body with his own.

For long moments Villard just watched them, hands curling and uncurling at his sides. A shudder racked him. He swallowed, blinked, wiped a hand over his forehead as though to clear his mind of something unwanted.

Finally he leveled an accusing finger at Alexandra. "This is not finished," he vowed. "By the eternal God, you'll pay for your treachery, for I swear I shall find it in my power to break you and make you suffer as you deserve." His eyes appeared glazed as they traveled over her. "You're nothing but a whore," he said, then turned on his heel and stalked out.

His footsteps faded. Clue's rigid body sagged with relief. Crouched over Alexandra, he stroked her shoulder with a shaking hand, the gesture to comfort himself as much as her. "Mrs. Pennington?" he asked in a hoarse voice.

She reached for his hand, and he helped her to stand, and they huddled together for reassurance like frightened children. "My God," she whispered.

"He's insane," Clue said.

Meeting his look, Alexandra barely managed not to weep at the sight of his battered face. Her voice cracked with emotion. "I'm sorry, Christopher. I'm so sorry."

"Never mind about me. Are you all right?"

"Yes."

Clue squeezed her shoulder, taking control. "Stay here," he said. "I'll make sure he's gone."

Left alone, Alexandra stood dazed, unable to stop trembling as she glanced around at broken glass, overturned furniture, spots of blood near the hearth. An eternity passed before Clue returned to the parlor. When he did, he was carrying her small pistol with the inlays of ivory and silver wire.

"The bastard's gone," he said, searching her pale face. "We'd better go tell the sheriff what happened."

"What will he do?" Alexandra cried. She hugged her arms in despair. "He has no authority left. Besides, he's afraid of Charles."

He should be, Clue thought grimly. "We have to do something," he said.

Numb with shock, Alexandra stared at the weapon he held, fighting to keep a grip on her presence of mind. She had expected resentment from Villard, but not barbarity. She shuddered to recall his enraged face and the horror of his fingers choking off her breath. Her hand rose protectively to her throat, which was sore and tender and bore red marks from his savage grip. The violence she had been dreading for so long had finally burst upon her, in a way she had never imagined, and with a sudden, appalling clarity she realized this was only the beginning. Villard had sworn to wreak revenge upon her, using all the power and influence at his disposal, and she imagined that no amount of punishment would be enough to heal his wounded vanity. She feared his vengeance, and because she did, Alexandra wept the tears she had been holding back.

When Clue embraced her, she clutched at him, drawing comfort from his nearness. "Damn him!" she cried, her body racked by huge sobs. "I did nothing to deserve his hatred. Nothing. I only wanted to be free of him."

"I know, ma'am."

"How could I have been so blind?" Tears were flooding down her face now. "He never cared about me. He's incapable of caring. He's an *animal*."

"I won't let him hurt you again, I swear it."

Eventually Clue's assurances helped restore her composure, but while she was grateful for his support, Alexandra knew he was no match for Villard. She thought of Dalton then, miles away and headed for unknown dangers, ready to fight for his beliefs. She thought of his arms around her and the fierce strength that was in him, and her own courage was suddenly sparked. Nothing in her life had been so important as the moment she declared her love for him, and no one, certainly not a brute like Villard, would stop her from having that love fulfilled. Determination rose in her, blunting the sharp edge of her fear. The devil take Charles, she thought, then drew away from Clue, wiped her eyes on her sleeve, and took a steadying breath.

She had made her choice. Against every crisis, she would stand by it. Given time, Villard's anger would pass, but even as she thought this, Alexandra knew the hope was empty. Something sinister had been unleashed in him. She had seen his madness, felt the power of his rage, and only a fool would not be wary of him. Sooner or later he would strike at her, and when he did she must be ready. Today he had caught her unaware, but she would never again underestimate him.

II.

The Gravedigger

Chapter Thirty

The oval-shaped ballroom held an assemblage of the most prominent Philadelphia Tories. As they raised their glasses in a toast, candlelight sparkled on jeweled, powdered hair, gilt-edged mirrors, and a score of great candelabra decorated in high relief silver and gold. Whisperings of silks and brocades faded to a hush as William Hamilton, the host of Woodlands, addressed his guests.

"God bless and preserve His Majesty's soldiers in New York. May their triumph over the misguided foes of America be swift and merciful, and may the wounds which divide us, friend from friend, parent from child, colony from motherland, be suffered to heal. And may God save the King of England!"

"*Hear, hear!*"

Alexandra touched her glass to her lips, then slowly lowered it without drinking the toast. Her attention was on Hamilton, one of the wealthiest men in the province. Not long ago, with the outbreak of the rebellion, Hamilton had espoused the rebel side and had even raised a regiment in this neighborhood of the Neck. But with the signing of the Declaration of Independence, the staunch Whig had resigned his commission on the grounds that, while he still supported the Continental Congress, he could not condone a complete break with England.

Now he stood in the elegant ballroom of his country seat, amidst ranking Tories, and celebrated a battle not yet fought and a victory not yet won. Hot-and-cold Hamilton, she thought. Like so many other Tories in the city, his loyalties ebbed and flowed with the circumstances of the moment. What tune would he be singing next week if, impossible though it seemed, the rebels succeeded in driving General Howe from Long Island?

Beside her, George Pennington murmured, "William certainly loves a display."

His remark made Alexandra smile as she glanced around at the retinue of liveried footmen carrying refreshment trays, the scarlet-clad musicians grouped at one end of the oval ballroom, the great porcelain urns filled with fragrant flowers from Woodlands's extensive gardens. Along the south-facing windows, exotic dwarf trees in silver-ornamented pots were arranged to simulate a woodsy grove. However inconsistent Hamilton's politics might be, his fondness for spectacle and entertainment was absolute.

The music for the ball was a French horn, an oboe, and two violins, and as the musicians struck up a slow march, Pennington offered Alexandra his arm. "May I have the honor?"

For a man of his age, he was a wonderfully enthusiastic dance partner, his dark eyes glinting with mirth as he led her through the steps of the march. The hot, dry summer weather seemed to agree with him, for his health had improved markedly over the past two months. Tonight he moved with the agility of a much younger man. There was even a tinge of color in his normally pale face.

After the march ended, Pennington's exuberance carried him through the minuet that followed and finally a lively jig to end the set. "By God, Alexandra!" he gasped as they applauded the musicians. "You wear a man out."

"It's your own fault for not conceding to Mr. Lindsay," she said. "He was trying to cut you out of the jig."

"Really?" Pennington seemed amused. "I didn't notice him."

"How could you miss him in that suit?"

Now Pennington pretended astonishment. "You mean that blinding blue specter was Stephen?" he asked. "Good Heavens! I thought he was part of William's decorations."

Alexandra laughed. Even amidst this colorful, shimmering crowd Stephen Lindsay stood out like a beacon, his plump figure swathed in iridescent blue silk.

Watching him thread his way toward the ballroom's main entrance, she was reminded of a strutting, preening peacock, albeit a tottering one. When he stumbled over his own feet, she shook her head pityingly. Then, as if drawn by a compelling force, her attention shifted from Lindsay to the arched doorway.

There stood Charles Villard. He was resplendent in an ivory satin suit trimmed with brown silk braid and lavish gold embroidery in a leaf pattern. He was staring at her, and even at this distance Alexandra felt the piercing hostility emanating from his chilly eyes.

She looked away, her pulse throbbing in her temples, heat rushing over her face. "Charles is here," she murmured to Pennington, who stiffened beside her and scanned the ballroom until he spotted Villard.

"Why, that young popinjay," he said, agitated. "It was my understanding that he wasn't invited here tonight."

"It doesn't matter."

"Yes, it does," Pennington said in a voice like iron. As he started away, Alexandra caught his arm.

"Where are you going?"

"To have a word with him."

"No, George," she insisted. "I have to face him some time. It may as well be now."

Hearing her determination, Pennington reluctantly yielded. "As you wish," he said. "But if he causes you the least annoyance, I shall plant his head in yonder French horn."

His seriousness made Alexandra thankful she had not told him the particulars of her last meeting with Villard. As far as Pennington knew, the attack on her had been only verbal, but even that was enough to ignite her brother-in-law's fury. More than a week had passed since the incident, yet Pennington seemed as angry now as when he had first heard about it. His eyes were fixed on Villard, who had entered the ballroom and was speaking with William Hamilton.

"It's uncomfortably warm in here, don't you think?" Alexandra asked, drawing Pennington's attention back to her.

A moment went by, then he sighed, offered her his arm, and steered her to a door which opened onto a lofty, white-pillared portico. They descended a flight of stairs into the formal garden and strolled among Hamilton's extraordinary collection of native plants and shrubs. Her thoughts adrift, Alexandra was hardly aware of Pennington beside her until he spoke.

"Forgive me for saying so, but I can't help feeling relieved about your break with Charles."

"You're forgiven," was all she said.

He gave her a sidelong glance. "You seem to be a hundred miles away," he said, smiling and frowning at once. "With someone in New York, perhaps?"

For a time the crickets filled the pause, then Alexandra revealed in a quiet voice, "I promised Dalton I would wait for him."

Pennington didn't bat an eye. "Are you lamenting your decision?"

"No," she said. "Only that I took so long to reach it." She was relieved to be able to speak freely and know that, no matter what she said, Pennington would not pass judgment or be anything less than a compassionate listener. She told him, "I pray every moment for his survival. Last night I scarcely slept for worrying about him. You may think the worse of me for this, but when Hamilton was toasting a British victory, all I could think was that Dalton would be safe at home if it wasn't for the King's stubbornness. I cannot believe he has allowed war to result from a stupid threepence on tea."

Pennington pursed his lips, absorbing her remarks. "To be sure," he said, "the Colonies expressed legitimate grievances that were foolishly ignored. But for every mistake of Parliament, the warm blades here have delighted in redoubling the insanity. This craving for independence is like a drug in their blood."

"It wasn't always so," Alexandra replied. "The rebellion might have cooled if England had negotiated instead of inflaming matters. My God, George. The King ordered his soldiers to burn our towns and hired foreigners to shed American blood. What does he expect to result from such actions?"

"Obedience to his laws."

"If you ask me, the Crown has its trade interests more at heart than our continuance as British subjects."

Sighing, Pennington glanced overhead at glittering featherstrokes of stars against the black sky. "Whatever the Crown's motives may be," he said, "the fact remains we are at war. The rebels are hopelessly outnumbered, and I expect they will learn a harsh lesson before long. But know this, Alexandra. I will add my prayers to yours that Mr. Philips returns home safely."

It was no small consolation he had given her. Her grip on his arm tightened. "Thank you, George."

Having come full circle to the house, they ascended the stairs to the broad portico outside the ballroom. From within came the strains of a lively gigue, accompanied by the shuffling of many feet, and when a footman opened the door for them, a score of whirling, brightly colored dancers was revealed.

Without wanting to, Alexandra found herself searching the ballroom for Villard. She spotted him among the couples on the dance floor. To her relief, he seemed completely intrigued by his young partner, the witty and beautiful Rebecca Franks, whose family wealth and prosperity had been derived from the favor of the Crown. A rigid Tory, Miss Franks was an advocate of law, order, and property, and was noted for her verbal abuse of rebel leaders. At the moment she appeared to have Villard in a trance, which suited Alexandra no end, for it spared her another dose of his contemptuous attention.

Noting the direction of her gaze, Pennington said, "We needn't stay any longer."

"It's still early," she replied, resolved not to run. "Anyway, it would be rude to leave without even a pretense at socializing."

"In that case, you had best prepare yourself for an ordeal, because Mr. Lindsay is headed our way." As Stephen Lindsay approached them, a glass dangling from his fingers, his wig askew, Pennington shook his head and grimaced. "By God, he defies the order of nature."

"Be civil, George."

"Must I?"

Lindsay arrived, reeking of rum, and bent over Alexandra's hand. "Greetings, sweet Alexandra. You've been hiding from me, you naughty woman." Straightening, he considered Pennington with vacant, bloodshot eyes. "Hello. I didn't see you there."

"Hardly surprising. How are you, Stephen?"

"Drunk, but otherwise splendid. Best punch in the world here." As if to prove it, Lindsay drained his glass and smothered a belch. "Debilitating, but tha's to be expected. I want you to know, Alexandra, I don't believe a word against you. Charles is jealous, tha's all. Pay him no mind."

Alexandra exchanged glances with Pennington. "Stephen, what are you talking about?"

"What? Why, your affair with that dirty rebel farmer, of course. You chose the wrong man to cuckold, sweet girl." Lindsay wagged his index finger at her. "But, as I said, I don't believe a word of it."

Just then a footman went by with a beverage tray. Quick as a snake, Lindsay's hand shot out and sequestered a fresh drink. Before he could raise it to his lips, Pennington gripped his arm and deftly confiscated the glass. "Hey!" Lindsay protested, then became aware of Pennington's blazing eyes. "No need to get upset, old man," he soothed. "This's a victory celeb—" he hiccuped "—celebration."

"It will be your funeral wake if you don't explain yourself. What poppycock have you heard about Alexandra?"

Lindsay stiffened with drunken dignity. "I'll not be a party to vicious rumors."

"It's too late for that, you twit. Speak up!"

"George." Alexandra laid a restraining hand on his arm, for several curious heads had turned to stare at them. Whispers were being exchanged, and she had the sudden humiliating sensation that she and Pennington were not the first people in the room to hear Lindsay's gossip.

Lindsay had stepped back a pace and his red-rimmed eyes were contemplating Pennington, who said to him, "If you were in any manner sober, I would thrash you to a pulp. Our discussion is not finished, Stephen. Rest assured you will see me on the morrow."

Lindsay stared at him a moment, utterly perplexed, then signaled to a tray-bearing footman and staggered away.

White-lipped with anger, Pennington told Alexandra to fetch her shawl. "We are leaving," he said in a furious undertone, then silenced her protest with, "Unless you would have me confront Charles here and now, do as I say."

Alexandra had never seen him so enraged. Being well acquainted with his impetuous temper, which had landed him in trouble on more than one occasion, she did his bidding without delay. But the idea of running away rankled her, almost as much as the speculative stares that followed her departure from the ballroom.

Minutes later, after saying goodbye to their host, Pennington ushered her into his coach and ordered his driver to return to the city. As the coach traveled the rutted road toward the Middle Ferry on the Schuylkill, Alexandra sat in silence, uncomfortably aware of Pennington's unseeing vigil out the window. Her face warmed as she recalled Lindsay's blunt statements. Annoyed at her own unsteadiness, she clenched her hands in her lap to still their shaking. She had expected Villard to stab at her reputation, but she had not imagined her nerves would fray so easily.

Tonight's trouble, she knew, marked the beginning of the vengeance he had sworn to exact. He had fertile grounds in which to cultivate his mischief, for her relationship with Dalton was bound to cause a shockwave among her peers. Let him salve his twisted pride with lies, she thought. No power on earth could diminish her feelings for Dalton. Their bond would carry her through whatever trials lay ahead.

Still, she had difficulty convincing Pennington to put his anger aside. "Whatever Charles says or does," she insisted, "I want you to ignore him, as I intend to do."

Pennington said nothing.

"George, you must. For my sake."

It was precisely for her sake that Pennington was so disturbed. To hear her maligned by a drunkard like Lindsay was intolerable. To let the worm behind the insult go unpunished was unimaginable. Alexandra, the daughter Pennington had never fathered, the widow of his beloved younger brother, had become the focus and joy of his life. Defending her was as instinctive to him as breathing.

He reached for her hand and pressed it between his own. "You are my family," he said. "Whoever strikes at you also

211

strikes at me. Charles will either eat his remarks, or by God I will squash him.''

As Pennington expected, she argued with him, pleaded with him, and finally railed at him. He stood firm. When they arrived at her town house and she refused to leave his coach, he lied to her. "I will sleep on the matter and reconsider my feelings in the morning.''

Alexandra watched him a long moment, doubt flickering in the clear depths of her eyes. "Promise me that you won't do anything rash.''

He nodded. "On my word.''

"Good," she said. "Now perhaps I will be able to sleep.''

After she went inside, Pennington despised himself for deceiving her, then thrust away his guilt and ordered his driver to return to Woodlands. Along the way he reflected on Lindsay's drunken innuendos and the pain in Alexandra's eyes when she had heard them. His outrage festered, his resolve sharpened to a hot, keen edge ready to cut down the man responsible for her distress.

At Woodlands, Pennington scanned the conveyances lining the drive and smiled with grim satisfaction when he spotted a large black coach bearing the Villard coat of arms on its door. Inside the mansion, he found the backbiter smoking a pipe and drinking rum punch in the library. Villard was not alone in the room. With him were Joseph Galloway, the former Speaker of the Assembly, and Enoch Story, both acquaintances of Pennington, both witnesses to the conversation that followed his arrival.

Pennington crossed the room and confronted his quarry. "What lies have you been spreading about Alexandra?''

"Lies?" Villard frowned, shrugged. "I don't know what you mean, George.''

"Shall I fetch Stephen Lindsay to refresh your memory?''

With calm deliberation, Villard drew on his long-stemmed clay pipe and exhaled a thin stream of smoke at the ceiling. He appeared unconcerned about having an audience of thoroughly interested men. If anything, Pennington noted, he seemed to be playing to them.

"Whatever Stephen has heard from me has been accurate," Villard said. "The fact is, while Alexandra was

212

engaged to me, she conducted a sordid affair with a criminal."

"Balderdash!" Pennington exploded.

Another shrug, the hint of a smile. "I'm afraid it's true," Villard said. "I should know. I found them together in Willowbrook's stable, in a position I shall not lower myself to describe for you. Suffice it to say that animals mate with more dignity."

Pennington was struck speechless. As his face darkened and hardened with rage, Villard went on in the same smooth voice, "So you see, George, if anyone is the injured party, you are looking at him. Alexandra used me as her cloak of respectability."

Pennington's glittering eyes raked him. "Respectability," he sneered. "What pathetic delusions you do have of yourself."

"Be careful, George."

Pennington's knobby-knuckled fingers were clenched into fists at his sides, his Adam's apple bobbing in his creased throat. "If you think I came back here to tread lightly, you're mistaken. For I fully intend to shut your lying mouth once and for all."

Villard considered him with eyes half-closed in pipe smoke. Then, as if disinterested, he sipped punch from his glass. "I have no quarrel with you," he said at last.

Seizing the glass from him, Pennington dashed its contents into Villard's surprised face. He was rewarded with a sputtered curse as the lemon-rum mixture stung Villard's eyes and streaked his carefully applied face powder.

"Now you do," Pennington said.

Chapter Thirty-One

Standing at the kitchen hearth, Mary Brock dipped a long wooden spoon into a bell skillet and scooped out a sampling of green turtle soup. The spoon was halfway to her mouth when the kitchen door burst open and Clue strode into the room.

"Good Lord!" Mary cried, a hand to her throat. "Do you have to scare a body to death?" A hissing sound made her look down to see her wooden spoon lying among hot coals. Dismayed, she bent down and rescued it. "You rascal. Look what you made me do." Then noting Clue's anxious expression, she forgot her annoyance.

"Where's Mrs. Pennington?" he asked.

"In the parlor." Mary pointed needlessly, for Clue was already gone. He sailed through the downstairs passageway to the parlor, startled Alexandra as much as he had Mary, then remembered to remove his hat in a lady's presence. He had run all the way from the High Street Market with his news. But now, as he stood before Alexandra and caught his breath, Clue was momentarily tongue-tied as he groped for words to soften the blow. Finally he blurted, "Mr. Pennington challenged Mr. Villard to a duel."

Stunned, Alexandra set aside the pillowcase she was mending. "Oh, my God," she said, hoping she had heard wrong or that Clue was mistaken. "Are you sure?"

He nodded. "I ran into Sammy Finn at the Market. The little skunk's telling everyone about it. He says they had an argument last night at Woodlands, and Mr. Pennington threw a drink in Mr. Villard's face and called him a coward. Now they're going to fight a duel." Clue gave a small, helpless shrug. "I doubt Sammy would be spreading the story around if there wasn't some truth to it."

So did Alexandra. A vision of George Pennington's wrathful face rose in her mind. He had broken his word to her. With shock, she realized he had never meant to keep it. But even worse than deceiving her, he now intended to risk his life to defend her reputation.

The devil he would.

Alexandra stood up. "Saddle my horse," she told Clue, then hurried upstairs and changed from her morning gown into a riding habit.

When she arrived at the small barn behind her town house, Clue had saddled her dappled-gray mare as well as his own horse. He led the mare to the mounting block and held her bridle while Alexandra climbed onto the sidesaddle. Without asking if she wanted an escort, he swung himself onto Sunshine's back and gathered the reins.

"Where to?"

"Oakwood," she said. "And possibly Sweet Briar."

Recalling his last encounter with Charles Villard, Clue felt a shiver of apprehension, braced himself, and followed Alexandra at a canter to George Pennington's house on Cedar Street.

While Clue waited in the busy kitchen and worried over the prospect of visiting Sweet Briar, Alexandra met with Pennington in the library. She found him absorbed in the novel *Tom Jones*. He seemed not to have a care in the world, his feet propped on a gout stool, a cup of tea at his elbow. Bright sunlight, streaming through a window, turned his powdered wig a glowing silvery-white. As he glanced up at her, his welcoming smile was so sedate that Alexandra wondered if Clue had been deliberately misled by Villard's servant.

"I've just heard a frightening rumor," she began, and when Pennington merely nodded, his unwavering eyes regarding her with purpose, she knew it was no rumor at all. Sinking into a chair, she stared at him in anguish. "George, how could you?"

Pennington closed his book and put it aside. "A more appropriate question would be: How could I not?"

215

"You could have ignored him as I asked!"

"There are some things which cannot be ignored."

"I don't care what Charles says about me—"

"I care!" Pennington snapped with sudden vehemence, then her stricken look pierced him and made him regret his sharp tone. His voice softened, vibrating with that particular warmth he reserved for her. "You mean the world to me, Alexandra. I would sooner perish than see you disgraced, which will surely happen if he continues to spread his vulgar lies."

Villard's lies, whatever they were, mattered little to her at the moment. Her concern was for Pennington. Intuition told her that an appeal to his emotions was useless, so she tried a practical approach. "Charles is only shaming himself with his talk."

Pennington grunted and looked unimpressed.

"If you really want to punish him, pay him no mind. That will cause him more agony than you can imagine."

"I doubt it."

"Don't you understand?" she implored, leaning forward, her fingers clenching the padded chair arms. "This is exactly what he wants—a public conflict, the attention of every scandalmonger in the city drawn to his petty arena. Deprive him of his show and this whole ugly mess will blow over. America and England are at war, for God's sake. With that to think about, what sensible person will give a damn about one man's injured vanity?"

"*This* person," said Pennington, jabbing a finger at his chest. "It's a matter of honor, yours and mine."

Infuriated by his stubbornness, Alexandra came to her feet. "Am I to feel honored if he blows a hole through your lunatic head?" she cried.

Pennington straightened, squaring his shoulders, and a hard gleam came into his eyes. "My dear girl, I happen to be an accomplished shooter. That is not a boast, but a fact. In the French war, I faced scalphunters and French barbarians in the wilderness, and I am still here to talk about it. God willing, it will be Charles and not I who is carried from the field."

Alexandra was struck silent by his forceful tone. Before her was a stranger, cold-eyed and utterly fearless. In his youth, she imagined, a provoked George Pennington had

216

been a formidable adversary. But age had slowed his reflexes, weakened his eyesight and, in Alexandra's estimation, robbed him to some degree of his common sense. Deep down he was a kind and dreamy old man, her beloved friend whose loyalty was an anchor. He had challenged a man less than half his age, a man whose skill with a pistol was considerable and whose cold-heartedness was purebred. Given the chance, Charles Villard would fell Pennington without a second thought.

As hot tears sprang to her eyes, Pennington's face blurred before her into a pale oval. It was hard for her to talk through her emotion. "The greatest injury Charles can inflict on me is to harm you."

"Don't underestimate him."

"George, I beg you," she said. "Call off the duel."

He searched her face with disturbingly calm eyes, then his gnarled hands reached for hers and held them tightly. "You rejected him with more kindness than he deserved," he said. "In return he has behaved in a cowardly, despicable manner, and by all that is sacred I shall make him answer for it. How fortunate he is that Mr. Philips is off to war, or else I would surely be spared the nuisance of having to kill him."

Alexandra lowered her head in despair.

"Tears will avail little," Pennington said gently. "I am committed. Whatever happens, you must never take the burden of my actions onto yourself, because the choice is mine and mine alone."

"I will stop this madness," she vowed, wiping dampness from her cheeks.

"There's nothing you can do."

Alexandra believed otherwise. And so, leaving Pennington to his novel and his stubborn resentment, she left Oakwood and rode along Cedar Street with Clue beside her. Every now and then, Clue glanced sidelong at her stony profile. From her silence and her reddened eyes, he knew things had gone badly with Mr. Pennington. Just how badly became apparent when, upon reaching the juncture of Fourth and Cedar Streets, she turned her mare south instead of north. They were going to Sweet Briar. Clue swallowed a protest and tried to mask his fear.

Unknown to him, Alexandra was equally apprehensive

about seeing Villard. She wondered what sort of reception to expect at Sweet Briar, what Villard would say to her if he deigned to speak with her at all. With a sigh, she looked over at Clue's grim face. "I couldn't talk any sense into George."

"So I gathered. I hate to say this, but you'll probably have worse luck with Mr. Villard. Knowing him, he'll stand behind his lies."

Her interest snared, Alexandra asked, "What has he been saying about me?"

Clue's face reddened instantly.

"Christopher, tell me. I need to know."

After a long pause, he did. "According to Mr. Villard, he's the one who broke off your engagement, on account of he caught you in Willowbrook's stable with Dalton."

Something burned in Alexandra's chest. "Caught me doing what?" she asked in a tight voice.

"You know, ma'am," Clue replied, his averted eyes and embarrassed shrug painting the picture more vividly than words could have.

Alexandra's anxiety about facing Villard was wiped away by a surge of anger. She was still seething when they guided their horses onto Sweet Briar's dusty lane and rode between rows of trimmed boxwoods toward the brick mansion.

Sammy Finn was exercising a sweat-lathered colt on the south lawn when he caught sight of them. Wheeling the colt toward the drive, he hurried over and cut them off. "What do you want here?" he asked Alexandra.

From his insulting manner, she deduced two things: Villard had anticipated her visit, and he had authorized Sammy to confront her. Puffed up with self-importance, Sammy eyed her defiantly.

"I came to see Mr. Villard," she said.

"Well, he doesn't want to see you."

Alexandra gauged Sammy a moment while the colt danced beneath him and his quick, experienced hands worked the reins, holding the frisky young animal in check. "Believe me," she told him, "I would sooner meet with the devil than your master. But I will see him. Where is he?"

His look hardening, Sammy tried to stare her down, but

her eyes refused to slant away and her contemptuous regard soon became more than he could bear.

The sudden, sharp *crack* of a pistol shot rent the still afternoon. The report came from somewhere behind the brick stable, and as its echo died away, Alexandra had a disturbing vision of Villard holding a sleek, smoking weapon, practicing his aim so that he could put a bullet in George Pennington.

"Never mind, Sammy," she said, urging her mare forward. "I'll find him myself."

Clue's heart bounced like a skipping stone as she started toward the stable. Overtaking her, he said in a low, urgent voice, "Mrs. Pennington, he has a *gun.*"

"Stay here."

"But what if—?"

"Mr. Villard is many things, but he is not stupid. He cannot murder me now and hope to get away with it. So please do as I say. And keep Sammy from following me."

She left Clue behind, rounded the stable, and saw Villard on the sloping, tree-dotted meadow beyond the building. Pistol in hand, he stood with his back to her, his figure silhouetted against rippling tan grass. A layer of heated air wavered above the meadow, blurring his outline and turning the far fields and patches of forest to a golden-green shimmer. The vista was peaceful, absorbing, but Alexandra's concentration was focused on the man with the weapon.

Dismounting, she tied her horse to the paddock fence and approached Villard on foot, her skirts rustling through sun-parched grass as she went. As she drew near to him, Villard suddenly turned and flinched in surprise when he saw her. In the unguarded moment when their eyes met, Alexandra glimpsed the vulnerable soul of a man riddled with insecurities. An unscrupulous man who had been taught to value status and money above human worth, including his own worth.

Then the moment passed. Villard firmed himself, and his eyes went slate cold as they swept her. He said, "I should have known better than to expect my servants to keep you at bay."

"Rest assured, Sammy was sufficiently rude."

"But obviously no match for your charms, otherwise

he'd have thrown you out in the road as I ordered him to."

"I came to talk to you about George."

"Do tell."

"I want you to call off the duel."

At that, Villard tipped his head back and laughed at the cloudless blue sky. It was several moments before he composed himself and looked at her again, and though his smile remained, his eyes were rock-hard. "Beg," he said, "on your knees. Then I might consider it."

Stung, Alexandra curled her fingers into her skirt to hide their unsteadiness from him. "If I were you," she said, "I wouldn't be so sure of walking away from a duel with George."

Villard cocked his head and looked scornful. Instead of replying, he knelt on the grass, opened a wooden cartouche box, and removed a paper-wrapped cartridge containing a measured powder charge and a lead bullet. As Alexandra watched, he loaded the pistol with swift, economical movements. First he bit off the cartridge end and poured the charge into the muzzle. Next he removed the ramrod and pushed the ball down the brass barrel until it was seated atop the powder. The wadded brown cartridge paper followed the bullet. Opening the flash-pan, Villard half-cocked the pistol, then primed the pan with fine powder from a shiny brass flask. Lastly he snapped the pan cover shut, tilted the pistol to the left, and tapped it lightly to ensure that a few grains of powder had entered the touchhole. All of this took less than a minute.

He was ready to fire. Staring at her, he thumbed the hammer to full-cock and Alexandra's blood froze in the hot day when she saw how pale his eyes were. But he merely gestured with the pistol at a stout maple tree about twenty yards away. Pinned to its broad trunk was a small square of paper.

In an amused voice, Villard said, "Watch and learn something, sweetheart."

Facing away from the tree, he took several deep breaths and shrugged his shoulders to loosen them. The pistol hung at his right side like an extension of his arm. As his handsome face relaxed, his eyes seemed to focus inward. Suddenly they sharpened to gray stones; his nostrils flared.

Pivoting a quarter turn, he presented his right side to the tree and his straight arm came up in the same fluid motion. With a loud *crack* the pistol bucked in his grip, gushing smoke and flame, and the acrid stench of burnt powder assailed Alexandra's senses.

Through a drifting white haze, she watched Villard walk to the tree and retrieve the paper. He was smiling as he brought it back and held it out to her. Dead center was a black, jagged-edged bullet hole.

"You may keep it as a souvenir," he said.

Alexandra swatted the paper from his hand. "You bastard! Why couldn't you leave him out of this?"

"Sweetheart, you're forgetting something. George challenged me."

"Because you provoked him with lies. For God's sake, Charles, let him be. He's an old man."

"Well," Villard shrugged, "I hope he's had a full life."

"If you hurt him, I swear—"

"Oh, spare me," he scorned. "You're no match for me, Alexandra. I've only struck a spark and you're all to pieces. How will you cope when the action becomes truly warm?"

Alexandra had to struggle for control. When she spoke again, her voice quivered with intensity. "I had hoped to appeal to your sense of fairness, or perhaps your compassion. But you possess neither." The contempt in her glittering eyes was magnificent. "I will pray for your miserable soul, Charles Villard, for you are surely going to hell." She turned and started away.

"One moment, Alexandra," he called after her. His quizzical voice made her pause and look back at him. "Do you plan to continue your affair with that farmer?"

"That's none of your concern."

"But I can't help feeling curious."

"I plan to marry him."

There was a pause. Villard studied a bare spot on the ground, then his eyes came back to hers. "If he survives the war, don't you mean? If he doesn't get blown apart by a cannon ball or hanged as a traitor." Villard seemed hopeful. He smiled and went on, "I understand he's a lieutenant in Mr. Washington's army of misfits. That's too bad, really, because when the rebels are defeated, their

221

officers will bear the brunt of the punishment. At the very least his property will be confiscated, and you'll be left with a worthless wretch on your hands." Sensing her dismay, his smile deepened. "I see the thought distresses you."

"Not nearly so much as the thought of spending one more instant with you."

She left him standing there with the pistol clenched in his sweat-slick hand and the small square of target paper fluttering on the grass at his feet. Rooted, Villard watched her return to her dappled mare. Against his will he found himself admiring her straight, proud figure, the graceful way she climbed onto the sidesaddle without the aid of a mounting block. She held herself as regally as a queen, marvelously confident, exquisitely beautiful. He waited, expectant, but she refused to look in his direction as she wheeled her horse around and disappeared from view.

His shoulders sagged. A ragged sigh escaped him. Despite all she had done to him, despite the humiliation and the pain she had heaped on him, it was not as easy letting go as he had imagined it would be. He missed her companionship, her quick wit, her unlimited capacity for tenderness. He detested the idea of her marrying another man. A nobody at that.

"Damn your eyes," he whispered, despising his weakness. Before he finished with her, she would understand how it felt to have her dreams shattered and her heart torn to shreds. Someday, somehow, he would teach her the true meaning of grief. Because if the war didn't kill Dalton Philips, he would.

Chapter Thirty-Two

For weeks the Patriot army had been hungry for a fight. For weeks they had ground their teeth and watched while the white sails of British men-of-war thronged lower New York Bay and Staten Island became an anthill swarming with redcoats. They had watched with a kind of fearful excitement when, under the cover of British warships, the Howes ferried twenty thousand troops across the Narrows to Long Island and began a slow, calculated march toward the American front on Brooklyn Heights. By the evening of August twenty-sixth, the British occupied the village of Flatbush below the woody heights, just a mile from the American lines.

The fearsome Bloodybacks had come to kick America's tail between her legs, and as Washington told his troops on the eve of the long-awaited battle:

> "The time is now near at hand which must probably determine whether Americans are to be freemen or slaves; whether they are to have any property they can call their own; whether their houses and farms are to be pillaged and destroyed, and themselves consigned to a state of wretchedness from which no human efforts will deliver them. The fate of unborn millions will now depend, under God, on the courage and conduct of this army. Our cruel and unrelenting enemy leaves us only the choice of brave resistance, or the most abject submission. We have, therefore, to resolve to conquer or die."

Daybreak of August twenty-seventh found Dalton crouched on a soggy field on the western edge of Long Island. Drums beat in the close, misty air. Enemy drums. Squinting into the white-veiled distance, he scanned the coastal road for movement, a glimpse of red, something to tell him how near the Lobsters were. He saw only the vague, dark shapes of stunted trees and marsh grass skirting the road. But the British were coming, and they were making a flourishing racket. The martial cadence of sticks on tightened skins vibrated the dawn. The rhythmic tread of thousands of boots was a pulse Dalton could feel with his heart.

He touched the smooth blue ribbon tied to his waistcoat. The satin was limp in the moist morning and soiled from the last night's sweaty work of strengthening the earthen fortifications at Brooklyn. Those protective redoubts were now far to the rear of Colonel Atlee's Pennsylvania battalion, Dalton's comrades-in-arms for the past two weeks. Assigned to the honorable rank of infantry lieutenant, he had given up his dream of a cavalry posting, for the disorganized American Army had no such force, nor did it seem in a hurry to form one. He had left Mercury across the river at New York, under guard with the army's remounts. It was just as well, he supposed, as horses would be next to useless on this boggy, pitted field where Colonel Atlee had deployed his troops.

A detachment of Lord Stirling's division, Atlee's battalion of musketeers had been on the move since midnight, and was presently formed for action beside the shore road leading to the Narrows. Advancing along the road from the south were two British infantry brigades, a Royal Highland Regiment and two companies of provincials. They were on a collision course with the American right wing under General Stirling, and the Pennsylvania battalion had the honor of being first to engage them.

As the sun crested the woody heights and the mist burned thin, the enemy became visible—first a blurred column of pink, then brightening to murky red and finally brilliant scarlet. A wall of scarlet, formed in line of battle opposite the Pennsylvanians.

Again Dalton's hand strayed to his ribbon. Lately he had come to think of it as his talisman against mortal

224

wounds. Now, awed by the spectacle of five thousand British regulars—a mere fraction of Sir William Howe's total force—Dalton knew he would need every fiber of the ribbon's luck to preserve him.

The bastards bleed, he told himself, same as me. Those red coats ain't armor.

But the British had the advantage of sheer numbers. And they had superb targets to shoot at this morning, for the Pennsylvanians were exposed on a swampy field at the foot of a fine rising ground. Colonel Atlee's orders were to oppose the enemy's passing the morass, thereby allowing time for General Stirling to form his brigade on the heights at the battalion's rear. It sounded simple enough, but without any kind of cover, the battalion could not hope to sustain fire for long.

Dragging his gaze from the imposing sight straight ahead, Dalton glanced down the line of perspiring faces to his right. Immediately beside him was a massive, bristly faced man named Forbes, who hailed from the west country. A bear-biter, Twigs would call him. Beneath Forbes's ragged fingernails was a garden of dirt. His deerskin hunting shirt and leggings were so thick with grease and black with campfire soot, they appeared to be made of metal, like the clothes of a statue. Forbes was typical of many men in the American Army, but he was by no means a standard, for the ranks were comprised of every discription and character of soldier. Some companies were in uniform, others wore civilian clothes. There were farmers in homespun and dandies in frock coats and white linen; there were tradesmen and shopkeepers who had left their families and businesses behind; there were convicts hoping for bounties and servants sent to fulfill their masters' patriotic obligations. They were the most disheveled, motley crew of men ever assembled. Untrained, undisciplined, ill-equipped, they were a mongrel fighting force, arrayed against the finest soldiers in the world.

The total American force on Long Island was eight thousand troops, mostly raw militia. Roughly half of them manned the defense works at Brooklyn. The remainder, including Atlee's Pennsylvanians, formed the outer defense perimeter along the heights. For reasons

Dalton could not comprehend, the main body of Washington's army was across the East River, guarding the city of New York.

Towns! Why in God's name was the General so obsessed with the idea of defending towns? They were just dots on a map, a waste of time, energy, and money, not to mention manpower. Surely Washington realized the danger of what he had done. A divided army was twice as vulnerable, twice as difficult to command. Not only were the Americans split in half, but a virtually undefended river, deep and a half-mile wide, lay between them. That river might as well have been an ocean.

Dalton chewed his lower lip and assessed the situation dead ahead. While the fog had been lifting, the British commander had positioned artillery on the elevated ground to the left of the road. The gaping muzzles of those cannon now commanded the field that Colonel Atlee's battalion had been ordered to occupy and defend.

Bloody hell, Dalton thought. Stirling's made us food for lions.

From the enemy ranks, a deep, burred voice roared a command. "'Tallion . . . fooorward!" A broadsword flashed in the sun, and five hundred red-clad infantrymen advanced as one entity toward the rebel lines. Above the rattle of drums and the steady tread of boots, Dalton could hear officers' spurs jingling, the creak of leather stirrup straps, the rasping ring of steel as swords were drawn from fine, silver-tipped scabbards.

"'Tallion . . . halt!" The Bloodybacks were now within a hundred yards of the Pennsylvanians. "Companeeees! Skirmish order!" Five companies of the elite Royal Highland Regiment—whose privilege it was to teach the rebels a well-deserved lesson in warfare—paced forward several strides and spread into staggered ranks, three rows deep. Fringed plaids and the black plumes of Scottish bonnets stirred in a light breeze.

"Companeeees! Fix bayonets!" Steel hissed, then came a symphony of clanking metal as sockets were slotted over musket muzzles and twisted into place. Sunlight glinted on a forest of sharpened bayonets.

In the Pennsylvania lines, a frantic energy charged the air, a fear so thick and ripe Dalton could smell it. As he unsheathed his saber, someone knelt beside him and touched his shoulder. He looked into Col. Samuel Atlee's narrow, hawklike face and obsidian eyes. Eyes that could be warm one moment, hard as flint the next. Dalton had been with the colonel's command only fourteen days, replacing a first lieutenant who was sick with dysentery, and in that short time he had been inspired by Atlee's confidence in his green Pennsylvania troops.

Now the Colonel's voice was quiet, his words meant for Dalton's ears alone. "Captain Marshall hasn't returned yet. That means this company is in your hands, Lieutenant."

"Yes, sir."

"Remember, most of these boys have never faced an enemy. They'll be looking to us to see how it's done, so let's give them a worthy show."

"Depend on it, sir."

Atlee smiled and clapped Dalton's shoulder, then peered hard at the Royal Highlanders. "There's something disconcerting," he said, "about soldiers wearing skirts and bonnets."

Before Dalton could reply, the morning erupted with the distant thundering of cannon. Every head turned toward the sound, which came from the direction of Flatbush village.

Atlee's mouth compressed in a grim line. "That will be the Hessians," he said, "saying good morning to Colonel Hand."

The American center under Colonel Hand occupied the strategic Heights of Brooklyn above Flatbush. The woods below the heights were thick with American sharpshooters, eager to test their skills on the enemy.

Colonel Atlee held up a hand and his booming command carried to every man of the battalion. "Listen, boys!" They did and heard the staccato pops of rifles interspersed with air-shuddering cannonfire. "Do you hear that?" Atlee yelled. "That's your brothers! Telling those hairy German rapists what we think of them! NOW LET'S GIVE THESE SCOTTISH BASTARDS SOME OF THE SAME!"

From hundreds of throats, a wild cheer burst forth and sent a tingle racing along Dalton's spine. Colonel Atlee continued down the line to offer encouragement to the next company, but Dalton barely noticed him leaving. He raised his saber high in the air. His voice rose in a tense command. "Steady, now. Make each bullet count." His eyes were fixed on the advancing companies of red-coated Highlanders, with their plaid skirts, plumed bonnets, and steel-tipped muskets. Dear God, he prayed, don't let me disgrace myself today.

"Front line!" he shouted. "Ready and aim. Pick off the King's pretty birds."

On the facing hillock, where British artillerymen were scrambling around field pieces, three puffs of smoke blossomed simultaneously and a heavy concussion pounded the air. Moments later, three clumsy iron balls zoomed overhead and bounced harmlessly on the field behind the Pennsylvania lines. The British gunners were finding their range.

Over to the east, at the American center, the big guns continued to crash as Colonel Hand's artillery answered the Hessian bombardment of the heights. Smoke from their firing drifted down from the woody hills. On the soggy lowlands, the Highlanders came on toward the Pennsylvanians. Now Dalton could see faces beneath Scottish bonnets, fixed eyes and grim mouths and clammy hands gripping muskets. He looked down the line at Colonel Atlee, waiting for his signal. Another staccato *boom-boom* rent the air; round shot screamed overhead.

Dalton saw the signal and yelled, "FIRE!"

One hundred muskets cracked in unison, sending a hail of lead into the enemy lines. Two officers and dozens of soldiers crumpled to the ground, but the rest continued to advance without breaking stride.

"Second line, forward!" Dalton yelled. "First line, reload. Do it quick!"

Another cannon blast roared from the hillock. Pieces of roundshot whistled past Dalton's head and plowed into the field beyond him. Sheathing his sword, he lifted his musket to his shoulder and sighted a redcoat down the barrel. "Take aim!"

The front row of Highlanders suddenly knelt and leveled their guns at the Americans.

"Fire!" Dalton screamed and squeezed the trigger. His

gun bucked. A bullet plucked at his sleeve as acrid smoke billowed into his face and scraps of ignited powder scorched his cheek. Waving the smoke away, he saw gaps in the enemy's front line, saw red bodies twitching on the grass and sucked in an astonished breath. Jesus God, they were giving it to them!

"Third line!" he shouted. "Get your asses forward and aim! Second line, reload! *Do it quick!*"

Just then, from the corner of his vision, he glimpsed movement that shattered his concentration. His head snapped to the left. His mouth slackened as he saw a large body of the enemy filing toward the woods that bordered the wide, marshy field. Within minutes, if left unchecked, the Bloodybacks would complete their flanking maneuver, and the Pennsylvania battalion would be caught in a deadly crossfire of cannonfire and musket balls.

But Colonel Atlee was not to be outsmarted. His orders sped down the line—battalion to file left into the woods and engage the flankers. They had accomplished their original task, for Stirling's brigade was now formed on the high ground behind them, and his artillery was giving the Lobsters a warm reception.

With cannon blasting from behind and in front, Dalton moved his company out. He urged them along at a swift trot, praising their bravery, giving orders to reload on the fly. Forbes, the leatherback giant, lumbered along beside him. "Jeezus Christ Amighty," he crowed, flashing Dalton a gray-toothed grin. "If that thar's the British Army, we got this thing licked afore it's started."

Forbes's lethargic stride and boastful tone stung Dalton like a slap in the face. The most dangerous thing the Americans could do, he believed, was take the enemy for granted. "They're trained soldiers," he reminded Forbes, "and they ain't afraid of dying."

"Right y'are, Lieutenant," Forbes agreed. "But they never tangled with the likes o' me. First 'un I git my hands on, I'm gonna rip his goddamn cock-sack out through his nose and feed it to him."

A cannon blazed, grapeshot sang over the field, and Forbes jerked as small iron balls ripped through his throat and smashed into his jaw. His massive body shielded Dalton, who felt warmth splatter his cheek. When Dalton looked over at the crimson pulp of splintered bone, teeth fragments, and stringy gobbets of flesh that had once been a face, his stomach convulsed.

Incredibly, Forbes continued to walk as blood spouted from his neck and coated his greasy shirt front a bright red. Dalton caught his arm, halting his momentum, and the big man toppled like a felled tree. His body gave one huge, terrible spasm, red froth bubbling from his ruined nose, then relaxed in death.

Several men of Dalton's company stopped and stared with stricken expressions at the bloody apparition on the ground. Their horror brought Dalton around.

"*Move!*" he shouted in their faces. "Before you end up like him!"

Startled into action, they ran on toward the treeline. Forbes was the only man lost on the swampy field that day. In the woods was another story. There, Colonel Atlee positioned his troops on the lip of a long, shallow gully to await the British flankers. No sooner was the battalion entrenched than two companies from Delaware, under a Captain Stedman, arrived on the scene. The captain carried orders for Colonel Atlee to file off farther into the woods and engage a second detachment of British that was threatening General Sitrling's left wing. Atlee gave the order to move out, and the battalion was once again in motion.

In Dalton's company, several men complained about having to leave the protective trench behind. "The colonel's going to get us all killed," one of them whined, loud enough for Dalton to hear. Drawing his saber, Dalton walked back to the loud-mouth and whacked him hard across the head with the flat of the blade.

"Quit your blubbering," he said in an undertone, "or next time I'll use the edge."

Cowed, a hand to his stinging skull, the soldier skulked off with the rest of the company, and the complaints ended. The British provided extra incentive to move quickly, for by then they occupied the swampy field at the battalion's rear, and the heavy crash of their muskets and artillery sent a storm of lead winging among the trees.

Seven men of the rear guard fell. Four died without making a sound. The other three, with hands pressed to bloody abdomens and chests, were borne moaning and screaming up through the lines.

Glancing back, Dalton saw bright scarlet tunics flitting among green foliage as British point men entered the woods. Unknown to the British, a string of American snipers was waiting for them, crouched behind trees and fern-covered hummocks. Flames suddenly stabbed in the gloom; redcoats howled in agony and clambered backward, tripping over logs and rocks. The rear guard fired another shower of hot lead at the scarlet invaders, and the enemy fled in disorder.

Atlee's battalion, reinforced by the two companies of Delawares, plunged on with renewed vigor until the colonel spied a hill of clear ground ahead and called a halt. Summoning his officers, he issued orders while cannon-balls zoomed overhead, splintering trees and showering debris on the Americans.

"We must gain control of that hill before the enemy does," Atlee said. "Lieutenant Philips, Captain Stedman, your companies will lead the advance. Wheel your men right and form abreast, then move straight to the summit. The rest of the battalion will follow at thirty yards."

The manuever was performed. Dalton, with his saber in his right hand, his musket in his left, ordered his company forward in line with Stedman's Delawares. Pouring sweat, gulping breaths of warm, smoky air, the Americans slowly ascended the grassy hillside. Twenty yards from the summit, a line of scarlet suddenly appeared on the crest above them. Scores of muskets were aimed at the rebels and a crashing volley ripped down the slope.

Most of the bullets sang overhead and tore into the trees below. It was a difficult technique to learn, the art of shooting effectively downhill, and it saved Dalton's men from slaughter. Still, several lead balls plowed into flesh. Bodies pitched backward and tumbled head over heels, leaving bloody smears on the grass. The survivors dove to the ground and lay prone, cowering in dread, for the enemy's position was formidable. The hill crest formed a natural breastwork from which the British again directed a heavy fire at the cringing Americans.

Colonel Atlee himself came to the front and ordered the advance party to retreat until they were beyond accurate

231

musket range. Crouched beside Dalton and Captain Stedman, Atlee gauged the hilltop, black eyes glittering with calculation as the guns above continued to blaze. Bullets hummed past and spit into the leaves below.

"There's at least a regiment up there," Atlee concluded. "If we don't stop them here, they'll rip General Stirling's flank to pieces."

Dalton waited, prepared to do whatever was asked of him. But Captain Stedman, his pale face streaked black with burnt powder, shifted nervously and wiped his smoke-reddened eyes.

"We'll attack," Atlee decided.

"No, sir," Captain Stedman shot back. "Not my men, Colonel. It would be suicide. My companies will withdraw and support the general as best we can."

Though senior in rank, Colonel Atlee had no say over the Delawares. He nodded, acknowledging Stedman's decision, but disgust was plain in his eyes. "Very well, Captain Stedman," he said, biting off the name. "You will be so kind as to inform Lord Stirling of my intention to secure this hill."

Stedman swallowed and offered a stiff, "Best of luck, Colonel." Then he was gone, bellowing orders to his men to retreat down the hill. The Delawares swarmed after him into the woods, grateful to escape the deadly firing from above.

"*Damn* his eyes," Atlee hissed.

"We'll do it without him, sir," Dalton said.

"That we will."

Atlee went below and rallied four companies to support Dalton's men. The reinforcements streamed up the hillside behind their brave colonel, who ordered a charge at the top of his lungs. Like veteran soldiers, the Pennsylvanians obeyed his command and surged howling and yipping toward the summit, their fearsome yells making them seem a thousand.

Withering fire blazing down on them, men stumbled and fell and vomited blood on the grass. The rest plunged on, picking their targets with care, conserving fire until a kill was assured. The ferocious charge must have looked unstoppable to the defenders of the hill, for when the Pennsylvanians exploded over the crest, they found the

232

redcoats fleeing down the opposite slope in disorder. The British left behind twelve dead and five wounded, including a lieutenant with a bullet lodged in his chest. Colonel Atlee lost his good friend and second in command, Lieutenant Colonel Parry, shot through the head.

The hill secured, Atlee quickly dispersed his men to defensive posts, and only then did he discover that Captain Stedman had drawn off a number of Pennsylvanians with his untimely retreat. The battalion was weakened, and the dull booming of enemy cannon was drawing nearer.

Dalton was forming his men on the left wing when he spied a group of soldiers stumbling up the hill from the east. Their leader, a pock-faced sergeant whose ear had been shot away, staggered the last few yards to Dalton and fell against him.

"General Sullivan's division . . . in trouble," he gasped as he was laid on the grass. "Howe outflanked him. Must've marched all night . . . took Sullivan by surprise."

"Jesus God," Dalton muttered.

"You'll be . . . surrounded if you sit here," the sergeant said between breaths. "Hessians coming right behind us."

Hessians. Monsters who hacked off the genitals of their prisoners, then watched them bleed to death. Barbarians who poked red-hot bayonet points into eyeballs and chopped off fingers and toes for fun. Such were the tales American enlisted men had been told about Hessians.

Dalton sprinted across the hilltop to Colonel Atlee and quickly related the sergeant's story. The colonel then dispatched his adjutant to request further orders from General Stirling, and the Pennsylvanians spent a nerve-racking half-hour awaiting the messenger's return. All the while the firing of artillery and muskets on their left flank grew increasingly warm.

Atlee's adjutant never returned. After a quick conference with his officers, the colonel ordered a withdrawal from the hill and the battalion set out to rejoin Stirling's brigade. The march to the heights was orderly, though the men were white-lipped and anxious and very much aware of their precarious situation. As the battalion approached Lord Stirling's position, Atlee sent Dalton ahead with a small scouting party to reconnoiter the woods.

Dalton found the heights deserted. Stunned, he crossed trampled grass that was strewn with abandoned gear and weapons and, every now and then, the mangled victim of a cannonball.

When Colonel Atlee arrived, he was equally astonished and infuriated at being left behind as an inevitable sacrifice. From the heights, using his spyglass, he had a clear view of Stirling's brigade retreating across a cornfield. The general's rear guard was being threatened by a large body of British grenadiers. A few courageous Americans had formed to oppose the pursuit, but they were hopelessly outnumbered.

Dalton did not need a telescope to show him what was unfolding on the distant field. "The general's in bad trouble," he said.

Compacting his glass, Atlee puffed up his cheeks and blew out a long breath. His eyes had a faraway look as he debated his next move—whether to save his battalion or rescue his general. Ordinarily, Atlee would not have hesitated to perform his duty. But Lord Stirling, without sending the least word of intelligence, had abandoned him.

"By God," he said, "I could almost find it in myself to shoot him for what he's done to us."

Instead, Atlee ordered the battalion to advance and attack the grenadiers. During the forced march to the cornfield, where roundshot and musket balls were flying, the troops glanced white-eyed at each other and cursed Colonel Atlee in low whispers. They cringed and instinctively ducked their heads with each booming cannon shot. But they continued to march because the Hessians were coming behind them, artillery was blazing on their right, and a brigade of British regulars commanded the shore road to their left. God alone knew what lay between them and the inner defense works at Brooklyn.

The trampled cornfield was soaking up American blood when Atlee's battalion arrived. They found a few tenacious survivors of Stirling's guard trading blows with Lieutenant Colonel Monckton's grenadiers, the cream of the British Army. At Atlee's tense command, the exhausted Pennsylvanians quickly formed behind a tree-lined fence and rested the heavy barrels of their muskets on the rails. The grenadiers were an unsettling sight in their tall, furred caps, hide-stiffened shoulder wings, and fancy white cross belts. They came charging across the cornfield behind eighteen-inch bayonets, cheering in impeccable Oxford voices.

When they were fifty yards away, Dalton cocked his musket. Sweat dripped off his chin to his chest and blood hummed in his ears as he watched Colonel Atlee, whose sword rose and pointed at the blue sky.

"Front line, take aim!" Dalton yelled above the hoarse shouts of the onrushing grenadiers. "Second line stand ready to fire! Wait for the word, boys!"

The grenadiers closed, making a heart-stopping racket, their colors streaming out in front. They were awesome to behold, fearless warriors descended from the finest English blood. They trod on mangled bodies as they ran. Bloodlust shone in their eyes and roared from their throats. But the Pennsylvania battalion held its ground, waiting, trembling, fingers curled against triggers. Twenty yards. Fifteen.

Atlee's sword flashed down.

"FIRE!"

The fence line blazed. The front row of grenadiers withered. The British flag-bearer sank to his knees and the colors fluttered to the dusty cornfield before being rescued and again borne aloft. Still cheering wildly, Monckton's blue-blooded regiment rushed on toward the fence, discharging their muskets at will.

"FIRE!" Dalton yelled, and a second volley of lead ripped into the red-coated lines and broke the furious charge. Grabbing their dead and wounded, the stunned grenadiers began to retreat.

Then, through a fog of dust and smoke, a British horseman spurred his sweating black charger to the front of the milling regiment. He was wearing the crimson and yellow coat of a high officer, with gold epaulets glistening at his shoulders, lace showing at his cuffs, and a bright silver gorget suspended around his throat. Colonel Monckton, brother of Lord Galway, leader of the most skillful and formidable soldiers in the King's service, rose in his stirrups and glared at his men. His deep, rousing, artistocrat's voice rolled across the field like ripples on a pond.

"Will the best soldiers of England give ground to these mongrel rebels?" he cried. "Will we shame our immortal and gallant King by turning back before a mob of farmers and shopkeepers? NO! On to the day!" Monckton's sword glittered above his head. "Advance on my word, lads!"

His challenging speech lashed the Americans with galvanizing force, touching off snarls and darkening faces along the Pennsylvania lines. An angry tremor shook Dalton. The gleaming silver gorget on Monckton's chest seemed to beckon him, so he fitted his musket to his shoulder and drew a careful bead on the gorget, sixty yards away. When his flint fell and his gun bucked back in billowing smoke, the whistling lead ball struck Colonel Monckton's left shoulder, pitching him backward off his warhorse.

There was a startled hush, then the Pennsylvanians cheered and shook their fists and took hopeful shots at Monckton's officers as they flocked around him. His brave speech forgotten, Monckton was carried off the field and his regiment withdrew to reconsider the gutsy band of rebels.

Colonel Atlee had his spyglass out again and was panning it over the distant fields for a sign of Stirling's rear guard. All he saw of them was the dust of their flight. The general's brigade had retreated out of sight, into what circumstance Atlee could only guess. His own situation was bleak. His battalion was weakened in manpower, fatigued from forced marches, and almost destitute of ammunition. Worse, Colonel Monckton's grenadiers, rather than mount another charge on the blood-soaked cornfield, were filing north to seal off Atlee's route to the brigade.

Lowering the glass, Atlee turned and saw Lieutenant Philips approaching at a trot. Despite his anxiety, the colonel found he could still smile. He stared into confident green eyes and said, "I would give my right arm to see that shot repeated."

"It was luck, sir," Dalton said, wiping gritty sweat from his forehead. He nodded at the grenadiers. "Anyway, you'll need all your limbs to break through them. It's that

236

or the Germans, I reckon, sir."

Glancing southward, Atlee felt a chill in the warm afternoon. Lines of blue coats were marching down from the wooded heights he had left behind. Within minutes, the Hessians would overrun the cornfield, and the Pennsylvanians would be trapped.

"Sir, with your permission," Dalton said, "my company will cover your back while you have another go at those flaming furheads."

Colonel Atlee blinked and looked away, a sudden thickness in his throat. It was a suicide proposal, yet from Lieutenant Philips's expression and tone of voice, one might think he was requesting a post of honor. Heavenly Christ above, Atlee thought. What I could do with a hundred such as he.

"Your men?" Atlee asked.

"They're with me, sir."

Somehow Atlee didn't doubt it. "Very well, Lieutenant," he said and squeezed Dalton's shoulder. "God willing, I'll see you at Brooklyn."

"Depend on it, sir."

Dalton and his company, reduced now to thirty-three men, took cover in a shallow, brush-choked ravine adjacent to the cornfield. While waiting for the Hessians, Dalton checked ammunition supplies and found that none of his men had more than three rounds left in his cartridge box. One hundred rounds to stop a regiment of blue-coated German fusiliers.

A fierce rattle of musketry signaled the beginning of Colonel Atlee's assault on the British grenadiers. Screams, howls, and curses swelled above the crashing of guns, causing a shiver of apprehension to race the length of the ravine. Blocking out the sounds, Dalton concentrated with all his being on the treeline at the field's edge. Colonel Atlee's fate against the grenadiers was out of his hands, but he could ensure that his commander was not ripped apart from behind by bloodthirsty butchers. Foreigners. Bought by King George's minions to spill American blood on American soil.

The Hessian advance party, marching forty abreast, slowly emerged from the woods and started across the cornfield. Oblivious to the guns lining the ravine to their left, the Germans moved directly into the path of fire. They were a polished-looking group, their blue coats faced with red lapels, their tall leather caps bearing fancy metal frontplates similar to the British grenadiers. But unlike the clean-shaven Englishmen, many of the Hessians wore thick, droopy mustaches which lent a sinister quality to their looks.

Leading the advance party, a strutting, mushachioed sergeant pointed with his halberd and barked orders in a gravelly voice. Though Dalton didn't understand a word of his guttural commands, it was plain the Hessians were bent on Colonel Atlee's destruction.

Exhaling a long breath, Dalton cocked the hammer of his musket, looked down the crude sights at the bushy-faced sergeant, and shouted, "Now!" Twenty muskets cracked as one and sent bullets plowing into the enemy's left flank.

Squinting through drifting smoke, Dalton whooped in excitement, for a dozen Hessians, including the spike-bearing sergeant, lay writhing in blood on the field. The remaining enemy, alarmed by the ambush and uncertain how many rebels occupied the ravine, broke ranks and began moving off to the right.

Dalton yelled, "Fire!" and thirteen more muskets spat flame and lead at the retreating Hessians. Red smears appeared on blue coats; more bodies flopped to the ground. A ragged cheer rose from the ravine as the Pennsylvanians quickly reloaded.

Across the dusty field, the blue coats were reforming, and from Dalton's viewpoint there looked to be hundreds of them. The surprise was over. The situation was hopeless and he knew it. But he called to his men, "Steady, boys. Remember what we're fighting for. This is *our* country, and those bastards got no business being here! So hold your ground!"

To his amazement, they did. Twice they turned back triple their number without losing a single man. But then their ammunition ran out, and they were reduced to bayonets, swords, and sheer guts for weapons.

Saber in hand, Dalton knelt on the lip of the ravine, his eyes darting from the field in front to the woods on his right. Blue coats were pouring from the trees onto the field, moving to surround the Pennsylvanians. To remain in the ditch would be to sacrifice his men to senseless slaughter. They had done all they could here.

"Fall back," Dalton said in a hollow voice and saw relief suffuse many faces. The withdrawal was fast-paced but orderly. With Dalton leading the way, the company waded a sandy creek, crossed a field of waist-high golden wheat, and climbed a hillock to get their bearings and form a plan of action. But once they gained the high ground and saw their predicament, the plan was decided for them.

Off to their right, a large party of grenadiers was marching to intercept them. Closing from behind was a company of German fusiliers, who would likely offer no quarter.

Motioning his men to gather around, Dalton knelt and quickly sketched a map in the dirt with his finger. "This is where we are," he said, pointing. "Here's the Bloody-backs. Here's the German fuckers, scum of the earth. And this," he tapped the spot for emphasis, "is the marshes west of us. Half a mile from here, I figure. On the other side is Brooklyn, and that's where we're going."

"Those swamps are deep in spots," said a doubtful voice. "I can't swim."

"Then those who can swim will help you across."

"We could give ourselves up to the British," someone suggested. "Better them than the Germans."

Muttered agreements followed this proposal.

Sitting back on his heels, Dalton surveyed the circle of anxious faces. "I ain't about to surrender," he said in a voice that brought instant quiet. "There's a girl waiting for me in Philadelphia, and I aim to marry her, not give myself up to be hanged." He came to his feet. "I'm for Brooklyn. Who's with me?"

Five men grounded their arms and declined to follow him. The rest, their sweat-streaked faces grim with resolve, set out after him at a swift pace.

A footrace to the swamps ensued as the British-German trap began to close around them. As firm ground gave way to sandy, boggy soil, a party of Hessians drew within musket range and began to pepper them with well-aimed shots. A screaming man arched his back, clawing helplessly at his spine where a bullet had lodged. As he fell, Dalton snagged his arm and half-dragged, half-carried him over a steep embankment rising from a small river. Bracing himself on the incline, waist-deep in swamp grass, Dalton drew his saber and motioned savagely to his panting comrades. "Bayonets!" he hissed. Blades were drawn from scabbards and quietly locked in place.

The rebels crouched in the tall grass, their eyes riveted on the crest above as rustling footsteps drew nearer and murmuring voices spoke words that none of them understood. A musket muzzle poked into view, then a dozen more with bayonets fixed and glinting. When the wounded man at Dalton's feet whimpered, the sound acted as a signal to the shaken, but determined Pennsylvanians.

Atop the bank, the Hessians froze as a blood-curdling chorus of howls split the air and a wave of wild-eyed rebels exploded over the crest. The fugitives became the attackers, stabbing steel through flesh, forking bodies aside and clubbing startled faces with heavy musket butts. The Germans fell back, firing in panic, but their aim was high and they overshot their targets. The Americans rushed on behind their tall, black-haired leader, whose saber was flashing and cutting like a surgeon's scalpel.

Dalton hammered a bayonet aside, then whipped his blade edge back across an unprotected stomach. As his opponent went down, spilling blue-tinged entrails onto the grass, a new threat snared Dalton's attention. He stilled, eyes wide with shock. Fifty yards away, a wall of blue uniforms was moving steadily toward him.

"Jesus God," he groaned, then recovered his wits and yelled, "Retreat!"

The order was unnecessary, for his men were already streaming over the bank in terror, leaving behind their dead and wounded. Leaping after them, Dalton skidded down the bank to the river and dove into its murky depths. The tide was up, the water was deep and pitch black. He stayed under as long as possible, surging and kicking toward the far shore until his lungs burned and bright points of light danced before his eyes. When he finally surfaced, gasping for breath, a musket volley roared behind him. Bullets hummed past his head like angry bees, kicking up tiny geysers of water.

Sucking lungfuls of air, Dalton went under again and

240

swam for his life. He stroked, kicked, and prayed until he ran out of strength and almost out of will. Suddenly his feet struck oozy bottom. Heedless of the German snipers at his back, he thrust his head above water and breath shot down into his cramped lungs like heavenly fire. Ahead lay a thick patch of reeds. Gasping, his legs shaking with fatigue, he dragged himself forward and clawed his way through the reeds to dry ground. Behind him, lying somewhere on the muddy riverbed, were his musket and his beautiful French saber.

Those of his men who were strong swimmers—and who survived the lead hail—made it across and came out of the river looking like pitiful water rats, their tongues hanging. Of the rest, some sank below the surface and drowned, too exhausted to stay afloat. Others were picked off like fish in a barrel as they floundered in deep water and mud. The brackish river turned red with blood.

Gathering what was left of his company, Dalton led them away from the carnage toward the rising ground of Brooklyn and the dull pounding of cannon. Before long, he saw that they weren't alone in the swamp. Small parties of stragglers—remnants of Stirling's and Sullivan's ruined brigades—were streaming into the marshes from adjacent fields and woods. Each group had been through its own horrors. They had seen their comrades surrounded and hacked to pieces without quarter. They had seen Hessians and Highlanders dispatch prisoners with bayonets and sword points. They had been powerless to save the multitudes of their countrymen who drowned and suffocated in morasses.

No one said much as the survivors banded together and slogged north toward the redoubts. They were beaten, their nerves shattered. They were fortunate to be alive and wondered how much longer that happy fact would continue. For as they staggered from the swamps and began to ascend to the plain, they were met by an unsettling sight.

The Brooklyn encampment—the last American line of defense on Long Island—was astir with frantic activity. Reinforcements had been ferried over from New York. Men were digging like gophers, throwing up fresh earthworks. Cannon were being wheeled into place.

Officers were shouting and hurrying troops to fortified posts. Less than a mile from the redoubts, a battle was raging on the Flatbush road. The road itself was choked with traffic—walking wounded, wounded on litters, artillery rolling in from the field, soldiers retreating to safety—all streaming into the American encampment.

Under a low, graying sky, the battered Pennsylvanians dragged themselves there as well. The situation was worse than any of them had dreamed. Lord Stirling and General Sullivan had both been taken prisoner, their brigades pounded to fragments. Munitions were short and the British were advancing in force.

Numbed by the news, Dalton searched in vain for Colonel Atlee, then finally reported to General Mifflin for orders. A little later, armed with new muskets and a meager supply of cartridges, Dalton and his men were huddled behind the redoubts. Waiting.

Clever Sir William Howe, whose envelopment of the Americans had worked to perfection, was expected to storm Brooklyn momentarily. If that happens, Dalton thought, we're lost. He despised himself for the thought, but the nighmarish day had demolished his faith in himself and the army. Terror and confusion were a thick stench around him. The dark stains he saw on dozens of breeches were not dirt, but the piteous result of men beshitting themselves in fear.

Fighting despair, Dalton put his head down on his knees and prayed for a miracle, for nothing less would save American liberty. Defeat was already an accomplished fact.

A raindrop struck his head. Another pelted him, then another. His head rose. He stared at the leaden sky with hope on his smoke-blackened face.

It began to pour. Large, cold drops that felt good on his hot skin, soaking his clothes and running down his chest, cleansing his grimy, upturned face. As the deluge continued and rivulets of water carved shallow trenches in the earthworks, the booming of cannon gradually lessened, then ceased. Blessed quiet descended.

In the enemy lines, the gentlemen soldiers from across the ocean squinted up at the sky, pursed their lips, and regretfully shook their heads. A good English general never fought in the rain. That would be undignified.

Orders were issued. The British lion sheathed its claws. The redcoats retired to their comfortable marquees, and the rebels who were still in the field stumbled dizzily back to their encampment, grateful for the divine intervention of rainfall.

Darkness fell. And Dalton, clutching his ribbon, curled up on the muddy ground behind the earthworks and slept.

Chapter Thirty-Three

On the morning of the duel, Alexandra awoke with a start in darkness. For an instant, before coming fully awake, she imagined that the quarrel between Charles and George was all part of a horrible nightmare. Then reality descended upon her, crushing her false sense of relief, and she groaned in apprehension.

Getting out of bed, she went to a window and parted the drapes. The marbled gray horizon suggested that daybreak was imminent, but the world was otherwise a dreary-looking place, shrouded in heavy mist. A fitting stage for a duel, she thought bitterly. Affairs of honor, men called them. But Alexandra could not conceive of deriving satisfaction, under any circumstances, from taking another life. Hugging her arms against a fearful tremor, she had a vision of George Pennington priming himself for a deadly contest, and her heart pounded with a premonition of disaster. How could she bear the loss of him if he died fighting on her account? It appalled her that a few malicious words could provoke rational minds to such extremes. Then again, she reminded herself, Charles had long ago lost his conscience—if indeed he had ever possessed one—and George was just tinder waiting for a spark.

Anger rose sharply in her, engulfing her despair. Damn their arrogant male pride! No vice was more self-destructive or had spilled more of the blood of fools. The potential for violence, she realized, was present in all men, and because of it there would always be duels, wars, and senseless deaths in the names of honor and glory.

Alexandra yanked the curtains closed, shutting out the dismal view. At her dresser, she poured cool water into a bowl, quickly washed herself, brushed her hair, and put on a blue linen gown. Going downstairs, she smelled coffee in the passageway and found Clue, who rarely stirred before mid-morning, sitting at the kitchen table with a steaming mug in his hands. One look at his troubled face made Alexandra revise her opinion of the nature of all men. This one was as distraught as she was about the duel.

With an absent greeting, she sat across from him and massaged the dull ache in her temples. "I don't believe I slept an hour last night."

"The same here. I made extra coffee." So saying, Clue went to the fireplace, lifted a pewter pot from a trivet, and poured her a mug. When he returned to the table, they drank in silence for awhile, each wrapped in grim thoughts. Then he announced, "I'm going to Rising Sun with Mr. Pennington."

By agreement between Pennington and Villard, the duel would be fought on a meadow near Rising Sun, a tiny village on the York Road, four miles north of the city.

"As soon as it's over," Clue said, "I'll come straight back and tell you. There's no sense you sitting here wondering for hours."

Overcome by rising dread, Alexandra rubbed a fist across her forehead as tears welled up. Never in her life had she felt so utterly helpless. "There must be some way to stop them," she implored, her glittering eyes fixed on Clue.

He reached over and gripped her hand. "You did all you could," he told her. "Whatever happens today, Mr. Villard is to blame. God forgive me for saying this, but I hope Mr. Pennington gives that bastard what he deserves. We'd all be better off without him."

"Nothing would be worth losing George," she said in anguish.

A few minutes later Clue left, and she sat alone in the silent kitchen, watching the fire burn down to coals on the hearth. She did not stir until the Brocks came downstairs a little after six. Mary started breakfast, and when it was ready Alexandra forced herself to eat something. No one said much during the meal. Afterward, Edward excused himself to run errands for the household, Mary washed the dishes with unusual vigor, and Alexandra, unable to bear the unspoken fear in the air, left the kitchen.

She set about her chores for the day, feeling strangely detached from the redundant motions her hands performed, as though her body was functioning in one world while her thoughts were suspended in another. Outside, the thick leaden clouds taunted her with occasional showers, but never a steady downpour. Never enough rain to turn gunpowder in flashpans to gray sludge and prevent pistols from firing.

Toward midday, Edward Brock returned from his errands. Entering the kitchen, where Alexandra and Mary were shelling peas for dinner, he laid an armload of packages on the sideboard and met Alexandra's anxious look. His normally impassive face betrayed worry.

"Have you heard something?" she asked, half-afraid to hear his answer.

"Nothing about Mr. Pennington," Edward replied. He sighed a little and seemed to brace himself. "I've just come from the State House," he said. "There was a battle on Long Island on the twenty-seventh. The rebels took a terrible beating. They lost almost a thousand killed and wounded, and hundreds more were taken prisoner. General Howe is expected to strike the finishing blow any time now, if he hasn't already done it."

For a moment Alexandra couldn't speak, could only watch Edward's grave face, seeing instead another visage with black hair, green eyes, and a quick, warm smile. At last she managed, "Perhaps Mr. Washington will have the good sense to surrender."

"God have mercy on him if he does," Mary moaned. "They'll hang him and all his officers."

Edward shot her a silencing look.

Willing herself to stand, Alexandra removed her soiled apron and let it drop. "I'm going upstairs for awhile," she said and quickly left.

In the quietness of her bedroom, she moved like a sleepwalker from the dresser to the window and finally to the bed, where she lay on her back and hugged her arms to still her trembling.

246

A thousand dead and wounded. Hundreds captured.

Her eyes spilled over, and hot tears ran down her temples into her hair. Dalton had promised to come back to her. He swore nothing would stop him. Alexandra's only defense was to hope, so she turned her soul northward to New York and focused all her being there in an effort to apprehend him with her senses.

After a time, as she lay very still, a feeling came into her heart, a sudden exhilarating sense that he was alive somewhere up there. She clung to the sensation, believing in it, because to think anything else was intolerable.

A soft tap came at her bedroom door. "Mrs. Pennington?"

Clue's voice brought her back to the room. As she sat up and wiped her eyes, the heavy feeling of dread returned in a rush. "Come in, Christopher."

The door opened, and Clue approached the bed, and Alexandra knew before he spoke what he was going to say.

"Mr. Pennington was shot."

In a gloomy hallway at Oakwood, Alexandra conferred in whispers with Dr. Francis Stone, the surgeon who had attended the duel on Pennington's behalf. "How badly is he hurt?" she wanted to know.

Dr. Stone scratched his head of bushy white hair and considered her question. Behind thick spectacles, his magnified eyes were bloodshot and somewhat vacant. When at last he spoke, he seemed bewildered.

"That depends, I suppose," he said.

"I beg your pardon?"

"Well, George and I aren't youngsters anymore. That's precisely what I told him when I heard about this business of dueling. A younger man, well, that would be different. The young have extraordinary recuperative powers." Dr. Stone sighed and looked wistful. "Oh, to be a young blade again."

Alexandra blinked, beginning to understand that the doctor was not all there. "What exactly is George's injury?" she asked in a tight voice.

More head scratching, then, "The ball broke a rib or two and lodged under his collar bone. I removed it promptly."

Dr. Stone was pleased with himself. "Right there on the field, mind you. Delicate work, and painful for him, but not to worry. He trusts me, you see. I've known George, oh, years and years."

Alexandra had known Dr. Stone barely five minutes, and already she did not trust his judgment or his abilities. His blue-veined hands shook as he smoothed the front of his satin waistcoat. He was either desperate for a toddy or afflicted by palsy. In any event, he did not seem in a condition to care for himself, let alone a gunshot man.

"I shall return this evening," he said.

"Thank you, Dr. Stone, but that won't be necessary." Taking his arm, Alexandra steered him toward the vestibule. "I'll see to George's care."

"Oh?" He seemed mildly surprised, but unoffended. "How good of you to take an interest. You're his niece?"

"His sister-in-law." She was thankful when Oakwood's butler materialized from a side door. Reading the unspoken message in her eyes, William took over as escort. "This way, Dr. Stone," he said smoothly, extricating the elderly physician from her arm.

Alexandra went the opposite direction to the kitchen, where Clue was pacing the floor. Seeing her, he stopped short. "How's Mr. Pennington?"

"I'll have a better idea after I speak with a competent doctor."

Clue frowned in puzzlement. "Shall I fetch one, ma'am?"

"George won't approve, but yes."

After sending Clue on his way, Alexandra went upstairs to Pennington's bedroom, eased the door open, and quietly crossed to his bedside. When she saw him up close, her breath drew in sharply as her fingers clamped a bedpost. Propped up on pillows, he appeared to be asleep, his head tilted sideways, his mouth slack, a thread of saliva connecting his chin to his bandaged chest. Spots of blood had seeped through the layers of gauze covering his left shoulder. His face was cadaverously gaunt and pale. The hollows of his eyes and cheeks were sunken in shadow, and there was a bluish tinge to his lips.

When she sat on the edge of the mattress, his eyelids fluttered. A few moments passed before he roused and focused on her. "Alexandra," he said hoarsely, his mouth twisting into a drawn smile.

"I'm right here, George."

"Yes, I know. I'm not blind, dear, just a little sore." Clearing mucus from his throat, he swallowed it down, then gave a deep, racking cough that brought tears of pain to his eyes.

Alexandra's own eyes were wet. "You're going to be fine, George."

"Of course I am. Francis removed the bullet, didn't he tell you?"

She nodded.

"A few bones were broken," Pennington said, "but nothing more serious than that. I shall be up to snuff in no time." Indeed, with each word he spoke, his voice gained strength and his eyes perked up as he watched her anxious fingers twist the bedcovers. He reached for her hand, wincing with the effort. "There, there," he soothed. "I'm all right, as you can see."

"I cannot see inside your head. If I could, I would probably discover a nest of insects or some such, but no brain."

"Goodness. And here I thought you came to comfort me."

Her face tense, Alexandra stared at their entwined hands. "I should disown you," she said.

"Before you do," he said, "would you mind terribly fetching me some brandy? It's right there on the dresser."

Alexandra retrieved the brandy, poured some into a glass, and held it to his lips, cradling his head while he drank. When the glass was empty, Pennington leaned back with a sigh and said, "The best medicine in the world."

"Are you in much pain?" she asked.

"A little," he admitted. "The bastard only pinked me, just enough to spoil my aim. Rest assured, I returned the compliment. If he weren't so damned slender, I'd have shot out his liver. The next time I shall."

His assertion chilled Alexandra like a plunge into icewater. Her hands curled into fists; her glittering eyes drilled him. "George," she said in a low voice, "you are my brother-in-law and my dearest friend. But I swear to you, if you pursue this matter any further I shall denounce you as both."

A smile tugged at his mouth. "Dear me."

"Damn you, George, I mean it! I'll move away if I must to keep you from fighting."

Pennington stared at her with an intense feeling of tenderness. How naive she could be when it came to the power of her own allure. If she fled to the ends of the earth, if she turned her back on him for eternity, he would still feel obliged to defend her memory. Any man would, he believed, once he had shared a bond with her. Even Charles Villard, in his own perverted way, was reluctant to let her go.

"I won't seek him out," Pennington said at last. "But nor will I tolerate any more of his lies. What happens next depends on him."

Alexandra had to be satisfied with that, for Pennington dismissed the subject with the firmness of a man whose mind was set. "I'll speak no more on it," he said, "but I would dearly love another spot of brandy." As she poured for him, he asked, "Where did Francis get to?"

"Dr. Stone had to leave," she said. "I sent for Benjamin Rush."

Pennington's eyes widened. "What the devil?" he demanded, outraged. "I will not have that rascally man in my house. He's a damned radical! He signed that infernal Declaration."

"Nevertheless, I want him to have a look at you."

Pennington braced himself with brandy. "An obnoxious troublemaker," he muttered, "that's what he is."

Alexandra smiled. "In that case, the two of you should get along splendidly."

She was wrong.

Dr. Benjamin Rush, when he arrived, was everything Pennington claimed—brusque, assertive, a rising young medical star inflated with self-importance. The trouble began the moment he entered Pennington's bedroom. "Well, George, who have you insulted this time?"

Pennington eyed him coldly. "I'm surprised to see you here, Benjamin. I rather thought you would be in New York, helping those poor fellows you urged there to be slaughtered. Isn't it curious that the blusterers among you

250

have skulked to the wings now that weapons have replaced words."

Silence hummed. Rush's face grew florid.

"George, please," Alexandra insisted. "Dr. Rush is here at my request."

"Against my wishes, I might add."

"So," Rush smirked. "You would rather suffer than be treated by a rebel doctor."

"You are not the only doctor in this city."

"True," Rush agreed, "but I'm the most qualified."

At that, Pennington snorted and rolled his eyes. "Exactly what you said about Mr. Washington, and look what a bungler he has turned out to be."

"Stop it, both of you!" Alexandra commanded. "For God's sake, can't you put your differences aside for one moment?"

"I arrived here perfectly willing to be of service," Rush said, his withering stare on Pennington. "But now, sir, I believe you are deserving of that wound. Frankly, I'm amazed it has taken so long for someone to put a bullet in you." Nodding to Alexandra, he gave her a curt, "Good day, madam," and stalked from the room.

Closing her eyes, Alexandra swore under her breath, then went after him. "Dr. Rush, wait."

He paused at the head of the stairwell and regarded her with frosty eyes. "I should have known better than to expect civility from him."

"He's in a great deal of pain—"

"He will eat his slur against *General* Washington, mark my words."

Alexandra went numb. Benjamin Rush, with his imposing connections, was a dangerous man to have as an enemy. A whisper in the wrong ear and George Pennington could wind up in a jail cell. "I apologize for his behavior," she said quickly, even though she felt Rush was as much to blame for the quarrel. "Perhaps I shouldn't have sent for you, knowing his mood, but I wanted him to have the best possible care. Frankly, I haven't much faith in his regular physician."

His ego stroked, Dr. Rush relaxed a little.

And Alexandra pressed her advantage. "I hope the unpleasantness will end here."

Rush considered her a moment, weighing his injured sensibilities against her imploring eyes, then finally nodded. "For your sake, it will. As for him," Rush glared toward Pennington's bedroom, "sooner or later he'll hang himself. He needs no assistance from me."

As September elapsed, and the warm, drowsy days gave way to crisp nights, Pennington's wound slowly healed. But the news from New York worsened.

Following that ghastly August twenty-seventh, the rebels had evacuated Long Island. The retreat was being called a masterpiece of strategy, but in fact there was nothing remarkable about it, except that the British seemed to have fallen asleep while it was happening. Aided by darkness, thick fog, and incredible luck, Washington had crowded his battered forces into leaky old boats and ferried them across the river from Brooklyn to New York. Nine thousand troops, plus artillery, horses, and supplies. It was an anxious, busy night, full of men cursing and climbing over each other in breathless panic, soldiers and horses thrashing in water when whole boatloads capsized in midstream.

When the sun rose and the pearl-gray fog lifted, the British vanguard swept down on Fulton Ferry only to see the last boats disappearing into the distance. The Bloody-backs saluted with muskets and field pieces, but the exodus of their prey was complete.

For the following two weeks, the rebels nervously occupied New York. General Howe returned the captured General Sullivan with peace proposals. Congress assembled to consider the proposals, but in the end Benjamin Franklin told Sir William Howe that America would submit on one condition only—England must recognize the independence of the United States.

The shaky truce was over. The hostilities resumed.

On September fifteenth, the British landed like an enormous paw on New York island. The assault began with the thundering of cannon as British warships pounded Kip's Bay, destroying the American earthworks there. British troops then landed and routed the rebels, who fled in terror into cornfields and woods, throwing away their knapsacks and guns as they retreated.

When Washington arrived from his headquarters, he ran into a disheveled mob of barefooted, wild-eyed soldiers who were panting and groaning with fear. The General drew a brace of pistols and commanded them to stand and fight. But nobody stood. The tall Virginian on the snorting white charger meant nothing to them. Ignoring his shouts and curses, a stream of men swept past him, stumbling and dizzy with terror because the British were coming at their backs, bayonets hungrily poised.

Washington shot at his own men. After emptying both pistols, he drew his horsewhip, spurred into their midst, and lashed right and left, burning stripes across the flesh of soldiers and officers alike. Still they ran. He chased them over a rocky field, his white horse prancing and rearing beneath him, his voice blistering the air as sweat poured down his face. General Mifflin and white-whiskered Israel Putnam also had their whips out and were trying to stem the maddened retreat, but it was hopeless.

At last Washington's wrath collapsed. Crushed with grief and shame, realizing he could not control the mob, he sagged in his saddle and watched his unarmed men whirl past him. He was a commander without an army. He would hang for high treason when the Crown caught up to him. Turning his horse toward the bay, he stared grimly into the guns of the advancing British vanguard. His eyes closed in despair. He waited, gaunt, reckless, and resigned.

Someone was shouting at him. He felt a tug on his arm and looked blankly into an astonished young face framed with jet black hair.

"Jesus God, General! Are you daft?"

Washington continued to stare, his eyes focused inward. "It's over," he said.

"No, sir! Goddamnit, you ain't giving up!" Ducking bullets, the young man yanked the reins from Washington's hands and led him away by force. Then one of Washington's aides spurred to his side and took over the reins, and the black-haired man, supported by a handful of courageous soldiers, covered their retreat with well-aimed volleys.

Pursued by the British, the fugitive Americans stumbled north to Harlem Heights. They were without a leader, without weapons, without supplies, and without hope. Once again, the redcoats were within an ace of crushing the rebellion and putting an end to America's bid for independence. The trouble was, the British were also without a general, for Sir William Howe and his entire staff of high officers, believing the Americans too far away for any decisive action, decided they were in need of refreshment. So they stopped at the house of Mrs. Robert Murray, and there they lingered for the entire afternoon, enjoying her wine and her cakes and her high-spirited hospitality. Their business with the dirty, sweaty rebels could wait until tomorrow.

When tomorrow arrived, the rebels were encamped along the northern ridge of a deep ravine called the Hollow Way. At dawn, a band of rebel scouts, led by the Indian fighter, Colonel Knowlton, became engaged in a sharpshooting contest with British patrols. The brisk air crackled with gunfire until Knowlton, realizing he was badly outnumbered, ordered a retreat.

The British swarmed after the rebels, running their prey. As Knowlton scurried across the Hollow Way to the American front lines, a fanfare of trumpets and horns mocked his flight. The impudent tune scorched the American encampment like an electric shock. *View, hallo!* Everyone understood what it meant. *Fox in view and on the run.*

Across the rocky gulf, redcoats appeared among the trees and taunted the Americans with laughter. Mutters and curses rumbled along the ridge, fingers tightening against triggers. Suddenly Washington galloped to the front on his white charger. When he heard the jeering and the insulting trumpets, anger scorched him. His enraged appearance struck a spark in men who only yesterday had fled like hysterical children before the Bloodybacks.

The General's sword came out. His steely voice rang in the crisp morning. "Turn on those dogs!"

Colonel Knowlton's men moved out. They crept around the hollow with the Third Virginia Regiment while Colonel Crary's men charged into the ravine for a frontal assault, using trees as a screen. The peals of rascally laughter stopped. The trumpeting died. The rebel foxes, lunging behind the steel fangs of bayonets, attacked with a feverish vengeance.

Washington, watching the fighting from the lip of the ravine, could scarcely believe what he was seeing. Suddenly he smiled. He raised his sword with an exultant shout. The savagery of his men was magnificent.

The British dogs fell back, pursued by a bayonet charge. Howling like demons, the rebels broke one stand after another and drove their enemy into a field of golden wheat. Reinforcements arrived on both sides, and the battle was on. For two hours the armies faced each other in close, hot combat, the air around them thick with smoke and leaden hail. Then, with snarls coming from their throats, a horde of rebels suddenly charged like rabid wolves and tore into the British lines, completely unnerving those disciplined English soldiers.

The unimaginable happened. The red-coated dogs broke and ran. They stampeded from the field, tripping over each other in confusion while the ragged Americans snapped at their heels.

When the battle of Harlem Heights ended, the British counted two hundred dead and wounded and some valuable cannon missing, along with a huge chunk of British pride. Sir William Howe was so dumbfounded he abandoned the offensive for almost a month. It unsettled him to have his crack grenadiers take such a whipping at the hands of rabble. Never again would he take the American Army for granted. The rebels, he had discovered, bit back.

And they had sharp teeth.

Alexandra had forgotten that it was her birthday.

She entered the dining room and froze in surprise when she saw the Brocks and Christopher Clue seated around the table. All three wore expectant smiles. In the center of the table stood a bottle of wine, a cake, and two paper-wrapped parcels.

"Good Lord," she said as realization struck.

"Happy Birthday, ma'am," said Clue, looking pleased as a well-fed cat as he came around the table and guided her to the place of honor.

The wine was poured, the cake served, then Alexandra was urged to open her gifts. The first package, the smaller of the two, was from Clue. Inside was a set of gilt buttons that she knew had cost him a pretty penny.

"They're beautiful," she told him and received a bashful smile.

"They'll be perfect on this," Mary said, handing her the second package. "From Edward and me."

Opening the package, Alexandra found a hooded mantle made of deep-blue velvet and fully lined with silk. Running her hand over the soft material, she said, "I dare not wear this in public."

Mary looked crushed. "Why not?" she asked in bewilderment.

"Because I have never seen finer workmanship. It's exquisite. If anyone finds out you made this, they'll bribe you away from me."

Mary's face glowed from the praise. "Not a chance, ma'am."

Her reply had a bracing effect on Alexandra. Warmth filled her as she looked around at their faces. "Thank you," she said. "You're all so thoughtful. No one has ever been blessed with kinder friends."

For the rest of that day and the next, the world seemed a little brighter, and her anxiety about Dalton lessened its grip. Then news of another disaster reached her ears.

A raging fire had destroyed part of New York City. In the lower Manhattan district, over a thousand houses were now piles of ash, their chimneys pointing like crooked, blackened fingers at the sky. No one knew who had started the blaze, but accusations were rampant. Washington was accusing the British, who in turn were blaming rebel scouts, saying they had deliberately destroyed the winter quarters of the King's troops. Regardless of who was to blame, the British, in rage, had grabbed anyone who looked suspicious and put them to death. Some were hanged by their feet and left to roast in the crackling inferno. Others had their throats cut and their bodies were pitched into the red-hot wreckage of buildings.

The British occupation of the city was said to be ungodly. Drunken Hessians and red-coated soldiers overran the streets after dark, whoring, brawling in taverns, clashing with citizens and rebel skirmishers. Almost every night, the narrow little streets would ignite with patters of gunfire. In the morning, corpses would be found in dank alleys.

The reports of British misconduct deeply disturbed Alexandra. She had expected decency from the King's soldiers, not flagrant disregard for American property and lives. If they showed so little regard for the local inhabitants whose homes they now shared, how on earth were they treating their prisoners?

She prayed the stories were the work of rebel propagandists. It was painful enough to imagine Dalton a prisoner, let alone to think of him suffering abuse at British hands.

The question of his fate gnawed at her and robbed her of sleep. One night, lying awake and tense in bed, she heard a thumping noise below and sat up abruptly. Opening a drawer in her night stand, she felt for the small pistol she kept there. Metal clicked in darkness as she thumbed the hammer. Getting out of bed, she slipped from her bedroom, moved quietly through the hallway, and crept down the stairs, her progress spearheaded by the pistol.

Another *thump*. From the kitchen? Frightened but determined, Alexandra approached the kitchen door and heard movement on the other side of it. A boot scraped against floorboards, then came a low curse.

Recognizing the voice, she sagged with relief. Damn him! Opening the door, she saw his dark form silhouetted against a moonlit window. "Christopher, what the devil are you doing?"

He spun toward her, lost his balance, and crashed into the table. "Hello, ma'am," he said, righting himself.

"Are you all right?"

"Juss fine."

As Alexandra moved closer to him, beer fumes assailed her. "What are you doing?" she asked again.

"Can't get my damn boots off," he muttered.

"Perhaps you should try it sitting down."

"There's an idea," he agreed and dropped heavily into a chair.

Alexandra lit a candle and carried it to the table. After a full minute of watching him struggle with buckles and straps, she knelt in front of him and pushed his hands aside. "Here, let me do it. You'll be all night."

As she pulled off his boots, Clue studied the ornate pistol lying on the table beside the candle. "Wha's this for?" he wanted to know.

"I thought you were a prowler," she explained. "I wish you would let us know when you plan to carouse about. I might have shot you."

"By God, tha' would've been a fitting end to a miserable night."

His flat voice and troubled expression took Alexandra by surprise. Concerned, she sat next to him and asked what was wrong.

For a long time Clue was silent. Then, with a deep sigh, he said, "Women." He sounded disgusted.

"What about women?" she prompted.

"Well, I have a girl—" He stopped, thought about it. "Had a girl," he amended, watching the flickering candle flame. "She kept saying, wait, wait. Two years I've waited, now she won't marry me."

"Why on earth not?"

"She won't marry a coachman, tha's why not. But tha's what I am, I told her. No better, no worse. It's her father, you see. He put it in her head tha' she can do better than me. Now she thinks money's all tha' matters."

"She's wrong."

"Tha's what I told her. She wouldn't listen."

Alexandra's heart went out to him. Never had he looked so morose. "I'm sorry, Christopher."

"Ah, well," he shrugged. "Best of luck to her. She'll find someone, I guess." His bleary eyes found Alexandra's. "I never told you this, ma'am, but I'm glad you didn't let a stupid thing like money come between you and Dalton."

Just hearing his name made Alexandra's pulse quicken. A thousand thoughts and feelings raced through her at once, but the strongest of all was a nagging sense of dread. Anxiety spilled into her voice when she said, "At first I did. In my heart I knew we belonged together, but I refused him because his prospects were poor." She paused, a raw ache in her throat. "I was such a fool, Christopher. I wasted so much time."

"Tha's all right. You'll make it up to him."

At that, the ache intensified, and Alexandra's voice fell to an agonized whisper. "Suppose it's too late?"

Clue stared at her a moment, then gripping her hand, he spoke with sudden clarity. "He's alive, ma'am, I know it. Dalton's a survivor. He's coming back to you, that's all there is to it."

Alexandra shivered with the hope that Clue was right.

Chapter Thirty-Four

In the cold rain of November, the American Army began a dark ordeal of retreat across New Jersey. They were a battered, dispirited band of men, their bright success at Harlem Heights a lifetime behind them.

In October, they had lost a hard-fought engagement at White Plains, New York, where British dragoons had paralyzed their infantry. It was the first time the rebels had faced a British cavalry charge—the great beasts galloping forward under whip and spur, nostrils flared and hooves thundering, the riders swishing sabers above their heads as blood-curdling battle cries tore from their throats. When the Seventeenth Light Dragoons came sweeping in against the American front-line trenches, militia units had panicked and scattered like frightened sheep. Washington ordered a withdrawal, and the Americans had turned tail for New Castle.

The next blow came with the fall of Fort Washington on the Hudson River. Three thousand Americans had been taken prisoner, doomed to rot in filthy ship holds and disease-infested prisons. A few days later, on the Jersey side of the Hudson, Fort Lee was seized by Cornwallis. The rebel garrison had narrowly escaped. In their flight, they left behind valuable artillery, their tents and blankets, and precious food stores.

New York was lost, and once again the rebels were in retreat, closely pursued by the British Army. Their route of march, the Hackensack Road, was a track of mud that sucked at shoes, hooves, and gun-carriage wheels. The weather was bitter cold. At night everything froze, including the damp clothes on weary backs. Along the road, men collapsed and lay trembling from hunger and exhaustion. Others slunk off through soggy fields without looking back. Food supplies were dangerously short. The army had not been paid for months, and the soldiers were living from hand to mouth. At home their families were starving, and without pay there was no way of helping them.

It was no wonder that men were deserting like flies. The air bristled with mutinous rumbles. Washington kept the whipping post busy almost every day, but the threat of "thirty-nine lashes, well laid on" was no longer a cure for disobedience. Men insulted and sometimes attacked their officers. The name of Washington had lost luster. His army, along with the dream of liberty, was evaporating.

Watching another stumbling figure disappear into the gray drizzle, Dalton ignored the impulse to go after him and drag him back. Five miles ago he might have done it, but now he was too bone-weary and disheartened to care. And Mercury, plodding along beneath him, could not be expected to chase down every man who had reached the end of his rope.

So Dalton looked the other way. At the moment all he wanted was some hot food in his stomach, topped off with a gill of rum. He had not eaten since last night's dinner—a strip of salt pork and a biscuit made from canel and peas-meal. The greasy pork had tasted rancid, the biscuit was hard enough to use as cannon shot. He wondered what delightful rations the commissary would scare up for tonight. Chilled to the bone, his stomach growling, he followed the straggling line of Pennsylvanians and tried to concentrate on something besides his hunger.

Like a drowning man clutching a lifeline, he thought of Alexandra. Only she could occupy his mind so completely that his misery was blunted. Three months ago, she had spoken the words he had never dreamed to hear. An eternity had passed since then, and he wondered, with a tight-throated feeling, if she thought of him as often and with as much yearning as he did her. He longed to do his heart's bidding and turn Mercury south toward home, but his conscience would sooner see him dead than a deserter.

Dalton awoke from his reverie as the stallion's ears

261

suddenly pricked forward. Peering into the rain, he noticed a commotion at the side of the road up ahead. It looked like a brawl between two soldiers, but spurring closer, he saw that only one of the two men was actually fighting. The other was curled into a protective ball on the ground, arms crossed over his head to shield it from vicious kicks.

"Get up, you bloody twit!" Another kick, a grunt of pain. "I SAID GET UP OR I'LL BASH YOUR BRAINS OUT!" The savage voice came from a tall, broad-chested officer, whose handsome face belied the brute lurking inside him. Dalton recognized Sergeant Beale of the first battalion. During the New York campaign, Beale had acquired a reputation as a cold, efficient killer. A good man to have beside you in battle; a nightmare to have as an enemy.

"You have five seconds to move," Beale warned the huddled figure on the ground, "or you're mine."

"Sergeant!" Dalton yelled, sliding from Mercury's back. "What the devil are you doing?"

"Getting this lazy bastard on his feet, sir."

"By kicking the shit out of him?"

"He refuses to march," Beale retorted.

"Leave him be."

At that, the sergeant found a new target for his animosity. His bright eyes searched Dalton's face, seeking a weakness to prey upon, but the look he encountered triggered wariness. He squinted, waiting.

"Move on, Sergeant." Dalton's command was all the more forceful for its softness.

Beale hesitated. "Lieutenant," he tried, "this man is my responsibility."

"Not anymore."

Piss on you, Beale wanted to say. But he now had the measure of this officer, so instead he skulked away, because the lieutenant's eyes were promising punishment if Beale did anything else.

With Beale gone, Dalton relaxed and turned his attention to the prone man at his feet. Looking down, he saw a round young face staring up at him, with dark hair plastered to pale cheeks and brown eyes drooping from fatigue. "Thank you, sir," the man breathed.

"Henry?" Dalton asked in surprise. "Henry Buckley?"

Henry blinked in puzzlement. "You know me, sir?"

"Indeed I do," Dalton said. But since Henry knew him only as Jack Flash, he did not bring up the circumstances of their meeting. "I've seen you around Philadelphia," he said. "I'm from there myself." Kneeling, he touched Henry's shoulder. "Did he hurt you bad?"

"Not him, sir. I was pushing a wagon that got stuck, and it ran over my foot."

"Is it broken?"

"Dunno, sir." Tears of pain suddenly glimmered in Henry's eyes. Ashamed, he dashed them away.

Dalton pretended not to notice. "Here, let me have a look." After a thorough inspection of the swollen foot, he concluded, "It ain't broken, but it must hurt like the devil. Can you ride, Henry?"

"I was born on a horse, sir."

Dalton smiled. "Bet that was uncomfortable for your mother." Hooking an arm around Henry, he helped him up and over to where the stallion obediently waited. "Two things," Dalton said, handing him the reins. "Mercury don't like being kicked, and his mouth is sensitive as a virgin's crack on her wedding night. So go easy on the bit, or he'll wrap you around a tree."

"I'll just walk him, sir," Henry said.

Dalton gave him a leg up, noted his natural posture in the saddle, the authoritative way he handled the reins, and was satisfied that Henry knew what he was doing. Mercury, too, seemed at ease with the stranger on his back. He moved willingly when Henry nudged his flanks.

"You been with the army long?" Dalton asked as they walked.

"Since White Plains."

"Just in time for all the fun, eh?"

Henry's smile was more a grimace. Curious, he studied his rescuer's profile. "You said you're from Philadelphia, sir?"

"Thereabouts. I got a farm on Wissahickon Creek."

Henry, listening to Dalton speak and watching the way he moved, felt a disturbing sense of recognition. "Have we met before, sir?"

Dalton hesitated for a second, then said they had.

263

"What's your name, sir?"

In the pause, Mercury snorted a sigh and nudged Dalton's shoulder with his muzzle. Dalton wanted to say he was someone else, because there was something very likeable about Henry, and the truth would undoubtedly earn his contempt. "Dalton Philips," he said.

Henry stiffened. Everyone from Philadelphia knew the name. A few months back, it had become synonymous with Jack Flash. His mouth slack, Henry recalled a snowy New Year's Eve when the robber had held a knife to his gut and demanded a strongbox of silver in return for his life. He took a closer look at Dalton's tall, powerful build. Same height, same stance. And that voice, with its undercurrent of steel . . .

Henry found himself looking into bold green eyes, the same eyes that had glittered at him from behind a black hood. "Now I remember you," he said, incredulous.

Dalton smiled a little. "Small world, ain't it?"

Henry just stared at him.

"I'm sorry about that night."

Disconcerted, Henry glanced away. For awhile he was silent, watching the ground go by. Then he said, "At least you didn't hurt me."

"Why would I do that?" Dalton shrugged. "You was the most obliging person I ever robbed."

Warmth flooded Henry's face. "What happened with the Whittakers, then?" he demanded. "They give you trouble, did they?"

Dalton walked several paces, then suddenly stopped and took hold of Mercury's bridle, bringing him to a halt. He locked stares with the younger man. "It wasn't me that robbed them," he said. "I did things as Jack Flash I ain't proud of, but I never hurt anyone."

Henry's thoughts were moving fast. He knew that Jack Flash had been granted unconditional amnesty and did not need to lie to protect himself. But what convinced him of the truth, even more than the honesty he read in Dalton's eyes, was that Dalton did not try to qualify or embellish his assertion.

Henry said, "You don't seem the kind of man to do a thing like that." The corner of his mouth lifted. "Is it true you gave the money you stole to the army?"

Dalton nodded.

"From the looks of things," Henry said, glancing around, "it didn't go very far."

Dalton was about to reply when he caught sight of a familiar white horse cantering along the road. The horse attracted notice because of its rider. General Washington cut a splendid figure, hard-muscled and big-boned, sitting erect and lean in the saddle. Heads turned to catch a glimpse of him, for there was something vital to be seen in his grave, windburned face, a strength both compelling and forbidding. The General called encouragement to the troops as he passed, beseeching them to hang on until nightfall.

Ragged huzzahs sprouted here and there. A few hats were waved. But for the most part the soldiers sighed in resignation and resumed the torture of placing one foot ahead of the other.

The General went past Dalton and Henry at a quick trot, his somber, hazel eyes absorbing a parade of desolate faces. Those eyes skimmed over Dalton, then came back, riveted. The Virginian's hands sawed the reins, wheeling his big white horse around so that his trailing aides almost collided with him. Hooves flashed in slippery mud. Steadying his mount with quick, absent movements, Washington took a long look at the black-haired man from the battle at Kip's Bay. The man who had called him daft, then dragged him beyond the range of British guns. Those desperate moments, though somewhat distorted, were branded in Washington's mind.

The nod he gave Dalton was barely perceptible, but the humility it encompassed was vast. Dalton responded by doffing his hat. Then Washington, the ghost of a smile on his stern face, spurred his horse and galloped off.

Watching him go, Henry said, "God Almighty," bewildered by what he had witnessed. "What was *that* all about?"

Dalton was staring after the General, his whole being transfixed. He felt as if he stood a foot taller. "Hard to tell," he said. "Maybe he was admiring my horse."

Chapter Thirty-Five

Philadelphia, 24th November, 1776

Dear Dalton,

I have no way of knowing whether or not you will receive this. I have heard none but distressing accounts of the war since you left and have no inkling as to your fate. If you should read these lines, I beg you to make some reply that I might know if you are alive.

Alexandra paused, twirling the feather quill in her fingers, and reread what she had written. Her brow furrowed as she stared at the desperate, morbid words. They could only have a demoralizing impact on a man already overburdened with tragedy and hardship. With a sigh, she put down the pen, crushed the letter into a ball, and drew a fresh sheet from her stationery box. Leaning over the paper, she began again.

Dear Dalton,

I have the pleasure to tell you that my betrothal to Mr. Villard is ended, and while the separation was disagreeable I felt not a moment's doubt for my decision. My choice was inevitable. In my heart it was made long ago, but my feelings did not become clear to me until that hour spent with you in my coach.

Better, she thought, then dipped the quill in an ink-pot and continued.

The months since you left have been long ones. I remain at my city house to be closer to news of the war, and Christopher spends half his time at the State House, listening for word of your situation. Not a moment goes by that I don't think of you and pray for your safety.

I don't know where this letter will meet you. Through the medium of Maj. Thomas Cooke (an express rider for Congress) I hope this will reach you, as he has promised to personally attempt its delivery. Nothing would delight me more than to hear from you and know that you are well.

Christopher, George, and the Brocks send their kindest regards. As for me, I wish only for your safe and swift return. Until then, believe me to be

Your love,
Alexandra

Lt. Dalton Philips
Pennsylvania Line
American Army, New Jersey

Waiting for the ink to dry, she summoned a memory of his face and tried to imagine him reading the words and drawing a measure of comfort from them. But the face she conjured was drawn, unsmiling, and tormented. She shivered with the apprehension that her letter would arrive too late. The worst, she supposed, was yet to come—the anxious days and nights awaiting a response.

Chapter Thirty-Six

December promised doom for the rebels. As they continued to retreat before the British advance, wagonloads of wounded and fever-stricken soldiers began to arrive in Philadelphia. Many died of wounds, hunger, and exposure to cold as the wagons transporting them lumbered into the city. The Pennsylvania Hospital, along with many private homes, was crowded with sick and dying men. At the Southeast Square, which had long served as a burying place for strangers, hundreds of soldiers were interred in unmarked trenches.

Another of the city's commons was also being put to use by soldiers. Glancing out the window of her coach, Alexandra saw a small company of militia drilling on the Centre Square. They were marching to the tune of "Jack, the Brisk Young Drummer," being played on fifes and drums by novice musicians. It seemed to be the only song the militia knew, and people living near the square claimed it was the rebels' most effective weapon to drive the enemy insane.

Some prominent Whigs were attempting to raise more militia companies in Philadelphia. Today was muster day, but turnout was poor. The sight of dead and suffering soldiers being carted into the city did little to inspire ablebodied men toward military service.

As the Pennington coach turned onto Eighth Street, a corpse-laden wagon rumbled across its path. The driver of the wagon, seeming half-asleep, was hunched over on the bench with the reins lax in his hands. But the draft horses needed no guidance. Conditioned by frequent such trips, they plodded unerringly toward the burial ground at Southeast Square.

Alexandra studied the wagon's grisly cargo with horror. The morning was in the grip of a heavy frost, the streets were criss-crossed with deep, rock-hard wheel ruts. As the wagon banged and lurched over the ruts, jostled bodies threatened to tumble over the sides like so much baggage. Sickened by the sight, Alexandra withdrew from the window and pulled her woolen cloak more closely about her.

Minutes later, Clue stopped the coach in front of Pennsylvania Hospital, a stately brick building with tall white columns framing its main entrance. After opening Alexandra's door and handing her outside, Clue asked, "Are you sure you want to go in there, ma'am?" Though the hospital's windows were closed against the cold, muffled screams could be heard.

"Yes," she said. "Please wait here for me."

She climbed a flight of broad stone steps and went inside. A shockwave of sounds greeted her—piteous wails, agonized sobbing, the shrieks of a man in excruciating pain. As the cries echoed from all directions and resounded off the lobby's high ceiling, Alexandra felt the noise like a physical blow. And the smells—urine, dung, blood, the putrid stench of flesh rotting on bones.

Unnerved, she flinched when someone touched her arm and a gruff voice asked, "May I ask your business?" The voice belonged to a bearish attendant with bloodstained clothes and lazy, hooded eyes that watched her without emotion.

"I'm looking for someone," she said.

"Everyone is," he said. "But you can't just go wandering around the building. It's against policy."

"I understand. Would you be good enough to see if his name is on your patient register?"

The attendant looked blank.

"You do keep a register of patients," she prompted him.

He shrugged. "The ones able to give their names are on the list. The rest are anybody's guess."

269

"Then how will I know whether or not he is here?" she asked, dismayed and annoyed.

The surly man made some reply, but Alexandra missed hearing it as a familiar figure entered the lobby and snagged her attention. "Dr. Rush!" she called.

Rush turned, distracted. His dark eyebrows were peaked with worry, his white surgeon's apron was spattered with blood to his shoulders. Recognizing Alexandra, his brooding look changed to surprise. He waved off the attendant, who had followed her across the lobby.

"Good morning, Mrs. Pennington. What brings you to this devil's paradise?"

"I'm looking for someone. An American soldier."

Curiosity glinted in Rush's eyes. "His name?"

"Dalton Philips."

If Rush had been curious before, his interest was now doubled. Noting the abrupt change in his demeanor, Alexander was at once hopeful and terrified of receiving an unbearable blow. "Do you know him?" she asked, her mouth dry as dust.

"We have a mutual friend," Rush said. "To my knowledge, Mr. Philips isn't a patient here. However, I haven't seen all the wounded and new ones arrive almost hourly. If you like, I'll check the wards for you."

"May I accompany you?"

Rush regarded her a long moment. Then, making up his mind, he said, "The choice is yours. But I warn you, what you'll see will make you shudder. You'll hear them blaspheme holy God and beg for death, which for many would be a blessing. Are you prepared for that?"

Alexandra said she was, though in truth she wasn't sure.

Every room of the hospital was crowded with the casualties of man's inhumanity to man. Where no beds were available, the sick and wounded lay on straw-filled pallets on the floor. They were of all ages, from graybeards to smooth-cheeked boys. Some were trembling and sweating with fever, others were whimpering or singing softly to themselves. The worst cases thrashed and screamed in agony and had to be restrained. A few lay stiffly silent on their blankets, filmy-eyed corpses awaiting removal. Attendants and nurses were on hand in every ward, dispensing relief wherever they could, but it was never enough.

As Rush led Alexandra through chambers that stank of vomit, festering flesh, and death, he was besieged with pleas and accusations.

"Doctor, help me! Don't let me die!"

"Where's my leg, you butcher?"

"Kill me . . . doctor, please kill me . . ."

Alexandra looked at every face, dreading to see Dalton's among them. If a patient's head was swathed in bandages, she looked for a bullet scar on the left thigh. The most horrifying case was a black-haired man who was missing both his left leg and part of his face. It was impossible to determine his identity from his ravaged features. With Rush's permission, she slipped a hand beneath the unconscious wretch, felt his feverish back, and shivered with relief to encounter smooth skin instead of ridged scars.

Eventually the moans and indescribable distress shattered her fortitude and drove her to escape into a hallway. Rush followed her. Taking her arm, he guided her to a window, jacked it open, and instructed her to take deep breaths. The clean, cold air felt good on her heated face. Control filtered back. With it came an acute sense of helplessness.

Composing herself, she met Dr. Rush's assessing gaze. "I hardly know what to say."

"It would melt a heart of stone to see them." The starched, self-conceited doctor was gone. Before her, Alexandra saw a man filled with compassion for the poor souls under his care. "Sometimes words are the only comfort we can give them," he said quietly. "But finding the right words . . ." His voice trailed off, he glanced out the window with a shrug. "What does one say to a dying man when he's counting on you to save him?"

Knowing Rush didn't expect an answer, Alexandra didn't offer one. "Have we seen all the wards?" she asked.

"Except for one, but I can't allow you in there. Putrid malignant fever," he explained to her inquiring look. "You've already been exposed to enough danger of infection. Anyway, I'm certain Mr. Philips isn't there."

271

Alexandra was relieved, for she dreaded to face another roomful of hollow-eyed, stricken men. When Rush said, "I'll take you back to the lobby," she went with him gratefully.

Before she left, he told her, "The sexton at Southeast Square is keeping a register of the soldiers being buried there, at least insofar as he is able to make an identification." Rush's expression was noncommittal. "His name is Hugh Jenkins. Perhaps you should speak with him."

"I will," she said. "Thank you for your kind help."

Returning to her coach, Alexandra told Clue to drive to Southeast Square, where fifteen bodies, encased in canvas sacks, had been delivered for burial. A crowd of mourners and gawkers was present for the ceremony, which was already underway when Alexandra's coach arrived at the square. Directing Clue to wait, she crossed the frozen, uneven ground and joined the gathering. Some of the spectators were weeping. Others were staring with unabashed curiosity at the corpses stacked three high in a trench.

The Rev. Samuel Aitken, of the Third Presbyterian Church, read the order for burial. His voice droned in the quiet morning. "O' Heavenly Father, have mercy on these brave souls who so valiantly gave their lives in the holy cause of liberty. Deliver them not into the pain of eternal fires, but raise them into the light and glory of life everlasting."

Alexandra was only half-listening to the minister. The rest of her was looking for the sexton, Hugh Jenkins. He was easy to recognize. Shovel in hand, he stood apart from the crowd, patiently waiting to perform his macabre work. He was flanked by two helpers, also armed with shovels.

When the prayer ended, Alexandra approached him. "Mr. Jenkins, may I have a word with you?"

Separating from his helpers, Jenkins joined her and removed his hat, revealing a head of thinning red hair. Dirt was packed beneath his ragged fingernails. "Yes, miss?" he inquired.

"Dr. Rush advised me to speak with you," she began. "He said you keep a register of the dead buried here."

272

"Who is it you're looking for, miss?" From his matter-of-fact tone, it was clear that Jenkins had been in this situation many times of late.

"Dalton Philips," she said.

"No," he said, shaking his head. "I know Dalton well, and I'm sure I haven't put him in the ground. Nor do I expect to, knowing that rascal."

Rejuvenated, Alexandra thanked Jenkins, then left the sounds of grief and the sickly odor of death behind her. Threading her way among gravestones and the stout, smooth trunks of silver beeches, her gaze was drawn across Sixth Street to the Walnut Street Prison. Inside those imposing stone walls, Dalton had spent two months chained like an animal, without a prayer of being released. Then a miracle had freed him.

She would never give up hope that he was alive.

As she thought this, a man stepped from behind a tree into her path, and Alexandra stopped short, the hair on her arms tingling as wintry eyes looked her up and down. Charles Villard smiled, but there was no warmth in his stare.

"Hello, sweetheart."

Locating her wits, Alexandra attempted to go around him, but he moved with her so that she almost ran up against him. Frightened but not about to back down, she watched his pale eyes in the shadow of his hat brim. He looked dangerous and tough. "Get out of my way, Charles."

"How is George these days?"

Alexandra said nothing, just watched him with loathing.

"Were you disappointed when he didn't kill me?"

Still no answer.

"To be fair, he did inflict a scratch. Right here," pointing to his midriff. "But the ball only raked me."

Again she tried to go past him, again Villard planted himself in front of her like a wall. He nodded at the distant trench, where the sexton and his helpers were dousing bodies with shovelfuls of lime. "Sad, isn't it?" he asked, but he sounded pleased. "The poor gravedigger says the rebels are dying so fast he can't dig enough holes for them

273

all." His mocking eyes bored into her. "I noticed you speaking with Mr. Jenkins. Were you inquiring about anyone in particular? Your stable cleaner, perhaps?"

With that, Alexandra's control was wiped away by a lacerating hatred so great it made her tremble. To Villard, persecuting her was a game, and she was sick to death of living in dread of his next move. Because she dared not relax her guard, sleep had grown elusive, and her waking moments were filled with the nerve-racking fear that he would strike not at her, but at someone she cared about. He had schemed to destroy Dalton, lashed out at Clue, goaded George into a duel. Now he was stalking her in broad daylight, and all her tension, bitterness, and anger of the past months welled up in one terrible surge.

"You vile bastard," she said, breathing deep with the effort to contain her rage. "I cannot conceive how you bear to live in your own skin. You're not a man, you're a monster. No shame is beneath you. When I think that I almost married you, I shudder in horror."

Amusement curved his mouth. "A feeling I suggest you get used to."

Alexandra's face paled. "Goddamn you, Charles. If you don't leave me alone—"

"You'll do what?" he challenged.

"I'll shoot you, Mr. Villard," said a voice behind him. Villard spun around and saw Clue standing several paces away, saw his part his cloak to reveal a cocked pistol. The muzzle was aimed at Villard's chest. "You stay away from her," Clue said in a low voice.

For a moment no one moved, then Villard chuckled. "Well, well," he said smoothly. "The servant boy has nerve. I'm impressed."

Ignoring him, Clue held out a hand to Alexandra. "Come on, ma'am."

She went to him, and they left the square with Villard's laughter ringing in their ears. After Clue handed her inside the coach, Alexandra leaned back against the seat and tried to calm her racing heart, but it was no use. Her body was as taut as a drawn bow. Her throat grew thick and her eyes flooded with the tears she had been holding back for hours, only now they were seasoned with an

274

overwhelming fury. As they streamed down her face, her fist beat the seat cushion while her thoughts darkened with malice. She ached to be rid of Charles Villard.

Slowly she collected herself from her turmoil and tried to decide what to do about him. To her despair, no easy remedy surfaced. The coach was now well away from the square, heading for her Fourth Street house, but in her mind she could still hear his derisive voice.

The rebels are dying so fast he can't dig enough holes for them all.

Eyes closed, Alexandra recalled the stench of decay at the hospital, heard again the groans of men struggling to live, to die, and covered her face with her hands. She felt their agony wash over her and allowed it to enter her soul, where deep within lodged a shard of guilt. Where was her own concern for their suffering? How could she continue to live as before, knowing that four blocks away men were in desperate need of comfort and caring?

Her head rose, her body swaying with the moving coach while her thoughts gathered in grim deliberation. Reaching a decision, she cleared her throat and wiped her damp eyes. She had no control over her vicious enemy, but at least one important thing was in her power to change for the better.

When the coach stopped at her house and Clue came to let her out, Alexandra asked him to drive back to the hospital. Arriving there, she climbed the broad stone steps to the main entrance, her mind set, her confidence restored. The attendant in the lobby, mindful of her acquaintance with the celebrated Dr. Rush, was courteous to her the second time around. "Back so soon, ma'am?"

"I'm sorry to trouble you again, but I must speak with Dr. Rush, if he can spare me a few moments."

"No bother, ma'am. Just have a seat, and I'll get him for you."

When Dr. Rush heard her proposal, he was flabbergasted. "You're serious," he said, as if he could not believe it.

"Quite serious."

"And what will your Loyalist friends think of your volunteering to nurse wounded rebels?"

"I couldn't care less what they'll think," she said. "I want to help."

His expression remained doubtful. "And you won't mind cleaning up vomit or changing soiled bedding or emptying chamber pots?"

"If it will bring one of these men a moment's relief, I won't mind at all."

Chapter Thirty-Seven

The British army had reached Trenton. Washington's spiritless troops had been driven across the Delaware River into Pennsylvania, and the Patriots feared that Philadelphia and control of the Delaware waterway was the new objective of General Howe.

On December twelfth, Congress passed a resolution providing Washington with "full power to order and direct all things relative to the department, and to the operations of war." They ordered him to defend Philadelphia to the last extremity. They wished him success in this endeavor. Then the nervous delegates fled to Baltimore.

Congress had abandoned the capital.

This act of timidity had a devastating impact on an army already shorn to pieces. Early on the morning of December thirteenth, an express rider galloped into Washington's camp with electrifying news—America was without a government. That same morning, Friday the thirteenth, the scattered remnants of the Grand American Army were dealt another blow—the capture of Gen. Charles Lee in New Jersey by a troop of His Majesty's dragoons.

After an unsuccessful attempt to rescue Lee, the three thousand soldiers in his command, now under General Sullivan, continued to march to join the main army. But their progress was horribly slow, as was that of Horatio Gates, who was coming from the north with a small body of reinforcements.

When all of them reported in, Washington estimated that he might have five thousand ragged troops on hand to face more than twelve thousand British and Hessian regulars. "In short," he wrote to his cousin, Lund Washington, "your imagination can scarce extend to a situation more distressing than mine. Our only dependence now is upon the speedy enlistment of a new army. If this fails, I think the game will be pretty well up . . ."

As far as many Whigs were concerned, the game was already over, for the rebels could no more stop a British assault on the capital than they could stem a flood tide.

Fearing an invasion, Philadelphia erupted in confusion. Militia drums beat; a martial appearance prevailed; shops shut down; all business except preparing to disappoint the enemy was set aside. Numbers of Whig families loaded wagons with their valued possessions and left town—men, women, children, and goods all flying from the city. Only the diehard Patriots remained in town as Philadelphia became a Loyalist stronghold. Watchmen still lit the lamps at night and patrolled the streets as usual, but by mid-December the city was dark, silent, and seemingly empty.

Then the unexpected happened. In America's bleakest hour, Sir William Howe once again declined to press his advantage. Each day that passed brought the winter storms closer, and Howe and his retinue were not about to shiver away the hours in some godforsaken crossroads town. The British were not cold-weather soldiers. New York City, with its large Tory population and its cozy, inviting taverns, seemed an excellent choice for winter quarters.

And so, one raw gray morning, rebel spies sighted a cumbersome, heavily guarded wagon train departing in the direction of Perth Amboy. The British left behind a chain of garrisons in New Jersey, lonely bastions that would become even more isolated and vulnerable when the deep and silent snows fell.

Pvt. Augustine Mattson seemed more dead than alive, his face almost as white as the pillow beneath his head. Leaning over him, Alexandra pressed a cup to his dry lips. "Gus?" she asked and was rewarded with a faint moan.

His eyelids fluttered. For long moments he watched her

278

without comprehension. Then, at last recognizing her, his sunken eyes livened and his thin lips and hollow cheeks drew into a smile. "Mrs. Pennington," he croaked. "We missed you yesterday."

Yesterday was Christmas, and Alexandra had indeed visited Gus, as she had every day since volunteering to help care for the wounded. But Gus's memory was failing along with his strength. He was a handsome young man with warm brown eyes, sandy hair, and long, tapered artist's hands. Tendrils of his hair clung damply to his feverish skin. His right leg had been amputated at mid-thigh, and he carried a lead bullet in his stomach.

When the bulk of the wounded had been removed from Philadelphia to safer regions, Gus and twelve others were left behind. Only the worst cases, who would not have survived a wagon journey, remained at Pennsylvania Hospital.

Dr. Rush had left town when the Congress bolted. He had not gone to Baltimore like most of the delegates, but north to Washington's camp, which lay ten miles above Trenton on the Pennsylvania side of the Delaware River. Rush's parting words to her had been brief, but bracing. "I didn't believe you would last a day, Mrs. Pennington. I want you to know, everyone here is glad you did."

For her part, Alexandra had never felt more useful. Working at the hospital had given her an increased appreciation of the Brocks and Christopher Clue, whose services she sometimes took for granted. After years of having her house cleaned, her meals prepared, and her property cared for by others, it was a gratifying experience to be using her hands to help someone else.

She again offered the cup to Gus. "Drink some of this," she urged, supporting his head with her hand.

After swallowing a mouthful of beef broth, Gus made a face. "No salt?" he complained.

"I'm afraid there wasn't any."

Salt was just one of the many shortages in Philadelphia. The city was feeling the pinch of British naval blockades, to the delight of some unscrupulous merchants. Since the outbreak of war, an orgy of profiteering had erupted, not just in Pennsylvania, but in every colony. The prices of many necessary articles, such as cheese, butter, and beef,

279

had risen to outrageous levels. The spirit of avarice was alive and well in America as vultures set about building their own fortunes upon their country's ruin.

Gus's gravelly voice broke into her thoughts. "Have you an answer for me?" he asked, looking hopeful.

"Gus, you are unbelievably persistent."

"I can't help myself. What do you say?"

"I told you," she said gently. "My heart is already given."

Gus sighed, a dragging, watery sound. "Ah, well. At least he's a Patriot and not one of those murdering redcoats."

The words came out before Alexandra could stop them. "English soldiers are not murderers."

"Not all of them," Gus agreed. "But a lot of them look on this country as fair game. They're killing and robbing innocent people and getting away with it."

In the silence, a man on a nearby bed stirred and moaned, labored breathing came from a darkened corner of the ward. Alexandra stared at a bloodstain on the wooden floor. She was thinking of the stories she had heard about British and Hessian atrocities against the inhabitants of New Jersey. The entire track of the British army's march was reportedly marked by a wanton destruction of property, and sometimes lives. Churches had been ransacked; homes had been looted, livestock driven off, families abused and left destitute; civilians had been murdered. The were many instances of married women and young girls being raped by British officers.

The effect of all this was to magnify the existing rebel hatred of General Howe's army and to horrify British supporters, who were counting on the Crown's protection.

"I know you don't want to believe it," Gus told her, "but it's the God's truth. I've seen it with my own eyes."

He was right; she didn't want to believe it. At first, she had written off the stories as more inflammatory propaganda. Now it seemed unlikely that all of the tales were false. And if just one was true, it was one too many.

Lost in thought, Alexandra was startled into alarm by sudden shouting in the adjoining ward. Moments later a wide-eyed attendant barreled into the room and yelled, "Washington beat the goddamn Hessians! He crossed the bloody river and took Trenton!"

Alexandra had to restrain Gus as he struggled to sit up. "When did this happen?" she asked the attendant, then listened in astonishment as the tale unfolded.

On Christmas night, under a dim, wintry moon, the rebels had crossed a swollen river jammed with floating ice. A strong wind was blowing from the northwest, the forefront of a severe storm that broke in full force in the midst of the crossing. Jagged chunks of ice banged the sides of the Durham boats, jarring the wedged-in loads of men and equipment, drenching huddled figures with freezing spray. As the strong current dragged at wooden hulls, threatening to capsize the boats, oars clutched frantically at patches of open water.

Incredibly, they all landed without mishap—2,400 troops, horses, and artillery—but they were far behind schedule, and the weather was worsening. It was four o'clock in the morning before the army formed up and stole silently along the River Road toward Trenton. Officers moved up and down the ranks, speaking in quiet voices, offering encouragement, reminding their men that the night's password was "Victory or Death."

By the first signs of daybreak, they were a mile from the lazy, sleeping village. Cloaked by the roaring storm, the rebels surrounded their prey like wolves in the twilight, hungry, desperate, and functioning by instinct.

The first shot was fired at eight o'clock when a Hessian officer stepped from a cooper's shop, which was being used as an advance post, and saw sixty raggedly dressed men trotting toward him. At first the stupefied German thought he was seeing a rebel raiding party, until the Americans fired a volley, then a second and a third, and the thundering of rebel cannon tumbled groggy Hessians from their bunks.

The defenders grabbed for weapons. They dashed from houses, pulling on boots and uniform coats and forming into small groups in the narrow village streets. They tried to resist the terrible onslaught of bullets, the cannonfire raking the streets and plowing into buildings, but the rebels attacked them from every quarter. Slipping and sliding in wet snow, still woozy from last night's celebrating, the Hessians retreated from house to house,

281

only to find more rebels at their backs.

The surprise was perfectly timed. It was devastating. Caught in a shattering fire, Hessian soldiers fell dead and wounded while their rattled officers ordered the survivors to close ranks and keep moving. But there was nowhere to go. Rebel snipers were firing from the cover of houses, picking off anything that moved. Rebel skirmishers were charging from three sides at once. Rebel cannon balls were slicing into the Hessian ranks, indiscriminately shearing off heads and limbs, turning the narrow village streets into an inferno of racket and confusion. Battle smoke and screams mingled together in the fierce swirling of the storm.

The battle of Trenton lasted two hours in sleet, hail, rain, and snow. When it was over, the whitened streets were tinged with blood, and the Americans had won their first real victory of the rebellion. No one went wild with joy, as they might have. It was too much for the rebels to comprehend just then. Their ordeal by ice and fire had exhausted them, and they had yet to recross the frozen Delaware River and return to camp.

They took prisoner almost a thousand Hessians, including thirty officers. More than a hundred Germans had been slain or wounded, and their commander, Col. Johann Rall, lay dying on a village church pew from two mortal wounds.

American losses were slight. Amazingly, in the furious fighting, only two officers and two privates were wounded. But there were three men, at least, who froze to death on the return trip across the Delaware.

The shockwaves of Washington's brilliant triumph were beginning to spread to New York, to Philadelphia, and soon to London, where Lord Germain would pound tables in fury and rail at General Howe for not following up the tide of success.

In the hushed hospital ward, where the news had just landed with sledgehammer impact, the air was charged with excitement.

"Lord in Heaven," Gus groaned, misty-eyed. "I wish I'd been with them. *God*, how I do!"

Alexandra's thoughts were tumbling over each other, pulling her in several directions at once. She was worried that events at Trenton would prolong the war. She felt vindicated because she knew Charles Villard must be seething. She was also aware of a nameless sensation curling in the pit of her stomach.

Gus's glimmering eyes were on her. His mouth twisted into the grimace that was his smile. "If I didn't know you better," he said, his gaunt face intense, "I'd say you look pleased."

With a start, Alexandra realized she was more than pleased. She was elated, not only for the men in this room, but for the battered rebel army itself. Despite every obstacle, they had pulled off the impossible—a stunning victory against the King, *her* King, and yet she couldn't help feeling thrilled. The rebels were unpredictable and daring, their courage was admirable.

"I'm glad you have something to celebrate," she told Gus, who nodded and gave a soft murmur of approval. When he held out his hand, Alexandra gripped it and felt a tremor pass through him. She didn't let go until he slept.

It was dark when she left the hospital and climbed into her waiting coach. She spent a restless night in bed, tossing under layers of quilts, unable to stop thinking about the rebel victory. Gradually her excitement wore down and sharp, familiar fear rose in its place. After more than a month, there had been no reply to the letter she sent Dalton.

Before dawn, Alexandra was awake, dressed, and anxious to return to the hospital. A sleepy-eyed Clue drove her there as the sun peeked over the horizon and cast the bluish shadows of trees against the snowy streets.

The hospital was chill and quiet inside. Whispers of noise floated through its corridors as the attendants on duty made their morning rounds. Alexandra put on her apron, scrubbed her hands with soap—one of Rush's strict guidelines when handling patients—and hurried to Gus's ward. She froze in the doorway with a choked cry.

His bed was empty, stripped to the mattress.

Chapter Thirty-Eight

Orders came in the dead of night. The darkness was filled with wind and biting cold as sergeants woke their sleeping men—*Get up! Get ready to march!*—and another raw, bone-numbing time of action began for the rebels.

The American Army, swelled to six thousand men by the recent arrival of Pennsylvania militia, was once again in New Jersey. Earlier in the day, Lord Cornwallis and eight thousand British regulars had pushed back rebel outguards on the Princeton Road, broken scattered resistance on all sides, and cornered Washington near Trenton. At dawn, Cornwallis planned to cross over the swollen Assunpink Creek and bag the fox.

But the bold fox was busy with his own gambit. Under a pink glow in the northeastern sky—the reflection of Lord Cornwallis's campfires—rebel horses were being harnessed. The wheels of gun carriages were being wrapped in rags to prevent the iron rims from singing out on icy roads like bells. Roused from sleep, soldiers huddled together for warmth. They stamped their sack-wound feet, blew on numb fingers, yawned, and groaned as their breaths frosted in the bitter night. Their stomachs were empty, their bodies ached from marching. Some were so exhausted they fell asleep leaning on their muskets. The officers had all they could do to form up the half-clothed troops.

Then, just after midnight, the final orders came. Leaving their campfires burning, the Americans began a fourteen-mile march around the British left flank. Their destination was Princeton, where Lord Cornwallis had stationed three infantry regiments and a number of cannon as his rear guard. Washington planned to smash the relatively small garrison, seize the British artillery, and obtain desperately needed supplies for his army.

The General and his staff rode ahead and disappeared into the blackness. Snorting in protest, the huge draft horses lumbered forward under the weight of heavy cannon. Straps creaked, snow crunched as the long file of shivering men moved off into the night. The ground they marched over was marked by the blood of soldiers' feet.

Due to the rutted condition of the road, there was no rhythm or uniformity to the march. Portions of the route led through dense woods where unshod horses slid on the glazed road and fell. The men broke through ice lying over hidden puddles and were soaked to the skin. Every now and then a cannon banged to a halt against an invisible tree stump, bringing everything behind it to a jarring stop.

Dalton, leading his company through a grove of pines, suddenly grabbed Henry's arm and pulled him upright. It was the second time Henry had gone to sleep on his feet. Dalton was feeling no less exhausted, cold, and miserable. He longed to have Mercury's smooth-gaited power beneath him, but only the most necessary horses had been ferried across the icy Delaware for the assault against Princeton.

"We're almost there," he told Henry, giving him a shake. "Wake up now, in case we run into some Bloodies."

Henry muttered something unintelligible and staggered forward again. Behind them, someone broke wind loudly, causing Dalton to turn and say, "I know that ain't a bullfrog." His narrowed eyes probed the gloom and picked out the rangy silhouette of Sgt. Tom Haney. "Must've been you, Tom."

"Sorry, sir."

"You keep that up, you'll give us away for sure."

"I can't help it, Lieutenant." No sooner did he speak than the sergeant proved his point with even more volume than before.

"Jesus God, Tom! Why the hell did we drag cannon all this way when we've got you?"

Snickers of laughter came from the darkness. Even Sergeant Haney smiled, grateful for any kind of diversion to take his mind off his tortured body.

Dawn blazed bright and beautiful, turning the sky above the winter trees to a cold, steely blue. Shortly after daybreak, two regiments of crack British infantry, under Colonel Mawhood, set out from Princeton and started south to join Lord Cornwallis. The colonel left behind the Fortieth Regiment to guard the town. His advance troops had just climbed a snowy ridge on the south side of Stony Brook when they caught sight of movement off to the east. There, on the far side of the stream, was a long file of men, horses, and artillery heading for Princeton.

Astonished by the sight, Colonel Mawhood quickly recovered, drew his sword, and ordered his strung-out infantry to wheel. Back they went, and a race for the bridge over Stony Brook ensued with a force of rebel infantry. The British were a step quicker. As redcoats poured over the bridge, the rebels ran through an orchard and ducked down behind a stone wall.

Snow was drifted deep along the northern bank of Stony Brook, forming a ridge which the British scrambled up. When they reached the top, a line of muzzles fired a devastating volley into their ranks. Snow flew on the little ridge; red-coated figures jerked and screamed and tumbled down the embankment onto the thin ice edging the stream. Another roaring volley shook the morning, and another scarlet wave toppled backwards. The rebels were firing with deadly accuracy.

But the disciplined British regulars, the flower of the Royal Army, had faced heavier odds. "Forward!" yelled Colonel Mawhood, and five hundred Bloodybacks charged in force, plunging over the ridge, driving down upon the rebels behind bright fangs of steel.

Two things about the redcoats terrified the rebels: their fearless cavalry and their infantry's legendary prowess with the bayonet. Faced with the awesome, blade-tipped charge, the rebels came unstitched. They broke and ran like scared rabbits, ignoring their officers, who shouted at them to turn and fight. Colonel Haslet of Delaware went down with a round hole in his temple. Gallant General Mercer, left behind by his stampeding troops, was surrounded by British grenadiers who mistook him for Washington and demanded his surrender.

Mercer drew his sword. "Surrender yourselves, god-damn you!" Snarling defiance, the fierce son of a Scots minister hacked at the encircling bayonets. He slashed arms and opened faces with cold steel, parrying and thrusting until a musket butt clubbed his head and knocked him to his knees. Bayonets plunged. The British ran Mercer through again and again until they left a bloody, twitching mess on the battlefield.

Meanwhile, at the edge of a woods, Capt. Joseph Moulder and a handful of his men had maneuvered two heavy guns into a position overlooking the field. They opened fire on the British with grapeshot. For several crucial minutes, Moulder and his two cannon were all that prevented the Bloodybacks from routing the retreating rebels.

Then Washington arrived with reinforcements. He rode to the front through a hail of bullets, seemingly charmed and invulnerable as lead plucked holes through his cloak and zinged past his ears. Swinging his troops across a ridge of deep, blood-reddened snow, he defied the British snipers sighting on him. With unshakable calm, Washington reined in and shouted encouragement to the fleeing swirl of men.

Watching him, Dalton's heart slammed with fear at the General's recklessness, but he took the example and roared commands at his terrified company. "Goddamn you bloody cowards! Get your asses back here and *fight!*" He chased them, kicked them, and dragged them until finally, by the sheer force of his will, he drove them back into formation.

Other officers were doing the same. The remains of Mercer's beaten force fell in line again. Hitchcock's New England Continentals came up and joined them. The frantic Pennsylvania militia stopped milling and began to form alongside a regiment of veteran Virginians. Within minutes, the rebel battle line was set, and General Washington waved his hat and ordered them forward against the shifting British line, which was still being flayed by murderous rounds from Moulder's two cannon. The Americans were now a formidale force, stretching the whole way across the hillside, and with guns at ready they followed their commander in chief into battle.

An order came down the line to Dalton, who repeated it to his men in a tense voice. "Hold your fire until the General gives the signal!"

The signal did not come until the Americans were just thirty yards from the redcoats. Washington, out in front of his army, directly in the line of fire, lifted his sword high, and Dalton held his breath until the bright blade flashed down.

"FIRE!"

Two thundering volleys came from the opposing armies, raising a screen of smoke that gradually cleared.

"Jesus God," Dalton breathed when he saw Washington still in the saddle, waving his troops forward.

Something happened to the rebels then. Their hesitation blew away like the smoke on the breeze. They swept ahead with a surge of excitement, then halted on command and delivered a blazing fire into the British lines. The terrible noise of battle rose to a crescendo—the concerted bang of musketry, cannon belching hot metal, flame, and smoke, rifles cracking with lethal accuracy, the wounded screaming and groaning as blood seeped into the snow beneath them.

Thrown into confusion by the unexpected reversal of roles, the disciplined British infantry broke ranks and fell back. They attempted to rescue their cannon, but the Pennsylvania militia overran the battery and captured the precious guns.

The Bloodybacks fled in disorder.

Like hounds on the hunt, the rebels gave chase. Washington rode with his men, his eyes glittering-wet to see British regulars in full flight across an open field, running before his fearsome mongrel warriors. He had wrested triumph from near disaster. Joy flooded him and burst from him in a shout. "It's a fine fox chase, boys!"

The rebels pushed on to Princeton, where some panicked redcoats took cover in Nassau Hall and fired on the advancing Americans. Soon, rebel artillery was blasting away at the big stone building, shattering windows, gouging walls, terrorizing the soldiers barricaded inside. When a cannonball streaked through the prayer hall and deftly decapitated a portrait of King

George II, the defenders decided they had seen enough.

A white flag fluttered from a window. The ferocious rebels backed off as the humiliated redcoats trooped outside and laid down their arms.

When Washington rode up, a wild, throaty cheering rose from thousands of Patriot throats. Princeton was theirs.

There was no time to bury the dead. After the wounded were brought off the field and carried to temporary hospitals, the red ground remained strewn with bodies. British losses were calculated at almost six hundred, including three hundred known prisoners taken at Princeton. In less than an hour, the best of the Royal Army—the crack 4th Brigade—had been shattered. The cost to the rebels was thirty privates and fourteen officers killed.

Washington's occupation of Princeton was necessarily short, for Lord Cornwallis was coming up from Trenton with fresh troops, and the tired rebels were in no condition to fight another battle. How far they could march was anyone's guess, pushed as they were to the limits of human endurance.

When the American Army pulled out, encumbered by confiscated military stores, prisoners, and wagonloads of booty taken from Tories, British skirmishers were already in sight near Stony Brook. By demolishing bridges in their wake, the rebels were able to outrun British pursuit. Just barely.

What galled Dalton most during the forced march was the haughtiness of the prisoners. They were a crabbed lot of men, sneering at their captors, and they grew worse with each mile the army traveled into the country. One redcoat in particular, Brigade Maj. Andrew Palmos, seemed to take pleasure in badgering his keepers. A musket ball had grazed the heel of the major's foot, and he was making the most of his injury, dragging himself along with an exaggerated limp.

"If you expect me to travel far," he announced to anyone who was listening, "you had best put me in a wagon." When no one answered or paid attention to him, he hobbled forward and tapped Dalton's shoulder. "Are you the officer in charge of this pack of vermin?"

Dalton swung around.

When Major Palmos saw the rebel officer's eyes, he recoiled slightly. Recovering, he demanded, "Well?"

"A well is a hole in the ground, and that's where you're going if you don't shut up and keep moving."

"You can't expect me to walk with a bullet in my foot!"

Dalton's pistol came out. "Ain't no bullet in your foot," he said, pressing the muzzle under the major's nose, tilting his head back. "But you'll have one in your brain in a minute."

"You wouldn't dare." The major had cannon balls, give him that. "I'm a wounded prisoner of war," he declared with dignity, matching Dalton's stare. "I demand to be treated as such."

"You want a wagon to haul you, is that it?"

"Precisely."

Turning, Dalton yelled back down the line, "Corporal Buckley! Bring that wagon up here!" The supply wagon arrived promptly, and Dalton told Henry, "Major Pompous is tired of walking."

The major bristled. "It's *Palmos*."

"Like I said, Henry. Major Penis wants a wagon to haul him, so tie him to the back by his wrists."

"Now, see here—"

"Do it," Dalton told Henry.

It was done. Henry climbed back onto the driver's bench and slapped the reins, and the wagon took off with the wailing, stumbling redcoat in tow. A quarter-mile later, Dalton and his company of Pennsylvanians caught up with the exhausted man. The major's curly brown wig was gone, his silk-lined uniform coat and snowy breeches were spattered with mud.

"Untie me," he gasped.

Dalton nodded to Henry, who climbed down and cut the bonds. Once free, Major Palmos sank to his knees and didn't move.

"On your feet," Henry said.

"I can't take another step."

"You'll step into hell if the lieutenant here says so." Getting no response, Henry hauled the major up and, to the delight of onlookers, booted his behind. "Move, goddamnit!"

Enraged, Major Palmos started forward, cursing under his breath, using words no proper British officer would dare utter aloud. He kept his gaze on the slippery ground so he would not have to see the amused faces around him. After a time, still fuming, he became aware of someone walking beside him and knew, without looking over, who it was. The barbaric lieutenant with the hard green eyes.

Major Palmos would never forget his face.

Following the rebel victories at Trenton and Princeton, the thinly stretched line of British outposts snapped. Marauding bands of rebels seized Hackensack, Newark, and Elizabethtown, forcing General Howe's outguards to fall back toward New York. In two astonishing weeks, Washington had liberated almost all of New Jersey.

But the boost to Patriot morale did not last long at Morristown, the peaceful village in the Watchung Mountains where the rebels went into winter quarters. Morristown was an unparalleled strategic position. From there, the rebels could protect the approaches to northern New York and New Jersey, and threaten the Brunswick-Trenton Road. Unfortunately, the only men who saw much activity were the far outguards and the roving patrols. The rest of the army sat in gloomy boredom on those unassailable heights, homesick and longing for spring.

As winter descended in earnest, the sounds of blazing cannon and musketry and the cries of soldiers became a dull memory. January saw the Continental Army hit rock bottom when only eight hundred veterans answered roll call. Some had gone home when their enlistments expired, others had deserted to the British, who were paying sixteen dollars in gold to every man who came over. The clink of gold coins was a huge temptation to soldiers who had not been paid in months and whose families were suffering at home.

The poverty of the rebel army was pathetic. For months no hard money had come through Washington's moth-eaten exchequer, and supplies had to be bartered or begged or paid for with worthless Continental currency, which was refused more often than not. While the war profiteers grew fat on luxury, the rebel ranks thinned, the pale soldiers despaired, and the Congress made vacant promises to clothe and feed the army.

"I heard we're having beef tonight," Henry told Dalton as they crossed the frozen parade ground one evening in February.

"You must be dreaming. Ain't no beef in this camp, unless you count the green stuff they tried to feed us last night."

"But the Virginians brought up some cattle."

"Two cows and a sheep," Dalton corrected him. "They'll go to the high officers."

The eating conditions for subalterns and enlisted men at Morristown were disgusting. The butter was rancid, the biscuits were rock-hard and moldy, the milk usually had a green tint. The commissary cooks would put anything into a pot of stew—dirt, leaves, bark, worm-eaten potatoes.

"It's a wonder more of us ain't sick," Dalton said, huddling deeper into the blanket that served as his coat. Another storm was coming, he could smell it in the whistling wind that bit through his clothing with needlelike teeth.

"Come play cards tonight," Henry urged him.

"No thanks."

"Why not?"

"Don't feel like it."

They were quiet a moment, their white breaths billowing behind them as they walked. Then Henry asked, "Is something wrong?"

Dalton glanced at him. "What do you mean?"

"I dunno," he said with a shrug. "You don't seem the same anymore." Henry watched the ground a moment, then added, "I'm not the only one who thinks so."

Dalton kept silent, waiting.

"I overheard some of the men talking. They're wondering if you're planning to disappear one night."

At first Dalton was shocked, then his face darkened and bright points of anger flared in his eyes. He seized Henry's shoulder and turned him so they were facing each other. "Is that what you think?"

"I think you'd shoot yourself first," Henry said, "and that's what I told them. But they're worried about losing you because you're the one keeping our company together. You're not just another officer to us. You make us laugh when there's nothing to laugh about, and God knows you showed us how to fight. We believe in you, sir," Henry said, quietly intent. "So if you need to talk, I'm here to listen."

For a moment Dalton just watched him, wrung with emotions, then the fire left his eyes. "It's got nothing to do with the army," he said, and the next thing he knew the words were pouring from him. "I left someone in Philadelphia. I know that don't make me special—we've all got someone waiting for us—but lately I can't stop thinking about her. I didn't know it was possible to miss a person this much, but there's no help for it." He stared into Henry's concerned eyes. "Much as I want to see her, I'm staying with the army till the end. Do you hear me?"

Henry nodded. "I hear you."

"Then do me a favor and pass the word along."

Smiling, Henry nudged his arm. "Are you sure you won't come to that card game?"

"All right," Dalton agreed, "but first I need some sleep."

"I'll come get you when it's time," Henry said and started away.

"Henry?"

He paused looking back.

"Thanks for listening."

"Anytime, sir."

It was a disturbed Dalton who returned to the crude log hut he shared with three other company officers. Outside the hut's entrance, the constant parade of men coming and going had turned the pathway to a brimming track of mud fringed with brown snow. Though Dalton negotiated the path with care, there was no avoiding the moisture that seeped through the splits in his boots and soaked his stockings.

Within the cramped enclosure, a small fireplace warmed the air and kept the earthen floor thawed. Crossing to his bunk, Dalton glanced around the little hovel that was home and saw a dingy place scarcely more cheerful than a cell at the Walnut Street Prison. He sat on his straw mattress, pulled off his mud-caked boots, and lay down with a sigh. Soft snoring came from two other bunks. Somewhere outside a whip cracked, a draft horse whinnied. Angry voices rose in the distance as yet another fistfight broke out. Dalton heard none of it. He stared at mud-chinked walls while his thoughts went elsewhere.

After a time his eyes closed, his hand straying to the ribbon tied to his threadbare waistcoat. The satin had faded to a pale shade of its former blue luster, and the ends were badly frayed. But the memories the ribbon evoked were as strong as ever.

She had promised to wait for him. Day after day that vow kept him going, but there were moments when he wondered if her feelings for him had ebbed. After six months of waiting, maybe she had changed her mind about wanting him. Maybe she had married Charles Villard.

Dalton shivered as the thought darkened in his imagination like a persistent wound. Wrapped in his blanket, tired, cold, and disenchanted of his romantic dream of war, he remembered those moments in the Pennington coach and ached for her.

Chapter Thirty-Nine

Alexandra told herself that the waiting and worrying could not get any worse. But when spring came and there was still no word from Dalton, she was plunged into a despair so deep there was no escaping it even in sleep. In her waking hours, she spent as much time as possible at the hospital, tending a new group of rebel soldiers who had been wounded in skirmishes with British troops in the Jerseys. She asked every soldier for news about Dalton, but to her frustration none of them had ever heard of him.

She tried to track down Major Cooke, the express rider she had paid to carry her letter to the American Army, but her inquiries about him led nowhere. One report listed him as captured, another stated he had been killed at Princeton, while still another source claimed he was on special assignment in Rhode Island. In any event he could not be located, which left Alexandra wondering if her letter had ever reached its destination.

Since the return of Congress to Philadelphia in February, Christopher Clue, at her instigation, had become a permanent fixture in the State House yard. With alert eyes and ears, he caught every whisper of news that dribbled to the public and often brought home disturbing stories.

"The British are murdering their prisoners," he told Alexandra one evening in April. They were sharing a bottle of Madeira at the kitchen table. Refilling their glasses, Clue went on, "Remember the committee that Congress appointed to investigate the British Army? Well, they turned in their report, and it didn't paint a pretty picture."

"Is there proof of the murders?"

"No clear proof," Clue said, "like written orders or anything. But some people in New Jersey testified that wounded American officers were tortured and killed on purpose. And a minister, who was never even in the army, was shot in cold blood at Trenton while he was on his knees, begging for his life."

"Dear God," Alexandra whispered.

"They were the lucky ones," Clue said. "The ones in prison are starving or freezing to death. At one prison, the poor fellows were kept four days without food, and when they were finally fed, the stuff wasn't fit for rats to eat."

Bracing herself with wine, Alexandra shed the last of her hope that English soldiers were above committing such cruelties. Because the melancholy truth was that too many well-founded reports—including statements from persons cool to the rebel cause—revealed otherwise. Further denial on her part, simply because the Royal Army was the accused, would be blind and foolish.

Plundering, raping, killing. She felt ashamed that British officers, who called themselves gentlemen, would prey upon the very people they were sent here to protect. What kind of general was Sir William Howe that he would allow his soldiers to make enemies of potential supporters?

"Then again," Clue said, breaking into her thoughts, "the rebels aren't blameless either. They've been doing their share of looting. But at least they haven't murdered anyone, and they're punished if they're caught stealing. And they treat their prisoners like human beings. That's what I've heard, anyway."

They were quiet for a time, sipping wine in disturbed silence. Then Clue asked, "How's Mr. Pennington?"

Alexandra forced a smile. "Crabby as ever."

"Did he get over his cold yet?"

It was more than just a cold, and if anything it was getting worse. Alexandra shook her head and said, "I'm worried about him, Christopher."

"He needs to get outside. Some fresh air wouldn't hurt him. It's bad for a body, being cooped up all the time."

Alexandra agreed. But Dr. Stone, on whose advice Pennington relied, had an acute phobia of cold air, claiming it caused sickness in the lungs. At his insistence, the windows at Oakwood remained closed even on the mildest spring days, and consequently the old stone house was damp and stuffy. Alexandra believed the stale environment was contributing to Pennington's poor health.

She said, "Dr. Stone has advised him to stay indoors until the middle of May."

"That's daft!"

"Dr. Stone is daft," she said. "But don't worry, I won't let it happen."

But it did happen, because George Pennington, besides being physically ill, was becoming increasingly stubborn. Finally, in late May, he came to her town house for dinner. Aided by Edward Brock's arm, he entered the front passageway, where Alexandra was waiting to greet him. Her throat ached at the sight of him. Pennington had urged her not to blame herself for whatever consequences arose from the duel, but each time she beheld his shockingly pale face, guilt stabbed her.

He had never fully recovered from the wound inflicted by Charles Villard. Even before the duel, Pennington's health had been fragile. But now, although his shoulder had healed, the rest of him seemed to be decaying. The bedridden months after the shooting, rather than restoring him, had robbed his body of what little vitality it possessed. His joints had stiffened from inactivity, and mucus had collected in his lungs. Lately he was plagued by a convulsive cough which he attributed to the deafness of his servants. "I must repeat everything twice," he complained, "and it makes me hoarse."

At least his sense of humor had not departed him. He paused in the hallway, peering hard at her. "What a long face," he said in a gravelly, phlegm-wet voice. "Why don't you simply wear black and be done with it?"

Alexandra went to him and hugged him. He felt like a bundle of sticks in her arms. "How are you, George?"

"Oh, getting around again. Just yesterday, in fact, William and I went to the market."

"And you didn't invite me along?"

"Heavens, no! You'd have fussed over me every moment."

Smiling, Alexandra linked arms with him and they followed Edward into the dining room. Pennington moved slowly, with obvious pain in his legs and back. Glancing down, she noted that the knuckles of his hands were swollen, the fingers permanently crooked. "I hope you brought your appetite," she said. "Mary fixed your favorite dish, roast duck. And brandied fruit for dessert."

"I'm famished," he declared. Indeed, he ate so much food that Alexandra wondered where in his thin frame he was putting it. Partway through the meal, Pennington leaned back in his chair, swirled wine in his glass, and said, "I saw Evelyn Wright yesterday."

Interested, Alexandra looked up from her plate. "What did she have to say for herself?"

"I said I saw her, I didn't speak with her. Frankly, I would rather speak with the hind end of Mr. Washington's horse."

Alexandra laughed, appreciating the jab. Since her break with Villard, Evelyn had been a constant thorn in her side. Not in any straightforward way—that wasn't Evelyn's style—but through every underhanded means known to a professional gossipmonger.

"Dear Evelyn was raising a racket at the Market Square," Pennington said.

"Whatever for?"

"A smutty little urchin snatched her parasol and ran away with it." He chuckled at the memory. "It was hilarious. I've never heard such shrieking, except from a stuck pig. Come to think of it," he said, frowning and tapping a finger against his lower lip, "there is a certain amount of resemblance."

"George, you're ornery as the devil."

"Thank you."

"Next you'll be telling me you paid the little thief to steal her parasol."

Eyes widening, Pennington rapped the table with his knuckles. "What a splendid idea! Why on earth didn't I think of it?"

"George . . ." she warned.

Changing the subject, he asked, "Have you noticed the inordinate amount of militia on the streets these days? Good God, they seem to be everywhere! Marching, singing, pounding those infernal drums of theirs. Don't they ever sleep?"

It was true, the number of militia companies in Philadelphia had doubled since the beginning of spring. Washington's winter victories had lifted the rebel cause on new wings. Recruiting parties that had been unable to find a single volunteer were now harvesting them in company-sized lots, and the rebel army was pushing up like new grass.

"They're all liberty mad again," Pennington muttered.

"After Trenton and Princeton, they have good reason to be."

Pennington watched her a moment. "You sound pleased about that."

"I'm not," she said quickly. "It will only prolong the war."

"By years, if you believe some estimates."

Those estimates were coming from England, where the King's minions were concerned about the growing support for the American Army. In particular, they worried about the proven capabilities of rebel leadership. The name of Washington was on everyone's lips, but no longer as the butt of jokes. Whereas it was once fashionable to disdain the rebels as ignorant, worthy only of contempt, they had now become a formidable enemy. Last winter, they had learned what a small, determined group of men could do, moving swiftly and unexpectedly against superior numbers. They had discovered the enormous effectiveness of a type of fighting that left British generals scratching their heads and grimacing in despair. Guerrilla warfare, it would come to be called, and Washington had no qualms about employing it at every opportunity. For months, small parties of his troops had been using hit-and-run tactics against British patrols and foraging parties in New Jersey. Whenever a large force of redcoats was deployed to attack them, the rebels would simply melt into the countryside, frustrating every attempt to draw them into an engagement. Then, just when it seemed they had quit the field, the raiders would reappear and harass the British all the way back to their base.

"If you ask me," Pennington said, "it's an unscrupulous way of fighting."

"No more unscrupulous than what the British have been doing to our country."

"Hearsay," he said with a dismissive gesture.

"I don't believe it is."

"The rebels are every bit as guilty of plundering."

"Perhaps," she conceded, "but their treatment of prisoners is at least humane. And I have not heard of one instance where a rebel soldier shot a minister or raped a young girl in front of her parents."

The mantel clock ticked in the silence. Pennington watched her with shrewd eyes. "Where are you getting all your information?"

"I hear things."

"From your friends at the hospital?"

"Sometimes," she admitted.

"I understand you're also using Christopher as your ears."

Her chin rose. "Why not? He has acquaintances in the right places."

"What you mean is," said Pennington, smiling wryly, "he spends all his time at the State House, rubbing elbows with radicals and catching whatever tidbits come his way. Really, Alexandra, it's unseemly for one of your servants to be constantly seen there."

Alexandra's tone was defensive. "Unseemly to whom, George?"

"You know exactly what I mean. People will form the wrong opinion of you."

"I don't give a damn what opinion people form of me."

"Stop being so naive!" he exploded, banging the table with his fist. A hush fell. And Pennington, his bloodshot eyes glittering, was suddenly intense. "When General Howe takes Philadelphia, the Tories will be in charge. Which means that our good friend Charles Villard and his cronies will seek punishment for things that are happening now."

"The devil take Charles Villard."

"That," Pennington said, "is an absolute certainty. But

until it happens, he will look to cause you trouble whenever he can."

"It isn't a crime to want news of the war."

"Have you forsaken the King?" Pennington demanded. Startled, Alexandra faltered.

"There, you see?" he said. "You hesitate."

"I believe we should remain under English rule," she shot back, "but I disagree with the way General Howe is going about it."

"In other words, you will not commit either way."

"I'm a Loyalist."

"Truly?" Pennington cocked his head. "Then you should look upon all rebels as traitors. When they are defeated, supose Mr. Philips is put to death for his part in the rebellion? How then will you rationalize your feelings?"

Alexandra stared at him, a sudden chill raising the hair on her arms. Averting her eyes, she concentrated on her plate while her thoughts caught fire and her hands balled into fists beneath the table.

After a time, Pennington said, "You look as fierce as ten Furies." There was amusement in his voice, coupled with sadness. "I know you don't appreciate my meddling in your affairs, but it's only because I care what happens to you. You cannot remain on the fence, Alexandra. Make your choice and protect yourself accordingly, because when the British Army comes to Philadelphia, there will be no such thing as neutrality."

Alexandra searched his grave face. "How do you know they're coming, George?"

He smiled. "I hear things, too."

She started to reply, then paused at the sound of footsteps hastening through the hallway from the kitchen. Clue entered the dining room, apologized for the interruption, and approached her chair. He was breathing hard, as though he had run a long way, and his face was flushed with excitement. "This just came," he said, waving a letter. "By army courier."

Alexandra stood and reached for the letter. Recognizing the wavering handwriting, her body began to tingle, her pulse raced. "Excuse me," she said in a faint voice and left the room with the letter clutched in her hand.

In the parlor, she sank onto the couch and stared at the soiled, torn paper a moment. Unfolding it, she saw there were actually two letters, written on opposite sides of the same sheet. One was addressed to someone named Twigs. But she was only interested in the letter which began:

Morestown, 30th April, 1777

Dearest Alexandra,

You can not emajin how good it felt to reseve your letter. I have read it a hundred times and know each line by heart, but I would give anything to hear the words from your lips. I think of you every day and hope you are well and that you miss me a little. I am well myself.

The page blurred as hot, joyful tears slid down her face and dripped onto the letter, smearing precious words. Heedless of staining her fine muslin dress with ink, she blotted the moisture with her skirt, then read on with utter absorption.

Your letter was lost and did not reach me until months after it was ritten, so please forgive the long wait for this reply. I hope your break with Mr. Villard was not very painfull for you, but no news has ever given me more joy.

I miss you more than I know how to tell you. The army is a terrible place to be when you miss someone. The food is bad, the nights are cold and long. Being a soldier is very hard duty. Not much grass grows under our feet, for we are always on watches and marches and sometimes our patrols have close rubs with the enemy.

We are awaiting the next move of Gen'l Hough. Everyone thinks he will make a pass at Phila. in wich event we are preyparing for its defence. We are becoming experts at defence. It seems we are forever going backward instead of forward.

I must ask a great faver from you as I am unable to do it myself. A friend of mine named Timothy Leeds lives at my farm and his health is not the best, so wold you please be kind enough to see if he is well? Also here is a letter for Twigs (the name I call him) and I wold be grateful if you wold read it to him.

Before I go, I must say something more. I still keep your ribbon next to my heart and it makes me feel closer to you, but sometimes I just need so much to hold you. Alexandra, my love for you is endless. You are the dearest person I know and I miss you and will always be

Faithfully yours,
Dalton

Alexandra read the letter again and again, overjoyed that Dalton was alive and that he loved her more than ever.

Chapter Forty

The lush, green Wissahickon Valley was sweet-scented with June. Majestic sycamores and groves of fruit trees had leafed out, soft winds had dried the fertile soil where crops now sprouted and wildflowers bloomed. Cows munched contentedly in pastures, birds twittered their morning songs in trees, brooks gurgled through fields and woodlands to feed the Wissahickon Creek, peaceful and shimmering in the sunlight.

It was the loveliest day in Alexandra's recollection. And it was today that she was visiting Dalton's farm and meeting his friend Timothy Leeds.

"If you think Mr. Pennington is crabby," Clue said, riding beside her along the creek road, "wait till you meet this character."

"He can't be that bad."

"He's worse. But I'll say this for him, he's loyal no end to Dalton."

That, in itself, was enough to endear Twigs to Alexandra before she ever laid eyes on him.

"Dalton's farm begins here," Clue told her, indicating a broad, sloping meadow dotted with buttonwood trees. "The property follows the creek quite a ways."

"It's beautiful. How long has he owned Downstream Farm?"

Clue shrugged and said, "Five years, at least."

Which made Alexandra frown. How on earth had Dalton—exiled from England, without a cent to his name—afforded this prime piece of ground? The obvious answer was Jack Flash's plunder, but she rejected the notion because Dalton had sworn to her that he never took money for personal gain, only for the rebel cause. There must be another explanation.

"Do you know how he acquired it?" she asked Clue, who shook his head.

"Can't say I do. But I recall he had an awful time getting established as a horse breeder. Somebody started a rumor that he was selling sick animals. It wasn't true, but it made folks leery of buying from him." Leaning forward, Clue patted his mare's neck. "He practically gave Sunshine to me, and she's sound as can be. The fact is, when you buy a horse from Dalton, you can be sure you're getting your money's worth."

The entrance to Downstream Farm was a narrow dirt lane that wound among cool, shadowy pines. Riding along the lane, Alexandra urged her horse into a canter, anxious for her first look at Dalton's home. The pines thinned, the farm buildings came into view, and her immediate impression was one of solidity. The two-storied farmhouse, built of local fieldstone, was modest and compact, with two large brick chimneys and a slate-tiled roof. Several of its windows contained oiled paper in place of glass panes. The awning overhanging the front door needed painting, as did the red fence surrounding the yard, but the house looked otherwise well-kept. Riding toward it, Alexandra breathed the smells of horses, new-mown hay fields, and the fresh, clean scent of the nearby creek, all reminiscent of the man whose lingering presence she could feel. She half-expected him to appear from one of the buildings.

Instead, a thickset, freckle-faced youth emerged from the stable with a pitchfork in his hands. Moving to greet them, he planted the fork's prongs in the ground and leaned on the handle. "Morning," he said, his watchful gaze moving from Clue to Alexandra. "Looking for someone?"

"Timothy Leeds," she said. "I'm Mrs. Alexandra Pennington, and this is my friend Christopher Clue. I have a letter for Mr. Leeds from Dalton Philips."

At once the youth straightened, eyes widening. "Wait here," he said and trotted toward the house.

When he was out of earshot, Clue muttered, "So much for a warm welcome."

305

"I'm sure Mr. Leeds will be more hospitable."

Clue just rolled his eyes.

A little later, the young man with the pitchfork returned and told them, "Twigs said to leave the letter with me."

Alexandra stiffened. "I'm afraid I can't do that. Please explain to Mr. Leeds that there is a letter written to me on the same sheet of paper, and I intend to keep it."

Frowning, the young man left again, and Alexandra drew a deep breath and let it out slowly. When she glanced at Clue, he was wearing such a smug look she could have crowned him. "Don't say a word."

"My lips are sealed."

"And wipe that smile off your face."

"Whatever you say, ma'am."

They waited five long minutes before Timothy Leeds came outside, and Alexandra noted with chagrin that his dour appearance supported Clue's assessment of him. From his scowling, sightless eyes to his turned-down mouth, Leeds had curmudgeon stamped all over him. He spoke like a man faced with an unpleasant task. "I'll handle this, Joe," he told the boy with the pitchfork. "Go back to what you were doing."

Joe headed for the stable, and Twigs confronted Alexandra and Clue, who were still on horseback. "You have a letter from Dalton?" he demanded.

"Yes," she replied. "He wrote letters to us both on the same paper. He asked me to read you yours."

"That was considerate of him, sending his greetings through a stranger."

Good grief. "I'm sure he didn't mean for you to feel awkward."

Twig's mouth twitched. "You don't know Dalton," he said, then beckoned her with a grudging wave. "Come inside, Mrs. Pennington."

Glancing at Clue, Alexandra received an I-told-you-so shrug, which heightened her annoyance. As they followed Twigs toward the house, Clue asked him, "Would you mind if I go look at the creek, Mr. Leeds?"

"Suit yourself."

Alexandra's eyes flashed at Clue. *Coward*, her look said, but she could not blame him for ducking out.

Promising to return shortly, Clue rode off, and

Alexandra followed Twigs behind the house and tethered her mare to the hitching post. With a wordless gesture, Twigs directed her ahead of him into the kitchen. He left the top half of the dutch door open to allow for ventilation and light while keeping animals out. As he moved to the table and sat down, Alexandra glanced around the room, consumed with curiosity. The rustic, spartan kitchen had a cozy feel to it, everything well-worn, yet tidy and clean. When her gaze fell on several bound volumes stacked on the fireplace mantel, she moved closer to read the titles. Poetry by Taylor, a novel by Smollett, an account of Caesar's victories in Gaul.

"Are these Dalton's books?" she asked.

"They wouldn't be much use to a blind man, would they?"

Her face burned at his caustic tone.

"Sit down, Mrs. Pennington."

Alexandra complied, feeling his hostility wash over her like a seething current. "Have you known Dalton long?" she wanted to know.

"Long enough," was his brisk answer. "Read me the letter, girl. I have things to do and you're keeping me from them."

At that, Alexandra's patience fled. "What do you have against me?" she asked in a tight voice.

As if he had been itching for the question, Twigs snapped a reply. "You're not his type."

"Who are you to decide what woman is his type?"

"I know the boy a lot better than you."

"He isn't a boy, Mr. Leeds."

"Not in years," Twigs agreed, "but he's far too trusting sometimes."

Then Alexandra understood the reason for his animosity. He suspected her of causing Dalton's arrest last year. She cleared the air without delay. "I've never broken his trust."

"You almost cost him his life," Twigs retorted. "You betrayed him to Mr. Villard."

Pierced by the accusation, Alexandra responded with equal adamance. "I have no doubt that Mr. Villard had a hand in what happened, but he did not learn about Jack Flash from me."

Twigs snorted a laugh.

"Think what you will," she said, eyes narrowing in anger. "What matters to me is that Dalton knows the truth."

"Like I said, he's far too trusting. Only a miracle saved him from the gallows."

"Why do you think his trial was postponed?" she demanded.

For a second Twigs seemed surprised, then his features hardened again with distrust. "Am I supposed to believe you had something to do with it?"

"I think you'll believe whatever bloody well suits you," she fired back. "I think you're bitter because Dalton made up his own mind about me and didn't listen to your petty advice." Alexandra leaned forward a little and her voice was low and intent as she warned him, "Make no mistake, Mr. Leeds. If your aim is to break us apart, you will fail. Because I will fight you or anyone else who tries to come between us."

Twigs was quiet a moment. Then, to her astonishment, his leathery face broke into a grin. "I'll be goddamned," he chuckled. "The boy has finally found his match."

All at once Alexandra realized he had been testing her, and she wasn't sure whether to feel angrier at him or relieved.

Twigs didn't give her the chance to decide. "Will you read the letter to me?" he asked without a hint of his former venom. If anything his voice was gentle, half-amused.

Taken aback by his sudden turnaround, she studied him warily, still offended by his behavior. At the same time she was intrigued, as a cat might be curious about the fluid movements of a snake. Opening her drawstring purse, she brought out the letter, unfolded it, and began to read to him.

Hello Twigs,
I am sorry for not riting sooner, but sometimes there is little time even to sleep and also paper is very hard to get. How are you? Well I hope, as I am. Murcrey was sick for awhile but he is better now after a long rest.

308

Soldiering is everything you said it wold be and sometimes werse, but we are in good spirits now and ready for fiting time. The Penna. Line is stronger than ever with many new Men who have joyn'd us. Gen'l Wayne who is back from the North now comands my battaleon. He is a brave officer and much respected, and I know he will not rest until we have Liberty.

I asked Alexandra to read this to you and I had no chanse to tell you that we have mended things between us. Please always remember my caring for her. I miss you and the farm and wold like nothing more than to be at home having a gil of rum by the hearth with you. Until then remember I think of you and that I am

Ever your friend
Dalton

When she finished reading, silence hung in the room. Twigs, his snowy head downcast, absently rubbed the table edge as a smile tugged his mouth. Uncertain what his smile meant, Alexandra waited for him to speak. As his head rose, something spanned the distance between them and banished her misgivings. Warmth emanated from the man who just moments ago had accused her of treachery, but whose blind eyes now shone with kindness.

"Will you have something to drink, Mrs. Pennington? There's no tea, but I do have a fine cider that I made myself."

"I would love some cider, thank you."

"I should warn you, it's a mite potent."

"So much the better."

Getting up, Twigs moved to a sideboard and uncorked a stoneware jug. As he poured two mugs of hard cider, Dalton's words blew around in his thoughts like an invigorating wind. The sentiments in the letter reinforced what Twigs already knew—the boy was in love with this woman. Which might have disturbed Twigs, except for what he had heard in Alexandra's voice as she read to him, for it was clear that Dalton was not alone in his feelings.

Twigs carried the mugs to the table and offered her one. "You're not what I expected, Mrs. Pennington."

"Please call me Alexandra," she said. "And I could say the same thing about you."

He smiled, liking her more and more. "Dalton says I meddle too much in his business," he said as he sat down. "He's probably right, but I'm just looking out for him. The boy's been trampled enough in his life." A moment passed as he sipped cider. "Him being a Patriot and you being a Loyalist is cause for concern in my opinion. But now I'm meddling again, and I know you didn't come here to discuss politics. I expect you want to hear about Dalton."

The door was open, and Alexandra wasted no time crossing the threshold. "How did he come to own this farm?"

"You must be wondering if Jack Flash had anything to do with it."

"The thought crossed my mind."

"He won it," Twigs said. "From Mr. Villard."

Surprised and exceedingly pleased, Alexandra asked, "In a horse race?"

Twigs nodded. "I'll never forget the day. It was the most incredible thing I ever saw." He sighed deeply, a distant look on his face. "It was back in seventy-one, you see, before I went blind. We were at the Indian Queen one night, and Mr. Villard was in the taproom with some of his friends. Drunk as a newt, he was, and twice as slippery."

Twigs paused and swigged cider, in no hurry.

"Mr. Villard was celebrating," he went on, "because his stallion won at Centre Square that afternoon. Lord, he was full of himself. Boasted for an hour that his horse was unbeatable. The way he talked, you might have thought he was an authority on horses. Anyway, he had an audience that night. You couldn't help but listen to him, loud as he was."

Another pause for cider, then Twigs said, "When Mr. Villard's father died, he left him several properties, including this farm. The buildings here were rundown, but this is prime horse country, and Mr. Villard fancied this place. That night in the taproom he told everyone he was going to restore Downstream Farm and start a racing dynasty here. He already owned the fastest horse around,

310

he said. Next thing you know, Dalton steps up and challenges him to a race."

Alexandra could envision it—Dalton with a daredevil gleam in his eyes, ready to take on the world.

"In those days," Twigs said, "Dalton lived out of his pockets and it showed. Mr. Villard looked him over, like he was nothing, then laughed at him. 'You couldn't afford to buy me another drink,' he said. Made Dalton hotter than hellfire. So you know what he did?"

Absorbed in his story, Alexandra asked what.

"He wagered his indentured services for seven years against this farm. Naturally, Mr. Villard wanted to see Dalton's horse before accepting the bet. So we all went outside the Queen, and Dalton pointed out his spindly little filly." Twigs shook his head with a smile. "You never heard such laughter. Everyone thought he was mad, including me. Not for a minute did I think that filly could win."

"Was it Secret?" Alexandra asked.

Twigs nodded. "Secret doesn't look especially fast, but she's a lightning bolt, and Dalton knew it. The boy has an uncanny eye for horses."

"Had Secret ever raced before?"

"Never."

"Good grief."

"That's how bad Dalton wanted this place. Fortunately, things went in his favor. The day of the race, Secret flew around the track so fast I thought Mr. Villard would shit marble." Twigs caught himself and looked ashamed. "Pardon me."

"It's all right," she said, amused. "You've given me a vivid picture of Mr. Villard's expression."

"You could have knocked him down with a feather. He took for granted that Dalton would end up indentured to him. Instead his wonder horse lost by ten lengths, and Dalton walked away with the deed to this farm."

"Dalton must have been thrilled."

There was a pause as Twigs ran a fingertip around the rim of his mug. "You should have seen his face after he won. The boy never owned anything in his life and suddenly," Twigs spread his arms, "all this was his. Took him months to get used to the idea."

311

"He took an awful risk for it," she said. "That seems to be a trait of his."

"The man who never dares succeeds at nothing," said Twigs. "To my mind, Dalton casts quite a shadow. He could use a dose of patience, but this war will temper him."

If it doesn't destroy him, Alexandra thought, her enthusiasm punctured. She drank cider from her mug, aware of its potent warmth spreading through her, relaxing her, and encouraging her to ask, "May I see the rest of the house?"

A knowing look stole over him. "His room's up the stairs, first door on your left."

Blushing, Alexandra stood up. "Thank you, Twigs."

She began her tour with the downstairs rooms, which were small, but seemed to multiply unexpectedly. There was little furniture to speak of—several sturdy tables, two cushioned chairs and a footstool before the sitting room hearth, a wooden bench in the passageway, where pierced tin lanterns hung on walls.

The stairs creaked underfoot. The smooth plaster walls of the stairwell were smudged from Twigs feeling his way up and down. Dalton's bedroom, like the rest of the house, was plain and sparsely furnished. Though she was tempted, Alexandra did not explore the drawers of his battered secretary. But she did open a large, ancient armoire and found a pair of striped ticking breeches and a linen shirt hanging inside. How lonely they looked in the otherwise empty closet. Her own wardrobe required five times as much space, and most of it never saw daylight.

Embarrassed at her extravagance, she closed the armoire and crossed the room to his narrow bed. The straw-filled mattress was slung on rope supports and rustled when she sat on it. Filled with remembrances, she ran her hand over the pillow and wondered how many long-ago nights, when Dalton lay here and she tossed on her bed at Willowbrook, their thoughts of each other had entwined.

Chapter Forty-One

Orders were flashing out to the scattered divisions of Washington's army—recross the Delaware with all haste, then march to the capital by the shortest route. The British fleet was sailing south, and a race for Philadelphia was on.

As Dalton cantered down a hillside toward the main American encampment at Ramapo, in northern New Jersey, the view reminded him of a colony of industrious ants. Wagons and artillery carriages were being hitched; field tents were being dismantled; soldiers burdened with gear were forming to the booming commands of their sergeants. But there was more than just energy in the air. Threading his way through the organized chaos, Dalton noted tension on many faces.

He located Henry Buckley without delay. "All present?"

"And ready to march," Henry said, then asked, "Is it true the Bloodies are sailing south?"

Dalton nodded, his face grim.

"Maybe they're headed for the Carolinas."

"Maybe," Dalton said, but he doubted it.

Since April, Washington's spies in New York had reported that small craft, laden with British soldiers, baggage, and stores, were constantly plying between the city's wharves and the enemy fleet. At first it appeared that General Howe was planning an excursion up the Hudson to join forces with Gentleman Johnny Burgoyne. Then came word that the transports were being fitted up with stalls over their main decks for the reception of horses. The extensive alterations to British ships augured more than just a feint to sea, prior to a dash up the North River. The Bloodies were gearing up for a major voyage.

Now they had put to sea, and Philadelphia was their most likely target.

Dalton handed Mercury's reins to Henry. "Look after him, will you? If I don't scare up something to eat, I'll croak."

"Afraid you'll have to croak, sir. General Wayne wants to see you."

Dalton had gone several paces. As Henry's words registered, he slowly pivoted, pointed to his chest, and mouthed a silent *Me?*

"You. Immediately."

"What for?"

"How the hell should I know?"

Puzzled and concerned, Dalton retrieved the reins from Henry and set out for Wayne's headquarters, a farmhouse on the outskirts of camp. Along the way, his anxiety increased until his shirt clung damply to his back and his palms felt slick in the warm July afternoon. It wasn't every day that a low-ranking subaltern was summoned before Brig. Gen. Anthony Wayne. This didn't feel good. Had he done something wrong? Offended a superior? Disobeyed some obscure order? But if such was the case, General Wayne would simply have issued a reprimand through one of his staff officers.

This definitely felt bad.

The stone farmhouse looked like a hornet's nest that someone had poked with a stick. Riders were galloping to and fro on the lane, baggage was being carried outside to a waiting wagon, horses were being saddled in the yard. Going inside, Dalton combed his fingers through his hair, conscious of his travel-worn appearance. Wayne, a stickler for neatness, demanded the best possible display from his brigade. War was serious business with him, and he knew that soldiers in dirty rags were viewed with contempt by other troops and soon began to despise themselves. Discontent produced desertion, so Wayne waged a constant battle with the Board of War to provide his men with proper arms and clothing. Unfortunately, the authorities didn't share his concern for the health and morale of his troops. Supplies were slow in coming and often inadequate, such as the time a shipment of thin-soled French dancing shoes arrived in place of much-needed boots.

Dalton was one of many soldiers who had yet to benefit from Wayne's diligence on behalf of his troops. To Dalton's embarrassment, his clothes were worn through in several places. Worse, he had been in the saddle since dawn and was covered with road dust.

In the farmhouse hallway, he saluted a ruddy-faced young captain in a smart new uniform. "Lieutenant Philips to see General Wayne, sir."

Sharp eyes glanced over him. "Wait here, Lieutenant." The captain disappeared into an adjoining room, where murmuring voices suddenly ceased. Moments later, four officers emerged from the room and swept past Dalton, whose watchful gaze took in handsome regimentals with impressive insignias of rank.

The spruce young captain brought up the rear. "You may go in now, Lieutenant," he said in a voice that imparted nothing.

Dalton went in.

Brig. Gen. Anthony Wayne was leaning over a table, his hands braced on either side of a map, his concentration absolute. Wayne was just thirty-two years old, but when his hazel eyes looked up, the light of hard experience shone in them.

Dalton stood at attention. "Lieutenant Philips reporting as ordered, sir."

Wayne straightened. Though not tall, he was lean and fit, and there was a warrior's intensity about him that was contagious. His fearlessness in battle was the talk of the Pennsylvania Line. The severer the pressure, the more complete Wayne's command of himself seemed to be. Two months ago, in an action at Brunswick, he had proved his merit against General Howe. As Wayne reported in a letter to his friend Dr. Rush, the British commander "had his Coat much Dirtied, his Horses head taken off, and himself badly Bruis'd for having the presumption at the head of 700 British Troops to face 500 Penns'as."

Now Wayne took a moment to study Dalton, then greeted him with, "I've heard much about you, Lieutenant."

315

Dalton blinked. "You have, sir?"

"Indeed." Wayne indicated a chair. "Please sit down." When Dalton was sitting, Wayne leaned back against the map table, arms folded, and said, "I haven't much time, so I'll be brief. Your enlistment expires next month. I want to know if you plan to abandon the army."

Dalton felt as if Wayne had punched him. His shoulders drew back, his nostrils flared as he gauged his commander. "Sir, I'm here until America wins her independence, or until I'm dead. Whichever comes first, sir."

A pleased gleam came into Wayne's eyes. "I'm told you fought well at Trenton and Princeton."

"I did my part, sir."

"You have a reputation as an exceptional horseman."

"I can a handle a horse, sir," Dalton replied, wondering where all this was leading.

"You have also demonstrated an ability to lead men," Wayne said. "So much so that Colonel Chambers put you in charge of several foraging expeditions this past winter. I have a report from him," Wayne rifled a stack of papers, lifted one, and scanned it, "advising me of a skirmish you had with British horse. The colonel states, and I quote: 'Although faced with a superior number of cavalry, Lieutenant Philips elected to attack rather than retreat.'" Wayne's stare drilled Dalton. "Why did you put your men at such risk?"

Jesus God, Dalton thought, here it comes. "It would have been more dangerous to withdraw, sir."

"Explain."

"Sir, the Bloodies would have chased us and probably outflanked us. We surprised each other, you see, and I saw right away how quick they could wheel around and cut us off. So I ordered a charge before they could form, hoping to confuse them. We split them in half and walloped their right, then ran like hell, sir."

Wayne glanced down at the report. Lieutenant Philips and his party had not only walloped the British, they had captured supplies as well. All without the loss of a man. On the surface the attack seemed reckless, when in fact the bold stroke had probably saved the foraging party from disaster. It must have baffled the British commander why so small a body would attack five times its number, unless

316

reinforcements were approaching or a trap had been devised. Hesitation on his part was therefore natural and reasonable, and was, Wayne imagined, exactly what Lieutenant Philips had anticipated.

"I believe you acted properly," Wayne said, "and I commend your bravery."

Coming from a man beloved for his courageous leadership, a man whose motto was "steel speaks for itself," the praise had quite an impact on Dalton. "Thank you, sir."

"Which brings me to the reason you are here. In all likelihood, we will soon be fighting for control of Philadelphia. To mount the best possible defense, this army needs scouts who know the environs of the city and who aren't afraid to tangle with the British Rebels."

Dalton smiled at the derogatory appellation.

"I want you to organize a special troop of light horse," Wayne went on. "You will withdraw twelve of the best horsemen from each of my regiments and form them into a company. Colonel Chambers will supervise the selection process. The primary tasks of this light horse troop will be reconnaissance," Wayne smiled and narrowed his eyes, "and sudden strikes at the enemy. You will operate as a detachment of my command and will report directly to me." He cocked his head. "Questions?"

Frozen in disbelief, Dalton stammered, "No, sir. I mean yes, sir." It was too much to comprehend—a light horse command of his own! "Where will the horses come from, sir?"

"Some will be drawn from the remounts. Colonel Chambers is working on procuring the remainder."

"Sir, that won't be no problem once we're near the city." Dalton's thoughts were leaping ahead. If need be, Twigs and his murky friends could scare up a whole herd of horses. "I breed livestock, you see, and I know others in the same business, sir."

"Whatever arrangements you can make will be helpful." But Wayne, far from looking appreciative, was frowning. The look in his eyes was calculating. "I'm curious about something, Lieutenant."

"Yes, sir?"

"Jack Flash."

Dalton's euphoria plummeted. For a moment he could only wonder why he hadn't foreseen this. Wayne lived a stone's throw from Philadelphia and moved in its highest social circles. Of course he would be well-versed on Jack Flash. When traveling the dark roads between the city and Waynesborough, his Chester County home, he had undoubtedly armed himself against an encounter with the robber.

"What about him, sir?" Dalton asked, his voice not as steady as he would like.

"I know you were arrested and charged." Wayne let the silence expand a moment. "Were you guilty?"

"Yes, sir."

A whip cracked in the farmhouse yard, wheels creaked and rattled as a wagon rolled down the lane. Wayne moved to a window and stared outside. "Bloody hell, Lieutenant," he said, shaking his head. There was amusement in his voice. "For a thief, you're remarkably truthful."

"Sir, I—"

"You needn't bother defending yourself."

Oh, fuck . . .

"I know where the money went. While I can't say I approve of your method of aiding the cause, I admire your audacity." Wayne faced Dalton again. "Which is precisely what will be needed if we're to save Philadelphia. That, and readiness. I expect you to turn those horsemen into the most disciplined and capable fighters in the army."

It was all Dalton could do not to sag with relief. "Depend on it, sir."

Wayne's assessing eyes swept him head to toe. "I've authorized a shipment of uniforms for you and your troop. With any luck, you'll have them before the war ends."

Still rattled, Dalton unearthed a smile.

Anthony Wayne smiled back. "Colonel Chambers has received written instructions regarding your assignment. You should report to him immediately upon leaving here. As for myself, His Excellency has ordered me to Chester County to organize the Pennsylvania militia. When I rejoin my brigade, I expect to see the results of your endeavors."

"You won't be disappointed, sir."

318

Wayne nodded and looked satisfied. "I have every confidence in you," he said. "Please present my best compliments to your men. That will be all, Lieutenant."

Dalton came to his feet. "Thank you, sir." The moment his back was to Wayne, a grin spread over his face. His heart was going full speed, his step was light as he went to the door, where Wayne's voice stopped him in mid-stride.

"One more thing."

Composing his expression, Dalton faced him. "Yes, sir?"

"These horsemen should be led by a captain. You may choose your own lieutenant, Captain Philips."

Chapter Forty-Two

Camp, Falls of Skuylkill
1st August, 1777

Dearest Alexandra,

The most amazing thing has happened to me. Gen'l Wayne has made me a Captain of Lite Horse! My troop is 48 men and myself and I have made Henry Buckley of Phila. my first luetenant. We are training for battle and must be ready for revue when Gen'l Wayne returns from forming the Penna. militia. It is hard work but no one minds sinse the British Rebels have threten'd to beat up our lines—*if we don't beat up thairs first.*

We are ordered to remain in camp unless given a pass to Phila. on special business. I miss you more than ever and being this close to you is enough to drive me Mad, but I dare not disobay orders.

I am just now sent for by Col. Chambers. If I can find a way to come to you I will be thair in a minit. Remember you are always in my heart and that I am

Always yours,
Dalton

On August third, at Falls of Schuylkill, the American Army was passing a pleasant Sunday. Divine services had taken up most of the morning. In the afternoon, Lt. James McMichael of the Pennsylvania Line sat under a tree on a grassy knoll and wrote in his diary. He was inspired to describe the setting—a high plateau east of the Schuyl-kill, overlooking a place where the river flowed around a large shelf of rock. Rivulets, cascading over the rock itself, gave the impression of a constant waterfall. Glancing up from his journal, McMichael saw not an army encampment, but an idyllic spot for lovers. Unfortunately, the only women thereabouts were the camp followers—vagabonds who carried their belongings on their backs and diseases in their crotches.

The lieutenant gazed southward. Less than five miles away was a whole city full of women, but Philadelphia was strictly off limits to the troops. Anyone caught there without permission would be punished with twenty lashes followed by a salt bath. The General was a stern disciplinarian.

With a wishful sigh, McMichael closed his journal. A moment later, he shot to his feet and stood at attention as Colonel Stewart ascended the hillock with purposeful strides.

The colonel was grinning like a fool. "We're under attack, Lieutenant."

"What, sir?"

"Three columns, approaching from the south on the Ridge Road."

McMichael was too bewildered to respond. How in God's name had the Bloodybacks gotten past the city undetected? Why had no alarm been raised? And why, blast his eyes, was Colonel Stewart laughing?

"Round up a scouting party, Lieutenant," Stewart said. "You have the honor of being the first to engage the attackers. When they have been properly subdued, parade them to my tent, if you please."

"I don't understand, sir."

"They're *women*, Lieutenant. From the city." Grabbing McMichael's arm, the colonel urged him on his way. "Hurry, man! We're about to be surrounded by a female horde!"

Within minutes, the scouting party was dispatched to intercept the "attackers"—Patriot women who had come to show their support of the army. It was, Lieutenant McMichael later wrote in his diary, "the largest collection of young ladies I almost ever beheld . . ."

The women, who had marched up the Ridge Road in

three columns, were a noisy, curious group that came to a standstill when confronted by Lieutenant McMichael and his patrol. "Ladies," he said, sweeping off his hat and bowing over his horse's neck. "I'm afraid the camp is off limits to civilians. However," he couldn't stop a grin, "I have been ordered to escort you to Colonel Stewart's marquee for refreshments. Please remain in your ranks and follow me."

McMichael and his men marched the women to the colonel's tent, where they were treated to a double bowl of sangaree. The colonel himself served up the sweetened and spiced wine while his officers paraded the regiment for the benefit of the visitors.

McMichael, somewhat dazed by the presence of so much femininity, was "standing guard" at the marquee when a voice behind him said, "Excuse me, Lieutenant."

Turning, he looked into a pair of the bluest eyes he had ever seen, belonging to a young woman of extraordinary charm. Momentarily tongue-tied, he removed his hat and bowed to her. "Good afternoon, ma'am. Lt. James McMichael, at your service."

"I'm honored, Lieutenant."

"How may I help you?" he invited.

"I'm looking for Capt. Dalton Philips. Are you acquainted with him?"

McMichael blinked in surprise. Captain Philips was a good fellow and a fine officer, brave beyond measure, but he was also somewhat coarse, so it was difficult to imagine him with this genteel beauty.

"Yes, ma'am, I am," McMichael said. As her face brightened, his eyes drank in sculpted features and dark, silken hair, piled in a luxurious mass of ringlets.

"Is he in camp?" she asked.

"I'm afraid I don't know offhand," McMichael said. "But I'll be happy to find out for you."

Her smile all but melted him. "Thank you, Lieutenant."

How could anyone refuse such an angel? McMichael started away, then turned back. "Who shall I say is asking for him?"

"Alexandra Pennington."

As the lieutenant moved off through the crowd,

Alexandra found herself unable to concentrate on anything except the prospect of seeing Dalton again. He had been away for a year, an eternity, and her overwhelming need to see him had inspired her to join the march to camp. To her relief, she had been warmly received by most of the women. But the more fervent rebel supporters in the group had regarded her with wariness, even hostility, and Alexandra knew they suspected her of being a Tory spy.

Someone must have communicated that fear to Colonel Stewart, for she saw him making his way to her, trailed by Lieutenant McMichael. The colonel offered a polite bow and introduced himself to her. His voice was soft, his manner reluctant. "Forgive my abruptness, Mrs. Pennington, but I must inquire the nature of your business here."

Her face warmed. She glanced at Lieutenant McMichael, whose eyes were full of apology. "As I told the lieutenant, I'm looking for Dalton Philips."

"Captain Philips is away on a training assignment."

Her hopes crumbled. "I see."

"If you wish, I'll pass along a message to him."

"Just tell him I was here, Colonel."

Colonel Stewart nodded, then glanced toward the parade ground, where the Pennsylvania State Regiment was performing close-order drill. His gaze returned to Alexandra's face. "While you are here," he said, "I must ask that you confine yourself to the immediate vicinity of this tent. Lieutenant McMichael will remain with you until your party leaves."

Never in her life had Alexandra felt so degraded. She knew the colonel was only doing his duty—preventing a possible informant from assessing rebel military strength—but that did not make his remarks sting any less.

"Believe me," he said, reading her chagrin, "it is my least desire to offend you. But I have my orders."

"I understand. I will, of course, do as you ask."

Throughout the exchange, Lieutenant McMichael had observed her reactions and was moved by her graciousness under fire. Her gaze was unwavering, her back remained straight, her head erect. Not for a moment did she lose her marvelous poise. After the colonel left, McMichael offered to bring her more sangaree.

"You're very kind," she told him. "But no, thank you."

He sensed no resentment from her, only sorrow. Pierced by her melancholy, he felt compelled to say, "I'm sorry, ma'am."

She turned her face from him then, but not before he saw a glimmer of tears. "So am I, Lieutenant," she said softly.

When the supply of sangaree was exhausted, the Patriot women were escorted back to the camp perimeter. Watching them retreat down the Ridge Road, Lieutenant McMichael was at once wistful and heartened. Their visit had been a rare pleasantry, an inspiring sight, and was proof of something else worth fighting and dying for.

Chapter Forty-Three

The British fleet was playing a puzzling game of hide-and-seek. Late in July, as elements of the rebel army had marched for a rendezvous near Philadelphia, the billowing white sails of British men-of-war had been sighted off the Delaware capes. The majestic ships were riding a fair wind toward the bay, and the question of Howe's destination seemed answered. Then, mysteriously, the fleet had pulled away from the Delaware estuary and once again put to sea. Howe's inexplicable maneuver threw the American camp into a riot of speculation. Washington feared he had been tricked and that the rebel march to Philadelphia was a grave strategical error.

Meanwhile, up north, Lt. Gen. John Burgoyne was pushing southward from Canada as part of a plan to divide the northern Colonies, then conquer the parts. With him was a proud and disciplined assembly of seven thousand British and German infantrymen, forty-two field guns, a contingent of Tories and Canadians, and four hundred Indians. Burgoyne's army had already taken Fort Ticonderoga, a crushing blow to Patriot morale, and had driven as far south as Fort Edward near Saratoga.

In Philadelphia, Washington agonized over what to do. With Howe's whereabouts and destination unknown, the American commander toyed with the idea of returning north. He argued with himself, argued with his officers and the Congress. Finally, fearing to have his northern army demolished, Washington withdrew his forces from the vicinity of Philadelphia and moved farther north, encamping twenty miles from the city at Little Neshaminy Creek.

The August heat grew intense. Tempers flared. The whole army was plagued with troubles that would have discouraged a lesser commander—desertions, lack of supplies, disciplinary problems, bickering among officers, the exorbitant prices exacted by merchants for necessary goods. To further complicate matters, lack of news about the British fleet held the army immobile and put Washington in a constant state of anxiety over Howe's intentions.

"His Excellency is exceedingly impatient," wrote Gen. Nathanael Greene, who, like his commander, felt that "this is a curious campaign. In the spring we had the enemy about our ears every hour—the northern army could neither see nor hear of an enemy—now they have got the enemy about their heads and we have lost ours."

At long last, the enemy was found. In mid-August, American watchers sighted the British fleet rounding Cape Charles into the sun-glittering Chesapeake Bay. By the time the news reached General Washington, the ships were partway up the bay, headed for a landing at Head of Elk, Maryland. After seven weeks and a thousand miles at sea, the inscrutable Sir William Howe had at last committed himself to capturing Philadelphia. But he faced a formidable task, for between his troops and the rebel capital lay fifty rugged miles, a maze of rivers, and an ill-trained, but tenacious foe.

"Christopher, you're moving as slow as a snail."

"Good Lord, ma'am, I'm coming." Wiping sleep from his eyes, Clue stepped outside and closed the kitchen door behind him. Six o'clock in the morning was not his best hour, especially after a bawdy Saturday night at the Blue Anchor.

Seeing his face in the daylight, Alexandra was suddenly concerned for him. "You look terrible," she said.

"Thank you, ma'am."

"Are you feeling ill?"

"I've been better." Clue managed a smile. "You look very nice this morning," he said to change the subject. On reflection, he thought she looked incredibly lovely in a fresh, crisp gown of floral-printed cotton. Her small matching hat, angled atop a profusion of unbound curls, was more a decoration than a head covering. For modesty's sake, her shoulders above the low-cut gown were covered by a fine silk scarf. Still, the long-waisted bodice and gathered skirt displayed her figure to distraction.

She had obviously taken great care with her appearance. Clue supposed she had slept little last night, if she had slept at all, because today the Grand American Army was scheduled to march through Philadelphia on its way south. And Dalton would be marching with it.

"Let's hurry," she said, setting out at a brisk walk along Fourth Street.

"Ma'am, we have a whole hour to get there."

Even so, Alexandra covered the eight blocks to Front Street at an unladylike pace, forcing poor Clue to expend an energy his throbbing body did not possess. Twice he stopped at public pumps to rinse his mouth and quench his raving thirst. Fortunately the morning was cool, with a light southerly wind. During the night a drenching thunderstorm had beat across the city, leaving in its wake some smoldering buildings fired by lightning. The refreshing breeze was tainted with the smoke of charred, wet timbers.

"I expected to see more people about," Alexandra remarked, eyeing the nearly deserted streets. She wondered at Mr. Washington's sense of timing. If his aim in staging the march was to reawaken local patriotism, he should have waited until a later hour. Sunday morning, when breakfast was on the table and people were getting ready for church, seemed an absurd time to hold a parade.

When she said as much to Clue, he reminded her, "The British are in Maryland, ma'am. My guess is, the General's more concerned about stopping them than impressing a big crowd."

As it happened, the nearer they drew to their destination, the more people they saw moving in an exodus toward the riverfront. Arriving at Front Street, they found both sides of its wide, well-paved middle thronged with spectators.

As she followed Clue's halting progress along the

congested sidewalk, Alexandra recognized several female faces from her visit to the rebel camp at Falls of Schuylkill. But there was a noticeable lack of young women in the crowd, and she knew it was because many of them were out of town. Responding to the state's appeal, they were at the Jersey seashore, sixty miles away, boiling potfuls of ocean water to make a coarse gray salt that the army needed to prevent meat from spoiling in the summer heat. Many rebel officers, groomed so admirably for the march, were about to be disappointed by the absence of their ladies.

Still moving through the crowd, Alexandra's pulse quickened to the distant sound of drums and whistling fifes. When she and Clue reached the Quakers Meeting House at Front and Arch Streets, he helped her onto a low stone wall so she would have an unhindered view of the march.

Twelve horsemen and a subaltern led the American advance. As a great cheer arose at their appearance, they smiled and sat up straighter in their saddles. Behind them, strung out in a long column, twelve men abreast, came Washington's Grand Army. The General and his staff, bedecked in gleaming regimentals, rode near the head of the column behind the advance party. They were followed by General Greene's division of infantry.

The soldiers marched with unaccustomed lightness, for Washington had freed them for the day from carrying cook kettles and bulky packs. He had also directed the camp followers, wagons, and spare horses to file away from the column prior to reaching the city. He wanted his men to appear as an army, not an encumbered mob, so the baggage train was traveling side streets and quaint alleyways to the bridge at Middle Ferry. The camp women hated it, but the General's orders had been explicit: "Not a woman belonging to the army is to be seen with the troops on their march through the city." This included wives, prostitutes, and servants.

Cannon were a different story. Big guns were impressive, and Washington desired to impress the inhabitants, Whigs and Tories alike. So each brigade had brought along its artillery and one ammunition wagon. The cavalry was divided upon the two wings, to the front and rear of the column.

From her vantage point, Alexandra watched the endless ranks of soldiers go by in their ancient hats and motley clothing. They were strange figures, marching briskly to the quick-step music of fifes and drums. They were outfitted in almost as many types of uniforms as there were men. Some carried flowers in their musket barrels. All of them, in a pathetic attempt at jauntiness and uniformity, wore sprigs of green in their hats. They were cheered by the people lining the sidewalks, leaning out windows, waving bright colors. A few brave Tories gave catcalls and boos, but the offenders were quickly isolated and silenced by the predominantly rebel crowd.

General Greene's division took forever to go past. General Stephen's took even longer. Suddenly Clue touched her arm and pointed. "Here comes General Wayne," he said above the revelry.

Contagious enthusiasm rippled through the crowd of Philadelphians, for Gen. Anthony Wayne was one of their own. He cut a dashing figure, lean and determined, braced up in his saddle as though to stretch himself. His cocked hat was edged with shining gold braid. Sunlight glinted off his boot spurs, his gold epaulets, and his sword hilt. When the crowd saluted him with boisterous approval, he smiled in pleasure. Anthony Wayne was one of those rare men who created excitement wherever he went.

Alexandra barely noticed him. As he went by, her concentration on his column of Pennsylvanians became intense. *There!* A troop of horse flanked the column, led by an officer astride a prancing chestnut stallion. Her breathing grew shallow, her fingers digging into Clue's arm as the stallion drew nearer and she could make out the rider's face beneath his three-cornered hat. He was wearing a new suit of regimentals—a dark blue jacket with scarlet facings, a white waistcoat, and soft doeskin breeches. A captain's fringed epaulette decorated his right shoulder; a gold strap, his left.

Watching him approach, Alexandra's elation soared to a dizzying height. She saw him rise in his stirrups to scan both sides of the street, searching intently, and she knew he was looking for her. She stepped down off the wall and pushed her way to the front of the crowd so he would see her. For a moment she wondered if anything had changed between them. Then he noticed her, and his attention fixed on her, and a feeling like electricity raced through her. Nothing had changed.

For Dalton, time came to a standstill. Beside him, Henry Buckley made a remark about the crowd, but Dalton heard nothing and saw only one face that had haunted him and sustained him for the past year. "Henry, lead the troop," he said without taking his eyes off her. "I'll catch up with you."

The army was under orders to put on the best possible show, with no breaking of ranks. Risking punishment, Dalton separated from his company and reined Mercury over to where Alexandra waited. A reprimand seemed a small price to pay in return for seeing her, if only for a moment. But when he reached her and saw her joyful face looking up at him, he knew that a hurried greeting would not be enough. To hell with orders, he thought. Eyes locked with hers, he slipped his foot from Mercury's stirrup, and reached down for her.

Alexandra didn't hesitate. Moving into his encircling arm, she put her foot in the stirrup and was lifted across the saddle in front of him. Supported by his chest, she felt his strong arms come around her, felt his body shift to make hers comfortable, and her heart overflowed with emotions. His deep, vibrant voice, close to her ear, was startling. "I knew you'd come."

"Nothing could have kept me away."

Dalton scanned the crowded sidewalk and spotted a grinning Clue, who signaled that he would wait where he was until they returned. Mercury was tugging on the bit, so Dalton gave him some rein, and they moved down Front Street to the sounds of applause and good-natured jeering. Anxious to escape the crowd, Dalton tried to think of someplace close by and private to take Alexandra. He didn't have much time, and he wasn't about to waste it.

Not far from the meeting house, he turned west into Pewter Platter Alley and followed the dingy thoroughfare toward Second Street. Along the way, he relished the sensation of having Alexandra in his arms. He nuzzled her hair, whispering her name. Her head tipped back against his shoulder, and he found himself looking at her upturned face, so close to his own. The scent and feel of her

330

invaded his senses, robbing him of all thoughts save one. He drew Mercury to a halt.

And Alexandra lifted her mouth for his fiercely tender kiss. She welcomed the warmth of his lips, tasted the saltiness of their tongues exploring and mating, trembled to the intimate way his body cushioned hers. Every nerve ending was afire as he dragged his mouth from her lips and rubbed it across her cheek, murmuring a husky, "I've missed you."

She buried her face into the curve of his shoulder and neck, straining to get closer to him, feeling his warmth spread to every part of her. She never wanted to stir again, never wanted him to let go. Somehow she must make this moment go on forever.

After awhile, still holding her tightly, Dalton nudged the stallion to start him moving again, and it was then Alexandra noticed the strip of faded blue satin tied to a button of his uniform coat. She lifted the ribbon and let its frayed ends trail through her fingers.

"That's been everywhere with me," he told her.

"You need a new one."

"It can't be replaced."

Smiling, she rubbed her cheek against the roughness of his coat, inhaling his heady male scent. "You look wonderful."

Dalton glanced down at himself. "Must be my new uniform," he said and heard her laugh gently. "I'm not used to wearing one. We just got them yesterday."

Alexandra fingered the gold fringe at his shoulder, then lightly caressed his jaw, her eyes drinking in every detail of him. "You make a very handsome captain."

He gave a bashful shrug. "Long as I make a good one."

They crossed over Second Street and entered Church Alley, which ran past the still, sunlit cemetery at Christ's Church. Just beyond the walled churchyard lay a wide, grassy plot shaded by ancient poplars and fragrant white pines. Guiding Mercury into the seclusion of the pines, Dalton eased Alexandra to the ground, dismounted after her, and tethered the stallion to a limb. Then turning to her, and with his eyes full of tenderness, he gathered her in and lowered his mouth onto hers.

Alexandra closed her eyes and reveled in the sensations

he drew from her, fiery feelings she hadn't known existed. She moaned softly as heat rushed through her and pleasure welled uncontrolled. Everything about her felt unsteady, yet her body had never been more certain of what it needed. Wanting more, aching to be absorbed by him, she swayed against him, and Dalton abandoned restraint and succumbed to the urgency that drove them both. His hands moved over her back to her waist, fingers spanning the curve of her hips. She was exquisitely formed. She stole his breath and filled him with a hunger that was new to his experience. He wanted her with a fierceness that staggered him.

Almost before he had begun, Dalton ended his wonderful explorations. It was the hardest thing he had ever done, but he was in love, and quick passion beside a cemetery was not what he wanted with Alexandra. With a ragged sigh, he held her against his chest and waited for his racing heart to calm down.

Against her will, Alexandra drifted back to reality, and hearing the beat of distant drums, sensing the power behind them, her euphoria turned to anxiety. The drums seemed to be signaling that time was slipping away. She wanted to be strong for Dalton, to encourage him, but she could feel the rebel army beyond the buildings, a bristling serpent flowing through the city on its way to do battle, and her mind fixated on the coming bloodshed. She clutched at Dalton's neck, drawing him tighter, telling him, "I would give anything if you could stay with me."

"Nothing would satisfy me more." His mouth moved along her temple, planting soft kisses. "But the British are coming, and the bastards want Philadelphia."

Bitterness seared her. "I've heard terrible stories about their conduct."

"Only the devil would be proud of them."

"I hope you send them back where they belong."

Dalton felt the faint tremor that shuddered through her. He drew back and saw that her eyes were wet, her face pale against the shadowy grove. "Alex," he soothed, laying the back of his hand gently to her cheek.

"Please come back to me," she whispered.

He drew her close again, pressing her head to his chest.

"I will, love." His voice was thick, revealing his torment. "I promise."

After that they said nothing, because there was nothing more to say. They held each other and seized what they could from their stolen time together, and the silence between them was bittersweet, yet full.

The Grand American Army took upward of two hours to parade past the Quakers Meeting House, where Clue was waiting. When Alexandra and Dalton returned there, the rear guard had just gone by with a flourish of drums. The noisy crowd ebbed toward Chestnut Street, moving in the army's wake, but a number of people were still on hand to see Dalton kiss Alexandra soundly before setting her down.

Keeping Mercury in check, Dalton lingered a moment and held Alexandra in a long look, full of promise and yearning, then he rode off with a clatter of iron-shod hooves on cobbles. Soon horse and rider were swallowed by distance, and part of Alexandra was swallowed with them.

Her concentration on Dalton was so keen, she failed to notice the man across the street, lounging in a tavern doorway. He was watching her, his face intent. After Dalton disappeared, the man caught Alexandra's attention. He stood out in his impeccable ivory-colored suit and polished pigskin boots. When their stares met, Charles Villard tipped his hat with mock respect, but his eyes were as flat and empty as death.

III.

THE LION'S SKIN

Chapter Forty-Four

On the wooded heights above Brandywine Creek, a scant twenty miles from Philadelphia, Gen. Anthony Wayne played his brass telescope over the smoke-filled valley below. To Wayne's right, a battery of American cannon was hammering British and Hessian positions across Chadd's Ford. British artillery, emplaced on an eminence opposite the rebel battery, was trading the Americans blow for blow. The warm September afternoon shuddered to volleys of man-made thunder. Cannonballs plowed into the earth on both sides of the creek, splintering trees and throwing clods of dirt fifty feet in the air.

Wayne's hazel eyes were afire as he lowered his spyglass. The steady bombardment, fierce though it was, had done little more than whet his appetite for a decisive battle. After hours of cat-and-mousing with artillery, there was still no indication of when the main course would be served.

"Gentlemen," Wayne addressed the cluster of officers around him, "whatever game they are at, I grow weary of playing it."

A few yards away, Dalton held Mercury's bridle and spoke softly to calm his nervous horse, but his eyes were fixed on his commander. Surrounded by anxious faces, Wayne was the epitome of self-assurance, strong and decided, the anchor to which his officers looked for stability. Earlier that day, when the general visited his entrenched infantry below the heights, grapeshot had shivered the trees and rained leaves on his head like a fierce autumn wind. Wayne's seeming indifference to the

337

blistering fire had earned mixed reactions from observers.

"I never saw such a piece of work as him," was Henry Buckley's hushed comment to Dalton. "Does he think his carcass can't be blown out of time like the rest of us?"

"He knows it. I saw him with the chaplain this morning, and they weren't talking about the weather."

"Then why is he risking his fool neck before the fighting even starts?"

"He's showing us how to behave when the Bloodies cross the creek."

"He's crazy."

"Maybe," Dalton said, "but I wish we had more like him. He don't fear nobody or nothing. Whatever he asks of us today, odds are he'll be leading the way."

The praise had come readily to his tongue, just as envy now possessed him as he observed Wayne's great calm in the face of peril. From his first day as a soldier, Dalton had harbored a healthy respect for bullets and cannon shot, as any sane man should. But somewhere between a quiet Philadelphia churchyard and this beautiful wooded valley, his respect had transformed into an awful dread, for a bullet could now deprive him of more than he was willing to lose—his future with Alexandra.

A short while ago, on Wayne's orders, he had taken a patrol across the Brandywine to reconnoiter the enemy's right flank. After fording the creek, the dangerous extent of his fear had struck home. He scarcely managed to conceal his condition from his men. Somehow he had accomplished his orders, crawling with Henry Buckley through prickly woods and damp ravines to spy on the redcoats, but all the while his urge was to flee like a scared rabbit.

He was back, with all his familiar, beloved parts still intact, but the sensation curling along his spine remained his relentless companion. He despised his cowardice, but could not seem to shake it.

Wayne's voice sliced through his disturbed thoughts. "Captain Philips?"

"Sir?"

Wayne, a telescope to his eye, was surveying the thick woods that screened the enemy from view. "How many troops do you estimate are across the creek?"

338

Dalton hesitated a moment. "No more than seven thousand, sir."

Lowering the spyglass, Wayne appraised him and seemed to appreciate what he saw. "If that is true, then His Excellency's scouting reports are wrong, and General Howe has indeed split his force." He looked back at the creek, his face grim. "In which case we may end up fighting Long Island all over again."

Hearing this, a tingling heat spread over Dalton's scalp. All afternoon, rumors of a British flanking maneuver had been flying, but the reports remained unconfirmed.

"Captain, what would you do?" Wayne's abrupt question caused several mouths, including Dalton's, to open in surprise.

"Sir?"

"About those seven thousand you spoke of."

Dalton felt the sharp stares of Wayne's regimental commanders. Was the general really interested in his opinion? Or was he keeping his officers on their toes by seeking the advice of a mere captain? Whatever his motivation, Wayne was waiting for an answer, and Dalton gave the first one that sprang to mind. "Sir, I wouldn't wait. I'd go over there and give them a snuff of gunpowder before help can reach them."

Disapproving murmurs arose. Wayne raised a hand for silence. "Suppose the rest of General Howe's army is waiting out of sight in those hills?" he said, pointing. "We would be driven straight into the Brandywine. Our losses would be tremendous."

"I don't think Howe's over there, sir."

Wayne stared at him, waiting.

"Sir, if he's in those hills, he must be asleep. I've been over there, and I didn't see the kind of dust nor hear the kind of racket fifteen thousand soldiers would be making. What I seen was a lot of pointless marching back and forth, like they want us to think there's more of them over there than there really are, sir."

At that, a bold light shone in Wayne's eyes. Without another word, he hurriedly penciled a message on paper, then handed it to his adjutant with a brisk, "Deliver this to His Excellency at once."

The messenger rode off toward Washington's command

post at Benjamin Ring's tavern, situated a mile east of Chadd's Ford. A new banner flew over the site. It was a gaudy thing with thirteen red-and-white stripes representing the Colonies, and a circle of thirteen stars on a field of blue. "Looks like a whore's petticoat," Henry had remarked when the flag was officially unfurled for battle.

Wayne's adjutant soon returned, bearing a message from the commander in chief. As Wayne read it, his hopeful expression hardened into a scowl. "Damn this caution," he muttered and stalked off.

Dalton was secretly relieved. Even though he had recommended crossing the creek, the last thing he wanted to do was wade through chest-high water while British snipers sent him lead expresses. Let them be the ones to come and get it, he thought.

They did come.

At four o'clock, a grim-faced courier arrived on a sweating horse with curds of foam dripping from its mouth. Dismounting, the messenger handed Wayne a dispatch from General Washington. As Wayne read the dispatch, his face darkened with such intense rage that every officer within sight of him fell silent. Even the gun batteries quit their hammering, as if the cannoneers had felt the brigadier's wrath.

Then the reason for Wayne's fury became apparent. In the momentary lull, the distant muttering of cannon and heavy musketry could be heard. Heads turned toward the heights of Birmingham, three miles behind the American lines, where a furious fire was being exchanged.

"Gentlemen," Wayne announced rigidly, "General Howe has gotten around our right flank."

"Great God," someone said.

"God had little to do with it," Wayne snapped. "Carelessness is the cause. Now we have the devil to pay."

To Dalton, the events of the next half-hour seemed to unfold with amazing quickness. Three American divisions, stationed along the Brandywine to Wayne's right, were deployed to Birmingham to oppose the enemy flankers. Then General Greene's division was withdrawn, leaving Wayne with roughly five thousand men to hold Chadd's Ford against seven thousand enemy regulars.

Leaving their horses under guard in a field behind the

lines, Dalton's company joined the light infantry behind the earthworks. Crouched on the lip of an entrenchment, Dalton stared across the Brandywine, alert for movement among the trees. Bitterness flooded him. What good were horsemen lying about in a ditch? Their real usefulness was past. A regiment of light horse, deployed on the army's right flank, would have exposed Howe's risky maneuver and given the Americans a golden opportunity to thrash the divided British force. But Washington, although a foxhunter and an excellent horsemen himself, seemed blind to the uses of cavalry. American horsemen were used as pickets, scouts, couriers and, to Dalton's immediate dismay, footsoldiers.

Beside him, Henry said, "I feel like I've been here before." He was fingering his firelock and watching the deceptively peaceful river. "I hope this isn't the place I'm supposed to die."

Dalton kept quiet. He was wondering the same thing himself.

"Do you have any eatables, sir?"

Dalton shook his head. His knapsack, like his rioting stomach, had been empty for almost two days. Yesterday he had tried to pilfer some apples from an orchard, but the farm's owner, a dyed-in-the-wool Tory, had chased him off with a pitchfork and a shouted curse. "Be gone or be dead, damn you! I'd sooner feed the devil than save a starving rebel!"

Southern Chester County, where the two armies were maneuvering, was unfriendly territory for the Americans. The scant rebel supporters in the area had fled their homes. The Quakers, who opposed any form of war, were unsympathetic to both sides. And the Tories, emboldened by the presence of fifteen thousand redcoats, were outright hostile and treacherous to Washington's forces. In all likelihood, Howe's enveloping stratagem was made possible by a helpful Tory guide.

"We're in for a tight scratch, aren't we, sir?" Henry asked.

"It's bound to be warm, but we'll give them a drubbing, just like General Wayne said."

"He'd say that if the sky was falling on us."

Lack of food and taut nerves took hold of Dalton all at

once. "For Christ's sake, cheer up or shut up," he lashed out. "You're glum as a duck shot through the head."

"Sorry, sir."

"Look at it this way. We'll probably all starve to death before the Bloodies can kill us."

Henry didn't answer. He was too busy cringing to speak as, across the creek, the enemy batteries opened fire in earnest. Cannonballs and grapeshot smashed into the trees along the redoubts, snapping slender trunks like matchsticks and gouging holes in the earth. As the air around him shuddered and the ground beneath him quaked, Dalton flashed on something Twigs had once told him. *Hope for the best, but prepare your soul for the worst.* Flattened against the ground, arms crossed over his head, Dalton said a silent prayer, expecting at any moment to be blasted to the world of spirits.

Suddenly the gunfire ceased. In the eerie, ringing hush that followed, the British Fourth and Fifth battalions tramped down to the water's edge and waded into the slow current. On their heels came a second scarlet wave, then a third.

Rebel cannon raked the water with grapeshot until a flotilla of torn bodies stained the Brandywine red. The survivors came steadily on, landed below the rebel artillery park and encircled it, then took the battery by storm, seizing a six-pound cannon, two four-pounders, and a howitzer.

As British gunners redirected the captured field pieces against Wayne's right flank, another contingent of British and Hessian troops poured over the Brandywine to engage the American left, where Dalton's company was entrenched. Watching the enemy approach, Dalton's fingers grew slippery on his musket; his mouth had a metallic taste in it. He heard a harsh voice yell, "Front line, make ready!" and glanced to his right.

Anthony Wayne had come into the trenches to rally his infantry. The fearless brigadier was standing atop a redoubt, a splendid target in dark blue and buff. "No soldier of this command will retreat one foot unless so ordered!" he shouted. "If any man so disgraces the name of soldier or the honor of the Pennsylvania brigades, I will personally put him to death!" The general held a saber in

342

one hand, a pistol in the other, and his eyes and stance said he meant every word of his threat.

"Front line, take aim!" Wayne roared.

Dalton singled out a Hessian captain, sighted on his broad, white-belted chest, and waited. His breath came shallowly, smoke seared his eyes and throat. His musket would not hold steady.

"FIRE!"

He missed by a mile.

"Second line, make ready!"

Dropping back behind Henry, Dalton reloaded with shaky hands, spilling gunpowder in his haste. Jesus God, get a grip on yourself, he thought. He had to live through this day, had to see her again and hold her.

"FIRE!"

Another musket volley beat the air like a thunderclap. Ears humming, Dalton returned to the forward position and saw great gaps in the advancing lines.

"Those hairy Germans look in need of a shave!" Wayne yelled. "Are your bayonets good and sharp, boys?"

The howling cheer that rose from the redoubts prickled the back of Dalton's neck. Breathing hard now, he aimed his piece and squeezed the trigger as Wayne's sword flashed down. "FIRE!"

The first wave of Hessians breached the breastwork. The rebels, crouched behind sharpened steel and spurred by Wayne's presence, were primed for them. The Hessians drove in so furiously, they almost ran themselves onto the waiting bayonets.

Dalton had abandoned his musket for his saber. The beautifully engraved weapon, taken from a British prisoner at Princeton, bore an inscription on its glittering blade: "Never draw me without reason. Never sheath me without honor."

He bloodied the blade four times before the rebels broke the charge and the enemy fell back in disorder. Afterward, listening to the exultant cries of his comrades, he felt himself shaking like a kicked dog. Three of his men lay dead, a fourth was writhing in agony from a bayonet wound. Then Dalton saw Henry on his knees, doubled over in pain, and ran to him.

"Henry?"

"I'm all right, sir," he gasped, raising his smoke-blackened face. "Just had the wind knocked out of me."

Relieved that his friend was unhurt, Dalton sheathed his saber, retrieved his musket, and formed his company in preparation for another bloody assault.

Then he saw General Wayne striding toward him. Wayne's voice and expression betrayed no emotion as he said in an undertone, "Captain, the main army is retreating toward Chester. I expect enemy reinforcements at our rear before long." It took Dalton a moment to grasp what Wayne was telling him. General Washington had been defeated at Birmingham, and British forces were now between Wayne's division and the main army.

Wayne calmly continued, "Take your troop to the Chester Road and support General Maxwell. Tell him I shall bring my brigades along directly and that he must protect the road until then."

"Yes, sir." It was the most welcome order Dalton had ever received. Wayne might be utterly fearless, but he was not an imbecile. The Chester Road was his only avenue of escape, and he was pulling out while he still could.

Dalton's troop mounted up and rode south. Arriving at the Chester Road, they found General Maxwell's light infantry battling a large British force for command of the road. When Maxwell heard Wayne's orders, he said tensely, "The general had better hurry. We can't hold them much longer."

Wayne hurried, but with the growing enemy buildup on the Chester Road, including artillery, and with three British regiments pressing at his back, his march to join Maxwell became a bloody contest. The enemy fell on the first Pennsylvania brigade from two sides, peppered them with whistling bullets, then rushed in to give them a clawing with swords and bayonets. Colonel Chambers went down with a ball in his stomach. Colonel Frazer, several of his officers, and scores of enlisted men were surrounded and captured. Dozens more were killed or wounded.

When Dalton learned of Wayne's predicament, he urged General Maxwell to send him help. Maxwell refused. "How can I send help?" he demanded, vexed. "My men are stretched so thin they're transparent!"

344

"Then my men will go, General." Only after he had volunteered, and Maxwell gave his consent, was Dalton knocked on his unthinking head by his own madness.

"Good luck, Captain," said Maxwell. He did not seem hopeful.

Wheeling Mercury around, Dalton rode off at a gallop and rejoined his troop before his nerve could desert him. "General Wayne's in trouble," he said, surprised that he sounded so calm. "We're going back."

As he led his troop up a narrow dirt road, he could hear the sounds of furious fighting ahead. Fear strummed every fiber of his being. I'm a fool, he thought. A dead fool. He wondered how Alexandra would take the news of his death.

The road snaked uphill through deep woods that were choked with battle smoke. Nearing the hill crest, Dalton pressed Mercury into a gallop, drew his saber, and ordered his men to ready arms. As the horsemen thundered over the hilltop onto the battlefield, they were greeted by a wild convulsion of elements—fiery explosions, rupturing earth, screaming metal. In the midst of the turmoil stood General Wayne, death flying all around him. The ground where he fought was so punctured by shot it looked like a ploughed field. His men were being cut up like cornstalks, their lead-riddled bodies jerking and collapsing on top of one another.

A green-coated regiment was bearing down on Wayne's position. The silver crescents on their black caps were engraved QUEEN'S RANGERS. They were American Loyalists. To the rebels, they were the most loathsome creatures on earth, and the sight of them plunged steel into Dalton's heart.

As the Rangers began to close the door on Wayne, Dalton gave the order to charge. Crouched over their sleek mounts, the small, gutsy band of horsemen swept down the hillside at their prey. They smashed into the Ranger's right flank with such fury that the Loyalist line broke in two places. Surrounded by green coats, Dalton twisted in his saddle, swung his saber in a vicious arch, and opened a pathway for Mercury, who plunged forward on command. Then Dalton saw an outstretched pistol take aim at him. Behind the weapon, a green uniform gleamed with gold

345

braid, but he saw only the gun's dark bore. The pistol snapped at him, the spark leaped to the pan. He swung his blade as powder fizzed and flame spit through the touchhole to the charge, detonating the bullet with a sharp crack.

A hammer walloped his head and flung him backward. As his body thudded to earth, pain flared red behind his eyes, knifed down his neck, and exploded through his chest. He heard himself moan as blood smeared the world crimson. His eyes closed. His arms and legs were useless weights. The pain in his head became so intense, his body forgot how to breathe. As the terrible yells and clashes of steel dimmed, he knew he was dying from a bullet in his brain and that he would never see Alexandra again.

Dalton opened his eyes. The pain was still there, lacerating his forehead with rhythmic strokes, but he was alive. He was lying on his back in deep grass, and the sky overhead was a washed out blue. Over the ringing in his ears, he heard muffled patters of gunfire, the sounds seeming to come from a great distance. He tested his legs and found they still worked. He curled the fingers of his right hand, then brought his hand up to explore the pulsing, sticky-wet ache that was his head. It felt as if someone was sawing through his skull with a dull blade.

Suddenly his view was filled by Henry's dark silhouette. "Can you hear me, sir?" When Dalton nodded, Henry's breath rushed out with relief. "You're going to be all right, sir. Just lie still."

Dalton tried his voice. It was thick and sluggish. "Am I shot?"

"A ball bounced off your head, sir." Henry grinned at him. "Lucky thing it's so hard."

As Dalton's fingertips discovered the deep, bloody furrow scored into his scalp, fragments of memory floated back to him. He recalled charging the Rangers, then seized upon why he had done it. Alarm gave his voice strength. "Where's General Wayne?"

"Over there." Henry pointed with his chin. "Don't worry, he's fine."

"Did we whip the Rangers?"

"Not exactly. Here, sir, I brought you some water."
Unstopping a wooden canteen, he held it to Dalton's lips
and supported the back of his head while he drank.

"Thanks, Henry."

Henry didn't answer. His face went rigid as he rose and
stared toward the Chester Road. "The Bloodies are
coming up, sir," he said tensely. "I'd better get you into a
wagon."

When Dalton raised his head for a look, the world
canted right, then left, then finally leveled out. On the
field before him, Pennsylvania brigades were hurriedly
forming for battle. Drums rolled, officers barked orders,
weapons clinked in readiness, then a familiar, resonant
voice silenced them all. "This ground is *ours*," Wayne
roared, "and no damn British Rebels are going to take it
from us! Now stand here and give those bastards fire!"

Dalton stretched a hand toward Henry. "Help me up."

"You shouldn't move. We'll put you in a wagon."

Ignoring him, Dalton gathered his shaky muscles and
pushed himself to a sitting position. Pain slammed
through his head and made him hiss. "Jesus God," he
whispered.

Kneeling in front of him, Henry peered into his glazed
eyes. "Captain?"

"I'm all right. Where's my horse?"

"Over there, sir. He's a loyal bugger. Stood over you
after you were shot."

"Bring him here."

Henry left and returned with Mercury. Fighting
Henry's grip on the reins, the stallion lowered his head,
nudged Dalton's chest with his muzzle, and nearly laid
him out flat again. With Henry's help, Dalton made it to
his feet, then sagged against Mercury's shoulder as bile
flooded up his throat and threatened to choke him. He
leaned over and retched on the grass.

After a time, still clinging to Mercury, he straightened
and saw a line of horsemen stretching off to his right in a
loose formation. His company was mounted and waiting
for orders. A cool, twilight mist hovered over the field. Out
of the white haze came the British Fourth Battalion, the
Seventy-First Regiment, and the Queen's Rangers.

Dalton's jaw clenched. "Bloody traitors," he said,

eyeing the Rangers' green coats. From somewhere deep inside, he summoned the energy to pull himself onto Mercury's back, where he swayed like a drunk. He looked down at Henry's worried face. "Mount up."

"You're going to get yourself killed."

"Piss off, Henry. I told you to mount up."

"You know what your trouble is, sir?"

Drawing his saber, Dalton aimed it across the field. "Those fuckers right there."

Henry smiled against his will. "You're the most pigheaded man I ever met."

And still bloody scared, Dalton thought, but ready to do what had to be done. And able to look Henry in the eye again without feeling weak and ashamed. "Are you coming?"

Henry fetched his horse, swung into the saddle, and took his place at Dalton's side.

Rising in his stirrups, Dalton looked down the line of horsemen. "Boys, let's skin some lions."

Chapter Forty-Five

Philadelphia was as dark and silent as a tomb. Even the watchmen were quiet, Clue noted, wondering if they had fled the city with the nervous Whigs. A few hours ago, the streets and ferries had been jammed with overloaded wagons, horses, and carriages, all heading for distant refuges. Congress had packed up its papers and run for York. On Washington's orders, rebel soldiers had carried off any materials that might be of use to the enemy. Six tons of church bells had been hauled away to prevent the British from seizing them and melting them down into bullets.

By light of the sputtering oil lamp, Clue manhandled Alexandra's portmanteau into the carriage house, then paused to catch his breath. What had she packed it with, bricks? The damn thing weighed a ton. As he hoisted the heavy trunk onto the back of the Pennington carriage, a groan escaped him.

"Need a hand?" asked a voice behind him.

Clue spun to face the intruder, who moved from deep shadows into the lamplight. Strange, fierce eyes glittered at him from a thin dark face. Clue said, "Jesus Christ, you scared me stiff!" and made Dalton laugh.

"How are you, Chris?"

His panic evaporating, Clue gripped the hand Dalton held out to him. "Glad to see you safe and sound," he said warmly. "I heard it was a bloody mess at Brandywine."

"We took a beating, but they knew they were in a fight."

"What happened to your head?"

"It re-enlisted."

Now it was Clue's turn to smile, but his amusement faded as he eyed Dalton's bloodstained uniform jacket and bandaged forehead. There was something different about him, something that went much deeper than his weathered appearance, but Clue could not put a finger on what it was.

Dalton nodded at the portmanteau. "Is Alexandra leaving the city?"

"She's going to Mr. Pennington's. He's in a bad way," Clue explained. "Lung sick."

"I'm sorry to hear that."

"Come inside," Clue said, picking up the lantern. "She'll be awfully glad to see you." As they left the carriage house, he asked, "Is the army treating you well, or is it as bad as they say?"

"It's worse. But thanks for asking."

"I thought you were at Reading."

"Not General Wayne's division. We're on special duty near Paoli Tavern. But that ain't common knowledge, so don't tell anyone."

"Mum's the word," Clue promised. "What's General Wayne like?"

"He's the bravest man I know, Chris. He laughs at things that would curl your hair."

"I heard he's a tyrant."

"Piss on whoever said that," Dalton shot back. "He's a good general, maybe the best we have. War ain't a holiday with him."

They entered the kitchen, where the smells of roasted meat and freshly baked bread made Dalton's mouth water instantly. A golden-brown turkey turned on a spit before the hearth. As he stared at the rotating bird, devouring it in his imagination, his shrunken stomach rumbled. Then he forgot his hunger as female voices rose in a hallway outside the kitchen.

"Did you remember to pack the camphor?" Alexandra asked.

"Yes, ma'am," Mary answered. "And a garlic and vinegar mash to help his breathing."

Alexandra came into the kitchen and froze when she saw Dalton.

"Hello, Alex," he said softly.

350

Uttering a low, choking sound, she crossed the room and flung herself into his arms. Dalton crushed her to him. She was even lovelier than he remembered, tall and fine, her dark hair like silk against his cheek. As he held her and rocked her, footsteps retreated from the room, the door to the hallway closed, and they were alone.

"Thank God you're safe," she whispered.

"I promised I'd be back," he said, pressing eager kisses to her hair, her cheek, her lips.

Alexandra clutched at his neck, drawing him tighter. This was no dream, but warm, living flesh. As his kiss deepened and his body clung to hers, it seemed as if they were swaying in a strong wind.

After a time, she drew back and let her gaze wander over him, absorbing every detail of him. He had lost weight, she realized, noting the changes in his face. His features were sharper, the bones more pronounced, yet he had never looked better to her than he did at this moment.

Her keen regard made Dalton glance down at his stained clothes and muddy boots. "I'm sorry for being such a wreck."

"It doesn't matter." Grimy or immaculate, a healthy Dalton answered all her prayers, but his bandaged head gave her concern. "You've been hurt."

He shrugged. "It's nothing much."

"What happened?"

As he recounted his scrape with the Queen's Rangers at Brandywine, Alexandra heard pride in his voice, saw it flare in his eyes, and thought he did not seem like a man who had been on the losing side of a battle. The picture he painted of the fighting was disturbingly vivid. A deep chill grew in her, although the room was warm.

"It must have been horrible," she said, then noticed him eyeing the roasted turkey with longing. "Are you hungry?"

"Starved."

"Sit down," she urged. "I'll fix you something to eat."

Unable to wait, Dalton went to the fireplace, tore a leg off the turkey, and took a huge bite out of it. Watching him wolf down the meat, Alexandra realized he was ravenous. She brought him a platter of sliced turkey, cornbread and butter, a cheese wedge, an apple, a bowl of chocolate, and a bottle of her best wine. Sitting next to him, exhilarated by his nearness, she watched him satisfy his hunger as fast as he could.

"Doesn't the army feed you?"

"Not if it can help it."

Her eyes narrowed. "That's terrible."

"King George is terrible," he said. "The army beggars description. I think our quartermaster's being paid by the British." Dalton ate every morsel and drank the wine like it was water. Finished, he leaned back in his chair, both hands pressed to his belly, and sighed with contentment. "That was a capital feast."

"There's more," she offered.

"If I eat another bite, I'll burst." Now that his stomach was full, he turned his attention to more important matters. His eyes grew tender as they watched her. He took her hand, and their fingers intertwined. "Tell me how you've been."

"Keeping busy," she said. "I was helping out at the hospital, but with the British so near, all the wounded had to be moved to safer locations."

"Those fellows were lucky to have you looking after them. If all nurses were as pretty as you, every man jack of us would be trying to get hurt." He smiled as she blushed, then grew serious again. "Chris said Mr. Pennington's sick?"

"He has influenza."

"That's bad at his age."

"He'll get better with proper care," she said determinedly. Reaching up, she lifted the edge of his bandage and grimaced at what she uncovered. "This is gorgeous."

"You should have seen it a few days ago," he said. "It was swelled up like a puffball."

Alexandra got up and went to the hearth. After hanging a pot of water over the fire to boil, she assembled lint, cotton, witch hazel, and shears on the table. Wielding the scissors, she cut through his soiled bandage and peeled it carefully away from the wound. The swollen, puckered furrow was infected and desperately needed cleaning.

"This should have been stitched," she said. "Who on earth treated you?"

"A battalion surgeon."

"He has the nerve to call himself that?"

Dalton nodded. "He wanted to cut a hole in my head and let out some blood. I told him if he tried it, his head would be the one bleeding."

"He sounds like a barbarian." Alexandra lifted the scissors again. "Hold still now." Working carefully, she snipped matted black hair from the lips of the wound, then cleaned away dried blood with witch hazel.

Dalton reveled in her gentle ministrations. It seemed the most natural thing in the world to slide his arms around her waist and lay his head against her. "God, you feel good," he murmured.

Alexandra was inspecting the damage done by the bullet, her mouth dry with dread at the thought of what might have been. Dalton was alive only because someone's aim had been off by half an inch. "You're incredibly lucky," she said in a low voice.

"My exact thought," he said, smiling and massaging the small of her back. Then he felt her trembling and looked up into her fearful, glistening eyes. "Alex," he said softly, reaching for her. He drew her down onto his lap and hugged her hard as she burrowed against him. "Don't be upset, love."

"I can't help it. I'm frightened for you."

"I'll be all right." As he held her and soothed her, all the moments they had spent together came crowding over him like a powerful current. His mouth sought hers. He kissed her hungrily until her fear was gone and the war became the farthest thing from their minds.

Alexandra was shocked by the wave of desire that swept her. Overcome by the need to be touched, her body pressed against him, throbbing to a flood of sensations until she thought of nothing but the wild heat of his mouth. She pulled his head down to deepen the kiss and moaned softly as he took his fill of her lips, tasted her neck, and nuzzled the tingling flesh above her bodice.

Finally he raised his head and gathered her to him. The groan that came from his throat was part frustration, part elation. Surrounded by his warmth, mesmerized by his hand moving through her hair, she closed her eyes and listened to his breathing slow down. His steady heartbeat was her pulse.

"I want you to leave Philadelphia," he said in a husky voice. When she drew her head back in surprise, he explained, "I don't think we can stop the British from taking the city. If you stay here, there's no telling when we'll see each other again. But if you go to York or Lancaster—"

"I can't leave George," she said with despair.

"Then take him with you."

"He's too ill to travel."

Deflated, Dalton looked away.

"Dalton, he needs me."

"I understand," he said quietly, even though his own need of her was tearing him apart. They were silent then, anguished by the thought of another long separation. Somewhere in the house, a clock rang out eight chimes. Dalton met her look. "I have to go, love."

Reluctant to leave his embrace, Alexandra moved off his lap and finished bandaging his wound, her hands going through the motions while her tortured thoughts moved ahead. Afraid of tears, she turned away from him and carried his soiled bandage to the fireplace to burn it.

Dalton's eyes followed her. He was acutely aware of her pain, for it mirrored his own at having to leave her again. He had no choice. Even if he could abandon his beliefs, he could not desert his family of brothers, whose hardships, dangers, and sufferings he had shared. Win or lose, the war for independence was his destiny, but the love of this woman was what he stayed alive for. Watching her kneel before the hearth, firelight bathing her in a flickering glow, the tenderness he felt for her was so great it made his heart ache.

"Marry me, Alexandra."

She came slowly to her feet. Her answer was a clear, steady, "Yes."

Dalton went to her and caught her in his arms, and there was joy in her eyes as she rose to meet his lips.

Chapter Forty-Six

They were calling it a massacre. The Paoli massacre. As its sad aftermath, two hundred men of Anthony Wayne's command were dead or severely wounded. Handbills describing the tragedy had been posted in every tavern, market building, and public square in the city, where murmurs of rebel reprisals had quickly become more than just talk. The night after the massacre, fire destroyed a Tory-owned warehouse on Front Street. In the smoldering ruins, members of the Union Fire Company discovered the charred, twisted body of the building's owner. The Loyalists might now reign in Philadelphia, but the Sons of Liberty still moved in its crevices.

At Oakwood, Alexandra learned about the massacre when William brought her a handbill bearing the ominous heading: GHASTLY NEWS! PATRIOT SOLDIERS BUTCHERED. "Someone left it on the doorstep," William told her.

As a warning for George, she thought fearfully. "Don't mention this to Mr. Pennington."

"Yessum."

"See that his pistols are loaded and put in the sideboard in the front passage."

William didn't bat an eye. "Yessum."

In the parlor, where Alexandra withdrew to read the handbill, her concern for George was wiped away by a vivid account of the carnage near Paoli Tavern.

In a dark, wooded ravine, just a few miles from his ancestral home, Anthony Wayne's encampment had been overrun by redcoats with bayonets fixed. Silhouetted

355

against their campfires, the rebels made perfect targets for the steel-tipped assault. The slaughter was horrific. Barefooted, half-clothed men running in confusion and falling from bayonet thrusts, men writhing on the ground and trying to shove their entrails back into their torn stomachs. Some Americans had crawled into their huts, hoping to escape the attackers, but the huts were fired and screaming fugitives were burned alive. Scores of Americans threw down their muskets and raised their hands in surrender. Defenseless men were stuck like pigs, their faces shredded with sword blades and bayonets. One British officer drove cold steel through fleeing bodies until blood ran out the touchhole of his musket.

Tory spies were being blamed for betraying Wayne's position to the British, who had left the American dead at the mercy of local inhabitants. Because the bodies were on Tory land, the owner refused to let them be buried at the site of the massacre. The dead had been borne to a crest overlooking the ravine and were laid in a common grave.

Hugging her arms against a shiver of horror, Alexandra reminded herself that the handbill's author was a rebel, and that the rebels were more anxious than ever to stir up anti-British sentiment. Still, she knew there must be some basis for the story.

"Excuse me, ma'am," William said from the doorway. "Mr. Pennington is asking for you."

Alexandra took a minute to compose herself before going upstairs. Though she entered Pennington's bedroom wearing a bright smile, he took one look at her and asked in a hoarse voice, "Has something happened?"

"Nothing of any importance," she lied.

He searched her face a moment, his breathing labored. "Pray tell me the truth."

Damn his perceptiveness. At times he seemed to know her mind better than she did herself. Sighing, Alexandra sat on the bed and held his hand. "I'm worried about Dalton," she said, staring at their entwined hands.

Pennington's bony fingers squeezed hers.

"When I saw him the other night," she said, "he asked me to marry him."

Wispy eyebrows rose. "What was your answer?"

356

Alexandra spoke as if there could be no other answer. "I said yes."

"Wonderful," Pennington breathed, his eyes growing misty. "I'm delighted for you, my dear. Mr. Philips is a fine man who will always stand by you. When will you wed?"

As soon as you are well, she thought and said, "General Washington has forbidden all leaves of absence, so we must wait awhile."

"Never fear," Pennington consoled her. "Once the cold weather arrives, General Howe will be too busy lying about to be bothered with campaigning." He paused to clear his throat, then was seized by a coughing fit that racked his inflamed lungs until he gripped his chest against jabbing pain. Gradually the spasms ceased. Pennington spat into a kerchief and sagged back on the pillows. When he could speak again, he said between breaths, "I predict a winter wedding . . . and I beg the honor . . . of giving away the bride."

Alexandra's eyes glittered with tears. "I wouldn't have it any other way."

She sat with him until he dozed off, making sure he stayed propped up on pillows so he wouldn't choke in his sleep. Easing off the bed, she picked up his soiled kerchief and saw flecks of blood on it.

That afternoon, Clue drove her to an apothecary's shop on Second Street. Known as the Pestle and Mortar, the shop offered a wide selection of European and West Indies medicinals, as well as local herbs. Inside, Alexandra inhaled a profusion of aromatic smells from confections, purges, salves, oils, and the like. Colorful jars and bottles lined the shelves behind the counter, where the owner-physician was wrapping packets of herbs. She purchased chinchona, which contained quinine to check Pennington's fever, and an opiate to control his coughing fits. While the druggist prepared the doses in separate bottles, she glanced out the shop window and saw Clue speaking with a portly man in a gaudy purple suit. Recognizing Stephen Lindsay, Alexandra tensed with apprehension. From Clue's angry expression and clenched hands, it was clear they were having an unpleasant conversation.

After paying for the medicine, she hurried outside in

time to hear Clue say in a warning tone, "Just go away and leave her alone."

Then Lindsay saw her and brightened. "Alexandra, thank goodness! This nervy boy is trying to prevent me from seeing you." He glared at Clue. "Someone must have put pepper in his snuff."

"I'll pepper you," Clue growled and stepped toward him.

"Christopher!"

He flashed her a look, then reluctantly backed down and stood glowering at his plum-colored antagonist.

Alexandra faced Lindsay. "What do you want, Stephen?"

Reaching inside his coat, he withdrew a wax-sealed letter. "As I told your incredibly rude coachman, I have a letter for you from Charlie."

Anger rose sharply in her. "Nothing Mr. Villard has to say is of any interest to me."

"Sweet heavenly God, Alexandra! Quit stabbing me with those dagger eyes. I'm simply trying to pass along a message."

"Which I don't wish to receive."

"But he—"

"You may as well save your breath to cool your porridge. Return the letter to him."

"But I can't," Lindsay explained. "You see, he left the city and went—"

"I don't care where he went," she said and started away.

"He said it was quite urgent," Lindsay called after her. "Something about settling an overdue account with you."

At that, Alexandra stopped short. Turning, she stared at the proferred letter in Lindsay's hand, then finally took it from him. "Good day, Stephen."

Clue opened the coach door for her. Seeing the menacing look he shot Lindsay, she said in an undertone, "Just leave, quickly."

"Yes, ma'am." Clue was glad to leave the jackanape behind, although he would rather have thrashed him. The spineless bastard was nothing more than a mouthpiece for Charles Villard. After handing Alexandra inside, Clue climbed to the driver's bench, slapped the reins, and drove to Oakwood at a fast clip. Arriving there, he stopped the coach behind the house and jumped down to let

Alexandra out. But when he opened the door, he found her weeping in a corner of the seat, Villard's letter in her shaking hand. Dismayed, he climbed in beside her and gripped her shoulder.

"What's wrong, ma'am?"

Her eyes were filled with agony. "He's lying," she whispered.

Deeply concerned, Clue took the letter from her and groaned to himself as he read it.

> British Camp, Bull Tavern
> 21st September, 1777
>
> Sweetheart,
>
> I loathe being the bearer of sad tidings, but I thought you should know Dalton Philips was killed last night near Paoli Tavern, run through with a bayonet. I have heard from a reliable source that he fought bravely. But alas, even the bravest of men are not invincible.
>
> My condolences.
>
> Your Everlasting Friend,
> Charles Villard

Clue looked up, at a loss for words.

"It can't be true," she said in a quavering voice, fixing on his face as though to read what he was feeling. Her horror-struck countenance begged reassurance from him.

Clue swallowed, thinking fast. "You know Mr. Villard wants to hurt you." He shook the letter like it was so much trash. "He made this up, the rotten bastard." Then thrusting the paper out of sight in his waistcoat pocket, he took her arm and urged, "Come inside, ma'am."

Alexandra went with him into the house and let him usher her to the parlor, where he poured her a liberal portion of brandy. The liquor felt like fire going down, dispelling the deep chill that had grown in her. When Clue refilled her glass, she made no objection but quickly drank the spirits down. Her condition of mind was such that oblivion seemed essential. With each vision of Dalton, the pain she felt in her breast was like a quick stroke from a dagger.

Clue left the room and returned a few minutes later wearing his riding boots and a light traveling cloak. He had armed himself with a pistol.

Seeing the weapon, Alexandra's gaze flew to his face. "Where are you going?"

"Paoli Tavern." As a protest formed on her lips, Clue hurried to silence it. "I'll be careful, I promise. But we have to know the truth."

Though she knew he was right, Alexandra felt more terrified than encouraged by his determination. She wondered if she could bear to hear the answer he brought back.

He was gone all night. In the morning, when he returned on his dust-covered mare, Alexandra rushed outside to meet him, her face pale from lack of sleep, eyes reddened from a night of torment. Clue dismounted and faced her, and from his dispirited look she knew his efforts had been futile.

"I couldn't learn anything, ma'am. None of the locals knows for sure who was killed; they just buried the poor fellows. They said the British took away about a hundred prisoners, most of them wounded."

Hearing this, Alexandra was torn between hope and a renewed surge of anguish. "The army must know who is missing," she said.

Clue nodded. "General Wayne will know. He'll make a report, and eventually word will reach us." Resting a hand on her shoulder, he held her gaze and said with reluctance, "Until then we'll have to wait and pray."

The morning air, filled with dust and light, suddenly seemed dim. Alexandra opened her mouth to speak, but no words came out. Everything inside her felt numb. In her mind, she realized there was no choice except to wait, but a part of her knew only that the source of warmth in her being had gone away, and that without it, nothing would ever again be the same.

Chapter Forty-Seven

The British were coming. Word spread like wildfire through the city. Sir William Howe and twenty thousand redcoats were advancing down the Schuylkill River toward Philadelphia.

At Oakwood, Alexandra received the news bitterly. While the rest of high society made lavish preparations to welcome the conquerors, she immersed herself in caring for Pennington and looking after his estate. She filled every moment with some task, any task, to keep from agonizing about Dalton's fate. Her constant worry affected everything she did, plaguing her day and night, so that she found herself going through the motions of life without really living. Only Pennington's need for her prevented her from giving up to grief.

After Pennington's health, her most pressing concern was that of obtaining enough food to feed two households. The rebels, in carrying off everything that might be of use to the British, had created serious shortages in the city. With William's help, Alexandra inventoried Oakwood's larder, and although the tally was worrisome, the situation was not yet desperate. But with two armies denuding the countryside of all available provisions, it was only a matter of time before Philadelphia's food stores ran out.

"I hope things improve when the British come," William remarked with a sigh. "Seems the rebels did all the mischief in their power before running off."

"They paid for most of what they took," Alexandra said, even though she knew the Continental money the rebels had paind with was virtually worthless. "And I haven't heard of them murdering anyone for a milk cow."

"Yessum, that's true."

"Or beating a farmer senseless in order to ravage his daughters."

Abashed at her directness, William mumbled, "Yessum," his irritation at the rebels blunted. Like Alexandra, he had heard the stories that were filtering down from the northern countryside. The reports of British and Hessian atrocities had a disturbingly familiar ring to them.

"If the British lose the war," she said with contempt, "it won't be on the battlefield. It will be in our homes."

Late that afternoon, patters of gunfire were heard in Philadelphia as British advance patrols pushed toward the city and skirmished with Pennsylvania militiamen. By nightfall, the British Army was encamped on the heights near Germantown, just three miles away. Fearing that rebel supporters would attempt to burn the city, Tory leaders went from door to door, warning everyone to remain indoors after dark or face arrest. In the morning, they said, when Sir William Howe made his triumphant entrance into the capital, the yoke of arbitrary power would be lifted.

But when morning dawned crisp and blue, Howe generously remained with his main army at Germantown and sent the Earl of Cornwallis to take official possession of the city. The thickset, grayish Cornwallis, resplendent in a scarlet and gold-lace coat, led a column of three thousand British and Hessian soldiers into Philadelphia.

Alexandra did not have to venture from Oakwood for a glimpse of the invaders. A battalion of British grenadiers took up quarters at the Bettering House, just three blocks from Pennington's mansion. Throughout the morning, Cedar Street echoed to the *tramp, tramp* of hundreds of boots and the roar of sergeants' commands. From a second-floor window, Alexandra and Clue watched redcoated soldiers march past Oakwood with machinelike precision, their polished metal cap plates, brass buckles, and musket fittings gleaming in the sunlight.

Redcoats in Philadelphia. The sight made Alexandra's skin crawl. Instead of spruce British soldiers, she saw the butchers of Paoli.

The grenadiers were followed by a cavalry squadron headed by Lord Cornwallis and his suite. Two men in civilian clothing stood out conspicuously among the bright red uniforms. From their animated gesturing and pointing, it was clear they were acting as guides for his lordship.

"Galloway and Story," Alexandra said scornfully, identifying Philadelphia's most rigid Tories. "What a surprise."

Clue was more interested in the dragoons. They were a dashing group, sitting boldly astride their powerful, well-groomed horses. He wondered what it would be like to face a thundering cavalry charge, to watch a wall of horseflesh come sweeping across a field at him, the riders fearsome and reckless, swishing razor-edge sabers above their heads. He decided he never wanted to find out. Suddenly he caught his breath and leaned closer to the window. His jaw slackened in amazement as he recognized several faces among the dragoons. They were Philadelphians!

"Damnit all to hell," he said, forgetful of himself. He grabbed Alexandra's arm and pointed. "That's Mr. Villard."

Alexandra looked. Her mouth went dry, her body tensed with revulsion. It was indeed he. He was wearing a scarlet jacket, white buckskin breeches, and boots of well-cured leather, polished to a high gloss. A crimson officer's sash showed around his middle. His plumed helmet bore a fancy metal frontplate with crossed sabers, and silver tassels decorated his pistol holster and sword scabbard. As if sensing her scrutiny, Villard looked toward Oakwood, his pale eyes shadowed beneath his helmet brim, and she felt his predatory stare like a cold hand around her heart.

Clue drew her back from the window, his thoughts in turmoil. Seeing Mr. Villard was never a pleasant experience; seeing him in a British uniform was downright unnerving, especially as the British had just seized Philadelphia by the throat. "God help us," was all he could think to say.

By dusk, British and Hessian troops were quartered in a semicircle around the city, protecting the whole, and the necessary guards had been posted. Then Philadelphia gave itself up to a round of celebrations. The high officers were given receptions in the drawing rooms of the rich. The common soldiers were received in lesser quarters where curtains were drawn and cheaply perfumed women ushered them upstairs. In one form or another, Loyalists prostituted for the British.

Alexandra awoke with a start, clutching the bedcovers to her chest. Feeling unaccountably frightened, she glanced around her dimly lit bedroom, wondering what had awakened her. A confused moment passed, then the morning shuddered to a distant, booming percussion that made her cringe. The thudding volleys came again and again in rapid succession, like an exploding bag of fireworks. Let it be thunder, she prayed, but she knew it was not.

Getting out of bed, she put on a robe over her linen shift and hurried downstairs to the kitchen just as William entered the back door. His expression was calm as he shrugged out of his greatcoat, but his voice betrayed nervousness.

"Those cannon sound just like a storm coming."

"How close are they?"

"I don't know," William said, "but I hope they don't come any closer. We're supposed to stay indoors, ma'am. Soldiers are running every whichaway out there. It's a wonder they can tell where they're going. The fog's so thick, you can't see across the street."

Moving to a window, Alexandra peered outside to find the world had vanished behind a curtain of dazzling whiteness. How a battle could be fought under such conditions she could not imagine, but the ominous muttering of artillery and crackling musketry signaled that one was indeed being waged just a few miles away. Meanwhile, the confusion outside Oakwood indicated alarm on the part of the British, cheering Alexandra no end. She suspected the rebels had launched a dawn attack, which put her in mind of their daring assaults on Trenton and Princeton. Recalling the results of those engagements, she hoped the redcoats would be driven from the city in inglorious defeat.

In any event, Philadelphia was at risk of becoming a

battleground. She couldn't just stand there, waiting for cannonballs to come crashing into Oakwood's parlor. In preparation for the worst, she helped William prepare a bed in the cellar for Pennington, in case they had to move him there, then readied emergency supplies of food and water.

Upstairs a little later, carrying a breakfast tray, she entered Pennington's bedroom and found him wide awake, propped up on pillows. He looked gaunt and worried, the flesh of his face as pale and translucent as fine parchment. "I knew it wouldn't be long before Mr. Washington attacked," he said.

"From all the commotion outside, it would seem General Howe was caught napping."

For an instant, she glimpsed the old George as he spoke in a raspy voice laced with scorn. "Damn him for a buffoon! Why is he content to let the rebels take the offensive?"

"Indolence?" she suggested. "After all, it took him eighty days just to get here from New York."

Sighing, Pennington glanced at the food tray and grimaced. "Porridge again? Have you no imagination?"

"Blame the British," she said, handing him a silver porringer and a spoon. "They stripped the city bare to feed themselves."

Pennington started in halfheartedly on his breakfast. "William said some soldiers ravaged my vegetable garden without offering a penny's compensation."

Meeting his look, Alexandra nodded grimly, and Pennington fell silent, toying with his porridge. After a time he handed her the unfinshed bowl and said with sad-eyed bitterness, "I never imagined the British would be so brazen or uncaring."

"They excel at both."

He patted the mattress beside him, commanding, "Sit down and tell me everything they've done."

Alexandra hardly knew where to begin. But once she started, she could not vent her pent-up anger at the British quickly enough. "At first they were courteous," she said. "They offered to pay for food and lodgings. Now they just take whatever they want."

Despite promises to the populace that their lives and

property would not be molested, looting by soldiers was continuous and wanton. Everything from wine to bedding was being stolen by red-coated thieves in the night. Foragers confiscated hay from barns and offered receipts for only one-tenth of what they took. The effect of all this was a growing disaffection among Philadelphians, in particular the neutral Quakers, who were beginning to feel more like victims than a people supposedly liberated.

Still and all, the British were being coddled by a majority of upper-class Tories, whose main passion seemed to be a desire to rekindle Philadelphia's social life, even if it meant overlooking British and Hessian licentiousness. Alexandra felt nothing but contempt for the fraternizers. Her days as a Loyalist seemed a lifetime behind her.

"Mr. Galloway has been appointed acting police commissioner," she told Pennington. "He has invented more rules for us to follow than a fish has scales. If we want to go out after dark, we need a pass. Neither river can be crossed without special permission. No wood can be cut and nothing can be sold without a British license. It's ridiculous!" she said hotly. "We might as well be prisoners. In effect we will be, just as soon as they finish building their damn redoubts."

The British were building a chain of ten redoubts, linked by entrenchments and a strong abatis, across the two-mile northern front that lay between the Delaware and Schuylkill Rivers. When completed, the line of fortifications would make the city impregnable to any assault from without. But Alexandra feared the defenses would also be used to contain the people of Philadelphia.

Unable to sit still, she moved off the bed and began to pace. "We mean *nothing* to England. We're chattel to be used at will. I once thought the rebels were mad for calling the King a tyrant. Well, he is one," she said fiercely, "and his army is composed of dregs." As she paused, wrung with emotions, the hush in the room was punctuated by the thudding of distant cannon. Her voice shook with despair. "I feel betrayed, George."

Shocked as he was by the portrait she had painted of the British occupation, Pennington was even more alarmed by her treasonous statements. And yet, surprisingly, he

366

found himself admiring her defiance of the Crown. While her peers turned a blind eye on British depredations and clung to what was safe, she valued the one thing that really mattered: the truth. That the little minds of a great empire cared more about America's bounties than the rights of her people.

With dismay, Pennington realized that his own loyalty was steeped in denial. He had labeled reports of atrocities as hearsay. He had written off stories of plundering, rape, and even murder as rebel propaganda. He felt like a dupe.

He started to say so, but was seized by a convulsive coughing that racked his sorry lungs unmercifully. Helpless to stop the torture, he clutched his chest as his face mottled with strain and tears of pain streamed down his cheeks.

When the spell finally passed, Alexandra had a vial of opiate ready. "Drink this," she coaxed, but he turned his head away.

"The damn stuff makes me insensible."

"George, don't argue with me. It's for your own good."

Sighing, Pennington took the vial and tossed down the medicine. "You're worse than a doctor," he grumbled. "At least I can insult them."

The opiate quickly took effect and soon his eyelids were drooping. He watched Alexandra, who stood at a window and surveyed the white-veiled morning. In a sluggish voice, he asked, "What is Charles up to these days?"

Just hearing his name made her seethe. Turning from the window, she met Pennington's glassy look and said quietly, reluctant to have him know, "He joined the British Army."

Pennington's eyes closed. "Good God."

"It seems he recruited a company of Loyalists and secretly trained them. Last month, they offered their services to General Howe. They call themselves the Philadelphia Loyalist Dragoons. From what I gather, they would do credit only to a band of ruffians. The Whigs are terrified of them, and with good reason. Charles and his bullies have arrested thirty people suspected of having rebel ties."

Pennington was a long moment responding. "For God's sake, watch your back, Alexandra."

"I intend to."

A short time later, Pennington drifted into sleep. Moving quietly, Alexandra collected his food tray, laid a clean kerchief on his nightstand, and left the room. Going downstairs, she heard loud conversation in the hallway below and recognized Clue's excited voice. When she saw him, his face was exultant.

"The rebels are thumping the British at Germantown!" he cried.

A thrill of disbelief raced through her. "How do you know?"

"I overheard some redcoats talking. They said the whole British center line collapsed!"

Hearing this, Alexandra began to envision not only an end to the occupation of Philadelphia, but to the war itself. Then her thoughts froze when Clue said, "I saw Mr. Villard and his troop flying up Second Street. From the looks of them, they were headed for the battle."

Alexandra stood unmoving, her eyes narrowed and glittering as she listened to nearby hammer-blows of artillery fire. To her mind, those zooming shells were now doubly significant, for one of them could purge an evil that had plagued her for too long.

Chapter Forty-Eight

The Walnut Street Jail was filled to capacity with prisoners—American prisoners of war. The upper floor of the State House was crowded with captured rebel officers, many of them suffering from festering wounds received at Germantown. Neutral Quakers and brave American sympathizers did what they could to sustain the prisoners, bearing food and other comforts to them, but most of what they brought was confiscated by the British for their own wounded.

Residents of Philadelphia who visited Germantown revealed the sad aftermath of the fighting. Scattered over the battleground, fallen rebel corpses were being stripped to their ragged underclothes by human parasites. The Wyck mansion and the Germantown Academy, converted into hospitals, overflowed with the wounded of both sides. On red-spattered dining tables, soldiers were held screaming and writhing beneath amputation saws, their only anesthetics whiskey and rum. Severed limbs were piled chin-high outside the makeshift surgeries and were dumped afterwards in a nearby quarry, where they fell prey to famished dogs.

Of the battle itself, the result was a bitter disappointment for the rebels. Owing to a drunken General Stephen and a blinding fog made worse by battle smoke, Washington's bold attack had ended in disaster. Stephen's troops, confused by his nonsensical orders, had mistakenly fired upon Anthony Wayne's men, shooting many in the back and causing a collapse of the Pennsylvania

Line at the moment of victory.

A surprised contingent of British infantry saw the enemy advance fall dead. The redcoats had been about to surrender. Instead, reformed and reinforced, they wheeled around and turned the American assault into a rout, driving the rebels deep into the countryside. Washington's battered, exhausted army had retreated to Pennypacker's Mills.

Philadelphia belonged to the British.

Philadelphians, Alexandra decided, were a fickle, spineless lot. Yesterday they were grumbling about food shortages, whining that their homes were being wrecked, and fuming because their daughters were being seduced by smooth-tongued English rakes.

Today they thronged the city's streets, rooftops, and windows by the thousands, cheering and applauding as the victorious British Army paraded into town. Sir William Howe, accompanied by bands playing triumphant music and surrounded by a glittering entourage of aides and general officers, led the column down Second Street into the heart of the city.

From a corner at Second and Chestnut, Alexandra and Clue watched in silence as the scarlet van went by. The redcoats looked healthy, splendidly equipped, and were clad in their best array. The contrast between them and the ragged American troops that had marched through the capital was striking, and caused Alexandra despair. Scanning rows of clean-shaven English faces, she wondered bleakly if one of them was Dalton's murderer.

Hot tears rushed to her eyes, blurring her view of the soldiers. Then her back stiffened, her chin rose. He isn't dead, she thought fiercely, and the war isn't over. For the past hour, rumors had been circulating through the crowd that rebel patrols were harassing the British rear guard, cutting off stragglers and taking prisoners. That kind of audacity was hardly the mark of a defeated army, she thought.

Clue nudged her arm. "Look," he said in a low

voice. "Hessians."

As though on cue, the fanfare and huzzahs around them dwindled to a polite, hesitant applause. The mustachioed Germans, fearsome and terrible in brass-fronted helmets, marched past to exotic, strident music that spoke better English than they could themselves. *Plunder, rape, pillage.*

The Hessian troops were followed by a regiment of British cavalry, the elite Sixteenth Light Dragoons. Despite her resentment, Alexandra could not help but admire their dazling uniforms, gleaming weaponry, and skillful horsemanship. After they passed, a huge cheer arose like a tidal wave, drowning out the resounding clatter of ironshod hooves on pavement. Standing on tiptoe, she strained to see the source of all the excitement and was rewarded with a glimpse of the Philadelphia Loyalist Dragoons. Soon the troop was close enough for her to observe the triumphant face of their captain.

Bitterness threatened to choke her. She felt cut to the bone by Villard's lofty demeanor. Beside her, Clue was equally chagrined. "Sod him," he muttered, then sighed. "There's no justice in this world."

"Perhaps not in this one," she said, "but there is in the next. God does not forgive his kind, Christopher. The devil will have him a thousand times over, and I, for one, shall rejoice." She gathered her skirts. "If you're ready, I've seen quite enough."

Clue, uncomfortable in the presence of so many soldiers and Tories, was happy to go with her. Leaving the noisy crowd and the trumpeting bands behind, they walked along Chestnut Street toward the Quaker School House, where they had left the Pennington coach. As they crossed the wooden bridge over Dock Creek, Alexandra noticed a lone, mounted British officer riding toward them. From the amount of gold braid adorning his uniform, she supposed he held an important post. He wore a courier's pouch on a shoulder strap and a confused look on his face. To her annoyance, he hailed them.

"You there!" he called, reining his horse across the dusty street to them. "I'm looking for the Bettering House.

371

Would you be so kind as to direct me there?"

Alexandra ignored him, but Clue cheerfully gave him directions, not to the Bettering House, but to a notorious brothel on Front Street. Nodding his thanks, the officer rode away.

And Alexandra gave Clue a delighted smile. "There are times when I absolutely adore you."

Pleased with his trickery, Clue started to reply, but the sudden pounding of hooves made them both turn and look toward the Dock Creek bridge. Following Clue's directions, the British officer had ridden onto the bridge, only to be surrounded by six British cavalrymen with their pistols drawn. While Alexandra and Clue watched in bewilderment, the protesting officer was disarmed, then herded off the bridge at gunpoint.

As the horsemen came toward her, Alexandra suddenly caught her breath and stared hard at one of the cavalry mounts—a splendid chestnut horse whose fire and elegance, once seen, were unforgettable. Her gaze flew to the rider's face, her heart expanded in her chest. For a split second she was stunned with shock, then a sound like a sob escaped her.

Dalton, disguised as a British dragoon and wearing a look of high excitement, was too intent on business to notice her at first. As he rode past her with his men, scanning the street ahead and behind for trouble, his gaze moved over her, then came back and riveted on her face. Eyes widening, he brought Mercury to a skidding, rump-down halt and hesitated in the middle of the street, grinning at her, then realizing the danger of tarrying, he wheeled the stallion around and galloped after his men.

Exhilarated, clutching Clue's arm, Alexandra watched the band of rebel raiders disappear up Chestnut Street with their prisoner. Her body was pulsing with fine tremors. Her voice, when she located it, shook with emotion. "Christopher, that was Dalton!"

"It sure as hell was," he said, equally astonished. "God Almighty, he has nerves of steel."

To Alexandra, the daring kidnapping of a British officer held little significance at the moment. Only one thing mattered to her. Dalton was alive. His image was burned into her memory—the surprise on his face, his reckless grin, the startling red of his stolen uniform. Her head was filled with him, and she wept with the sheer joy of knowing that he lived, because she had never felt more gloriously alive herself.

Chapter Forty-Nine

Cannon fired downriver, shuddering the air. Day and night, the Delaware River forts were being hammered by British land and naval batteries. Sir William Howe, dependent upon his ships to bring him supplies, was desperate for control of the waterway. Philadelphia's food stores were nearly exhausted, and his army could not survive on fodder.

Alexandra prayed the rebel forts would hold. If they did, Howe's game here would be up. He would have to go reeling back to New York as best he could, and getting out of Philadelphia would probably cost him more than getting in. She wanted nothing more than to see the backside of him.

But it was not to be.

In late November, Howe's warships finally dropped anchor at Philadelphia's fortified wharves. The British fleet could now safely navigate the Delaware River. Across its broad expanse at Red Bank, a vagrant breeze wandered the ruins of Fort Mercer, stirring ribbons of smoke from its smoldering palisades. Mercer's garrison had withdrawn, the yawning mouths of its cannon were silent. As silent as George Pennington, who lay still and withered on his bed at Oakwood.

Clasping his chill hand, Alexandra felt his fingers twitch against hers, then watched the light fade from his eyes. Her own eyes stung as she brought his hand to her cheek and held it there, her heart aching with grief.

Pennington had known what was coming. For weeks he

had drifted in and out of delirium, too feverish at times to recognize her. But a short while ago, in an unexpectedly lucid moment, he had spoken his last words to her. "Don't weep on my grave, dear. Remember our happiness."

Now he was gone, and the anguish she felt was too great to contain. "Oh, George," she whispered and began to sob brokenly.

Standing behind her, at a loss how to comfort her, Clue held her shoulders as she wept. "His pain's over, ma'am."

She nodded, immersed in sorrow.

"He knew you were with him at the end. He always knew you cared."

Alexandra knew her affection for George Pennington was eternal. For that reason, she was able to honor his last request when, two days later, he was buried at Christ Church cemetery. Black-garbed and dry-eyed, she bade him a silent farewell as his coffin was lowered into the ground. The press of mourners at his graveside was considerable—friends, business acquaintances, a sprinkling of distant cousins. His immediate kin had all gone before him, making Alexandra the closest person he had to family. While the minister droned on about God's will and the frailty of man, she reminded herself that George was now safe from harm, free of suffering and worry, and protected from the likes of Charles Villard.

But his property, she discovered, was not.

Returning to Oakwood after the funeral, she went upstairs to the guest room and fell asleep in exhaustion. At noon, a company of British soldiers arrived at the house, and within minutes the yard was piled with military baggage of every description. Startled awake by coarse shouting outside, Alexandra hurried downstairs to see what the commotion was about. As she reached the front foyer, the door burst open, admitting a rush of chilly air and Charles Villard.

She stopped short when she saw him. Eyeing her coldly, he closed the door and came toward her, and though her pulse hammered, she held her ground. "How dare you come here?"

"I dare on the King's business."

"What do you want?"

"I should think that's obvious." Amusement lurked beneath his stony look. "I'm commandeering George's house to quarter our troops."

Her eyes glittered with hatred. "You couldn't even wait until he was cold," she accused.

"Sweetheart, I couldn't wait until he was dead."

Fury exploded in her. She tried to slap his mocking face, but Villard was ready for her. He caught her wrist in an iron grip and pulled her roughly against him, twisting her arm behind her back until she gasped in pain.

"Hold still," he said, "or it will hurt worse."

Alexandra quickly learned he was right. "Let me go!" she said through her teeth.

"In a minute. Then you can pack your things and leave."

"Go to hell!" she cried, trembling with outrage. "You won't get away with this, you bastard. I'll report you to General Howe!"

"Sweetheart," he cooed, his thumb stroking her cheek. Alexandra jerked from his touch as though burned, then stilled again as he increased the pressure on her throbbing arm. "Allow me to educate you," he went on in the same, soft voice. "At Germantown, I saved the life of a British major after his horse was shot from under him. At great personal risk, I plucked him right out from under the rebels' noses." Villard chuckled, enjoying himself. "It turns out Major Palmos is an aide to General Howe."

Alexandra absorbed the news with a sinking feeling. Villard's scarlet uniform had suddenly taken on new meaning.

"As you can imagine," he gloated, "we've become quite good friends."

"How unfortunate for him."

Villard's eyes lost their humor. All at once he shoved her from him with such force that she had to grab the banister to keep from falling. Straightening, she rubbed her sore shoulder and watched him warily as he reached inside his coat.

"Major Palmos agrees with me that this house should be impounded for our troops." With that, he handed her a document bearing Sir William Howe's seal and signature,

376

authorizing him to take possession of Oakwood.

After reading the order, Alexandra threw it back at him, consumed with loathing for him. She longed to defy his authority, but Villard held the advantage of a direct link with Howe, whose word was law. Knowing it was pointless to argue, she asked numbly, "What about George's things?"

"The spoils of war, sweetheart. But," he shrugged, "for old time's sake, you may remove whatever you can carry. Just be quick about it, or I'm liable to change my mind."

In the end, she collected a few of George's belongings to take with her, items that were of little value to anyone except her. Among them were a brace of pistols, his medals from the French war, and several well-worn books. But the greatest treasures she carried with her from Oakwood were her memories of a beloved friend. No one could take those away from her.

A few weeks later, on a raw December morning, Alexandra sat down to breakfast at her Fourth Street house. With the arrival of British supply ships, food shortages in Philadelphia had eased, and she savored the fresh eggs, bacon, and coffee that Mary had prepared for her. A fire snapped on the dining-room hearth, warming her against the cold. In the quiet, she listened to Mary moving about in the kitchen, then heard Clue humming an off-key version of "Liberty Tree" as he came in from feeding the horses.

Sipping coffee, Alexandra was startled by a sudden hammering as someone with a heavy hand banged the front-door knocker. The disturbance continued without pause until Mary went to answer the insistent summons. Moments later, she entered the dining room, her face apprehensive. "It's Mr. Villard and a British officer," she said, wringing her hands.

Alexandra's unease gave way to slow, smoldering anger. It took a few moments to bring herself under control.

The two men were waiting for her in the parlor. Villard, immaculate in a scarlet uniform with blue facings, greeted her casually. "Good morning, Mrs. Pennington." His voice was taunting, his look triumphant. "As always, it's a pleasure to see you."

Coldly ignoring him, Alexandra faced his companion and saw a uniformed man of average height, slender except for his waistline, which betrayed on overindulgence in good living. Like Villard, he was meticulously groomed. His red coat bore two gold epaulets, signifying an aide-de-camp to a British general officer. He might have been handsome, but for his eyes. Small, close-set and glittering black, they appraised her without seeming to, evaluating her breasts before finding her face. Tucking his cocked hat under his arm, he bowed formally to her and introduced himself as Maj. Andrew Palmos, aide to Gen. Sir William Howe. From his tone, he expected awe from her.

"What do you want, Major?" she asked in a voice like ice.

Surprise flitted across his face. As he darted a look at Villard, Alexandra watched his eyes and was reminded of a rodent. She thought the two men made a fitting pair.

Recovering his composure, Palmos flashed her an ingratiating smile. "I understand you have several vacant rooms here."

Alexandra heard presumption in his tone, realized what was coming, and felt enraged. Aware of Villard's keen regard, she refused to meet his look. She wondered what he had told Palmos about her, for the major's eyes had taken to roaming again.

"As you probably know," Palmos said, "decent lodgings are scarcer than hen's teeth in the city. Therefore, I'm thinking of quartering myself and a servant here. I trust we can work out a suitable arrangement. Captain Villard assured me of your generous hospitality."

"Mr. Villard is an ass."

There was a strained pause. Villard, enjoying the scene, folded his arms without comment. But the major's lofty expression had fallen flat. "See here, Mrs. Pennington—"

"Find somewhere else to stay," she cut him off. "You are not welcome here."

Palmos stiffened. "Pray, don't force me to become unpleasant."

"How so?" she demanded, eyes flashing. "By serving me with an order signed by General Howe?"

"Your compliance would be preferable to such a measure."

"I would sooner burn this house down around your ears."

Pierced by her withering scorn, Palmos strove to retain his air of authority. Had Villard not been standing there, the major might have softened his approach, for Mrs. Pennington was an intriguing creature, a dark angel, and he had no desire to earn her contempt. Rather, he was envisioning her as a warm, sensual diversion from what promised to be a bitterly cold winter. But Palmos's arrogance would not allow him to bend.

"My dear woman," he said curtly, "you needn't behave so offensively. Consider yourself fortunate to have an officer and a gentleman moving in with you, and not some vulgar sergeant." His obsidian eyes narrowed at her. "Which could easily be arranged."

Now Alexandra looked at Villard, and as their stares clashed she could feel the force of his exultation beating against her. The urge to strike his smug face was overwhelming, but then a greater sensation supplanted her rage, for the challenge in Villard's eyes brought home the enormous danger of his newfound power. No one in this house was safe from him. She thought of Clue and the Brocks, innocents caught in the middle, and fear for them held her in check.

As if reading her mind, Villard cautioned, "It would be in everyone's best interest if you would cooperate."

Alexandra held his gaze with a sinking feeling, reduced to bitterness by her impotence. Once again he had defeated her. She looked back at Palmos's expectant face, and though her voice was level, her body shook with despair. "Very well, Major. The house is yours."

Pleased by her capitulation, Palmos relaxed a little. "You have my word I'll not disrupt your household," he said. "In fact, you'll hardly know I'm here."

"I'm sure I won't."

"Splendid. Then it's settled."

"Yes," she agreed coldly. "I shall move out this very afternoon."

Palmos blinked in surprise. "It's unnecessary for you to leave, Mrs. Pennington."

"On the contrary," she retorted, "it's a matter of life and death. Because I would rather be dead than share my house with a friend of Mr. Villard."

Chapter Fifty

On New Year's Eve, a crackling fire warmed the public room at the City Tavern, where drunkenness was the order of the evening. Smiling, bright-eyed barmaids served hot punch and tankards of foaming ale while fending off the pawing hands of soldiers. With the city's defenses in place, British officers had little to do beyond guard duty, so they gave themselves up to amusements. Gambling in the city had increased. Balls and parties were everyday occurrences.

Philadelphia's high society embraced the gala season with enthusiasm, but a few brave Americans, mostly women, openly expressed their displeasure with British rule. They complained bitterly to Howe about the deplorable conditions at the Walnut Street Jail, where the British provost marshal was growing rich on the bodies of the dead and the starvation of the living. By all accounts, Capt. William Cunningham was a monster. It was said he regularly beat and kicked his prisoners, often to death, and sold their food to enhance his own pockets. In a few short months, he had earned the nickname "Bloody Bill."

Maj. Andrew Palmos, in his capacity as Howe's official buffer, had heard earfuls about the mistreatment of rebel prisoners. "I don't see what all the fuss is about," he said above the tavern din. "They're prisoners of war, for God's sake."

"They're traitors," said Villard. "They should all be executed. It would save us a lot of needless expense."

Smiling and bleary-eyed, Palmos wagged a finger at

him. "I like the way you think, Charlie." A pause to swill spicy ale. "Anyway, the rebels have no room to complain. When I was their prisoner after Princeton, I was shamefully mistreated."

"Indeed?"

"Terribly so! I was wounded in the foot, you see, and they denied me medical care. Not only that, they forced me to walk for miles with a bullet in my foot. When I dared to complain, do you know what they did?"

Whether he wanted to or not, Villard knew he was about to find out. Andrew Palmos, he had discovered, liked to talk about himself almost as much as he liked to drink and chase after women.

"I demanded to be put in a wagon," Palmos explained, "and this bastard of a lieutenant tied me to the back of one, then dragged me until I was unconscious."

Villard's narrowed eyes affected concern. "And the rebels call us brutal."

"If ever I should meet with that low-life dog again, I'll teach him the meaning of abuse."

"How is it you're not still a prisoner, Andrew?"

Sitting up straighter, Palmos puffed out his chest and said with pride, "I escaped."

"Really? How?"

"The rebels stopped at a village and crowded us all into a church for the night. I overpowered a guard, attired myself in his odious rags, and passed myself off as the enemy. Clever, don't you think?"

"Oh, better than that. Ingenious."

"I daresay it earned Billy's attention. He was rather impressed with my resourcefulness."

"So he made you his aide," Villard said before Palmos could get the words out.

Palmos grinned. "Prisoner one week, aide to General Howe the next. Isn't life ironic?"

Ridiculously so, Villard thought.

Just then a serving girl arrived at their table with heaping platters of food. As she set the plates down, Palmos boldly caressed her buttocks, then withdrew his hand when she raised a fork at him.

"Lecher," she said and moved away, hips twitching beneath her gathered skirt. Palmos stared after her a

382

moment, then picked up his knife and fork and dug into his meal.

Across the room, a group of Queen's Rangers began singing a ballad written by one of their captains. Called "The Rebels," its lyrics ignited the partisan crowd.

The arch-rebels, barefooted tatterdemalions,
In baseness exceed all other rebellions,
  With their hunting-shirts and rifle-guns.
To rend the empire, the most infamous lies
Their mock-patriot Congress do always devise;
Independence, like the first of rebels, they claim,
But their plots will be damned in the annals of fame,
  With their hunting-shirts and rifle-guns.

A roar of approval followed the verse and each verse thereafter. Even Villard applauded the singers, amazed that in their bleary condition they could remember so many words. Eventually the furor died down; Villard returned to eating his dinner.

Major Palmos was sawing energetically on a tough piece of meat. "Damn!" he exclaimed. "I haven't sampled a decent piece of flesh since arriving in America. And I don't mean bullock beef. A shame Mrs. Pennington ran off. Now *there* was a rare delicacy." He chewed, sighed, resumed carving his steak. "Had I known how she would react, Charlie, I never would have let myself be seen with you. Whatever did you do to earn her revulsion?" Glancing up, Palmos encountered a look that could kill.

"It wasn't what I did, but what she did."

"Oh? What was that?"

"She became a whore."

Palmos was intrigued. "Perhaps I took the wrong approach with her."

"She prefers a baser breed of men, I'm afraid."

"It never hurts to try," Palmos said with a shrug. "Where do you suppose she went?"

Villard knew exactly where Alexandra had gone. He had made it his business to find out. "She's staying at her country house."

"Which is where?"

"On the Ridge Road, a few miles beyond the redoubts."

383

"She has nerve moving to that lawless neck of the woods. Still," Palmos's eyes gleamed roguishly, "it isn't so far that I couldn't pay her a visit."

"In that case, I would advise an armed escort, or you might find yourself taken prisoner again."

The remark made Palmos grimace. Although the British army was secure in Philadelphia, protected by fortifications on the north and surrounded by water on all other sides, the rebels ruled the countryside. Bands of mounted raiders patroled country roads, preying on foraging parties and preventing Tory farmers from carting food into the city. Even the supply caravans escorted by British soldiers had come under attack.

"It's a damn nuisance," Palmos scowled. "Billy's so infuriated by the interference with his supply lines, he can hardly sleep nights. He wants the culprits caught or killed, but it's like trying to apprehend ghosts. They simply vanish into the woods." Palmos suppressed a belch, then signaled for more ale. "A rebel deserter said some of the raids are being led by a local man, Dalton Philips. Have you heard of him?"

Villard tensed. After a moment, he said he had heard of Dalton Philips. Then he was silent, his eyes cold and forbidding.

Oblivious to his mood, Palmos went on, "Captain Philips is on Billy's blacklist. Whoever dispatches him is sure to earn a promotion."

Villard didn't say so, but he had his own death list, and Dalton Philips was at the top of it.

Chapter Fifty-One

The air was so cold it hurt to breathe. Empty stillness shrouded the snow-covered woods, where creeks lay frozen in their beds and even the hardiest animals were loath to leave their burrows.

The supply wagons could be heard a long way off. There were four of them, rumbling over the road to thudding hooves and the low whine of iron rims in icy ruts. Flanked by redcoats, the caravan made an eye-catching scarlet splash against the whitened landscape. The soldiers and drivers were heavily bundled up, black fur caps pulled down low over their necks, their breaths billowing in the frosty morning. Nervous heads turned to and fro, eyeing the snow-crusted road ahead and behind for movement. When nothing stirred, there were sighs of relief all around.

Then, out of the hushed woods, came a rush of mounted riders. The calm exploded with the crash of gunfire and clashing sabers, the shouts, screams, and curses of a ferocious attack. Draft horses sprawled in the road, overturning wagons and dumping precious stores onto the ground. Steel hissed and rang, bullets whipcracked and thudded into flesh. Then came the groans of dying men, vomiting blood in the snow. As the roughriders laughed and flourished swords in triumph, the remaining British horseguard fled for their lives.

A cowering farmer was dragged from beneath a wagon and hauled before the rebel captain, whose voice was as hard and unforgiving as the saber in his hand. "Do you know the penalty for trading with the British?"

"Please," the farmer begged. "Don't kill me."

Unmoved by his plea, Dalton glanced at Henry. "What should we do with him, Lieutenant?"

"Hang the fucker, sir."

"Ready a rope then."

"No!" the man cried, sagging to his knees. "Have mercy. I have a wife and five children at home."

A long silence followed as ruthless green eyes appraised him. "What's your name?"

"John Turner."

"Turner," Dalton said with contempt. "A fitting name for a bloody stinking turncoat. Where do you live?"

"Dilworth."

"You came a long way for British gold." The tip of Dalton's saber rose and poised at Turner's throat. "In my opinion, hanging's too good for you."

Turner swallowed, aware of his captors pressing closer. Wild-looking they were, wearing tattered trousers and beaver hats, their cracked fingers sticking out of mittens, gripping cold muskets. Many were without greatcoats and boots, their feet wrapped in rags or gunnysacks. They stared at Turner with weathered faces that seemed to be chiseled from marble.

"Take off your coat," Dalton ordered him.

Jarred into action, Turner stood up and shrugged out of it.

"Empty your pockets."

Turner did as he was told, producing a folded kerchief, a leather purse, and a pocket watch, all of which Henry confiscated.

"Now turn around."

Turner hesitated, eyeing Dalton's bloodied saber.

"Do it, fuck-pig!"

With a murmured prayer, Turner presented his back to Dalton. Trembling uncontrollably, certain he was living his last moments on earth, he waited to feel the killing blade.

"If I ever lay eyes on you again," Dalton told him, "I'll cut you in two. Now get out of here before I change my mind about letting you live."

Stunned, Turner took two shaky steps, then broke into a run, slipping and stumbling over the rutted road in his

386

haste to get away. Watching him go, the rebels howled with laughter.

Henry grinned at Dalton. "You scared the blazes out of him."

"Lucky for him it was us and not McLane's men that caught him." Moving to a wagon, Dalton inspected its freight and found casks of beef packed in brine, barrels of flour and salted shad, and several small kegs of rum. His mouth watered at the sight of so much food and spirits. Beckoning two of his men, he told one, "Diddle, knock the bung off that keg and give each man a gill of rum."

Diddle's face lit up. "Yes, sir!"

"Pauley," Dalton told the other, "watch that Diddle don't nip while he's pouring."

"Right, Captain," Pauley grinned.

After the rum was distributed, the overturned wagons were righted, the enemy dead were piled atop captured supplies, and the caravan turned around and headed north for Valley Forge, with Captain Philips spurring ahead.

Toward nightfall, Philips's Raiders passed the sentry posts on Gulph Road and began their ascent into the strong hills that shaped the western horizon. Riding beside Henry at the head of the column, Dalton produced a flask of rum, trickled some down each boot to keep his feet from freezing, then passed the flask to Henry, who did likewise. Scattered over the ridge ahead of them, campfires winked like stars in the darkness. The air was permeated with the pungent odor of woodsmoke.

Valley Forge camp, where wolves howled at night and the moaning wind rivaled the groans of suffering men and animals. Where famished soldiers wanted for everything—coats, hats, boots, underwear, trousers, blankets, and bedding. And food. There was never enough food.

Washington's army was dwindling, ravaged by killing cold and epidemic diseases. The slab-floored hovels that served as camp hospitals were overflowing with victims of smallpox and putrid fever. The rising death toll had been too much for some men to bear. Scores of soldiers had deserted to the British in Philadelphia.

The rest shivered, starved, and suffered. Men existed for days on nothing but firecake—a pasty mixture of flour and water, baked on flat stones set by a fire. Beef came in trifles and was often spoiled or so thinly sliced that, as one camp joker declared, "You could see the butcher's breeches through the meat." Forage was also in critically short supply, and horses were dying by the hundreds, their carcasses rotting and fouling the whole camp.

By the time the huts of the Pennsylvania brigades came into view, Dalton's mood was grim. The captured supplies, measured against the needs of the camp, amounted to a drop in the bucket.

Hearing the wagons approach, groups of hollow-eyed soldiers materialized from the darkness and gazed hopefully at the food casks. Col. James Chambers emerged from a crude log hut and grinned when he saw Dalton. The colonel's face was streaked with fireplace soot, his nose reddened from the cold.

"Saints be praised," he said, then cupped a hand to his ear and pretended to listen. "You must be the most wanted man in both camps, Captain. I can hear Billy Howe ranting from here. He wants his goods returned."

"I'll return them, sir. Right up his flaming arse."

The gathering of soldiers cheered and hooted.

As Dalton started to dismount, the colonel checked him. "General Wayne wants to see you right away."

Although exhausted and numb with cold, Dalton was heartened by the thought of seeing Wayne. Leaving Colonel Chambers in charge of the wagons, he set out for Little Trout Run, half a mile south of the outer breastworks, where Wayne had found accommodations in one of the several stone houses bordering the creek.

In December, despite a racking cold and splintered breastbone suffered at Germantown, Wayne had refused to indulge in comforts, living out-of-doors with his men until all of them were hutted. Only then had he allowed himself to rest and recuperate from a grueling, dispiriting campaign. While his body had mended, he wrote incessantly to the Board of War, the Council of Safety, and the Clothier-General, badgering and pleading for supplies. He expended forty-five hundred pounds of his own money to purchase uniforms, only to have them withheld by the Clothier-General because no definite date had been set for their release. After that, Wayne's letters had grown increasingly blistering, anguished, and moving.

"I never pass along the line but objects strike my eye which give a painful, melancholy sensation. They almost induce me to wish that I was past either seeing or hearing. Indeed, sirs, nothing but the doubtful state that we are in keeps me in a service that has become intolerable."

When Dalton tapped on the door to Wayne's chamber, he heard a sharp, "Come!" from inside. The general was sitting at a mahogany writing table, scratching away with a quill pen by the light of a candle. A decanter of wine stood at his elbow. Glancing up, his scowling face smoothed into a smile, his eyes gleaming a welcome as he rose.

"So," he said, "you're still in one piece."

"Only because all my parts are frozen together, sir."

"Come thaw yourself out," Wayne urged, gesturing to a chair before the hearth.

Dalton sank into the chair, removed his ice-encrusted mittens, and stretched his hands toward the flames to warm them. After pouring two tumblers of wine, Wayne joined him. He glanced Dalton over and shook his head. "My God, you look a wreck."

"General, you should see the British Rebels we tangled with."

Wayne laughed, pleased and intrigued. "Tell me everything," he insisted.

As Dalton described the attack on the caravan, Wayne hung on his every word, for even the smallest victory was reason for celebration these days. Afterward, Wayne toasted his success. "You're the backbone of the commissary department."

"Thank you, sir."

Although not under specific orders to lead raiding parties, Dalton made it his business to harass, attack, and generally alarm the enemy, wherever and whenever possible. The risks he took were not lost on Wayne, who had great respect for Dalton's bravery and battle sense. Dalton had become one of his favorite officers and, despite the difference in their social stations, a close friend.

Likewise, Dalton had grown to revere his commander. At the Brandywine and again at Germantown, Anthony Wayne had fought like a panther, seeming to be everywhere at once—shouting orders and encouragement, wheeling his troops into position, risking his life to be at the forefront of battle. The butchery of his men at Paoli had scorched him. The tragedy had also created a warrior filled with the need for revenge. Now, whenever the enemy was mentioned, Wayne displayed all the calm nervousness of a cat stalking prey.

Tonight his ferocity was directed at Congress. "I sometimes think they're our worst enemy," he confided, then swept a hand at the unfinished letter on his desk. "My fingers are cramped and my patience is burnt down from trying to reason with those unfeeling dolts. They oppose me at every turn with red tape and nonsense. I sent a letter pleading for some of the shoes stored at York, and the Clothier-General wrote back that he cannot send them because Congress neglected to vote on their distribution!" Bolting down his wine, Wayne stood up and paced before the hearth. "This camp is crisscrossed with bloody footprints, hogsheads of boots and shoes are mildewing at York, and those damn fools are so busy lying and making up excuses, they have no time for action!"

"Say the word, sir, and I'll raid the Clothier-General's warehouse."

Dalton's seriousness and the pathetic irony of his statement made Wayne sigh in frustration. Then, remembering something, he went to his desk, opened a drawer, and removed a wax-sealed letter. "I almost forgot. This came while you were away." He passed the heavy stationery beneath his nose, inhaling its perfumed scent. "From a lady, I should think."

Dalton came to his feet, eyes glued to the letter.

"Read it here, if you like," Wayne said, handing it to him. "I'll not disturb you." So saying, he sat at his desk, dipped his quill in ink, and resumed writing a scathing reply to the Clothier-General.

Dalton broke the seal on the letter and read by fire-light.

390

Dear Dalton,

So much has happened since I last saw you, I hardly know where to begin. George died the 25th of November, and the dear soul was barely in the ground before the British confiscated Oakwood. My Fourth Street house also fell into British hands. They are the worst scoundrels I have ever had the displeasure to encounter, and there will be no peace until they are gone from here forever.

To that end, I am happy to report that you've become quite famous—or infamous, as the case may be—for your refusal to leave the poor British lions alone. I applaud you, my love, but I beg you to be cautious as their patrols are constantly on lookout for you. They often stop here, demanding food, drink, and whatever else they feel entitled to, which is to say everything. After we came to Willowbrook, Christopher spent several nights outdoors for fear they would steal my horses, and consequently he took ill with fever. He is just now regaining his strength, and the British came and took possession of my horses after all.

But that won't prevent me from traveling. As soon as I can arrange transportation, I am coming to Valley Forge to be with you. Until then and always, I am

Your love,
Alexandra

Chapter Fifty-Two

Wearing a blue satin gown, Alexandra stood before a long oval mirror in her bedroom and studied her reflection in beveled glass. The gown's material was a deep, sapphire blue and shimmered in the candlelight as she moved. The bodice and cuffs were edged with fine Flanders lace; the slashed skirt revealed a quilted floral petticoat. Too elegant? she wondered.

Perhaps not. Rumor had it that General Washington was fond of entertainment, especially dancing. He was, after all, a Virginia aristocrat. An occasion might arise at Valley Forge camp when she would need a good dress. Anyway, it never hurt to be prepared.

Slipping out of the gown and petticoat, she packed them carefully into her portmanteau, along with matching jeweled slippers, then put on a flannel sleeping shift and a robe.

Now to select the rest of her wardrobe. She wished Mary were there to help her, but yesterday the Brocks had left for Lancaster, where they would spend the remainder of the winter at their son's farm. Their departure had been marked by a characteristic burst of tears from Mary and a touching glimmer of moisture in stolid Edward's eyes. But while Alexandra knew she would miss them deeply in the weeks ahead, just now her thoughts only went as far as Valley Forge.

By this time tomorrow, she would be with Dalton. Summoning his image, she shivered with the sweetest longing she had ever felt. They would be married right away, without fanfare. They would wed for love, and their days and nights would be filled with tenderness and sharing.

"God, give me his children," she whispered in a voice full of hope. After years of trying, John Pennington had died fatherless, but Alexandra could not accept that the fault lay with her. She refused to believe that her strong, young body would remain barren after mating with Dalton's. Something different and wonderful would take place between them.

A knock on her bedroom door interrupted her reverie. With a fond smile, she called, "Come in, Christopher."

He was bundled head to foot in heavy clothing, with only his face exposed. It was a remarkably healthy-looking face, she thought, considering how pale and sunken his features had been a few weeks ago, when she had feared for his life. So sick had Clue been, shuddering with fever and vomiting up everything that passed his lips, Alexandra had refused to leave his side for even a moment. She had slept on a pallet beside his bed. She forced mutton broth and warm milk into him, changed his soiled bedding, and kept the fire in his room stoked around the clock.

One morning she had awakened to find him clear-eyed and smiling. "Please don't tell Dalton," he said.

She thought he was delirious again. "Tell him what?" she asked gently.

"That you slept in my room. He'll kill me deader than a doornail."

Then she had known Clue would recover.

Now, watching him remove his mittens and hat, hearing his teeth chatter as he said, "Christ Almighty, it's freezing out there!" she was overwhelmed with affection for him. As he crossed to the fireplace, flashing her a shy grin as he presented his backside to the heat, she realized they had transcended the bonds of mere friendship. They were as close as a brother and sister could be.

"You shouldn't have stayed out so long," she admonished him.

"I was checking over the harness. I hope it doesn't snow again tomorrow. I'd hate to get stuck halfway between here and Valley Forge."

Alexandra didn't say so, but if need be she would ride

393

bareback through a blizzard to reach Dalton. "We'll get there," she said.

"One way or another," Clue agreed, then glanced at her portmanteau, grimacing at the thought of wrestling it down the stairs. "Are you still packing?" he asked, amazed that it was taking so long.

"I'm almost finished."

"At this rate, you should be done by spring." Ignoring her insulted look, he said, "I heard a patrol go by on the road a little while ago. They were headed for the city, thank God. I wish the redcoats would stop coming around here like they own the place. They give me the shivers."

"After tonight," she reminded him, "we'll be too far away for them to bother us."

"Not if you don't finish packing, ma'am."

That made her laugh and erased the tension that surfaced whenever the enemy was mentioned.

After warming himself at the fireplace, Clue fitted his hat over his head and pulled on his mittens.

"You're not going out again?" she said.

"Just for a bit. The horses seemed nervous about being in a strange barn."

That afternoon, Alexandra had purchased two cart horses from a Derby tanner. Aging, worn down from hauling heavy loads, the animals had still cost her plenty. Horses were at a premium these days. Before Philadelphia was surrendered, General Washington had sent troops to requisition, by force if necessary, all the available livestock they could find. Then the British had arrived and confiscated what was left. Alexandra felt lucky to have found the two horses.

"I'll give them some grain," Clue told her, "and make sure they haven't loosened their blankets. It's going to be a bitter night."

After he left for the barn, Alexandra continued packing, humming softly as she worked, her mind flirting with visions that would soon be realities. Suddenly she stilled to the sound of hoofbeats entering the yard. Many hoofbeats. Not again, she thought irritably. Another cold, thirsty group of soldiers, anxious to track mud and snow into her house.

Carrying a candle, she went down to the front passage,

determined to turn the patrol away. The door knocker banged, heightening her annoyance. With her mouth compressed in anger, she opened the door fully prepared to dress down a young, smooth-shaven subaltern.

Maj. Andrew Palmos was lounging against the door-jamb. Seeing her, he straightened, removed his cocked hat, and sketched a teetering bow. "Mrs. Pennington," he slurred. "How delightful to see you again."

He reeked. He was drunk. His vacuous smile deepened as he watched her, deviltry in his eyes. The heavy scarlet cloak that draped from his shoulders made him appear larger than she remembered. As he leaned toward her, his swaying form seemed to fill the doorway. "Aren't you going to invite me in?"

She tried to close the door, but he caught it with both hands and shoved hard, flinging her backward into the hallway. Following her inside, Palmos shut the door, leaned back against it, and wagged a finger at her. "That was quite rude."

"Get out."

"Come, come. You don't mean that."

"Get out," she demanded. As his glassy eyes prowled her body, fear and revulsion triggered the hammers of her heart. "If you come near me, I'll kill you."

Palmos laughed. "For Heaven's sake, calm down!"

Alexandra just watched him, wondering if Clue had heard the patrol arrive. She doubted it, or he would have come at once.

"I came to apologize for chasing you from your house," Palmos said, but his attitude was hardly apologetic. "I wish you had stayed. Just think of all the fun we could be having."

A sideboard stood a few feet to Alexandra's right. Keeping an eye on Palmos, she edged to the table and set the candlestick on it, freeing her hands. "I told you to leave, Major."

"Oh, don't be so tedious! I *hate* difficult women," he said, then looked past her down the darkened hallway. "Isn't that so, Charlie?"

It was an old ploy, but it worked. As Alexandra glanced toward the kitchen, she felt Palmos lunge, felt it first with her heart, then with her body as his powerful arms clamped around her. Twisting wildly in his grasp, she kicked his shin and heard him hiss, but he only tightened his hold, fingers clenching in her robe. The robe tore as she fought him, desperate to get loose. Finally Palmos lost his balance, but still refused to let her go. With his arms locked around her, he crashed into a wall, then pinned her against it with his body weight.

"Just be still," he commanded, breathing hard. "I'm not going to hurt you. I don't enjoy that."

Warm, sour breath fanned her face. When he bent his head and nuzzled her neck, Alexandra shuddered. The major might be drunk, but he was rock-hard against her. "I'm going to pleasure you," he said as his mouth grazed her cheek, "and warm you." His knee forced itself between her shaking ones. "There's a good girl. Don't be afraid."

Alexandra was more enraged than afraid. She suffered his pawing, waiting her moment. When she lifted her face to him, Palmos lost himself in her glittering blue eyes. "God, you are exquisite," he whispered. Lulled by her warmth, drawn to taste her soft, quivering lips, he covered them with his own, and when she responded he moaned and fed her his tongue.

She bit down sharply. As Palmos jerked back with a cry, tasting blood, her knee drove upward and hammered his testicles. He dropped like a sack to the floor and lay whimpering, unable to do anything except cup himself and wait for the bolting pain to subside.

Alexandra backed away from him. Hearing footsteps behind her, she spun toward the sound, ready to defend herself again, but it was Clue coming from the kitchen. He took in the scene with open-mouthed astonishment that quickly changed to fury. Opening a drawer in the sideboard, he brought out a pistol and leveled it at Palmos.

"Christopher, no!" Alexandra took the weapon from him. If anyone was going to kill the bastard, she was. Circling behind Palmos, she kicked the small of his back and ordered, "Get up. Get out of my house this instant, or I'll shoot you dead."

At her prodding, Palmos made it to his knees, then to his feet, then lurched to the door. Clue was there to open it for him, and the major stumbled outside to sprawl face-down

396

in the yard. Alexandra and Clue followed him as far as the porch.

A half-moon rode the horizon, blurred by a thickening veil of clouds. In the pale light, Alexandra made out a dozen mounted redcoats in her yard, all staring in wonder at their prone commander. Hearing him moan, watching him clutch his wounded groin, several men snickered, but Palmos was too lathered and in too much pain to notice. One of the redcoats, a lieutenant, directed two soldiers to help the major onto his horse. No sooner did Palmos's rump hit the saddle than he slumped over his mount's neck and began vomiting. Faces turned away, hiding grins.

But Charles Villard was unsmiling as he spurred his horse forward. "Who dared to assault him?" he demanded, his cold stare on Alexandra, who blanched upon seeing him.

"Captain Villard," the lieutenant said wearily, "I don't see that it matters."

Villard's head snapped toward him. "A British officer has been attacked."

"Rightly so, it appears."

"It is your duty to make an arrest."

"My duty is quite clear to me, and it does not require me to answer to you." The lieutenant's authority was practiced, effective, and was underscored with absolute disdain. Villard was, after all, only a provincial in a British uniform. His captaincy meant little to British regulars, who were ranked above provincial officers, a fact that came across in the lieutentant's condescending tone. "You may stay if you wish. The rest of the patrol is leaving."

With that, the lieutenant touched his hat to Alexandra. "Good night, ma'am," he said pleasantly, as if nothing out of the ordinary had occurred. At his command, the soldiers rode off with Major Palmos in tow.

Villard lingered, watching Alexandra by thin moonlight. "You've been spying on us for Dalton Philips."

His accusation earned a short, bitter laugh. "As far as I know, Dalton died at Paoli Tavern. Or so you wrote and told me."

Silence crackled. "Be careful of the company you keep, sweetheart."

"I try, but you leave me no choice. Every time I turn around, there you are. You're worse than a plague."

With strained composure, Villard studied the pistol hanging at her side. Noting its small size, he asked scornfully, "Is that your toy?"

"It's my protection if need be."

"Then I suggest you purchase something larger if you intend to do any damage."

There was a sharp click as she thumbed the hammer to full-cock. "It will certainly knock you off your horse at this distance."

Villard measured her. Although the urge to call her bluff was strong in him, he decided against it, for she looked capable of pulling the trigger, and her soft voice carried an ultimatum. "Don't come here again, Charles."

He watched her a moment longer, a muscle twitching in his cheek, then said, "Remember my warning." Wheeling his gelding around, he rode off at a canter.

As horse and rider melted into the night, relief swept Alexandra. Her shoulders sagged; her breath expelled in a rush. Beside her, Clue said, "Wait here, ma'am."

"Where are you going?" she asked with renewed alarm.

"Just down to the treeline. I don't trust him for a second. He might try to double back."

"Take this," she said, pressing the pistol into his hand. "And for God's sake be careful."

He squeezed her arm and was gone.

Shivering with cold and fright, Alexandra waited on the stoop for what felt like an hour, expecting at any moment to hear a pistol snap and see it flash out in the darkness. The moon vanished behind scudding clouds. Probing the gloom with her senses, she strained for a glimpse of Clue and listened for his footsteps in the stillness.

As she stood there, it began to snow, small, stinging crystals that struck her face and clung to its warmth like tears. "Christopher, where are you?" she whispered, hugging her arms against a rising, icy wind.

There! As a dark form took shape on the driveway and came toward her, there was no mistaking his spry step or the wavy outline of his hair.

Clue was out of breath when he reached her. "I didn't see any sign of him, ma'am," he said, taking her arm. In the house, after bolting the door behind them, he studied her with concern. "Are you all right?"

"Yes. Just shaken up."

"I'll get you some brandy."

But Alexandra declined the liquor. "I'm fine, Christopher. Truly, I am." To his worried look, she forced a smile and eventually convinced him that no real harm had been done to her, except to her nerves. "But it's over now," she told him. "The devils are gone, and tomorrow we'll be out of their reach."

"Thank God for that."

"If I'm to be ready to leave, I had better get busy," she said. "Believe it or not, I still have packing to do."

"I believe it," he said with a wry smile. "I'll be in the kitchen if you need me."

Maintaining her calm, Alexandra retreated to her bedroom, where the fire had burned low on the hearth. Once the door closed behind her, she shed her brave front and allowed herself some frightened tears. Sitting on the bed, plagued by the memory of Villard's hate-filled eyes, she buried her face in her hands and fought to control her trembling. "You black-hearted bastard," she wept. "Goddamn your soul, you filthy by-blow of a pig!"

"Alexandra?"

The soft voice scalded her and spun her off the bed with a cry. As she backed toward the door, her heart slamming with fear, a figure moved from the shadow of her armoire into the firelight.

"By God, you're a fine curser," Dalton said.

Chapter Fifty-Three

She couldn't move at first. His name filled her throat and came out in a whisper. He was smiling, caught up in the same elation that held her transfixed. As he came slowly forward, the glow of firelight revealed his gauntness and the shabbiness of his clothes. His eyes, beneath a sheen of rejoicing, had a haunted look in them. He seemed so changed. But when his arms came around her, enfolding her against lean warmth, he felt familiar and comforting, and Alexandra felt a joy greater than any she had ever known. Her body shook to soft, slow sobs that could not be contained.

Dalton's voice was husky with emotion. "God, I've needed you."

The need was mutual, electrifying. He bent his head as she lifted her face to him, and his kiss nourished her and made her strain to bring him closer.

Without warning, the bedroom door burst open and crashed against the wall like an explosion. Framed in the opening was Clue, looking murderous as he leveled a pistol at Dalton, who thrust Alexandra from the line of fire and raised defensive hands. "Whoa, Chris! It's me."

Clue blinked in amazement. "Dalton!"

"Yes," he agreed, nervously eyeing the pistol. "You can put that thing down."

Clue lowered the gun. "Jesus Christ, I could have shot you!"

"Believe me, you stopped my heart."

"How did you get in?"

"The back door," Dalton said. "I knocked, but nobody

answered, so I let myself in. You should do something about that latch, by the way."

"When I heard voices," Clue said, "I thought Mr. Villard had come back."

In the sudden hush, Dalton surveyed Alexandra's tear-stained face, the torn shoulder of her night robe, and his eyes blazed with comprehension. "Did that son of a bitch hurt you?"

There was vengeance in his look. Fearing he meant to act on it, she shook her head. "He just stopped here with a British patrol."

Dalton touched her shoulder. "Then who did this?"

"One of the redcoats. He was drunk . . ." Her voice trailed off when she saw Dalton's savage expression. "He didn't harm me," she said quickly.

"What's his name?"

Alexandra hesitated.

"Tell me, Alex."

"So you can go looking for him?"

"I won't be just looking. I have something specific in mind to do."

"Just let it go," she implored him.

Dalton looked at Clue. "Do you know the bastard's name?"

"Maj. Andrew Palmos."

Alexandra shot Clue a withering look as Dalton brooded over the name. "Palmos," he mused, then recognition dawned on him. "Jesus God," he said and asked, "Snotty man? Bump in his nose and rat's eyes?"

Clue grinned. "Sounds like you know him."

"You can say that. He was my prisoner after Princeton, but the slippery snake got away. Can't say I was sorry to lose him."

"He isn't worth your trouble," Alexandra insisted. "I told you, he didn't harm me. And besides, I'm going to Valley Forge with you—"

"No, Alex."

Struck silent, she thought for a moment that she had heard wrong. "What do you mean, no?"

"I mean you're not going there."

Her face grew distraught. "Why not?"

Pierced by her anguish, Dalton glanced at Clue. "Chris,

401

could you give us some time alone?"

"Of course."

"Mercury's behind the carriage house. If you have something for him to eat, he could use it."

"I'll look after him, don't worry."

When the door closed behind Clue, a heavy silence throbbed in the room. Then Alexandra asked, "Why don't you want me to go there?"

Dalton looked at her, and something twisted inside him. God, she was lovely, standing there with her hands clenched at her sides, her expression bewildered. He could not imagine her at the camp. He would hate for her to see how he lived, no better than an animal. Above all, he was worried about her safety, so he tried to explain the hell that was Valley Forge. "Because it's a mean place," he began. "It's dirty and cold."

"I don't care what it's like."

"*I* care. It's no place for you."

"My place is wherever you are," she said, hating the resolve in his eyes. They were bleak, heartbreaking eyes.

"Alex, you mean everything to me," he said. "I won't risk losing you there."

"It can't be that terrible."

Dalton stiffened, the muscles in his jaw flexing. "It is," he said, and the pain in his voice made her want to put her arms around him, but he moved away from her.

He went to her portmanteau and saw her blue satin gown lying atop a pile of equally fine clothing. As he lifted the dress, Alexandra was struck anew by his ragged appearance. His coat was threadbare at the elbows and shoulders, its collar and cuffs frayed. Mortified at her extravagance, she watched him examine the beautiful gown and was stung by the contrast of rich satin against stained wool and cheap ticken.

Dalton rubbed the soft material between calloused fingers, then ran his thumb down a row of glowing pearl buttons. Sighing, he laid the dress back into the trunk. "It's a pretty name, Valley Forge. Makes you think of a warm, cozy place, don't it? Hard to imagine what goes on there."

"However bad it is, I can take it. I'm not as fragile as you think."

402

Somewhere inside him a dam burst with surprising force. His throat tightened up, and he felt a sudden, overwhelming urge to shout some sense into her. He hardened his expression and let his anger run loose, let it toughen his voice. "Can you take smallpox and the bloody flux?" he demanded. "Could you eat soup made from boiled shoes? I've seen men do it. I've seen them spoon rotted fish out of a barrel and eat it raw, then swear it was the best food they ever had."

Alexandra was silent, watching him.

"Half the army walks around barefoot. Have you ever seen feet freeze and turn black?" Dalton prowled her bedroom as he spoke, touching her beautiful belongings, leaving his mark on them. He lifted a silver hairbrush from the vanity and fanned soft bristles with his fingers. "The night pickets have it the worst," he said without looking at her. "When they don't report in, we know they either deserted or froze to death. It wouldn't happen if we had enough shoes and coats to go around."

Alexandra was aghast. "Why can't you get them?"

"General Wayne's been trying since December. They'll probably come when the weather warms, that's how the army is. That's how the high-and-mighty Congress makes it be. They put themselves first. We're nothing but a poor second."

Dalton glanced up and stopped talking when he saw the look on her face. His anger fled as he realized how deeply she was hurting for them both. After so much time apart, this was not how he wanted to spend his moments with her, spouting rough words, evoking images of misery. Suddenly he ached to hold her again and know that what she felt for him was real and undiminished.

He returned her hairbrush to the vanity, closed the distance between them and gathered her in. "I'm sorry."

"Don't be."

"I just want you to understand."

"I know," she murmured, her face buried against his throat. He felt the tremor that shook her and heard the catch in her voice when she said, "Dalton, I love you so much."

His fingers spread in her hair, tilting her head back for his kiss. He tried to satisfy himself on her soft lips, but it wasn't enough, not when her mouth was as anxious as his. Not when she was touching him with the same urgency that drove his hands to explore her and pull her against him where he was straining forward, needing more of her.

When she drew back and held his gaze, whispering, "Stay with me tonight," the look in her eyes set him afire. He couldn't conceive of leaving her then. He kissed her again and felt hard animal desire clench in his loins, felt the warmth of her seep into him until his aroused body found the limits of restraint.

Stepping back from her, he shrugged off his coat, unbuttoned his shirt and whipped it over his head. With his next shallow breath, he felt her trembling fingers unfasten the top button of his breeches. His own impatient hands took over the task.

While Alexandra waited and watched in the yellow pulse of firelight, he finished undressing, and the haste in his movements matched the burn in his eyes whenever they touched her. Then he reached for her, and as he took his fill of her mouth, liquid heat pooled between her legs. She ached for him to touch her there, fill her there. She needed him embedded inside her. "Love me," she whispered against his mouth.

Dalton longed to please her slowly, in all the ways he had imagined through all his solitary nights. He needed control now. Instead he was anxious, unsteady, his body too long denied to measure up to his intentions.

The buttons of her flannel shift gave him fits. There were so many of them, nestled in frilly lace, a row of shiny tormentors descending between her breasts. Slowly the shadow of her cleft was revealed, then the rising swells of pale flesh, warm against his knuckles. At last he drew the shift off her shoulders and let it fall, and for an instant his eyes drank her in. Then lifting her in his arms, he carried her to the bed and followed her down onto the mattress.

Her arms stayed around him. He kissed her neck as his hand stroked down across her stomach to the thick, soft thatch of hair at the apex of her thighs. He claimed her with the gentlest of touches. As his finger slid into her, she shuddered with a mew of approval. Before long her breath came in soft gasps, her hips moved of their own will. When he bent his head to her breast, she rose to meet him, offering as much of herself as his mouth could hold, and the raw sounds that came from her throat nearly put Dalton over the edge.

He took his place between her thighs and thrust forward to feel hard muscles contract around him. Her fingers bit into his flesh, pulling him deeper into a pleasure so agonizing he could only do its bidding. As his burning pressed into hers, she tightened all over, lifting herself to his possession. Her throaty keening flooded him with sensations. When he felt her arch up, sobbing with joy, Dalton soared with her to an intense oblivion. He felt it coming and planted himself deep, and as it exploded over them in a wave after wave, he locked his arms around her and held her fiercely until it was done.

Breathless, adrift in euphoria, he took his time coming back. As he did, he let his mouth and body tell her what words could not, and her answering caresses were full of equal tenderness and wonder. In the quiet comfort of her bed, Dalton buried his face in her hair and held her tightly to him, determined to lose himself in her for as long as he could. She was everything he needed in the world. Just her, nothing else.

Chapter Fifty-Four

Midnight came. As snow whispered down and coated the world a fine, powdery white, the temperature plunged outside Willowbrook's stout walls. But inside, exchanging soft words and loving touches, Alexandra and Dalton were bathed in the healing balm of firelight.

They lay beneath the covers with their limbs entwined, their bodies utterly sated. Cradled against him, Alexandra pressed her lips to his neck and tasted salty dampness. He was watching the fire with heavy-lidded eyes, absorbed in the dancing yellow flames that flirted into blue.

"What do you see in there?" she asked.

"A dream."

"What dream?"

"Being home again. Waking up one morning, in the spring when it's warm, and having you next to me." His arms gently squeezed her. "Just like this."

She smiled, envisioning the scene. "I like your dream."

"I'm going to make it real." After that he was quiet for a time, lost in the hypnotic power of the flames. Then he said, "I want you to go to York as soon as possible."

Panic stabbed her. She clung to him, swept by a cold, gut-wrenching premonition that signaled danger not for her, but for Dalton. "I'm staying here," she said. "I want to be near you."

Sighing, Dalton propped himself on an elbow and lightly stroked her neck, his fingers spreading sparks over her skin. "It's easy to listen to your heart," he said, "but your gut is almost always right. And my gut is telling me you should go to York."

Alexandra was afraid that if she did, she would never see him again. "It's a hundred miles from here," she said. "I might as well be on the other side of the world from you."

"You'll be safe from pigs like Major Palmos."

"I can handle Major Palmos."

"What about Mr. Villard?" he asked and read her apprehension. When she averted her eyes, he caught her chin and made her look at him. "You're afraid of him."

"He's only trying to intimidate me."

"So far," Dalton pointed out. He smoothed dark hair from her forehead, but while his touch was tender, his eyes were sharp with worry. "I know his kind, Alex. He thinks he can do whatever he bloody well pleases and get away with it."

"He won't come here anymore."

"What will stop him?"

Alexandra flashed on her small pistol. "I will," she said, then stilled his protest with her fingertips. "I won't be driven away from you. If I'm here, you'll come see me."

"It's dangerous for me to come here."

"So is going mad from needing you." She held his face and kissed him, and once again Dalton was amazed at the feelings she produced in him. He would never be able to get enough of her, the smoothness of her body, which was graceful and slender, the flavor of her mouth, which was drowning him with sweetness. When she drew back, it took him a moment to recover his train of thought. His worry returned, and with it came a cold realization: something had to be done about Charles Villard.

"General Wayne promised me leave in a few weeks," he said. "Then we'll go to York together."

Her face brightened with enthusiasm.

"And be married," he added softly.

"Yes."

"And afterward," authority hardened his voice a little, "I want you to stay in York. Do it for my sake, because I need to know that you're safe."

His concern for her was so acute, Alexandra could not bring herself to deny him. When she gave her agreement, Dalton felt slightly better, then better still as he leaned down and nuzzled her face, her throat, the curve of her shoulder. Her fingers caught in his hair as his mouth came

407

back to delve hers for long moments. It was all very tender and thoroughly arousing.

"I love the way you feel," he whispered, running his hands over her suppleness. "Your breasts are perfect." He cupped them reverently, his thumbs stroking her nipples. When he drew one into his mouth and gently tugged on it, her body arched to him, shaking with desire. Only after he let go was Alexandra able to breathe again.

"I have a confession to make," he told her.

Curiosity flared in her a moment, then dissolved as his mouth moved to suckle her other breast, the sensual friction of his teeth and tongue igniting a slow burn in her abdomen. A purring sound came from her throat. Too soon, he took his mouth away and said, "I've seen you naked before."

Startled, she looked into his mischievous eyes. "What?"

"It's true."

"When?"

"A long time ago at Sweet Briar. Remember the night I stole your necklace?"

Alexandra nodded.

"I was looking around your room, see, and I heard some maids coming, so I hid under the bed. Then you came in and got undressed."

A moment went by as she watched him. "You scheming rascal."

His mouth twitched. "It wasn't on purpose."

"You could have looked the other way."

"I considered it, but you made me all eyes. You were a sight I never forgot," he said, and before she could utter another word, he lowered his mouth to hers and stole her thoughts.

Alexandra closed her eyes and opened her senses to him, every part of her stimulated in every imaginable way. His strong body seemed to radiate heat; his touch was overpowering. When she could wait no more, when she thought she would die of wanting him, she implored him to love her again, and moments later welcomed him with a husky cry.

Dalton told her, sometime later, that he could not imagine a future without her. He lay with his head on her stomach, a drugged smile on his face as he hugged her like a pillow. Propped on a feather pillow, Alexandra massaged the crook of his neck and shoulder, kneading his flesh with smooth, sure strokes. He seemed exhausted. After a time, as she continued her gentle ministrations, his eyelids began to droop.

"Don't let me fall asleep," he murmured.

"Sssh." Her thumb followed a tendon down his neck. "Just rest."

"I can't be here when it gets light."

"I'll wake you in time."

His eyes closed. In the dying light of velvety embers, she noted again a new harshness in his face, lines etched there by strain. She longed to bring him relief, however small and brief it might be, and that longing went into her touch.

His breathing slowed. The muscles of his face relaxed, smoothing away the hardness. As he drifted off, she thought he looked vulnerable in repose, his mouth slack and innocent as a child's, eyelids fluttering as he dreamed. Beguiled by his tranquil face, her mind removed layers of time, unveiling the orphaned boy who had fended for himself in order to survive. She imagined him as a wary youth, stripped of trust, his outlook tempered by the lessons of betrayal, injustice, and pain. Hard living had shaped a man strong enough to endure whatever life dealt him. But inside him, she knew, was a well of need.

She had never loved anyone as she did him. Being with him felt so natural, so right. He would never wonder about the depth of her commitment, she vowed, because she would always be there for him. She would defy the world for him, and his enemies be damned.

In the space of several hours, Alexandra and Dalton adopted a new form of communication, on a level beyond words. A single look or touch between them spoke volumes. Not even Twigs, with his uncanny perception, had ever probed as deeply into Dalton's soul as the blue eyes that watched him now.

"That's the longest face I've ever seen," he said.

Managing a smile, Alexandra leaned into his comforting embrace. They were in Willowbrook's kitchen, and he

409

was ready to leave. For long moments he did nothing more than hold her, as though to absorb her, then he sighed and Alexandra knew it was time. "I have to go, love."

"I know," she said, surprised at how calm she sounded. Withdrawing from his arms, she dug into the pocket of her robe, took his hand, and pressed a small leather purse into it.

When Dalton heard coins clink and felt the weight of them on his palm, he recoiled slightly. "I can't take this," he said.

She closed his fingers around the purse. "I want to help."

"I know, but—"

"Please. I can afford to part with it."

Dalton stared at the purse with a hollow feeling. He hated taking her money, but in the end he couldn't refuse it because he knew it would save lives. He tucked the purse inside his coat, then wrapped his arms around her and pressed her body to him, imprinting the feel of her on his memory. Later on, in the miserable hours when cold numbed him and hunger rumbled in his belly, he wanted to be able to summon her soft shape. She was brightness in a gray, hostile world, and somehow he had to find the strength to walk away from her.

"I love you," he whispered.

Alexandra swallowed her anguish, wanting to be strong for him. She felt him kiss her brow, then cold seeped into her where his warmth had been. Eyes burning, she watched him cross to the door and open it, and for a moment he was silhouetted against blurred whiteness.

Dalton stepped outside into the quiet fury of a blizzard. Although dawn was still an hour away, the panorama of woods and fields was luminous beneath a powdery blanket. Watching the thick flakes swirl down, he remembered how he used to love the snow.

Movement caught his eye. Squinting into the storm, he saw Clue coming toward him from the barn, leading Mercury. Lashed behind the stallion's saddle was a heavy greatcoat, a blanket roll, and a bulging sack. As Clue handed him the reins, Dalton knew without asking what the sack contained, for he could smell the food strongly.

Moving to Mercury's flank, he brushed snow from the

410

greatcoat and rubbed thick, excellent wool between his fingers. "Is this yours?"

"It was her husband's."

Dalton was quiet a moment, his breath forming frosty plumes. Then he came out of himself. "It's time I was going. Look after yourself, my friend."

"And you be careful," Clue replied worriedly. "The redcoats would love to get their hands on you."

"That," Dalton said, "will be a cold day in hell." With grim resolve, he swung onto Mercury's back and headed him for the woods beyond the barn.

Unmoving, Clue watched as the storm swallowed them, and for no reason that he could comprehend, he knew Dalton was wrong.

Chapter Fifty-Five

The first person Charles Villard ever killed was his father, Richard. On the night it happened, Charles was eighteen. Richard Villard was a callous fifty-two, and no match for his son, unless one counted his razor-edged tongue and endless reserve of scorn. Both were contributing factors to his death.

"A man's worth is measured by his successes." Richard's favorite maxim. "Your mother died bringing you into this world," he would say, "and in return you've accomplished nothing. When will you make me proud of you, Charles?"

Never. Not because he didn't try, but because it was impossible to attain the level of perfection his father demanded from him. At twelve, Charles was doing complex sums in his head, could recite pages of dramatic verse word for word, and understood Franklin's single-fluid theory of electricity. His tutors called him brilliant, clever, remarkable.

But that wasn't enough for Richard.

And so Charles strove to excel physically as well as mentally. He sharpened his reflexes with fencing lessons and hardened his muscles with hours of horseback riding, hunting, and sculling. He was a natural athlete. His sinewy prowess made him the envy of his male peers and a sought-after suitor.

Still Richard was unsatisfied. One day he complained, "You gamble too much."

"No more than my friends."

"Friends? You spend your time in the company of

knaves. I heard you were drunk the other night and had to be carried from the Queen. You expect my approval, yet you behave like a fool." Richard hooked a thumb at his chest. "*I* was taught that respect must be earned. I could have been given a life of ease; instead I was given backbone."

"Father, I—"

"Shut up when I'm speaking!" Richard raised a hand as though to strike his son, then lowered it without touching him. He rarely touched him, even in anger, and never with affection. "You're a wastrel, a failure. No one admires a failure."

While his father ranted on, Charles kept quiet. He watched Richard's lips move and bore his scorching contempt. And he thought about killing him.

"You'll never amount to anything," Richard scorned.

I despise you.

"You don't deserve to be called a Villard."

I want you dead.

"I pray your mother cannot see what a good-for-nothing you've become."

What Charles prayed for was the courage to obey the voice in his head.

Late one night, the courage came to him. Richard Villard, well-known for his restless sleeping habits, got out of his bed at Sweet Briar and went to fix himself a nightcap. As he left his bedchamber, all was still. The household slept.

Except for Charles, who was waiting at the head of the staircase, his shadow disturbing a slender spindle of moonlight that slanted from a window.

Richard paused, squinting into the gloom. "Who's there?"

"It's me, Father." Though he heard himself speak, Charles did not recognize his own voice. He stood frozen, balanced on a giddy brink.

Until Richard spoke as he always did to his son, sharp and insulting. "What the devil are you doing? Lurking in the dark like a common thief. Have you been drinking again?"

Charles felt the words like a physical blow. His feet

413

carried him forward. "Shut your vile mouth," he hissed. "I never want to hear you again!"

Their struggle was brief and one-sided. Charles's powerful hands shot out, seized his father's head, and twisted savagely until bones popped and snapped. When the deed was done, he flung the body over the banister to the floor below.

He slept like a baby that night. In the morning, a frantic servant summoned him downstairs to the main hall, where Sweet Briar's master lay in a crumpled heap, his neck turned at an impossible angle.

Richard's death was ruled accidental, the tragic result of a fall. His funeral was a well-attended affair, through which Charles showed the public what it expected to see— a grieving son, deeply wounded by his loss. While the dirge moaned and the casket was lowered into the ground, he stood with his head bowed, rejoicing.

A few days later, at the reading of the will, Charles was named the sole heir to a vast estate. He inherited everything belonging to Richard Villard, including his unlimited capacity for cruelty.

The farm had once belonged to him. Six years had passed since he lost it on a foolish gambit, yet the buildings still looked the same, solid and compact, in need of some repairs. Beyond the farmhouse, featherstrokes of moonlight shimmered on Wissahickon Creek, curling below the black silhouettes of steeply rising hills.

Such a peaceful scene, so harmless-looking a dwelling. But this was an outlaw's lair, a place where furtive figures came and went in the night. It was here that Jack Flash had hatched his daring schemes, and it was here that Dalton Philips now plotted treason against the Crown.

Villard drew a pistol from beneath his greatcoat. He was wearing civilian clothes, and his head was covered by a dark hood with holes cut for his eyes. The horsemen with him were similarly attired and, like Villard, were anxious to draw blood. With a sharp motion, he dispatched five of them toward the creek, then led the remainder around behind the stable, moving as quietly as possible. At his prearranged signal, the raiders would converge on the farmhouse.

Twigs heard them coming. Crouched in a hedgerow near the paddock, he listened to the scuffling of hooves on hard-packed earth and tried to determine the number of his stealthy visitors. Tory marauders were nothing new in the area. Wearing masks and armed with swords and muskets, roving bands of desperadoes ravaged the countryside after dark. Whippings, beatings, and theft were their trademarks. Most were in the pay of the British.

Twigs flinched as a pistol cracked, then hunched deeper into his hiding place as horses thundered past the hedgerow toward the house. Four riders, perhaps five? More coming from the creek. The farmhouse was their focus, and their search of it was furious and swift. Wood splintered as doors were kicked in, boots thudding on planking and stairs. Before long Twigs heard angry shouting, then cringed at the shock of exploding glass. The sound came again and again as every window in the house was smashed.

Suddenly Twigs heard and smelled what he most dreaded. *Fire*. The sons of bitches had set the house ablaze. Within minutes, flames were roaring from its shattered windows, and gusts of heat whipped sparks aloft to shower the treetops. But the raiders were just getting started. They fired the sheds, the storehouse, and finally the stable.

As clouds of choking smoke rolled over him, all Twigs could think was that Dalton's dreams were burning. The boy would be devastated. Then a new sound tore the fabric of Twigs's heart—the terrified screams of horses trapped in an inferno. He could distinuigsh their individual cries as easily as he could human voices. Secret, the broodmares, and Mercury's foals were about to be roasted alive.

Unable to bear their cries, Twigs left the bushes on all fours, slipped through the paddock fence, and made his way behind the stable. Guided by finely tuned senses, he moved quickly over familiar turf, skirting obstacles with the ease of a sighted man while listening for the raiders. His sharp ears detected no footfalls, but he could hear hooves thrashing wildly inside the barn, splintering stall doors and pounding the earthen aisle.

Reaching the sliding rear door of the barn, Twigs unhooked the heavy chain lock, grabbed the door handle with both hands and yanked hard. As the door slid aside, the cold darkness sucked heat from the cavernous building, and Twigs was engulfed in a blast of super-heated air. With it came a stampede of horseflesh. Caught in their path, Twigs was bowled over by a charging broodmare, and his ribs felt the bite of her sharp hooves. Snorting and bellowing in fear, the horses plunged into the night, leaving him stunned where he lay, exposed in a flood of angry amber light.

Moments later Villard found him. Eyes glittering behind his hood, Villard regarded his catch with immense satisfaction. He had missed the wolf, but snared the fox. "Get up, old man."

Still shaken, Twigs pushed to his feet.

"Where is Dalton Philips?"

"How should I know?"

Grabbing a fistful of white hair, Villard shook him like a dog. *"Where is he?"*

"Are you deaf, Mr. Villard?"

Villard stilled in surprise, his hold loosening. The sightless old beggar had identified him. As Twigs pulled free and retreated several steps, rubbing his sore scalp, Villard said with fury, "Perhaps your memory will improve in prison."

"Perhaps," Twigs replied. "But you'll never put Dalton there again."

A tremor shook Villard. As he searched the wizened face before him, blind eyes seemed to return his scrutiny, piercing him to the core. "Philips is a walking corpse," he vowed. "I don't care what hole he crawls into, I'll find him and watch him die."

Twigs's laughter split the night. "You're not man enough!" he scorned.

Something in the air changed. Twigs felt it, and although he could not see Villard's face, his quickening pulse told him what was there. Madness. With his mind's eye he probed a killer's soul, sensed cold-blooded intent, and turned to flee.

416

Villard's pistol rose. He took aim and shot Twigs in the back as he ran. Spine arching, mouth opening in a soundless scream, Twigs clawed at the bloody smear and pitched onto his face. He lay unmoving as Villard, in no hurry, walked over to him and stood listening to his dragging, watery breaths.

"Dalton," Twigs gasped.

"Don't fret, old man. He's coming."

Chapter Fifty-Six

The narrow, grass-grown road was in excellent shape for a horse race. A March thaw had made the ground slightly springy, giving the horses a good grip as they galloped hellbent through a thickly wooded valley. Rounding a sharp bend, Dalton and Mercury hugged the turn and closed the gap on their quarry—a young British officer running for his life.

The redcoat had made the mistake of venturing beyond the redoubts without an escort and now found himself cut off from help by a band of rebel cavalry. His sleek bay mare had left most of the rebels behind, but glancing back, he saw a chestnut nightmare clinging to him like a burr.

Mercury stretched out his neck and sped on, a tuned, powerful racing machine with the devil for a jockey. Even on her best day, the mare was no contest for the stallion, but bullets were another matter. Dalton nearly ate a pistol shot as the fleeing man turned in his saddle and fired.

Lead fanned hotly past Dalton's cheek. Mercury's fluid strides continued without pause, surging over the road. The stallion seemed tireless, but the mare was flagging. Curds of foam dripped from her mouth; sweat lathered her heaving chest. Realizing the futility of his flight, the redcoat suddenly drew a short sword, hauled his horse to a skidding halt, and turned on Dalton, who was ready for him.

Dalton wanted him alive, so when he brandished his own saber and maneuvered Mercury to meet the onrushing charge, his hissing blade was aimed to engage steel, not flesh. Swords clanged in the still woods. The horses grunted and circled as their riders sawed on reins, jockeying for position. As he had been trained to do, Mercury suddenly wheeled and rammed his chest into the mare. The exhausted horse stumbled, the redcoat grabbed for her mane, and Dalton caught a flailing sword with a ringing blow and sent it flying.

Seized with panic, the redcoat righted himself, saw a bright blade poised at his throat, and froze. Swallowing, he met a pair of glittering green eyes. "It seems I'm your prisoner."

"It don't seem," Dalton told him. "You are."

Just then more rebels came into view and galloped up. Surrounded by hard-looking men, the redcoat was dragged from his saddle and searched. In one of his pockets was a fancy invitation card bearing Sir William Howe's embossed crest. After studying the invitation to a ball at Sweet Briar, Dalton regarded his prisoner with heightened interest. "Who are you?"

"Lt. Thomas Calvert, of the Fourth."

"The Fourth, my ass. You work for General Howe."

"I'm only a messenger."

"For headquarters," Dalton supplied, his look intent. "You must hear lots of important talk."

"I'm not privy to matters of military importance."

But Dalton wasn't interested in learning about military matters. He said, "I reckon you know all about the raid on Downstream Farm," and something flickered across Calvert's face that gave him a jolt.

"I've no idea what you're talking about."

Still gripping his saber, Dalton stepped closer to him. "Lieutenant, I'm going to let you in on a little secret. I hate liars." Receiving no reply, he sheathed his saber and said, "Henry, get me the shovel."

Shovel? Apprehensive, Calvert watched Henry walk to his horse and open his saddlebag, from which, sure enough, he withdrew a short-handled spade and brought it to Dalton.

Shovel in one hand, pistol in the other, Dalton indicated the woods with his chin. "Let's go, Lieutenant." He followed close behind as Calvert pushed his way through dry underbrush to a small, winter-bare clearing. Halting him, Dalton threw the shovel at his feet. "Start digging."

Calvert just stared at him. "What am I digging?"

"A hole. Don't have to be deep, just big enough for you."

"Now see here," Calvert protested. "I'm a prisoner of war, and I demand—"

"You lot of British bastards are all alike," Dalton said with sudden fury. "You think you deserve special treatment, but you treat us like dogs. Well, I have my own rules, Lieutenant." He took aim at Calvert's chest. "Tell me what I want to know, or I'll bury you here."

The lieutenant's face was bloodless. "That would be murder."

"That would be too bad."

A moment passed. Then Calvert, eyes glued to the gun's dark bore, said, "I did hear something that might interest you."

When they emerged from the woods a little later, and Henry saw Dalton's face, uneasiness swept him. Dalton shoved Calvert at him with, "Tie him up and get him on his horse."

"Yes, sir."

Trailed by Mercury, Dalton walked to the edge of the road and stared unseeing into the trees. After a time, he felt Mercury's head come alongside his face and felt warm, moist breath fan his skin as a velvety textured muzzle nibbled his cheek. His eyes squeezed shut against burning moisture. Looping an arm around the stallion's neck, he pressed his face into the warm curve behind a massive jaw and gritted his teeth against grief.

His farm was in ruins, not a building left standing. By some miracle, his horses had been spared. He had found them wandering the lower pasture, their coats singed in spots from firebrands, badly spooked but otherwise unhurt. The broodmares and foals had been moved to a neighboring farm for safekeeping. Secret, who had greeted him like a long-lost friend, was now at Valley Forge, a fresh, reliable mount in case he should need one.

The thought of having to replace Mercury dragged Dalton deeper into his depression, because he knew his wonderful horse was irreplaceable. Just as he knew there was no substitute for his beloved old mentor, the man who had taught him to dream, to believe in himself, and whose passing had left a gigantic hole in his heart. Nothing in life had prepared him for the shock of finding Twigs with a bullet in his back. And now he knew whose hand had struck the blow.

Agony seared him. His fingers clenched in Mercury's mane. "The bastard killed Twigs," he whispered. "God-damnit, it was me he wanted."

"Captain?"

Looking around, Dalton saw Henry standing a few feet away.

"We're ready, sir."

"I ain't going back with you."

Henry was incredulous. "What?"

"I got something to settle."

Fearing the something was dangerous, Henry tried to dissuade him. "General Wayne told you to quit taking so many risks."

"I know what he said," Dalton retorted. "He said it to me, so that makes me the best judge of what he meant." His tone carried a warning, but Henry, concerned for him, ignored it.

"What are you going to do?" he insisted.

Dalton was only half-listening. The rest of him was eyeing Lieutenant Calvert, noting his height, his build, his crisp, neat uniform. Suddenly inspired, he said, "I'm going to have another word with that prig."

Chapter Fifty-Seven

Philadelphia had changed. Quaint old neighborhoods, victims of the British army engineers who designed and built the city's fortifications, were almost unrecognizable. Fences and walls had been torn down to make room for soldiers' huts. Lush yards had been excavated for the mounds of earth needed to build redoubts.

Aside from the work of destruction, the redcoats had added something else to the capital's beautiful avenues. Garbage littered the central gutters, permeating the air with the stench of decay. Human dregs fouled the taverns and were a common nuisance on the streets. British patrols, charged with keeping the peace, were kept busy day and night by disorderly offenders, but punishments were rare. General Howe's strictures had grown ridiculously lax, for he, too, was immersed in the city's sins.

The luxury-loving Howe had kindled what was jokingly called "scarlet fever" in Philadelphia. Daughters of well-to-do Tories and Quakers had fallen under a red-coated spell. What with the British, the Hessians, and the Queen's Rangers filling the city to capacity, the high-coiffured, hoop-skirted belles, decked out in gaily colored costumes, had no lack of partners at the endless rounds of parties.

Tonight's gala was at Sweet Briar on the Neck. Hidden in the gloom beneath an arbor, Dalton studied Charles Villard's candlelit mansion, where bright red uniforms flocked to a glittering ballroom, there to flirt, preen, and dance in the trappings of wealth. In the formal garden, British dandies were hard at work seducing coy young women. A score of couples wandered the pathways and groped each other in shadowed intimacy. Feminine laughter floated on the night, grating Dalton's nerves and firing his resentment.

Waiting to make his move, he plucked bits of hay from his gold-braided uniform, a gift from Lieutenant Calvert. The pieces of hay were souvenirs from his nerve-racking ride into town, concealed in the false bed of a farmer's wagon. The farmer, a Son of Liberty and a friend of Twigs, had been eager to assist Dalton's unauthorized mission.

To Dalton's mind, the invitation card in his pocket was authorization enough to be at Sweet Briar, where tonight he would put an end to Charles Villard. He would use the dagger in his boot and dispatch him in silence. All he needed was a few moments alone with him, and Villard was as good as dead.

Leaving the arbor, Dalton strolled along softly lighted pathways, scrutinizing the couples he passed. No one paid him a bit of attention. With any luck, he would locate his prey outside, execute him without fuss, and be long gone when the body was discovered.

But Charles Villard was not in the garden. Common sense told Dalton to bide his time. Instead, restless, he approached the mansion and climbed the stairs to the veranda outside the ballroom. The ballroom's double doors were open to the unseasonably mild night, and as he glanced inside his blood quickened at the sight of so many redcoats. He began having severe second thoughts, until he remembered Twigs's body sprawled on the ground, felled by a cowardly shot. Right now Twigs would be calling him a fool. But Dalton knew that if the situation were reversed, if he were the one lying in a grave, Twigs would stop at nothing to avenge him.

Hands clasped behind his back, he sauntered the length of the veranda, peering through the rippled glass of tall windows, eyes searching. Going past one window, he suddenly stopped in his tracks. His fingertips went to the glass, his body tensed as he beheld an arrogant face that summed up all the evil in his life. There was his prey. Now to figure out a way to get to him.

"I say, isn't this a splendid evening?"

423

Startled, Dalton glanced at the owner of the voice and a shock wave paralyzed him. For an instant, as he stared into Major Palmos's liquor-glazed eyes, recognition flickered in them.

"Yes, quite," Dalton mumbled, then brushed past the puzzled officer with, "Pardon me, sir."

"Just a moment."

Dalton kept going. Reaching the head of the staircase, he froze looking down. Evelyn Wright, a scarlet-clad escort on each arm, was ascending from the garden. So Dalton did an about-face and grabbed Major Palmos by the arm. "Sir, I need a word with you," he said, steering him toward a darkened corner of the veranda.

"Do I know you?" Palmos demanded.

Dalton kept his face averted, kept Palmos moving. "Unlikely, sir."

Without warning Palmos seized Dalton's shoulder, yanking him around so the yellow light struck his features. He gaped in astonishment. *"You!"*

Caught out, Dalton smiled a little, his eyes like shards of glass. "Hello, Major Pompous," he said and rammed a fist into his stomach. As Palmos doubled over, Dalton landed another shot that broke two teeth and knocked the major senseless.

Sensing movement behind him, he spun in a crouch, whipping the dagger from his boot, and was confronted by Evelyn Wright and her gawking companions. Evelyn's shrieks pierced the night with such force, even the ballroom musicians fell silent.

"Rebel traitor! Stop him!"

Dalton vaulted over the balustrade and hit the ground running. Alerted by Evelyn's cries, the garden swains came to life, responding to the alarm with the martial instincts of soldiers. A dozen redcoats took up the chase. Their fleeing quarry was easy to spot, but he was also as fleet and sure-footed as a deer, hurdling walls and hedges without breaking stride.

Dalton ran with a wildly thudding heart. As angry shouting rose behind him, his folly struck home with sledgehammer force. He was trapped on a veritable island bottled up with twenty thousand redcoats who would hunt him with the tenacity of bloodhounds. The dark alleys and warrens of the city would have afforded him numerous hiding places, perhaps even a helpful friend or two. But to reach them he had to cross the ruined landscape of the Neck, which was patroled by British cavalry, bored men looking for action.

His best chance was to steal a horse, ride for the Schuylkill, and swim the animal across the icy current. That much decided, he changed direction for Sweet Briar's stable and covered the distance there at a ground-eating pace. Rounding the paddock, he pulled up in dismay. A troop of mounted cavalry officers was in the stable yard. Lantern light glinted on drawn sabers and pistols.

"You there! Stop or I'll shoot!"

Jesus God.

It occurred to Dalton, as the cavalrymen advanced and pursuit closed in on him from behind, to use his dagger on himself. He was in enemy territory, wearing an enemy uniform, which made him not an assassin, but a spy in British eyes. Spies were denied an honorable death by firing squad. They were hung from a gibbet, and he refused to die that way, dangling piteously from a noose. But neither could he bring himself to take his own life.

He charged the dragoons, determined to either draw their killing fire or topple one from his saddle and seize his horse. Selecting a target, he ran straight for him, but as he gathered himself and leaped, the rider's horse reared up on command and lashed out with sharp hooves.

Iron shoes struck hard, jarring flesh and bone, and Dalton thudded to the ground, in a haze of lancing pain. He rolled away from stomping hooves, heaved to his feet, and was kicked again, this time by a steel-tipped boot that caught him flush in the face, lacerating his cheek. His face streaming blood, he tumbled backward into clawing hands that bore him down and pinned him to the ground. Then a redcoat knelt with a pistol, which he used to beat Dalton unconscious.

"You have been charged with spying." General Howe's voice resonated in the silent room. "How do you plead?"

Dalton swallowed a sigh. It was the morning after his arrest, and a board of twelve general officers had convened

425

t British headquarters to hear his case. From their mplacable faces, he knew his response to the charge was of no account. The trial was a mockery. Military protocol required one, so he had been brought here to face his accusers, whose uniforms boasted enough gold braid to ransom a king. Sir William Howe presided, grave and heavy-eyed, but whether his expression stemmed from the seriousness of the matter or the earliness of the hour, Dalton wasn't sure. He only knew the board of gentlemen soldiers had already passed sentence on him.

Figuring he had nothing to lose, he said, "I ain't a spy."

Howe, contemplating his prisoner in the pale light of morning, was unmoved. An elusive troublemaker had been bagged, and the British commander smelled blood. "Explain to the court why you are dressed as a British officer."

"So I could kill the bastard that murdered Timothy Leeds. You remember, don't you, General? The blind man who was shot in the back by one of your maggots."

Uncomfortable looks were exchanged, but Howe's face remained unreadable. "It is the contention of this court that you disguised yourself as a British soldier in order to gain British military intelligence."

Dalton fell silent. Chains clinked as he bent his head and rubbed a blood-encrusted knot above his right ear.

"Send in Major Palmos," Howe told his adjutant.

Dalton perked up again. When the major came in, and Dalton saw his swollen, discolored jaw, he felt a measure of satisfaction. But the feeling was short-lived, ending as soon as Palmos took the witness chair and began his testimony, which spun more fiction than fact.

"Last night," Palmos said, "at Sweet Briar, the defendant approached me in the guise of a British lieutenant." He eyed Dalton coldly. "I thought it odd when he began asking questions about our defenses at Chester and Wilmington. Naturally I declined to answer his inquiries, and when he persisted, I became suspicious of him."

Dalton stared back at Palmos. "You lying sot."

"The prisoner will be silent," Howe commanded.

And so it went. Several more witnesses were called and sworn, including Evelyn Wright, whose glittering black eyes and pinched mouth spat venom throughout her deposition. When all the evidence had been heard, Dalton was removed from the room while the board deliberated his fate. It took them five token minutes to reach a guilty verdict. The sentence of death by hanging was given. After the order was signed in Dalton's presence, Sir William Howe, with a dismissive wave, remanded him to prison to await execution.

Outside Howe's headquarters on High Street, a wagon and six armed guards were waiting to escort Dalton to jail. As he was put in the wagon, a small but buzzing crowd gathered on the sidewalk for a glimpse of him. A shackled prisoner was a common sight in Philadelphia, but this one wore a British uniform and his tall, erect figure demanded notice. His eyes were piercing to behold, an intimidating deep forest green, and many curious stares fell under his keen regard.

Riding along High Street, Christopher Clue looked into those eyes and drew his horse to an abrupt halt, his heart squeezed in a vice, his errands for Alexandra forgotten. When Dalton gave no sign of recognizing him, but instead looked the other way, Clue understood that he was being warned off. He hesitated a moment more before wheeling his horse around and heading back to Willowbrook.

And Dalton, trying not to imagine Alexandra's reaction, felt suddenly crushed. His shoulders sagged as the defiance drained out of him. Head bowed, he heard a whip crack and felt a rough jerk as the wagon set out for the Walnut Street jail, where Bloody Bill Cunningham awaited him.

No one knew how many deaths Cunningham had been responsible for in his reign as British provost marshal, but the grave mounds at Potter's Field put estimates in the hundreds. To Cunningham, every rebel prisoner was a potential source of income and amusement. When Dalton arrived at the jail and Bloody Bill heard his sentence, he laughed. "One less rodent to feed," he said.

Going down into the foul-smelling bowels of the prison, Dalton felt the bite of a blackjack between his shoulder blades and heard Cunningham growl, "Keep moving. Try anything and I'll break your skull."

At the end of a murky corridor, a cell door stood open. Lantern light spilled from within. Shoved inside the cell, Dalton's shackle chains became entangled with his feet and tripped him up. He went down heavily on cold stone and was slow to recover, too worn out to move quickly. As he came to his knees, a shadow fell over him. He looked up expecting to see Cunningham's jowled face and pig-lidded eyes.

Charles Villard stared back at him. "Welcome home," he said with menace.

Like a cat Dalton sprang at him, tackled him around his knees, and dropped him like a sack on the hard floor. Surging forward, he went for Villard's throat, but as his hands closed around it, something slammed into the back of his head and sent him reeling. Cunningham's blackjack delivered another vicious shot, and Dalton went limp.

When he roused again, Cunningham hauled him up, secured him to a thick iron staple set in stone, then left the cell with Villard. Out in the gloomy corridor, gold exchanged hands. Villard's pale eyes drilled Bloody Bill. "Are you certain there will be no repercussions?"

"He refused to be put in his cell," Cunningham said with a shrug. "Happens all the time."

His answer pleased Villard, who returned to the cell wearing a smile. Closing the door after him, Cunningham leaned a shoulder against it and stood watch in the corridor while listening to the muffled sounds of a beating. When at last the savage blows drew a grunt of pain, he stifled a yawn.

Chapter Fifty-Eight

The city was graying with dusk when Alexandra's coach stopped before her Fourth Street house. Lamplight glowed in the downstairs windows. The once-beautiful yard had been trampled by hooves and boots into a slop of mud, and rubbish was strewn in the mire.

Setting the coach brake, Clue climbed down from the bench, walked briskly to the house, and rapped on the front door. When it swung open, he beheld a colossus of a man, well over six feet and thickly muscled. Looking into his severe and forbidding face, Clue said, "I'm looking for Maj. Andrew Palmos."

"Not here," was the gruff reply. In contrast with his gigantic size, the redcoat's voice was hoarse and weak, undoubtedly the result of the jagged pink scar running down his Adam's apple. His uniform was linty, his shirt a sweaty gray. Reaching beneath his jacket, he scratched his hard, flat belly while considering Clue with flinty eyes. "Who wants him?" he asked, nodding at the lantern-lit coach.

"Mrs. Alexandra Pennington. She owns this house." And a sorry place it had become, Clue noted, eyeing the trash-littered hallway beyond the redcoat's towering hulk.

"What's her business with him?"

"It's a private matter."

That won a smirk. "All his whores think they're something special to him. Better tell her not to hold her breath. She's his third cunt today. He probably couldn't get up a cockstiff for Venus." Appraising the waiting

429

coach, the redcoat glimpsed a sleek, winsome face at the window and added, "But I could."

Clue silently seethed. "Where can I find Major Palmos?"

"Try the City Tavern. He's there every night like a fly on shit."

Clue left without thanking him. "Bugger you, bunghole," he muttered, crossing the yard. "Venus would puke up if she saw your ugly face."

He opened the coach door to speak with Alexandra. In the soft rays of the coach lanterns, she looked to him like a dark-haired princess, her elaborate coiffure aglitter with jewels, the shimmery, wine red silk of her gown defining delicate contours. The gown's modesty piece had been removed, bravely baring the upper swells of her breasts, which were softly powdered and seemed to be straining for release. Hard-pressed not to gander there, Clue felt a strong, protective urge to reach over and pull her cloak closed, concealing the feminine confections that were sure to engage Major Palmos's attention, not to mention his lecherous hands.

"He's at the City Tavern."

"Damn," she swore softly.

"We could wait for him."

"He might be there for hours," she said, then debated a moment, her eyes calm and purposeful. "One place is as good as another, I suppose. Drive to the tavern."

When they arrived at the brightly lit building on Second Street, the sounds of a celebration reverberated from within. After Clue entered the taproom in search of Palmos, Alexandra glanced down at her daring display of flesh and her face burned with embarrassment. Her instinct was to cover herself. Instead, with a deep breath, she tugged the gown's bodice even lower, until the suggestion of rosy nipples appeared.

Minutes later, Clue emerged from the tavern with disconcerting news. "He's drunk as a newt, ma'am."

"Is he coming out?"

Clue nodded. "So he says."

Eventually Palmos did come outside, and when Alexandra took stock of his condition, she almost wished he

430

hadn't. He walked to her coach with a weaving stride. As he climbed in beside her, she saw that his left cheek was discolored and swollen to the size of a walnut. If he harbored any ill will toward her for their last encounter, it was not apparent from his greeting.

"Well, hello," he crooned, lifting her hand for a wet-lipped kiss. "What a marvelous surprise."

His liquored breath made her throat tighten against a rush of nausea. She thought he might be too lathered to notice her provocative display, but then his stare focused on her half-clad breasts and for awhile he seemed unable to look anywhere else. At last he raised his bloodshot eyes to hers. "As always," he said, "you look enchanting."

Alexandra lowered her gaze and thanked him.

"What happy fate brings you here this evening?"

"I need your help, Major."

His eyebrows shot up. "Oh?" As he leaned toward her, his thigh pressed hers, his hand moved along the seat cushion to the nape of her neck. "My help with what, pray tell?"

At his touch, her mouth went dry as ashes. A trickle of perspiration started down between her shoulder blades as she formed her next words. "General Howe values your counsel, does he not?"

"Absolutely. We're very close, Billy and I. He seeks my advice regularly." Palmos curved his fingers around the top of her shoulder, kneading taut muscles. "Come now, it's unlike you to be timid. Just tell me how I can be of assistance."

"By stopping Dalton Philips's execution."

There was a pause, then Palmos exploded with laughter. "So Charlie was right! You *are* infatuated with that bumpkin."

"He's a valuable prisoner," she said quickly. "He could be exchanged for someone of equal importance."

"Him?" Palmos sneered at the notion. "My dear woman, he's worth far more to us dead than alive. You've no idea how much Billy is looking forward to watching him swing."

"You could change the general's mind."

"And let Philips go unpunished? I think not."

431

Alexandra's blood froze when Palmos drew away and reached for the door handle. "I shall make it worth your while," she said.

Silence invaded the coach. Palmos turned, his expression intrigued, and looked her over with maddening slowness. By the time his questing eyes returned to her face, her cheeks were aflame. "I don't think you realize what that would entail," he said. "I'm a man of, shall we say, unusual tastes."

"Major, have you ever been in love?"

He grinned wolfishly. "At least once a day."

"You mean you scratch the itch between your legs?" she inquired wryly.

"At every opportunity."

"Are you cruel in bed, or merely as selfish as you seem?"

Palmos cocked his head, eyes agleam. "That depends."

"On how far I am willing to go?" she supplied, then answered her own question. "As far as you wish. Because as difficult as this may be for you to grasp, I love Dalton Philips. If he dies, I won't care to be alive anymore. So I'll do whatever you want, for as long as you want, if you'll persuade General Howe to spare his life."

Beside her, Palmos was riveted, his mind gorged with lustful images. This was too good to be real.

"What do you say, Major?"

His stare devoured her breasts. "Payment first."

For a heartbeat neither moved, then Alexandra swayed toward him, and in the next moment he was squeezing the breath out of her with a crushing embrace. As his mouth swabbed hers, forcing her lips apart, the rank flavor of him made bile rise from her stomach until she had to gulp it down.

At last his mouth released her. "Shall we retire to my quarters?" he said, panting softly. "I'm sure you'll feel more comfortable in familiar surroundings." Without waiting for her reply, Palmos rapped on the coach roof and told Clue to drive to her Fourth Street house. Then he lowered the leather window shades, plunging the coach into murkiness, and with a groan renewed his impassioned assault. He dragged her down onto the seat and levered his body across hers.

432

There was nowhere to go and nothing to do but suffer his mauling hands. In desperation Alexandra summoned memories of a wintry night spent with Dalton, imagining his clean-mouthed taste and musky scent, the incredible ardor of his lovemaking.

Palmos freed her breasts, his head bent to slaver them, and she closed her eyes against burning moisture. Tears of mortification squeezed through her lashes and ran into her hair, and as his hand probed beneath layers of petticoats and silk, it was all she could do not to strike him. When he sat back on his haunches and began to unfasten his breeches, panic shot fire into her limbs.

"Not here," she gasped, struggling to sit up, but he pressed her back down on the seat.

"Having second thoughts?"

"No, but—"

"I can have your Yankee-Doodle executed tonight, you know. One word from me and snap goes his neck."

"You could at least wait until we reach my house."

"Never fear," he said. "By then, I shall be ready for you again." Just then the coach slowed to a halt, and Palmos froze in surprise. "We can't be there already," he muttered, fumbling to right his trousers.

Alexandra pushed herself to a sitting position and straightened her own clothing with trembling hands. "Indeed we are," she said, a hard edge in her voice.

Suddenly the door behind Palmos swung open, spilling lantern light into the coach. He looked, gaped, then shrank back as a fearsome-looking apparition sprang at him and jabbed a pistol into his gut, making him grunt.

"Don't even breathe," the gunman warned.

Palmos held still, his eyes round as shillings. It crossed his mind to grab for the weapon, but the notion shriveled, for the stranger wore a murderous look and his compact figure gave the impression of hard-bitten strength and sureness. He was mud-spattered to his muscular thighs. Beneath a dark stubble of whiskers, his face was youthful but weathered, with fine squint lines around his eyes.

He grinned at Alexandra. "Good work, ma'am."

Palmos was dumbfounded. Forgetful of his predica-

433

ment, he glared at her in disbelief. "You treacherous little bitch."

That was the all the provocation Henry Buckley needed to coldcock him. Henry made it look easy, first with a bone-crunching left jab, then a finishing thud from the butt of his pistol. "There," he told the unconscious man, "now your face matches." He looked at Alexandra, who was visibly shaken. "Are you all right, ma'am?"

"I am now," she said.

A line of dark clouds slid across the descending moon, and beneath its shadow a group of riders traveled north on the Gulph Road toward Valley Forge. Alexandra, riding astride on Secret, had never felt so bone weary in her life.

Beside her, Henry said, "We're coming to the last picket post. We'll be in camp soon."

Thank God, she thought. She could hardly wait to get out of the saddle. They had been riding for over five hours. Before that, crowded together in a stolen rowboat, the rebel kidnappers and their prize had crossed the wide expanse of the Schuylkill, rowing hard against the current while cat-and-mousing with British sloops of war. Somehow they had avoided detection by the warships, but in doing so they had missed their landing site and wound up slogging through a half-mile of marshland to reach the Derby Road, where more of Dalton's men were waiting with horses.

Now, after a grueling journey, Alexandra was getting her first glimpse of Valley Forge, and her immediate impression was one of beauty. Straight ahead a line of strong hills stood outlined against the twilight, with clusters of campfires scattered like stars over their heights. Henry had sent Private Diddle ahead to announce their arrival, and when the riders reached the last sentry post before camp, a guard detail was waiting to take charge of Major Palmos. As he was led away, sullen and slump-shouldered, Alexandra's worried gaze followed him. A nagging thought made her shiver. Suppose General Howe refused to trade Dalton for him?

Brig. Gen. Anthony Wayne, who was waiting for them

at the huts of Pennsylvania brigades, did not share her uncertainty. To his mind, an aide-de-camp of Sir William Howe was a powerful bargaining piece. And so, the moment Palmos's capture was confirmed, Wayne dispatched a courier under a white flag to the British lines, with a letter bearing His Excellency's seal. General Howe, Wayne imagined, would be chewing his fingernails for breakfast.

Despite a sleepless night, Wayne's hazel eyes were alert and full of confidence as he greeted the riders. He shook hands with Henry, "Well done, Lieutenant," then helped Alexandra dismount and guided her to a seat on a nearby log bench. "From what Private Diddle has told me, you have earned yourself an honorary commission in the Pennsylvania Line."

Wayne's praise was a balm to her nerves and softened her resentment toward him. Yesterday afternoon, when she met with him in a Buck's County farmhouse and presented her desperate scheme, his skepticism of her resolve had cut deep. She had been counting on his support. Instead, he had patronized her.

"This isn't a parlor game we're playing, Mrs. Pennington. The British shoot real bullets."

"Yes, I know," she replied, eyes flashing at him. "I helped remove some of their bullets from your wounded at Pennsylvania Hospital. I would be a liar if I said the British don't frighten me, but nothing will stop me from trying to help Dalton. As I see it, his only chance is a prisoner exchange, so I'm going after Major Palmos, with or without your assistance."

As it turned out, Wayne was almost as anxious as she was to get Dalton back, and had assigned ten capable men to the task. Men who were willing to die for their captain. They crowded around her now, their clothing in tatters, their shoes worn out, looking more like weatherbeaten scarecrows than soldiers. Wayne, dapper as ever in dark blue and buff, did not seem out of place among his ragtag warriors, but rather like their beacon.

On his order, a small keg of whiskey was produced, cups were filled, then Wayne made a solemn toast. "To freedom for our brother, Captain Philips, and for all our brave comrades in enemy hands. May God protect them and deliver them from the British Rebels."

A cheer arose on the hillside.

Alexandra, sitting on a rough-hewn bench in a crudely built log town, drinking fiery spirits from a tin cup, was stirred to her very soul. Scanning the rugged faces around her, she thought she had never been in more worthy company.

Chapter Fifty-Nine

The pain was so intense Dalton thought he would faint from it. Even the slightest movement shot red-hot bolts through his battered ribcage and made his lower back throb violently. It hurt just to breathe.

He had no idea why he was at British headquarters, in the same room where a board of high officers had condemned him to death. Silent and watchful, he studied Sir William Howe, who was sitting behind a wide, mahogany table, and wondered why the British commander seemed so disturbed.

"Can you read?" asked Howe's red-coated adjutant.

Dalton nodded, then hissed in agony as strong hands seized his arms and propelled him forward to the table. When the hands let go, he swayed drunkenly but stayed on his feet. General Howe pushed a sheet of paper across the polished surface to him.

"Read this."

Gripping the table edge, Dalton struggled to bring the paper into focus. His left eye was purplish black and swollen almost shut. He could not see much with that eye, but with the other he made out the heading *Oath of Allegiance*, which was enough to make his blood simmer.

"You have a choice, Captain." Howe's voice was like stone. "Pledge allegiance to the Crown or be executed."

The adjutant placed an inkwell and quill pen within Dalton's reach. Trembling, a sheen of perspiration on his face, Dalton stared at the document and told himself the oath was meaningless, just words on a page. He could sign his name to it and be saved. As he thought this,

Alexandra's image rose in his mind, and the ache he felt in his heart had nothing to do with his injuries. He gulped down a groan, picked up the pen, and dipped the point in ink.

The pen scratched in the stillness. Across the table, Howe's lips moved in a smile. Finished, Dalton straightened with a sharply drawn breath and looked at Howe, who reached for the paper and drew it in. Scrawled across the bottom was GO TO HELL.

Anger hardening his features, Howe looked up with frosty eyes. "I had hoped you would be reasonable."

"Fuck reasonable," Dalton said. "As long as British soldiers are here, I'll fight."

Chapter Sixty

On a field by the Wissahickon Creek, near the ruins of Downstream Farm, a band of rebel cavalry waited for a rendezvous. Waiting with them, Alexandra shaded her eyes against the afternoon sun and stared across the field, willing the enemy to appear. But the meadow remained empty, and the chill wind rippling its surface rushed like ice water over her despair.

"Something is wrong," she told Henry, who was watching the field with equal intensity.

"They'll be here," he said. "From my experience, General Howe never does anything on schedule." It was lame reasoning, but Henry felt compelled to reassure her, or perhaps himself, because a premonition of disaster was gnawing at him. "Excuse me, ma'am," he said and walked over to where Diddle was holding the captain's stallion.

Diddle's face was grim. "This doesn't feel good, Lieutenant."

"Keep your voice down," Henry said, though they were well out of Alexandra's earshot. "What time is it?"

"Four o'clock, sir."

The rendezvous had been set for three. Beseiged with worry, Henry patted Mercury's neck. Like everyone else, the stallion appeared to be concentrating on the field, just watching, watching, which made Henry wonder if the horse possessed a special awareness where his master was concerned. When the stallion's ears pricked forward and a low, eager whinny swelled from his throat, hope surged up Henry's spine. He stared hard at the meadow. For a moment nothing changed. The wind blew, the dry grass shivered, Mercury tossed his head. Then, at the far treeline, a flash of color stained the landscape.

"Boys?" Henry called over his shoulder. "Look sharp."

Alexandra held her breath as a troop of redcoats rode into view under a truce flag. Trailed by a rumbling wagon, they advanced to mid-field and stopped, waiting.

"Pauley!" Henry barked. "Get his lordship mounted up. Diddle, show the Bloodies the white flag."

As Diddle unfurled the flag, there was activity on the field. Alexandra, her emotions seesawing wildly, saw two redcoats climb into the back of the wagon and haul a shackled man to his feet. Even at this distance she could tell he was hurting. Arms folded protectively over his ribs, he stumbled getting out of the wagon. After his captors laid him on the grass, he didn't move. A terrible, numbing fear compressed her heart. She picked up her skirts and began to run.

"Mrs. Pennington!"

Henry's shout only made her go faster. She forgot her promise to follow his orders, forgot everything but the still figure on the grass, and she ran as if her life depended on reaching him.

Henry mounted up and gave chase. "Mrs. Pennington, stop!"

She kept going, listening to a surge of hoofbeats coming behind her, then thundering alongside her. Henry shouted again, but she paid no attention. She covered the remaining yards to the redcoats, shoved her way past them, and fell to her knees beside Dalton. For a moment she could only stare at him, then rage exploded over her.

"You bastards!" Her face was grimly set and her eyes, looking up, held hatred.

"It's his own fault," one of the redcoats said. "He resisted arrest."

"Unshackle him!"

They did.

As Dalton stirred, swimming up through layers of red-hazed misery, he was dimly aware of someone bending close to him. Recognition sharpened his senses. He knew the feel of those hands, knew the fragrance of her hair and skin. He opened his eyes and saw her, and though it hurt like hell to move, he reached for her.

Chapter Sixty-One

Spring came to Valley Forge. The dogwood and cherry trees blossomed, and the grass grew deep, soft, and green where short months ago men had frozen to death under bitter skies. Warm sunshine and fresh air worked wonders for coughs, colds, and itches. By the grace of divine luck and the inspired indolence of Sir William Howe, the rebels awakened from a season of famine and began to prepare for the fighting time.

As fresh recruits poured in from all over the Colonies, the mood of the camp changed dramatically. Laughter was heard. Gaunt faces filled out and grew keen-eyed. Soldiers with full bellies and new uniforms played at rounders—a game of ball and bat, with posts for bases—and held marksmanship exhibitions.

In early April, word leaked from Philadelphia that Howe was about to be superseded as British commander by his deputy, Sir Henry Clinton. Unlike Howe, Clinton was a puncher who burned to deal the rebels a fatal blow. He had his work cut out for him, thanks to a portly German aristocrat named Baron von Steuben.

Since his arrival at Valley Forge in February, Steuben had stiffened discipline and restored esprit de corps to the straggling American troops. Appalled to see soldiers using bayonets as cooking spits, he had made bayonet practice a daily exercise. He taught them the deadly art of the blade— the feint, the quick thrust, the sickening twist of steel in a man's guts. From dawn till dusk, his booming voice dominated the parade ground, where he had the whole army drilling in unison.

By April's end, Steuben molded an untrained, independent-minded band of men into a formidable fighting force. Regiment by regiment they were now equal, if not superior to any troops the British could put in the field.

May sixth was a day of resurrection for the American battle spirit. Every soldier at Valley Forge was relieved of his duties as the army celebrated France's official recognition of American independence. The whole countryside turned out for the festivities. Wine and rum flowed from flagons; fifes and drums accompanied a high-stepping parade of soldiers with flowers in their hats. Washington, riding to the high ground overlooking the Grand Parade, could scarcely believe his eyes as he beheld the superb precision of his army.

They saluted him with a glorious *feu de joie*. It began with thirteen thunderous cannon shots, fired from the artillery park on the heights, and was followed by a blank cartridge fusillade. At a signal from Steuben, a volley of musketry rippled from left to right, then from right to left along the beautifully aligned ranks of soldiers. The procedure was repeated until ten thousand men had participated in the running fire. When it was over, the General had tears in his eyes.

After the grand review ended, the officers marched thirteen abreast to open marquees for a feast. They fed on bread and beef, pork and beans, and soaked themselves in quantities of rum and cider. At sundown, the festivities at the marquees came to a close, and another celebration began at the site of the Pennsylvania brigades.

"Do you, Alexandra, take this man Dalton to be your lawful wedded husband, to love, honor, and cherish, for as long as you both shall live?"

"I do."

The moments were passing quickly for Alexandra. She watched Dalton's face and thought how handsome he looked with his black hair gleaming, his uniform cleaned and brushed. Beside him, serving as best man, Gen. Anthony Wayne was bedecked in gold-braided regimentals. On Alexandra's side stood Christopher Clue, looking somewhat more relaxed than Wayne. As well he

442

might, she thought, after sneaking a gill of rum with Henry Buckley.

Ranged around them were the men of Dalton's company. Like their captain, they were clean-shaven and spruce, and Alexandra could smell horses and whiskey on them, and the ever-present tang of woodsmoke. Weddings in camp were always well-attended. This one was no exception, for beyond the inner ring of Philips's Raiders stood scores of men from the Pennsylvania Line. Spurs jingled in the quiet, leather belts creaked, boots shuffled, and voices whispered. Some of the voices belonged to women, wives of Pennsylvania officers and enlisted men who had traveled to the camp with the warm weather.

Alexandra had not expected such a turnout. Nor had she dreamed of being married by the flickering light of campfires, against a backdrop of rustic log buildings, surrounded by a host of rebel soldiers. But given a choice, she would not have wanted to be married anywhere else.

The chaplain was prompting her again, and she looked at Dalton and said, "I, Alexandra, take thee Dalton to be my lawful wedded husband . . ." As she pledged herself to him, he was solemn and intent, with pure sharing in his eyes.

Moments later, he slipped the gold band onto her finger. "With this ring I thee wed." He kept her hand in his warm one and kissed her for the first time as his bride, and Alexandra felt as radiant as a sunrise.

When the kiss ended, the hush erupted with the applause and cheers of well-wishers, who wasted no time getting to the revelry. Kegs were opened, spirits were poured, and it seemed to Alexandra that dozens of toasts were made, led by General Wayne's magnificent voice.

"To the bride and groom, long may they live!"

"Hear, hear!"

"Long live the King of France!"

That sparked a roar of approval.

"Long live His Excellency Gen. George Washington, the father of American Liberty!"

The cheer for the General was deafening.

Then someone shouted, "Now for the music!" and Private Diddle, an accomplished fiddle player, brought out a battered black case. After he tuned up and tucked the

443

instrument under his chin, Alexandra discovered there were many fine dancers among Dalton's men, and tonight they were full of ginger.

As Diddle sawed and his fiddle squealed, the soldiers took turns dancing with the bride, with the other wives who were present, and with each other. Before long they were swooping and whirling in shirtsleeves, baying like hounds while trying to outdo everyone else's fancy steps. Even General Wayne got into the act. In fact, anyone who stood too long in one place was grabbed and forcibly dragged onto the packed earth dance floor.

During a lively jig, Alexandra wound up on Clue's arm and laughed as he whirled with her. "Christopher, I didn't know you could dance!"

"Neither did I!" He was clumsy, but what he lacked in finesse he made up for with enthusiasm. When the jig ended, he hugged her hard. "I wish you all the best, ma'am." His voice was hoarse, and when he drew back and held her shoulders, his eyes were glittering wet. "No one deserves happiness more than you."

Moved by his caring, she embraced him again, inciting the delighted whoops of onlookers.

After Clue departed to refill his cup, Alexandra felt an arm encircle her shoulders and looked up at Dalton. The bright firelight clearly showed the scar on his cheek, the only remaining mark of his ordeal at British hands. As he smiled warmly at her, the scar formed a groove in his cheek. He smiled a lot these days, she realized with contentment.

Just now he seemed a little woozy, but under control. Every man of his company had been plying him with liquor, and considering their persistence and his reluctance to refuse them, Alexandra thought he was holding up remarkably well.

"You look different," he said, searching her face. "Before you were only beautiful, now you're magnificent."

He sounded so serious, Alexandra had to bite a smile from her lips. "And you're getting tight."

"Me?" He squeezed her shoulders. "Not tonight, love. There's a warm bed waiting for us, and I plan to do more than just sleep in it."

Under the gown and all the petticoats, Alexandra's body responded to that hopeful desire. He must have felt her tremor, for an intimate gleam came into his eyes, suffusing her with a full measure of awareness. He was her husband. Reaching up, she touched a finger to his cheek, tracing his scar. "I shall hold you to your word."

"Mrs. Philips," he said softly, as though to see how it felt to say the name. "You can hold me however you want."

Chapter Sixty-Two

At the City Tavern, Charles Villard shut out the noise around him and stared across a drink-littered table at Major Palmos. "Is the rumor true?"

"What rumor is that, Charlie?"

"That Clinton has orders to evacuate Philadelphia."

When Palmos shrugged, pretending ignorance, Villard wanted to throttle him. "Don't toy with me, Andrew."

"Even if I knew the answer, I would not be allowed to discuss the matter with a civilian."

Stung, Villard drew his head back. "I'm an officer in the King's service."

"A provincial captain," Palmos pointed out, "not regular army. Oh, for heaven's sake, don't look so offended!" With an exasperated sigh, he leaned forward a little and his voice lowered conspiratorially. "Can you keep a secret?"

Villard nodded, his face intent.

"The King has ordered the army to withdraw to New York."

Villard blinked. "When?"

"I don't know. Soon."

"You mean we're to just hand Philadelphia back to the rebels?" Villard was incredulous.

"As the ministry sees it, we should never have come here in the first place. We should have gone north to support Burgoyne."

"This is absurd!"

"Charlie," Palmos raised a cautioning finger, "not one word. Now brace up your chin: you're attracting flies.

There's a good man. Shall I order us another round?"

Numb with shock, Villard declined with a shake of his head, but the major signaled a barmaid to bring him a fresh tankard.

"John Andre has planned the most spectacular celebration in honor of Billy," Palmos said, then sighed at the thought of Howe's imminent departure from America. "Lord, I shall miss him. He's been like a brother to me."

Villard could not have cared less about Palmos's woes. He stared blankly at the tabletop, his mind leaping ahead. The British were about to abandon the capital, which meant that thousands of Loyalists, whose support the Crown had practically begged for, would be left at the mercy of the rebels. Their properties would be confiscated, their lives forever ruined. Many would have to flee or face imprisonment, perhaps even execution. Villard knew he could expect no quarter. He would have to leave Philadelphia with the British.

And Palmos had the gall to look unconcerned. Villard trembled with outrage. What a lopsided trade it had been, Philips for this dolt.

The barmaid who brought Palmos's drink was young and rosily pretty, with a ripe figure and a halo of bright golden curls. Palmos could not resist groping her. After swatting his hand away, she hefted a foaming tankard. "Did you order this?"

"Indeed I did. But you make me warm for more than just ale, my dear."

When he reached for her again, she emptied the tankard in his lap. "That should cool you off."

Bravo, Villard thought as she flounced away. He watched Palmos, who was cursing and mopping his crotch with a napkin. "Your luck with women has certainly taken ill."

Palmos's head snapped up. Gone was his former nonchalance. "You can mock me after being jilted for a bumpkin?"

The air around them hummed. "Be careful, Andrew."

"No, *you* be careful. I'm sick to death of your drivel. My God, but you Colonials do assume airs! The way you carry on sometimes, one might think you were indispensable to us. Well hear this, my posturing friend. You can be

447

replaced," Palmos snapped his fingers in Villard's face, "like that."

Villard's pulse was throbbing in his temples; his eyes were blistering cold. He pushed back his chair and stood up. "Good night, Major."

After he left, Palmos brooded over their conflict for awhile, then dismissed Villard from his thoughts and continued to marinate himself in ale. "Billy, Billy, Billy," he lamented into his mug. "We shall all become dullards without you to inspire us." Just like Clinton, he thought, with his bunchy paunch and jaundiced eyes. Dull, dull, dull. The fat bore would never be caught reveling in a dance or shivering with excitement at a faro table or laughing full-throated in a theatre. His hair was perpetually on end.

Draining his mug, Palmos suddenly became aware of a pressing need to answer nature's call. "To pee or not to pee," he intoned, "that is the question." In answer, he pushed to his feet and went out back to relieve himself.

At midnight, saturated to his eyeballs, Palmos staggered outside for a final time and made his way to his quarters on Fourth Street. The house was completely dark. Crooning a dittie he had composed at the tavern, he stumbled up the walkway to the front door.

> They toasted my honor and gave me a star.
> They boasted my bravery from near to far.
> They granted me riches, no prize did I lack,
> But I gave it all up for a tit and a crack.

Groping blindly through the downstairs passageway, he heard someone snoring and realized it was Captain Lambert, who shared the house with him. Lambert, sprawled on the parlor couch, was dead to the world. Fast approaching the same state, Palmos lurched up the stairs, into his bedroom, and fell fully clothed across the bed, where he immediately passed out.

For awhile the house was still. Just after three, a fire broke out in the kitchen. It began with a *whoosh* and spread with deadly swiftness, aided by a dousing of lamp oil on dry floor boards. Kitchen furniture ignited like matchsticks, curtains caught fire. Flames curled upward to lick at the beamed ceiling, then exploded into the lower hallway, sending lethal black clouds throughout the house. The fire leaped onto the banister and was sucked up the stairwell like smoke up a flue. Within minutes, tongues of crackling orange flames were shooting from second-floor windows.

Major Palmos never stirred. The boiling black smoke killed him long before the inferno roared into his room and consumed his body.

By dawn, the house was a smoldering brick shell, and Charles Villard felt temporarily vindicated.

Chapter Sixty-Three

"Dalton, you're being unreasonable."

Dalton was thinking the same thing of Alexandra. He kept the thought to himself, because he could see that she was working herself up into a fine anger. "I just want what's best for you," he said.

"Then stop treating me like I'm made of glass! I won't break. Haven't I proved that since I've been here?"

He had to admit that she had adapted surprisingly well to camp life. She had set up housekeeping in this mean little hut, which could fit into a corner of Willowbrook's spacious parlor. She pinned her clothing with thorns, prepared meals with inadequate utensils, and cooked bread on hot stones. In the evenings, she darned old stockings and patched torn uniforms by firelight. Much of her free time was spent doctoring minor ailments among his men. With the skillfulness of a professional, she cleaned and bandaged cuts, made salves for burning itches and sores, and brewed tea from sassafras blossoms to purify the blood. She tackled every task with cheerful enthusiasm. But despite doing a fair share of work, her stay at Valley Forge had passed in relative comfort.

"Alex," he said, "the past couple months have been easy on everyone, but that will change as soon as we march. Then you'll wish to God you were home."

"How do you know what I'll wish for?"

"Because you never had it rough. You won't last a week on the road."

Too late Dalton realized he had said the wrong thing. Her nostrils flared, her eyes glittered, and he could almost hear her thinking, *We'll see about that*. She rose from the bunk and began to snatch on her underclothing.

Watching her dress, her breasts gently swaying, her smooth, alabaster skin agleam with sunlight, he was torn between frustration and sharp desire. She wasn't the least bit self-conscious of her nudity, which only heightened his arousal. At first he flirted with the ebb and flow in his loins, letting it tantalize and clutch at him, until finally it gained its own impetus and took control.

"Come here," he said quietly.

She ignored him and continued to dress. "If you think I'm about to spend months waiting to hear from you again, you're out of your mind."

"Alex, look to me."

Instead, she turned her back on him and opened her portmanteau. At a loss how to calm her, Dalton set his jaw and watched her cover her inviting flesh. He knew every inch of her suppleness as intimately as he knew himself. He could make her sing like a raptor and shudder with pure joy. But with a jolt he realized how little he understood the workings of her woman's mind.

Again he tried to reason with her. "The army's the worst kind of life you can imagine," he said, and that was as far as he got.

"No, it isn't." She faced him again. "The worst kind of life is wondering every day whether you're alive or dead. It's feeling helpless and useless while others do what needs to be done." She buttoned her bodice as she spoke, her voice low, all her energy in her eyes. "This may come as a shock to you, but I can fend for myself. I'm quite good at it. And another thing. I won't be just tagging along, I'll be pulling my weight. I happen to be an experienced nurse."

A skill that would take her close to the battlefield, Dalton imagined. "You're not going," he said, "and that's final."

She left the hut then, closing the door harder than necessary. As her footsteps faded, Dalton rolled out of bed with a curse and began to pull on his clothes. One way or another, he had to get through to her. Ever since she had learned that the British were stirring at Philadelphia, she had been all nerves. Sure worry was eating her, but he wished she would put herself in his place for a minute.

451

Dalton caught himself, remembering her words, the keen edge of pain in her voice. *The worst kind of life is wondering every day whether you're alive or dead.*

How would that feel? he asked himself. What horrible visions tortured her when news of a battle reached her ears? He could pretty well guess what she felt and imagined, because he knew all about fear and how it could tear your heart out. With a shaky sigh, he sat on the bunk and rubbed his forehead, feeling as if all creation was up-heaving inside him. Maybe he was the unreasonable one after all.

He got up and went to look for her. She was easy to track, for her feet had left a dark path through the shimmer of last night's dew. Not far from the hut, he found her in a wooded glade where the sun reached down under the treetops and made an island of light. Caught in that light, she was sitting on a large mossy rock with her knees drawn up, her look bitter. She was hurting.

When he entered the clearing, she didn't stir or look up. He sat down with her, took her hand, and said, "This ain't the best way to start a marriage."

"Is there any best way to conduct a marriage in the middle of a war?"

He studied her profile a moment. "I guess not."

"Then what are we to do?" she asked, turning agonized eyes to him. "Because I can't bear to watch you leave again."

"I guess you'd better come with me." After saying the words, Dalton wanted them back. He saw her face brighten and felt her come into his arms, and he hoped to God he had made the right decision.

Chapter Sixty-Four

One night in June, the British finally stirred from their winter quarters. Tents were struck in darkness, the garrison marched south into the Neck, and thousands of troops were ferried over the Delaware River to New Jersey. At dawn, Philadelphians awoke to an eerie quiet and found the city deserted of soldiers. As one resident put it, "The British did not go away, they just vanished."

But Clinton's army could not hide their maneuver from rebel scouts, and when the last boatload of redcoats disembarked below Gloucester, a race across New Jersey began with Washington's forces.

Hampered by a huge baggage train eleven miles long, the British war machine moved at a crawl through the sandy, boggy countryside. As wagons creaked and banged over rutted roads, Clinton cursed the heavy, clumsy transports, which were full of food, booty, officers' mistresses, and other useless things. Moving at scarcely a mile an hour, the column was easy prey for rebel snipers, who needled the British flanks at every opportunity. The Jersey Blues got busy with axes, compounding Clinton's nightmare. Felled trees littered the roads, crucial bridges were destroyed, and drinking wells were filled with sand and rocks.

For all that, rebel harassment took a minor toll compared with the ruthless weather. Thunderstorms crackled. Rain poured in sheets, turning roads into quagmires and fouling guns with mud and rust. When the clouds parted, the sun generated a ferocious heat that broiled the marching red column. As temperatures soared into the nineties, steam rose from heavy woolen uniforms and sodden packs. Clothing refused to dry out and hung like limp weeds on exhausted shoulders.

Pushed over the brink, soldiers collapsed by the roadside, writhing with dreadful head pains and babbling with the delirium that comes from sunstroke. A horde of Jersey mosquitoes settled like a black plague on their exposed flesh. Several men died, their faces so bloated with mosquito poison and purpled from the intense heat that it was impossible to identify them. Almost hourly, deserters went over to the rebels.

The Patriot army, shadowing the British along parallel roads to the north, fared somewhat better during the march. Unhindered by wrecked bridges and needless baggage, the light-clad American troops were able to outpace the British while putting pressure on their flanks. Still, the blistering heat exacted its price, and many rebels sank by the wayside in exhaustion.

Alexandra was fortunate enough to be traveling in a covered wagon which carried medical supplies belonging to the Seventh Pennsylvania Regiment. She had made a seat among the piled baggage, just behind the front bench, and could look out past the driver at the twisting, dust-raising column ahead. The wagon's tarpaulin roof, stretched over ashwood hoops, kept off the worst of the blazing sun, but the midday air was suffocating. Her clothing was soaked through with perspiration; her hair was plastered to her cheeks and neck. The skin of her face felt flushed and fiery hot.

Riding with her in the wagon was sturdy, red-headed Jenny Barnes, a camp follower whom Alexandra had befriended. A year ago, Jenny had given her two children into her mother's care, left her home in Allentown, and joined her husband Matthew, a gunner with Proctor's Pennsylvania Artillery. Jenny was twenty-seven, but looked forty. Her hands were calloused as a dog's pads, her muscles toughened by the rigors of camp life. Inside, however, she was soft as clay.

"You don't look so good," she said, squeezing Alexandra's arm. "Are you all right?"

"My head feels awfully warm."

"It's hot enough to kill a person, that's the truth. Here,"

Jenny dug in her apron pocket and brought out a tin flask, "this might help."

But Alexandra declined the rum, remembering Dr. Rush's admonition that liquor made a body more susceptible to heat and cold. Had the opposite been true, she still could not have swallowed a drop of the stuff. The fumes alone were making her gag. Eyes closed, she swallowed a rush of nausea and felt Jenny's steadying hand on her shoulder.

"Breathe through your nose," Jenny coaxed. "Quick like a bunny, that's it."

Slowly the queasiness abated. Alexandra straightened and wiped her brow.

Jenny, sipping from the flask, watched her speculatively. Leaning forward a little, she lowered her voice so the driver would not hear her ask, "Are you pregnant?"

The very word made Alexandra tingle. "I hope so," she said fervently, then related the recent changes she had noticed in her body—the discomfort in her lower back, the odd, metallic taste in her mouth, the episodes of morning sickness and spells of extreme fatigue. Most encouragingly, her menses had not occurred since the end of April.

After hearing all this, Jenny said, "Well, if you don't bleed pretty soon, I'd say you're gonna have a baby."

Despite feeling ill, the idea that she might be carrying Dalton's child made Alexandra ecstatic. "Are you sure?"

"'Course I'm not sure, but you got all the signs. And that husband of yours seems healthy as a bear. I doubt he's firing blank cartridges."

Alexandra smiled. A few miles up the road, Dalton and his light dragoons were riding with the advance column toward Princeton. Looking eastward, she directed her thoughts to him, and with that strange awareness that sometimes came to her, she sensed that he was thinking of her too.

"Have you told him?" Jenny asked.

There was a pause. "Not yet," Alexandra admitted. "I want to be absolutely sure first, so please don't say anything to him."

"Wouldn't dream of spoiling your surprise."

But Alexandra was wrestling with more than just the thought of surprising him. She knew Dalton, and she

455

knew what his reaction would be if he suspected she were pregnant. He would insist on sending her home. For the baby's sake she would go, if indeed there was a baby to worry about, but for now she planned to sit tight. She only wished her stomach would do the same.

To her amazement, Jenny managed to doze off in the lumbering wagon, sprawled like a rag doll among hard-edged baggage. Worn out from the heat, Alexandra tried to follow her example but could not get comfortable enough to fall asleep. She was thankful when, arriving at a bridge over Stony Brook, the driver stopped the wagon to rest and water the team. Like a moth drawn to light, Alexandra got out and made her way down the sun-parched embankment to the stream. Sitting on a rock, her bare feet in the shallows, she splashed tepid water over her face, neck, and wrists, gasping at the relief it brought her heated skin.

"Mrs. Philips!"

The familiar voice made her glance downstream, where a group of thirsty soldiers was descending from the road for a drink. With them was Christopher Clue. He waved amicably to her, his sunburned face as cheerful as ever. A musket was cradled in his arm and bundled at his belt was a uniform jacket of the Seventh Pennsylvania Regiment. Alexandra still could not get over the fact that he was a Continental soldier.

Dalton had broken the news to her. On their last day at Valley Forge, he had entered the hut with his face set and grim, his eyes looking everywhere but at her. Right away she had known something was wrong, but she never dreamed he would say, "Chris signed enlistment orders last night."

Stunned, she sank onto the bunk. "Was he drunk?"

"From what I heard, he couldn't have found his pecker with both hands, but he managed to scratch his name on the indentures."

"For how long?"

"Three years."

"Oh, my God," she whispered. "Christopher isn't cut out to be a soldier."

"He is now."

Surprisingly, Clue seemed happy with his lot. "I feel like I belong with these fellows," he had told her

456

"Anyway, it's high time I did my part for America. But after the fighting's over, I'd like nothing more than to come back to work for you."

Alexandra was quick to assure him, "You're family. You'll always have a home with us."

Now, shielding her eyes against harsh sunlight, she watched Clue kneel and plunge his face into the cooling stream. The soldiers with him were doing the same, guzzling water with the gusto of parched livestock. After drinking his fill, Clue shouldered his piece, fell in with his compatriots, and marched off to rejoin his regiment. Alexandra's worried eyes followed him. As he disappeared from view, she prayed for his safety because she knew the chances were good he would soon have to snuff some gunpowder.

When the wagon master signaled that it was time to go, she put on her stockings and shoes and started up the embankment. Partway to the road, she paused on legs that were suddenly weak and uncooperative. In the scorching afternoon, a damp chill prickled her skin. Fighting dizziness, she sat on the grassy bank, hoping the spell would pass, but a great heaviness dragged her down, down, until she was drowning in nothingness.

"Just hang on," Jenny soothed. "We're almost to Hopewell."

Hopewell. After so many grueling hours on the road, it sounded like paradise to Alexandra, whose only wish was to lie flat and still until the pain throbbing behind her eyes went away.

Thanks to Jenny, her wish was fulfilled within minutes after reaching Hopewell, a tiny village near Princeton where the main army was encamping for the night. Jenny's first order of business was to prepare a pallet for her friend. Spreading straw over the sandy ground, she covered the bedding with a blanket, then rigged stretcher poles and sheets to form a privacy screen.

To Alexandra, no bed had ever felt more comfortable. In the gathering dusk, she lay with her eyes closed and listened to the bustling activity around her—the bite of axes chopping firewood, horses whinnying to be fed, the

457

clanging of camp kettles as meals were prepared and hungrily devoured. The energy and efficiency with which supplies, equipment and people were settled for the night served to emphasize her own feebleness. As the ache in her head lessened, guilt took its place. She was glad Dalton was not there to see her lying about like a good-for-nothing.

She could not begin to imagine all that he had been through since becoming a soldier, but after today she had an inkling. For two years he had faced the fright, pain, and death of battle, the agonies of forced marches without rest, the grinding responsibilities of a command. He had endured times of belly-twisting hunger, often going two, three, and even four days without a mouthful to eat. He had suffered through two hellish winters, shivering in inadequate shelters while trying, somehow, to improve the welfare of his men. All of this he had done without losing his courage or hope.

As the camp quieted and cookfires glimmered on the field, Alexandra forced her eyes open and battled exhaustion, determined to be awake if Dalton came looking for her. The campfires, stoked with green wood, created a smoky haze intended to ward off mosquitoes. But while the smoke gave protection against the droning insects, it also irritated her eyes. When they began to burn, she closed them for a moment.

The next thing she knew, her eyes were opening again and Dalton was with her. He was sitting cross-legged on the ground beside her pallet, his face calm against leaping firelight. "I shouldn't have woken you," he said, smoothing her hair.

Alexandra came fully awake. "I'm glad you did."

With a sigh, he stretched out beside her and pulled her close, and despite the hot, sticky night, she was grateful to have his warmth against her.

"Was your day rough?" he asked.

Knowing she looked a wreck, Alexandra didn't try to evade him. "I'm afraid the heat got to me."

His embrace tightened, telling her wordlessly of his concern. "It was wicked, wasn't it?"

"Like an oven."

"A good night's sleep should fix you up."

"Your being here is the best medicine of all," she said and was aware of sudden tension in him.

"I can only stay a few minutes," he told her. "The generals had a council of war, and they're sending some regiments ahead to Englishtown, including part of the Pennsylvania Line. General Wayne did me the honor of choosing my company to go with him."

Alexandra drew back, saw resolve on his face, and her whole being went numb. "To attack the British?"

He nodded. "Before they reach the high grounds, otherwise they'll get away without a fight."

She shivered against him and felt him draw her head to his shoulder, where she buried her face in his shirt. They stayed like that for a time, neither speaking.

Then he said, "The army's stronger and better trained than it's ever been. This time we'll win, don't you worry."

"I love you."

Dalton hugged her hard, and she felt the roughness of his beard against her face, then his lips. "Whatever happens," he whispered, "you've made me a happy man."

When he left a little later, Alexandra held back tears. She watched him cross the camp with his long, sure strides, until he was swallowed by the darkness beyond the fringe of firelight. Returning to her pallet, she curled up on the blanket with a hand pressed to her abdomen. The camp was hushed, but the muggy air was charged with apprehension, a collective nervousness so thick she could feel it with her heart. A battle was coming, and despite Dalton's assurances, there was no certainty of a rebel victory, only the promise of casualties and of lives forever changed.

Chapter Sixty-Five

Alexandra had heard rumblings of cannonfire before, but never at such an alarming proximity. Inside Old Tennant Church, where the army surgeons had set up a hospital, there was no time to dwell on the battle taking place just a mile away, for stretcher bearers were bringing in patients in droves. With each rumble of heavy guns, the air thickened with smoke, medical instruments quivered on tables, surgeons flinched but continued their critical work. The acrid smell of gunpowder mingled with the odors of blood and perspiration, making for an awful stench. Flies droned in the sweltering heat. If yesterday's weather had been brutal, today the air seemed too hot to live in.

Assisting Dr. Ross of the First Pennsylvania Battalion, Alexandra tightened a fillet-and-stick tourniquet around the thigh of an unconscious man, then averted her eyes as a curved knife flensed around the leg, parting flesh, muscles, and sinew. Moments later the amputation saw lowered and rasped through bone. Mercifully, the patient stayed oblivious, but tiny moans came from his throat and his body jerked spasmodically throughout the procedure. A surgeon's mate stood ready to pin him down in case he awakened, for the strength of a man under the saw could be vicious.

When the worst was done, the mate removed the severed limb to a growing pile outside the meetinghouse. Dr. Ross readied ligatures, then lifted a long needle with a crooked end. While Alexandra kept the tourniquet tight, he began tying off the arteries. "Loosen," he said after a time, watching closely for leakage. Seeing none, he placed two round pledgets of lint over the bone end, covered the stump muscles with fine linen, and bound the dressing with long strips of cotton. A woolen cap covered the whole. The unconscious man was then transferred to one of several hospital tents outside the meetinghouse.

Wiping her brow, Alexandra glanced around the room at the organized mayhem. Only the most necessary amputations and operations were being performed. Otherwise it was emergency care only—removing bullets and grapeshot from wounds; stopping bloodloss with compresses, ligatures, and tourniquets; splinting fractured bones and applying dressings.

From the cries and mutterings of the wounded, she suspected that Gen. Charles Lee was at least partly to blame for their agony. Lee had been in command of the American advance when it attacked the enemy's rear guard. Exactly what had transpired during the attack was still unclear, but the end result had been a Patriot rout, and Lee was being called everything from a traitor to a coward for ordering a retreat.

If there was one art of warfare the American soldier had mastered, it was that of retreat. Lee's troops, gasping for breath, their clothing soaked with sweat, had stumbled back in confusion before a counterattack. Some had broken into panicked flight, scattering in all directions, and for a heartbreaking time it had seemed that yet another American defeat was in the making.

Then General Washington had arrived on the scene. Mounted on his white charger, he rode along the lines firing commands with the smooth precision of a rifle, restoring the fighting spirit of his troops by his voice and example. His broad face and keen gray eyes were a nucleus of calm in a maelstrom. The result of his presence had been almost miraculous. Their blood up, the Americans had regrouped and formed a strong battle line, spearheaded by Anthony Wayne's Pennsylvanians.

The two armies were now trading each other blow for blow, and the casualties were mounting. In preparation for the next one, Alexandra wiped down the operating table. Across from her, Dr. Ross was cleaning his saw blade of foreign matter. Without looking up, he said, "Go

461

outside and get some air."

The last thing Alexandra wanted to do was sit idle. Only when her hands and mind were occupied could she control her fear for Dalton. "I would rather stay here," she said.

"It wasn't a suggestion." Ross's voice was quiet but firm. "You've been going hard for hours. Most of these poor fellows will need a second round of treatment, and you'll be of no use to me unless you rest. So off with you," he said, shooing her away.

Alexandra went outside. Incredibly, the meetinghouse yard was more hectic than the surgery had been. Soldiers designated to transport the wounded were hurrying to and fro with their charges. Ambulance wagons were coming off the battlefield, which lay just beyond a smoke-wreathed rise to the east. Besides wagons, the stretcher bearers were using whatever biers were handy to retrieve injured soldiers, including wheelbarrows, carts, and sleds. Alexandra shuddered to think of the agony such transportation caused to splintered bones and gunshot wounds.

A sudden, pitiful screaming rose above the din and made her look toward the road. There, bouncing along in a wheelbarrow, was Henry Buckley. She thought she had seen every kind of wound imaginable until she rushed to his side.

The British were firing shrapnel from their field pieces—scrap iron, chains, broken sword blades, and the like. A large belt buckle, fired from a cannon mouth, had caught Henry flush in the stomach. When Alexandra pulled his hands aside and saw the damage, a moan escaped her. At her direction, Henry was placed in the shade beneath a maple tree, then she knelt with him and lifted his head into her lap.

"Henry?" she asked, but he seemed not to hear her. "Henry, it's Alexandra."

His breath hissed; his gaze sharpened. She stroked his face and watched his bloody mouth try to speak. As his dying eyes looked into hers, she realized that he wanted urgently to tell her something, but his throat kept filling with blood and all he could do was gasp for breath.

Finally he gurgled, "Dalton," and fear constricted her heart. Henry swallowed and tried again. "Tell him . . . my privilege."

462

Moments later, Alexandra closed his glazed eyes. Feeling a hand press her shoulder, she looked up and saw Private Diddle weaving on his feet, his right arm hanging like a broken stick at his side.

"Is he dead?"

When she nodded, Diddle sank to his knees beside her, his features contorting with grief. "Ah, Lieutenant," he groaned, wiping blood from Henry's cheek. "I never thought they'd get you."

"I'm sorry, Diddle," she said.

Haunted eyes stared at her from a smoke-blackened face. Diddle spoke as if in a trance. "I fell off my horse and broke my arm. I thought I was food for the Rangers, but Captain Philips and the lieutenant come back for me." He paused, shivering in pain. "We almost made it. We was coming across a bridge when their cannon opened up on us. The lieutenant got the worst of it."

Alexandra's mouth had gone dry. "Is Dalton all right?"

"His arm got sliced to the bone. It's bleeding something awful, but he won't leave the field. His noodle must be baked."

Getting to her feet, Alexandra looked toward the battlefield where Wayne's brigades were said to be holding tenaciously to their position in an orchard. For all she knew, Dalton was bleeding to death only a mile away.

"Diddle," she said, "you'd better have one of the surgeons look at your arm."

As she started across the yard, Diddle's puzzled gaze followed her, and when he saw her climb into the back of an ambulance wagon, his eyes widened with alarm.

"God, don't," he breathed, struggling to his feet, but it was too late to stop her. The ambulance driver slapped the reins, and the wagon headed for the battlefield at a fast clip. As the vehicle was enveloped by a thick haze of smoke, Diddle murmured a prayer for the captain's wife.

Alexandra was also praying. Pale with apprehension, she gripped the back of the driver's bench and surveyed the view ahead. After skirting a wooded rise, the wagon descended the gently sloping terrain toward Middle Brook, a shallow stream running through a deep, narrow ravine. As they neared the brook, the rattle of musketry intensified; the screeching of grapeshot was blood-chilling. Smoke hovered like fog in the sultry air. Squinting through the haze, Alexandra saw soldiers across the stream and realized they were Americans. They were formed in line of battle along the edge of a ploughed field, and facing them were rows of distant red figures. British grenadiers, looking like so many toy soldiers.

When the wagon stopped on the lip of the ravine, two attendants got out with a stretcher. Indicating the Americans across the way, Alexandra asked the driver, "Are those General Wayne's men?"

"That's Ramsey's regiment," he said. "Wayne's men are over toward the bridge."

Alexandra left the wagon. Following behind the stretcher bearers, she half-slid, half-clawed her way down into the ravine and crossed the brook with them. On the far side, they were met by several Marylanders carrying two wounded soldiers. One of the wounded men was already dead, his chest riddled with grapeshot. The second man's arm had been sheared off at the elbow by a heavy saber blade. A hasty tourniquet had been tied above the stump, but he was bleeding profusely.

Crouching beside him, Alexandra applied pressure to stop the flow and said, "Someone find me a stick." One of the soldiers quickly obliged her. As she retied the tourniquet and began to twist it tightly, a volley of cannonballs suddenly zoomed overhead, splintering trees with deafening crashes and gouging up hunks of earth. Cowering instinctively, Alexandra felt an overwhelming urge to flee, to get as far away as possible from the horrifying sounds, smells, and sights of destruction. But the anguish of her patient kept her there.

Dalton had been unable to put Henry from his mind. In his heart, he knew his friend was dead. No one could survive the kind of wound Henry had suffered, and no one could have borne the agony with more bravery. It had been a tormenting thing to watch and a humbling example of just how much a body could endure.

So when pain lanced Dalton's bound forearm, he gritted his teeth and remembered Henry's courage. The pain was the best part of his injury. Thanks to a sharp sliver of steel, the fingers of his right hand were almost numb. He had removed the fragment, but his grip was so impaired he could not clench his pistol with enough strength to aim the weapon effectively. Against such a dilemma, he had practiced his marksmanship, as well as his swordplay, with his left hand. But while he believed he could use both hands with equal ease, his left-handed skills had never been put to the test. A fact that was about to change.

Looking out over the battlefield, he beheld a breathtaking spectacle of color—the flashing red of British grenadiers, the Scots in green plaid, white-wigged Hessians in blue coats, and fierce-bearded German Jaegers wearing green and gold.

On the Patriot side were Virginians in dark blue and yellow, and Massachusetts men in pale blue and red. The soldiers of the Pennsylvania brigades, ranged behind a hedgerow, wore a multi-colored variety of uniforms. In almost every regiment were soldiers in rags, men with nothing but their shirttails to adorn their nakedness. But with the sun burning overhead like a brilliant white cannonball, the half-clad warriors were to be envied.

Glancing right, then left along the rebel lines, Dalton marveled at what he saw. From a collection of misfits, thieves, and scoundrels of every sort, from high-born smugglers, lawyers, and silk-stockinged gentry, an army had been forged. Disciplined, toughened by loss, blooded to each other, the Americans were set to prove their worth as soldiery.

"Ready arms!" Wayne's voice rolled down the hedgerow, eager and rock-steady. The general was in his element. "They look hungry, boys, so let's give them a bellyful of lead!"

They were Lt. Col. Henry Monckton's Royal Grenadiers, Britain's *corps d'elite,* advancing with steel-tipped muskets and razored swords. Watching them come on, Dalton remembered a long-ago day on a Long Island cornfield, when a band of untrained Pennsylvanians had challenged Monckton's warriors and sent them reeling. He burned to do it again.

Pistol in hand, he moved down the ranks in a crouch. "Hold your fire, boys. Wait for the word." Sighting a familiar figure, he hunkered down beside a pale Christo-

465

pher Clue and patted his shoulder. "How are you, Chris?"

"Scared stiff."

"Well, good. At least you ain't daft." Dalton nodded at the grenadiers. "But they are. Look at them, lined up like bull's-eyes. Just pull the trigger, you're bound to hit something."

"I aim to knock down an officer."

"Attaboy."

The grenadiers had closed to within thirty yards, black boots tramping in unison, weapons aglitter under the blazing sky. Their famed colonel was leading the way with his sword raised. In true Monckton fashion, he called a halt, boldly presented his back to his foes, and in a resounding voice delivered a speech that raised hackles on both sides.

"You are the finest regiments in the King's service! These are but ruffians arrayed against you, mongrels without honor or gallantry! Immortal glory awaits, so forward, my brave fellows! THIS DAY IS OURS!"

Wayne, pacing like a panther, his hazel eyes relentless, flicked up his sword tip. "Steady, boys!" His command whipcracked with intensity. "Aim for the King's birds."

The British gave a furious cheer and charged the thick hedge.

"FIRE!"

American muskets poured death on the grenadiers. Monckton went down with the first volley, half his face torn away, but his column surged forward.

"Second line, present!" Wayne yelled. "FIRE!"

The hedgerow blazed. The ripping volley staggered the British charge, but failed to halt it.

"Bayonets at ready!" Wayne aimed his sword at the oncoming redcoats. "Remember Paoli!"

Steel teeth glinted along the hedge, poised to engage the attackers. Then the British wave swept in, and the fighting became close and desperate. Thanks to Steuben's endless drills at Valley Forge, the Patriots wielded their bayonet with deadly efficiency. Bright blades combed like fang into flesh until the ground before the hedgerow wa littered with redcoats. The fashionable beaus of the Britis Army, the darlings of Philadelphia society, were being cu to pieces by the farmers and tradesmen they had so loved t

466

imitate to amuse their mistresses.

Finally the stunned grenadiers broke off the attack, and their officers called a retreat. Withdrawing to a safe distance, they hurriedly regrouped.

Watching them form, Wayne's narrowed eyes noted a redeployment of strength to the British right wing. Quickly grasping their intention, he signaled Dalton, who trotted to his side. "They're going to try to outflank us. Alert Colonel Ramsey to watch the woods to his left."

"Yes, sir."

Dalton ran to Mercury, vaulted into the saddle, and was off at a gallop to find Wayne's wing commander. On Washington's orders, Colonel Ramsey and his troops had been rushed to Wayne's support, and the reliable Marylanders had held their ground like granite ever since. Approaching their position, Dalton was looking for Ramsey when a heart-stopping sight caught his eye.

Alexandra? "Jesus God!"

His duty forgotten, Dalton changed direction and galloped over to where she was tending a wounded man. Several soldiers were with her, and as Dalton reined Mercury to a halt, his blistering eyes raked them. "Who in bloody hell brought her out here?"

Alexandra came to her feet, elated by the sight of him. To her relief, he seemed none the worse for his injury, but the furious face looking back at her belonged to a stranger. "I came on my own," she explained quickly. "Diddle said you were hurt."

Wrath and fear made Dalton's voice menacing. "You and you," he said, pointing to two of the Marylanders. "Get her out of here, or so help me I'll kill you both." As they moved to do his bidding, his stare drilled Alexandra. "This time stay put, do you hear me?"

She nodded, not about to argue with him. With a last look at his angry face, she went with her escorts toward the ravine, trailed by the stretcher bearers with her patient.

Pressed for time, Dalton rode off in search of Colonel Ramsey, located him, and delivered Wayne's message, then headed back to the Pennsylvania brigades.

In the smoky ravine, one of the stretcher bearers lost his footing and went down heavily, wrenching his ankle in his attempt to keep the litter from overturning. "God-

467

damnit!" he cried, gripping his leg with both hands.

After a quick examination, Alexandra feared he had fractured his ankle, but before she could voice her conclusion, the enemy's artillery opened up with another furious barrage. Missiles whined overhead and slammed into the far bank, shooting geysers of debris into the air. The soldier beside her yelled, "Down!" but Alexandra was already flattened against the embankment, listening to the whiz and thud of cannon shot as British gunners pummeled Ramsey's position.

As abruptly as it began, the bombardment ceased, only to be followed by the heavy crash of musketry. Bullets hummed like hornets into the ravine. From the continual firing, it was clear the Marylanders were caught up in a hot engagement.

Alexandra lay frozen, her fingers digging into sandy soil as she waited for a lull and chance to escape. But with each passing moment, the shouts, curses, and screams of fighting men grew louder, until it seemed as if Ramsey's troops were almost on top of her.

Suddenly they came streaming into the ravine, their smoke-streaked faces wild with panic, their officers hurling orders. Scores of soldiers took up defensive positions along the crest of the embankment.

Cringing between her two escorts, Alexandra heard the steady tread of British boots, the clank and hiss of steel blades, the simultaneous clicks of numerous firelocks. Then a deep voice bellowed, "Have at the rebels, lads! NO QUARTER!" And a bloodthirsty huzzah poured from hundreds of throats.

The Americans managed one stinging volley, then the unseen enemy loosed a hailstorm of lead at the ravine. Bodies tumbled down the slope into the stream, staining the water red. When Alexandra found the courage to raise her head, she saw that her escorts had deserted her. All around her soldiers were retreating in disorder, for the redcoats were coming on at a trot, yelling at the top of their lungs. As they stormed the ravine in waves, forking bodies aside with gleaming bayonets and firing into the backs of fleeing men, Alexandra curled up in terror and remembered to pray.

Footsteps thudded close to her. With her heart beating

468

on her ribs, she looked up to see a British soldier aiming a bayonet at her chest. His ruthless eyes locked with hers for an eternal instant, and she understood what was coming. One moment he was towering above her, the next a bullet slammed into his forehead and lifted the top of his skull away. The redcoat stood for a moment, his face frozen in a puzzled expression, hands still gripping his musket, then with a moan of escaping breath, he slowly fell across her.

Chapter Sixty-Six

The Americans were in danger of being rolled back by the ferocious British advance. Wayne's soldiers, panting and grimed, too parched from heat and thirst to even curse, continued to fire and reload feverishly while American cannon were lugged up Combs Hill, the highest prominence on the battlefield.

Gamely pressing his offensive, Sir Henry Clinton ignored the danger of attacking a horseshoe-shaped defense and threw his best strength at Washington's center—his guardsmen, grenadiers, fusiliers, and light infantry. Against Wayne's weakened left, he dispatched a battering ram of light dragoons. Thundering toward the rebel line, their colors streaming out in front, the wave of horsemen swept forward to the killing.

As the British came on, fuses were lit on Combs Hill, flames dipped to touchholes, and rebel cannon roared from the heights. The American gunners fired with deadly precision. One round was so perfectly aimed, the whirring cannonball stripped the muskets from the hands of an entire platoon, then felled their drummer as he rattled a martial cadence. Volleys of grapeshot sprayed the scarlet ranks. Men were flung about like puppets, their limbs and faces shattered, their blood leaking into the hot Jersey sands.

Still the British came on.

Dalton, crouched over Mercury's neck, sped along the fighting lines as red-coated infantrymen took hopeful shots at him. Mindless of the danger, he raced toward the ravine where he had last seen Alexandra. Sweat stung his eyes, the flat taste of dread in his mouth. He should have stayed with her, should have made sure she got out. Fear for her deadened his caution, and when a small band of grenadiers rushed to cut him off, he cocked his pistol and rode straight for them. Bayonets flashed in readiness. A musket cracked. Mercury snorted in pain as the bullet creased his rump, but his stride never faltered. With a maddened yell, Dalton fired his pistol point-blank at a surprised face, then used the empty weapon to club a ducking head. Spurring clear of the scattering foot-soldiers, he holstered his pistol and drew his saber. Eyes searching frantically, he bore down on the ravine where heavy fire was being exchanged.

Through a fog of battle smoke, a red-coated dragoon rode forward to challenge him, and when Dalton recognized the face beneath a plumed leather cap, every nerve and muscle in his body reacted. Hatred blew in his veins like a storm wind. Rising in his stirrups, he whipped his saber above his head and charged.

Villard fired his pistol at Dalton, who felt the ball fan hotly past his neck. A moment later, their horses collided with a grunt. Steel parried steel, ringing and hissing as the two men probed each other's skills at close quarters. Dalton caught a vicious blade across his basket hilt and shoved it back, exerting all his country-bred strength to lever Villard off balance.

At the last instant Villard broke away. He circled, eyes intent. He now had the measure of his foe, whose sleeve was bloodied and whose right hand was having trouble with the reins. Spurring his gelding, he came at Dalton's weakened side, and again the two horses thudded together. Villard slashed and hacked with frenzied determination, seeking an opening in his opponent's guard, but the door was closed. Then he saw his chance and thrust hard, aiming for the heart. To his astonishment, his sword found only air, and he had to clutch his horse's mane to keep from pitching to the ground. With a gasp he parried the saber flashing toward his throat. Sparks flew as the blades ground together. Too late, Villard read Dalton's feint, saw the saber flick out, and felt a white-hot burning as his face was laid open from ear to chin. Hunching over his horse's neck, he pressed a hand to the wound and fled.

Dalton urged Mercury in pursuit, intent on catching Villard before he could rally. As the distance closed and Villard glanced back, wild-eyed, Dalton got ready with his saber. Across the field, a British cannon flashed out its long orange tongue, round shot came screaming toward the ravine, and Mercury staggered and went down as though poleaxed, a great crimson hole in his chest.

As the world upended around him, Dalton flung his feet from the stirrup irons and tried to leap clear of his tumbling horse. They fell with a crash onto the sandy ground. Winded, his head spinning, Dalton blinked up at the bowl of blue sky overhead, aware of a tremendous weight pressing on his left leg. He raised up and saw Mercury's heaving ribs lying across him, holding him immobile.

He touched the stallion's lathered neck. "Up, boy!" But his beautiful horse was never going to rise again.

In desperation Dalton dug in with his elbows and heaved backward, trying to get free. No good. He wriggled his foot, hoping to slide it from its boot, but his leg was pinned beneath his shuddering horse.

"Philips, you bastard!"

The savage voice raised the hair on his arms. Looking around, he saw Villard rein in and dismount, a glittering sword in his hand. Then Dalton spied his own blade lying a few feet away. Twisting toward it, he stretched his injured arm as far as it would reach, clawed for the saber's hilt, and missed by a fraction. He lunged again, his face contorting with effort, and felt a sharp pull in his forearm as his wound reopened and spilled warm blood. His fingers brushed the hilt, scrabbling clumsily.

Villard kicked the saber out of reach. His bloodied face was raging with triumph. "Damn your eyes, now you die!" he cried and raised his sword with both hands.

In the instant it took the weapon to reach its zenith Dalton embraced a thousand sensations. Then the bright blade sliced down.

A red splotch burst on Villard's chest. He stumbled back and dropped the sword, mouth open in shock, eyes staring down at the spreading stain on his jacket. He touched the wound as if he could not believe it was real.

Dalton was equally amazed when he turned his head

and saw Alexandra lowering a smoking musket. Her face pale, she dropped the gun and ran to him.

Villard's knees buckled. He sagged to the ground and slowly collapsed onto his side. From there he watched as Alexandra dug frantically with her hands to free Dalton, scooping soil from beneath his trapped leg. As her fingers darkened with dirt, Villard was astounded by her tenacity. Alexandra Pennington digging in dirt, wearing a look of desperation, willing to die on the spot for a farmer.

She had killed for him. As he thought this, Villard shuddered with the realization that he was dying.

All at once Dalton's leg slid free, and Alexandra helped him to stand. There was pain in his ankle, but it bore his weight as he limped to Villard's gelding and caught the dangling reins. Swinging onto the horse's back, he reached down and pulled Alexandra up behind him.

As they started away, Villard raised a hand in feeble protest. Blood bubbled from his lips as his hollow eyes followed their flight. He watched them ride down into the ravine, splash across the brook, and surge up the far bank as bullets kicked up dirt around them. He saw how tightly Alexandra was holding on, and then their images blurred as thick smoke enveloped them.

Villard coughed, squinted. The sun seemed to be blinding him. Its brilliance leeched color from the world until everything around him was flat, soundless, and graying at the fringes. He felt himself sliding to somewhere and fought to hold onto the last bit of light, but darkness bled over him and bore him away.

Chapter Sixty-Seven

Nightfall forced Washington to call off an attack aimed at routing Clinton's exhausted army. Before dawn of the next day, anxious to renew the contest, he sent his spies out in force to reconnoiter the enemy encampment. They found it deserted. Under the cover of darkness, the British had stolen away. Here and there were fresh pits where their dead had been hastily buried. Most of their wounded had been carried to Monmouth Court House and left in the care of local inhabitants.

Riding Secret, Dalton led a fast troop of horsemen to scout up the enemy. They shadowed the redcoats toward Middleton, following a route of march that was littered with discarded knapsacks, firelocks, and broken tools of war. The British moved with all speed. At the Shrewsbury River, the rebel patrol finally overtook the fleeing army as it crossed a pontoon bridge to reach the protecting heights. In their haste and extreme fatigue, dozens of redcoats fell into the water and had to be rescued. From a nearby hilltop, Dalton and his men surveyed the disorganized spectacle with enjoyment. It was a heady feeling to be the pursuers and not the pursued.

When the crossing was completed, the British lions drew together, formed into a ragged column, and slunk away toward New York. Watching them retreat, Dalton's satisfaction was intense.

Run, you bastards. Remember what happened yesterday.

Yesterday, American soldiers had fought like veterans. They had responded instinctively to booming commands,

474

wheeling into line as if on parade, throwing back charge after charge by superior numbers. Wayne's infantry, the guts of the rebel army, had shone like polished steel under fire. His officers were able to check hysterical retreats and turn their soldiers back into battle. For the first time since the war began, Washington had ended a general engagement without being defeated and was possessor of the field.

To Dalton's mind, the hot, bloody hours of Monmouth had been defining ones for the Americans. He imagined the tyrants across the ocean would tear their hair when they learned that the King's mighty army was beaten into withdrawal, and he smiled to think of the French reaction to the news. Soon all the world would feel the shock wave of a demonstrated truth—America was armed with courage.

During the long ride back to Monmouth, exhaustion and an aching body brought his grand outlook back into perspective. A rough road lay ahead, full of conflict and pain aplenty for those who undertook the fight for independence. Liberty was still a dream, and victory would not mean the end of the struggle, but the beginning of a new one to balance freedom with justice. The toughest sacrifices had yet to come, Dalton imagined. But no matter the cost, he would honor the cause to which he had pledged his life.

It was dark when he rode into camp and reported to Wayne, who was bitterly disappointed over the enemy's escape. "We could have finished them had they not run off with their tails between their legs."

"They won't run far," Dalton said.

A hard light danced in Wayne's eyes. "Nor will they ever forget how we bloodied them. I anticipate a monument will be erected here, telling how the pretty redcoats humbled themselves on the plains of Monmouth. And of course it shall be noted how Pennsylvania showed the way to victory."

Dalton smiled at the general's cockiness. If anyone had a right to boast, it was Anthony Wayne, whose brave display throughout the battle had been nothing less than brilliant.

"Dalton, you look half dead," Wayne observed. "Go and get some rest. And please present my best compliments to your wife. I understand she has been instrumental in caring for our wounded."

Suffused with a warm glow of pride, Dalton went to look for her. On the way, he saw Christopher Clue sitting cross-legged before a campfire, roasting a piece of meat on a stick, and went to greet him. As he sat down with him, the first thing he noticed was the tremor in the hand holding the stick. Then Clue's shock-filled eyes turned his way, and Dalton recalled his own bewilderment after his first taste of war.

"You fought well yesterday," he said.

Clue's gaze slanted away to watch the fire. "I did my best."

"That's all anyone can ask."

The flames danced as Clue struggled with unwanted visions. "It was the most horrid thing I've ever been through in my life," he said at last. "I never counted on seeing their faces and then having to shoot them. God knows what made me think I was ready to kill redcoats."

"They're killing Americans for King George," Dalton reminded him, "and we can't let our brothers die for nothing. We've got rightful cause to be in this war, Chris. That don't make killing easy, it just makes it possible."

Meeting his look, Clue shuddered a sigh. "How in God's name have you lasted this long?"

"One lousy day at a time," Dalton said, finally extracting a smile.

"I'd take my hat off to you, but I lost the damn thing."

Dalton smiled back at him. Clue was shaken, but intact. In time he would be all right, and he would come to realize that it was only the urge to kill, the craving to destroy, that made a man sinister.

Leaving him to his dinner, Dalton continued on to Old Tennant Church, where the army's hospital tents glowed softly in the darkness. After making inquiries, he was directed to a maple tree in the torch-lit yard, and beneath its spreading branches he found Alexandra asleep on the bare ground.

Unaware of his tender regard, she stirred in the throes of a dream, murmured something, then was quiet again, her chest gently rising and falling. Dalton stood for long moments and just watched her, held in place by the sight

476

of her grimy face and tangled hair, her blistered hand tucked beneath her chin. She seemed thinner, dark under the eyes. She was the loveliest picture he had ever seen. Her endurance amazed him. Not once since leaving Valley Forge had she complained to him.

When he lay down beside her and fitted himself against her, Alexandra came slowly awake, saw his face in the dim light, and burrowed closer to him. "I was dreaming about you," she said in a sleep-filled voice.

"A good one, I hope."

"All my dreams of you are good ones."

His arms gently squeezed her. "You picked a hell of a place to sleep."

"I was so tired, I didn't care where I lay down." With sudden awareness, she tipped her head back to look at him with anxious eyes. "Where are the British?"

"Still flying from shadows. They must have heard we were arming our women."

Alexandra smiled. "They must be in shock, you mean. They may never recover from losing their laurels to *rebel* officers."

"We knocked the fight out of them, didn't we?"

"Just as you promised," she said and felt him sigh with contentment. Closing his eyes, he got comfortable against her, and for a time they lay quietly together. Then Dalton spoke in a drowsy voice. "I was wrong about you."

Alexandra was suddenly alert.

"You're a true soldier, Alex," he said, pressing a kiss to her brow. "You're the best part of my life." Then he hugged her tight and close in the flickering darkness, and Alexandra could feel the warmth of him surrounding her and could hear his steady pulse where it beat beneath her cheek. Everything she wanted was with her now, this man who held her. She thought she would rather die than let him down. After a time, as his breathing grew slow and deep and his body relaxed against her, she knew he was sleeping.

Her own eyes closed, but sleep eluded her as her mind became busy with planning, dreaming of things to come. There was so much to look forward to. Dr. Ross had examined her today, and in his opinion a life was growing inside her. Even if it turned out he was wrong, she no

477

longer felt right about keeping something so important from Dalton. Tomorrow she would tell him that the chances were good he was going to become a father.

After thinking this, Alexandra smiled to herself, envisioning his reaction—first elation, then concern. He would want her to return immediately to Willowbrook. If she hedged, he would argue with her and refuse to change his mind. He would probably win. Whatever he did, she would love him forever.

Author's Note

Monmouth was the last major battle fought in the northern colonies during America's war for independence, and was a turning point for the rebel cause. The American spirit displayed on the hot plains of Jersey sent a grim message to British Parliament: the ragged rebels were indeed a formidable foe. Clearly, a single, culminative battle would not crush Washington's army—a new one would simply rise in its place—and the might of British arms was stretched too thin on a vast battleground.

Adopting a new strategy, England shifted its operational emphasis southward, to Virginia, the Carolinas and Georgia, with an eye toward salvaging its holdings from the Chesapeake capes to Florida. The British southern campaign ravaged property and destroyed many lives, including the hundreds of slaves lured from plantations with the promise of freedom, only to be discarded like excess baggage when Cornwallis's army was surrounded at Yorktown, Virginia, in the fall of 1781. Beseiged by allied American and French forces, Lord Cornwallis was forced to surrender his entire army of 6,000 men.

The Yorktown victory stunned the world. In truth, the miracle could not have happened without the French, whose land and sea forces played critical roles in the siege. Most assuredly, the war would never have been won—

indeed, *begun*—were it not for the incomparable courage, fidelity and valor of America's men-at-arms.

This book is dedicated to the Patriots who suffered, fought and died so that a nation of free men might be born.